A Tale of Pond Life

# Mr. Big

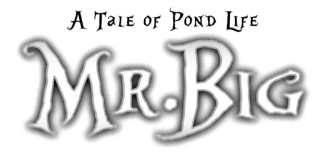

# A Tale of Pond Life

# Mr. Big

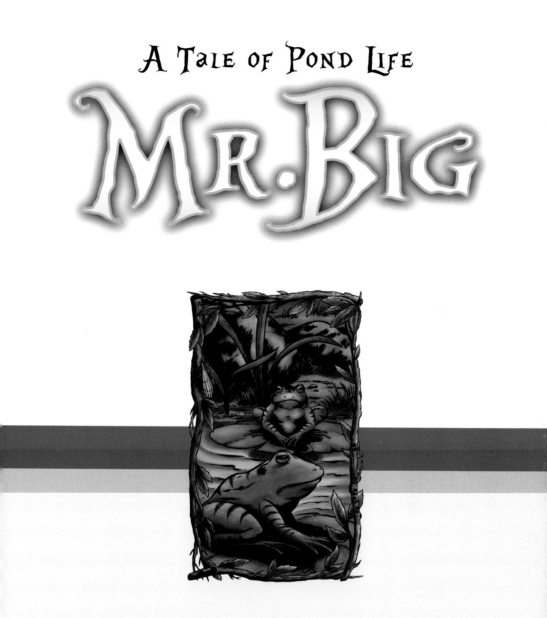

## CAROL DEMBICKI & MATT DEMBICKI

### COLORED BY JASON AXTELL

Sky Pony Press
New York

Sky Pony Press books may be purchased in bulk at special discounts for sales promotion, corporate gifts, fund-raising, or educational purposes. Special editions can also be created to specifications. For details, contact the Special Sales Department, Sky Pony Press, 307 West 36th Street, 11th Floor, New York, NY 10018 or info@ skyhorsepublishing.com.

Sky Pony® is a registered trademark of Skyhorse Publishing, Inc.®, a Delaware corporation.

Visit our website at www.skyponypress.com.

10 9 8 7 6 5 4 3 2 1

Manufactured in China, May 2012
This product conforms to CPSIA 2008

Library of Congress Cataloging-in-Publication Data

Dembicki, Carol.
 Mr. Big : a tale of pond life / Carol Dembicki and Matt Dembicki.
     p. cm.
 Summary: Pond dwellers make a plan to rid the pond of the destructive snapping turtle, but what does that mean for the delicate balance of the pond ecosystem, especially when a new and more vicious predator is found lurking in the deep?
 ISBN 978-1-61608-967-2 (pbk. : alk. paper)
 1. Pond animals--Juvenile fiction. [1. Pond animals--Fiction. 2. Pond ecology--Fiction. 3. Snapping turtles--Fiction. 4. Turtles--Fiction.] I. Dembicki, Matt. II. Title. III. Title: Mister Big.
 PZ10.3.D384Mr 2012
 [Fic]--dc23
                              2012013454
Editor: Julie Matysik
Production Manager: Sara Kitchen

To Adam and Roman,
Our little acorns . . . remember from
small things come great wonders.

# FOREWORD

My favorite place to collect insects is a little pond (or a large ditch, depending on how you look at it) behind the baseball field of the small college where I work. This is an unlikely place to experience the wonders of nature. A supermarket is only about a hundred yards away, the Doppler shifts of car wheels hum on the road up the hill, and the ground is covered with rusting bits of metal. And yet, in this pond, dragonflies hunt, small frogs sing love songs, and fish dart among the reeds. And a huge snapping turtle hides in the muck. I only saw her once, a living island that disappeared the minute I tried to get a better look. But knowing she was there, unseen and powerful, was fuel for my imagination. I returned to the pond several times throughout the summer to get another look, but I never saw her again.

And then, with a fateful "kaplunk!," I discovered Matt and Carol Dembicki's *Mr. Big*. Matt and Carol are excellent storytellers who take you deep into their wonderfully realized pond and allow you to get up close to the snapper and gaze into its unblinking eyes. The pages themselves are alive with swirling and bubbling panels. In Mr. Big's pond, you will discover strange new faces speaking in familiar voices and struggling with the idea of a power beyond their control. Where do they fit in the world? Is Mr. Big the terror of the pond creatures or their protector? The difficult answer is that he is both, but not because he has chosen either role. Mr. Big just is. And in the hands of a talented cartoonist like Matt Dembicki, we get to experience all of the wonder and terror and complexity of his world.

This lovely book will allow us to return to Matt and Carol's pond whenever we want and watch the frogs skitter away from circling crows or see the crayfish give wisdom on the pebbly bottom. Or, perhaps, you'll return for the same reason I will— to get another glimpse at that big snapper and let his stare spark your imagination. When you do, remember that it was the elegant imaginations of Matt and Carol Dembicki that made your visit possible.

—Jay Hosler

**Jay Hosler** is the six-time Eisner Award nominee and Xeric Award– winning creator of *Clan Apis* and *The Sandwalk Adventures*. He teaches biology at Juniata College in Huntington, Pennsylvania.

# INTRODUCTION

In high school, I volunteered as an aide for a youth camp with children of physical exceptionalities. As many of the attendees were wheelchair bound, planning camp activities took some effort. One activity that was greatly anticipated by the entire camp was the induction of three newly acquired ducks for the camp pond. We lined up the children to ensure the best vantage point for them to witness the ducks' release. As the three young ducks began their first swim, the audience watched in horror as the last duck was silently and efficiently pulled under the water. Of course, the younger kids immediately began to cry, while the older ones began to ask questions. The head counselor attempted to say the duck was diving for food, but the children insisted on waiting for the duck to resurface. After fifteen minutes and many tears, the counselor confessed that the duck was probably serving as a meal for an unknown underwater predator. What could have caused so much terror and destruction? A snapping turtle.

Twenty years later, Matt and I found a relaxing spot at a small pond tucked away from the biking trail that runs near our home in Northern Virginia. We would spend lazy weekend mornings lounging on the pond's dock, feeding the resident population, and watching nature unfold. During one of our visits, we spotted a giant snapping turtle slowly making its way toward us in the murky water. It occasionally surfaced to breathe and to observe the surroundings. The closer the snapping turtle got, the more animals seemed to flee, despite the number of breads and cereals floating on the water. It seemed like the pond critters were aware of the snapper's presence and knew to get out of its way (unlike that poor duck so many years ago). We enjoyed watching the turtle—whom we dubbed "Mr. Big"—and his habits that seemed to challenge natural rhythms given the impact of human interference (such as ours).

It was during one of our visits that I mentioned doing a little comic about what we witnessed. Matt liked the idea, so we did. The original concept was to create a one-shot, self-published comic with full-page panels. But a funny thing happened. The people who purchased the short comic liked it. In fact, we received emails inquiring about more installments. So, Matt developed the next book and soon the trials and tribulations of our "Mr. Big" began to unfold.

This book serves as a collection of the *Mr. Big* minicomics in a larger format. We hope you enjoy it.

—Carol Dembicki

A Tale of Pond Life

# Mr. Big

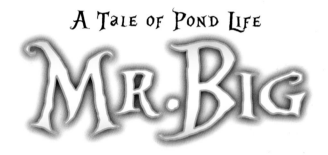

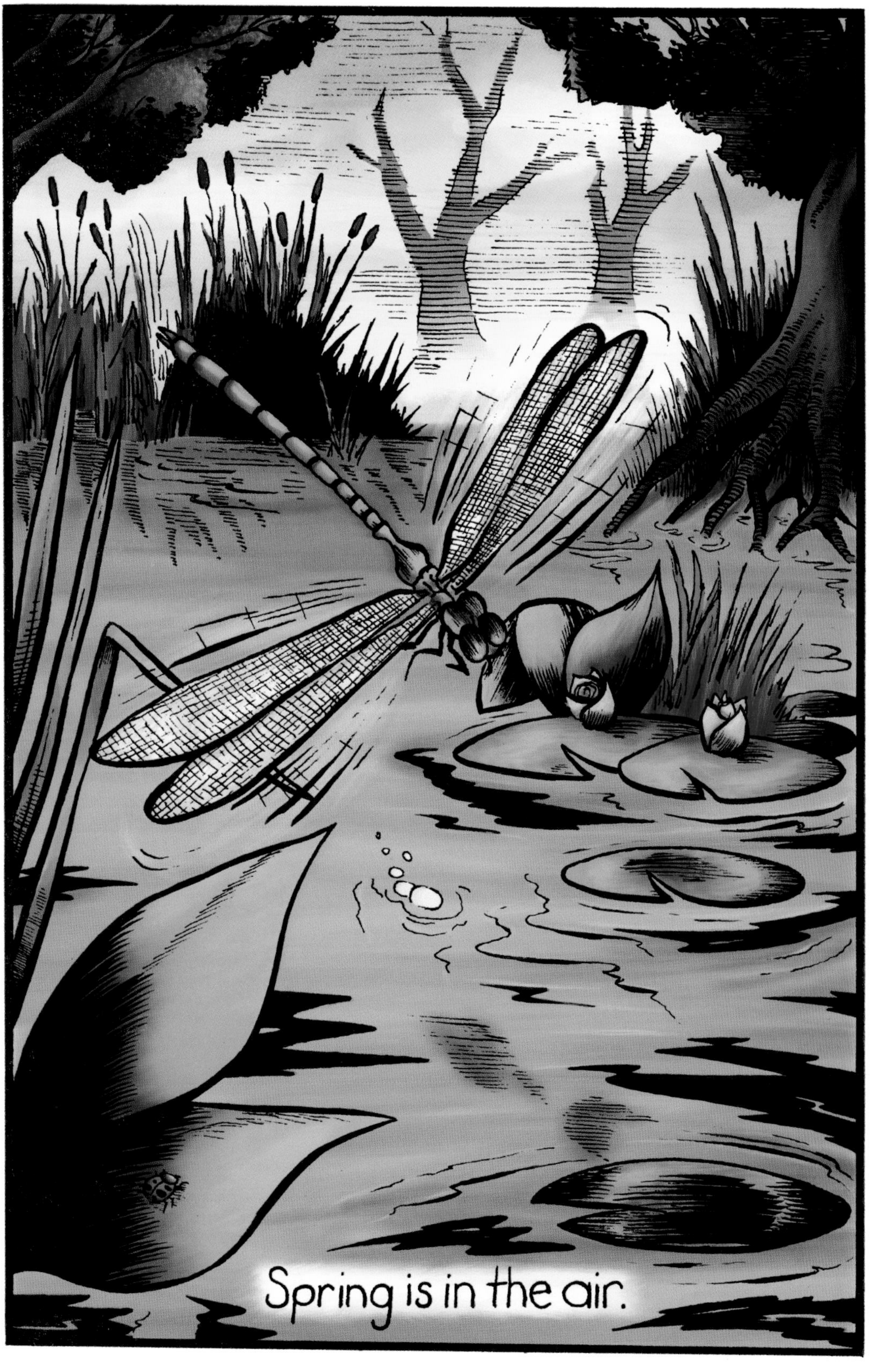
Spring is in the air.

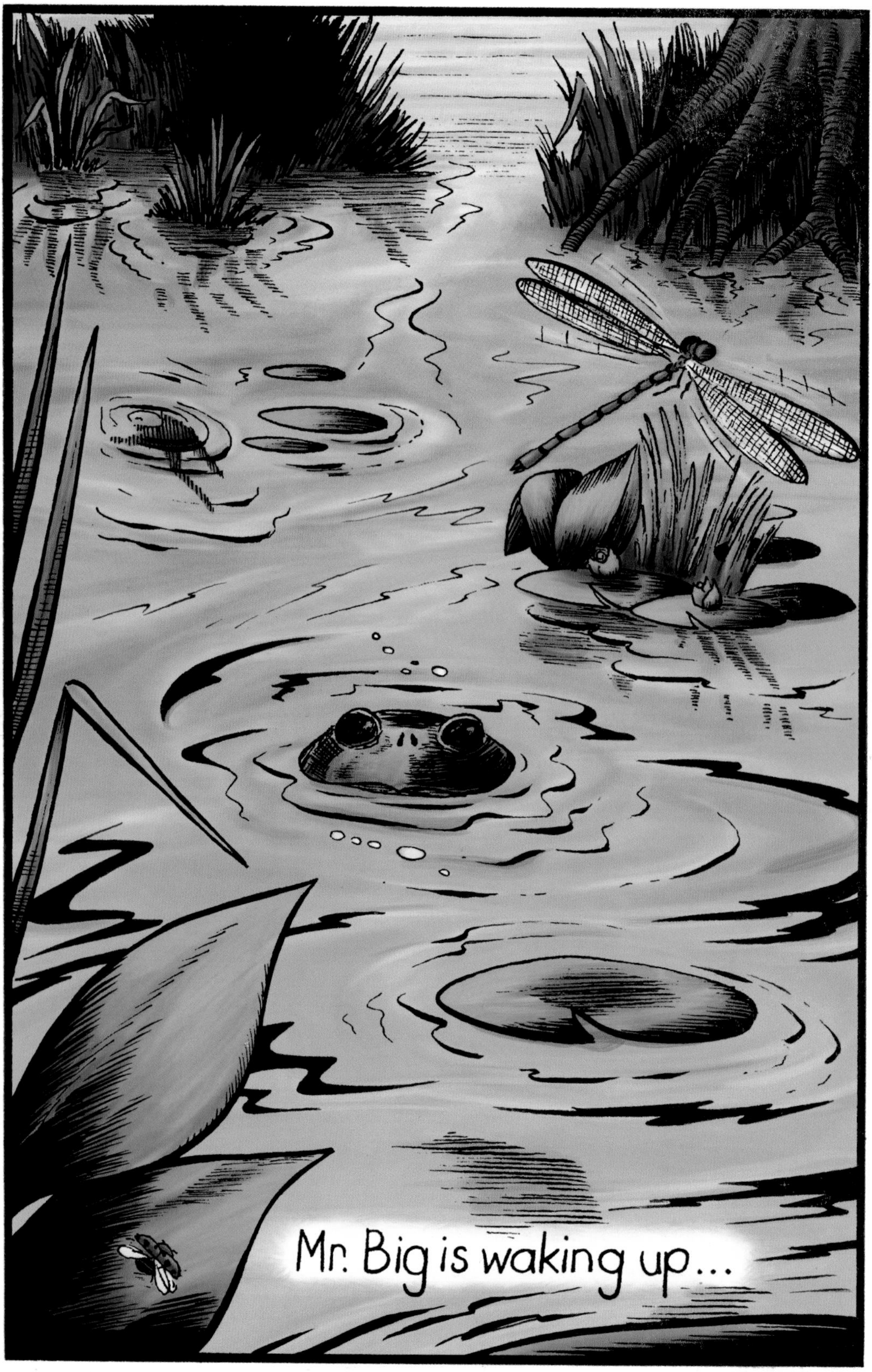
Mr. Big is waking up...

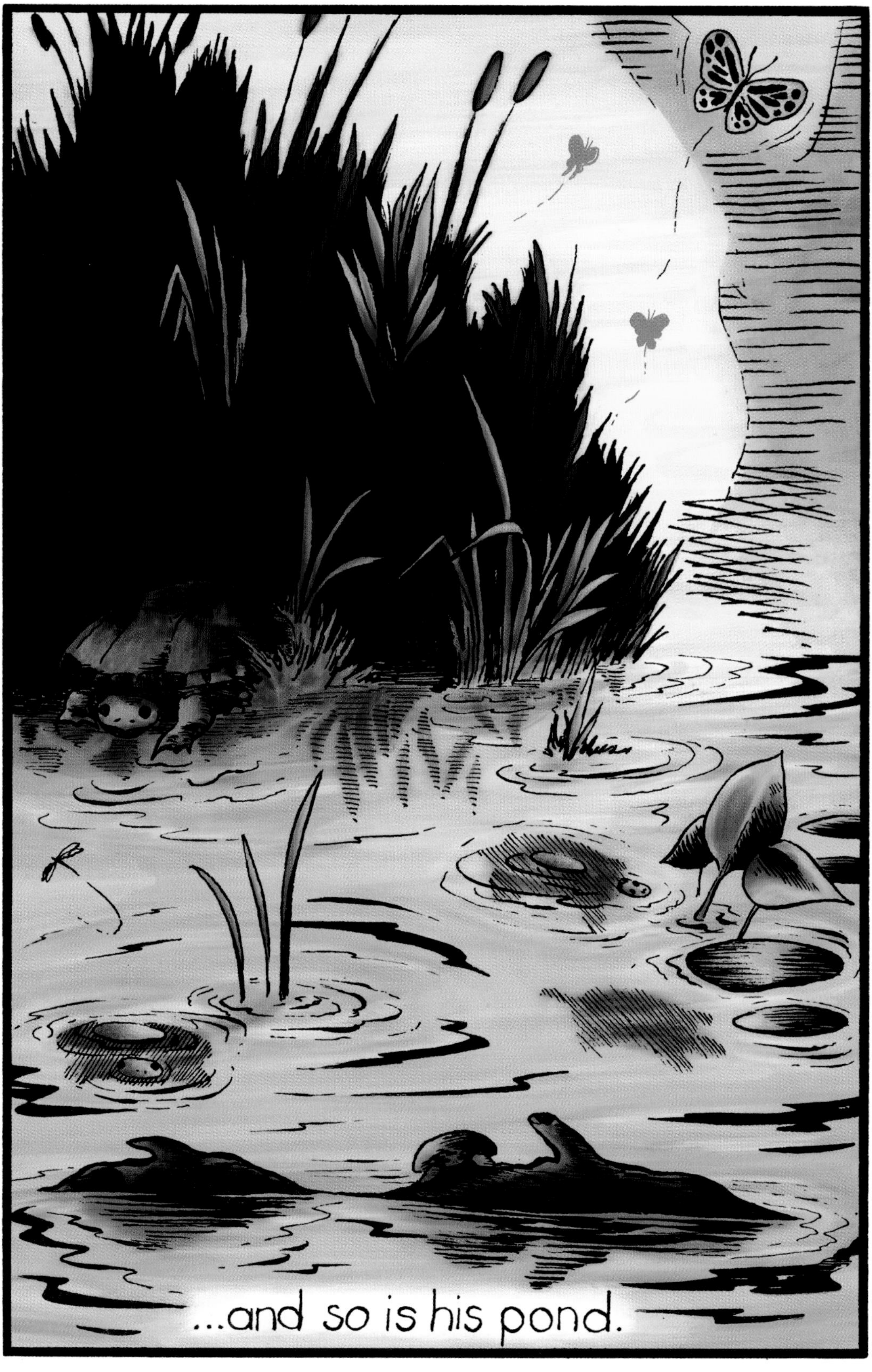
...and so is his pond.

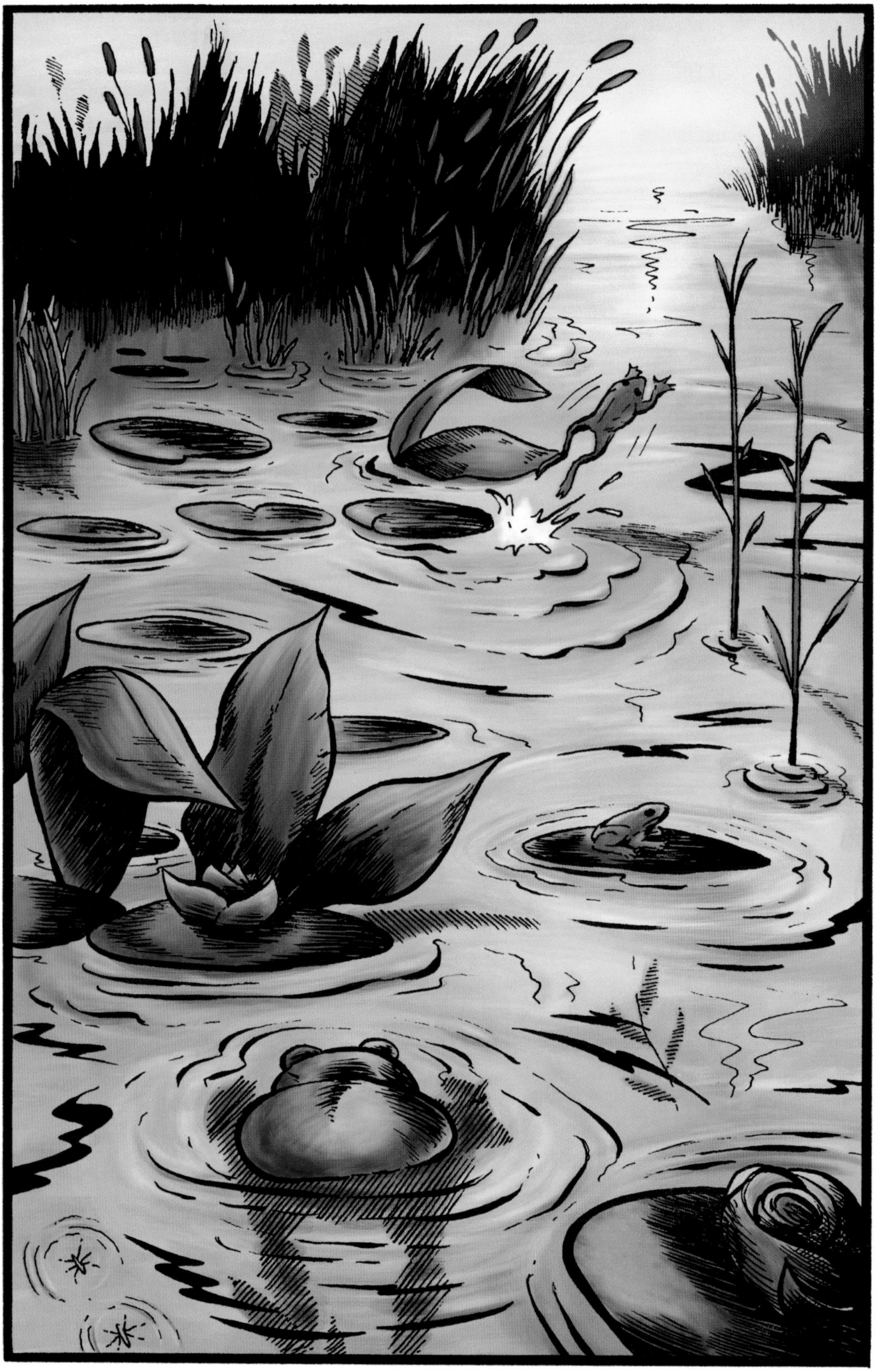

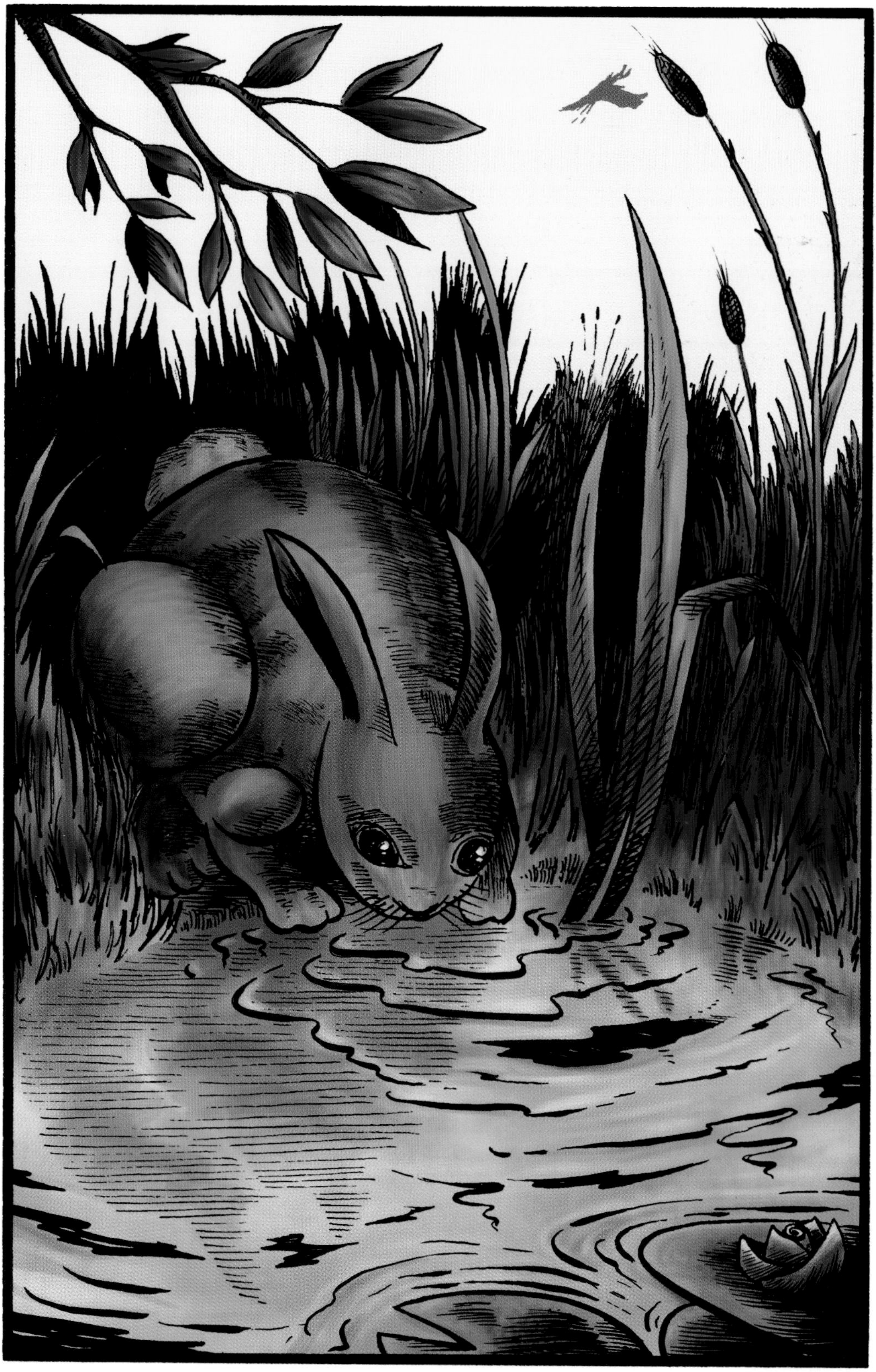

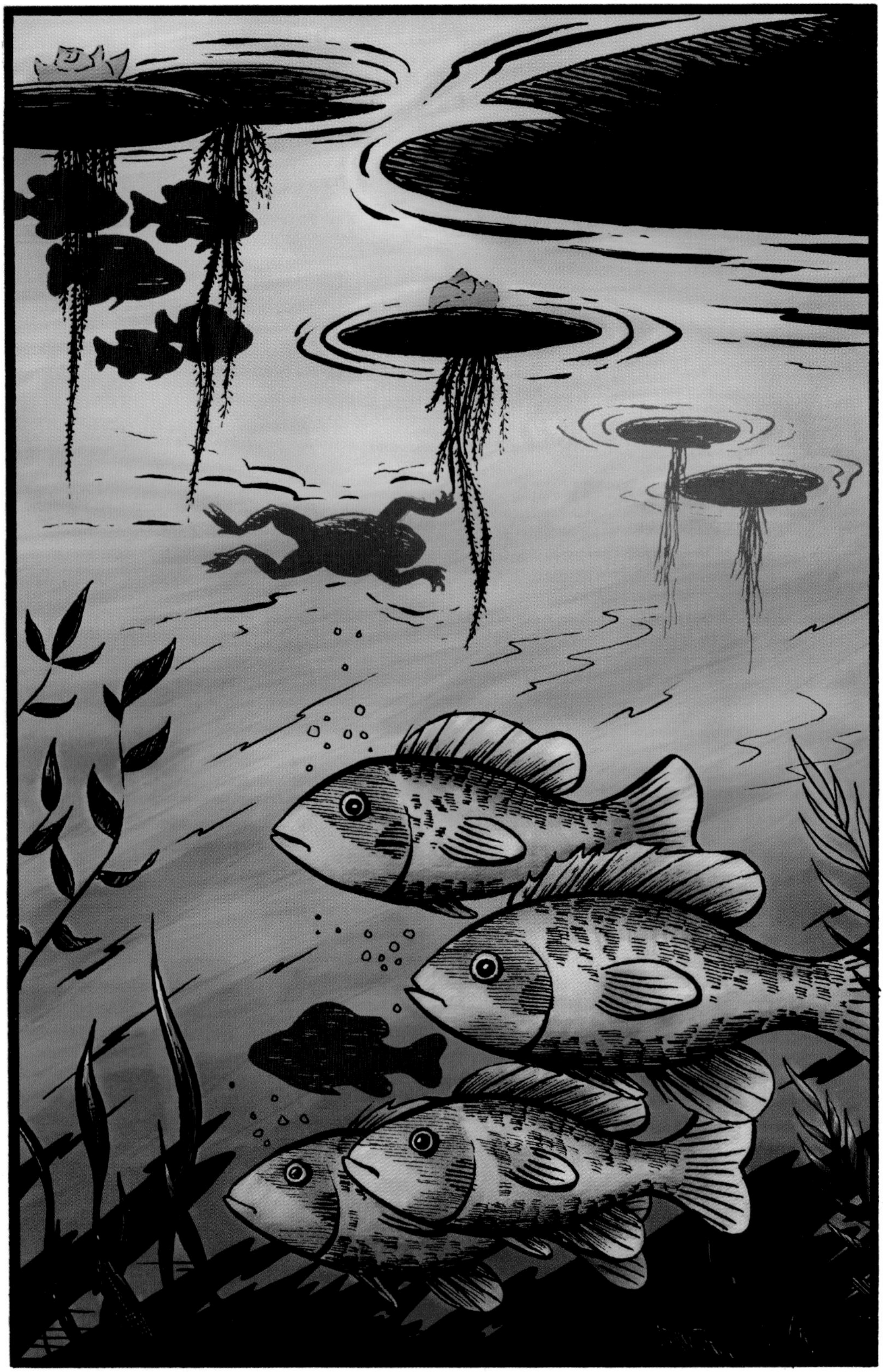

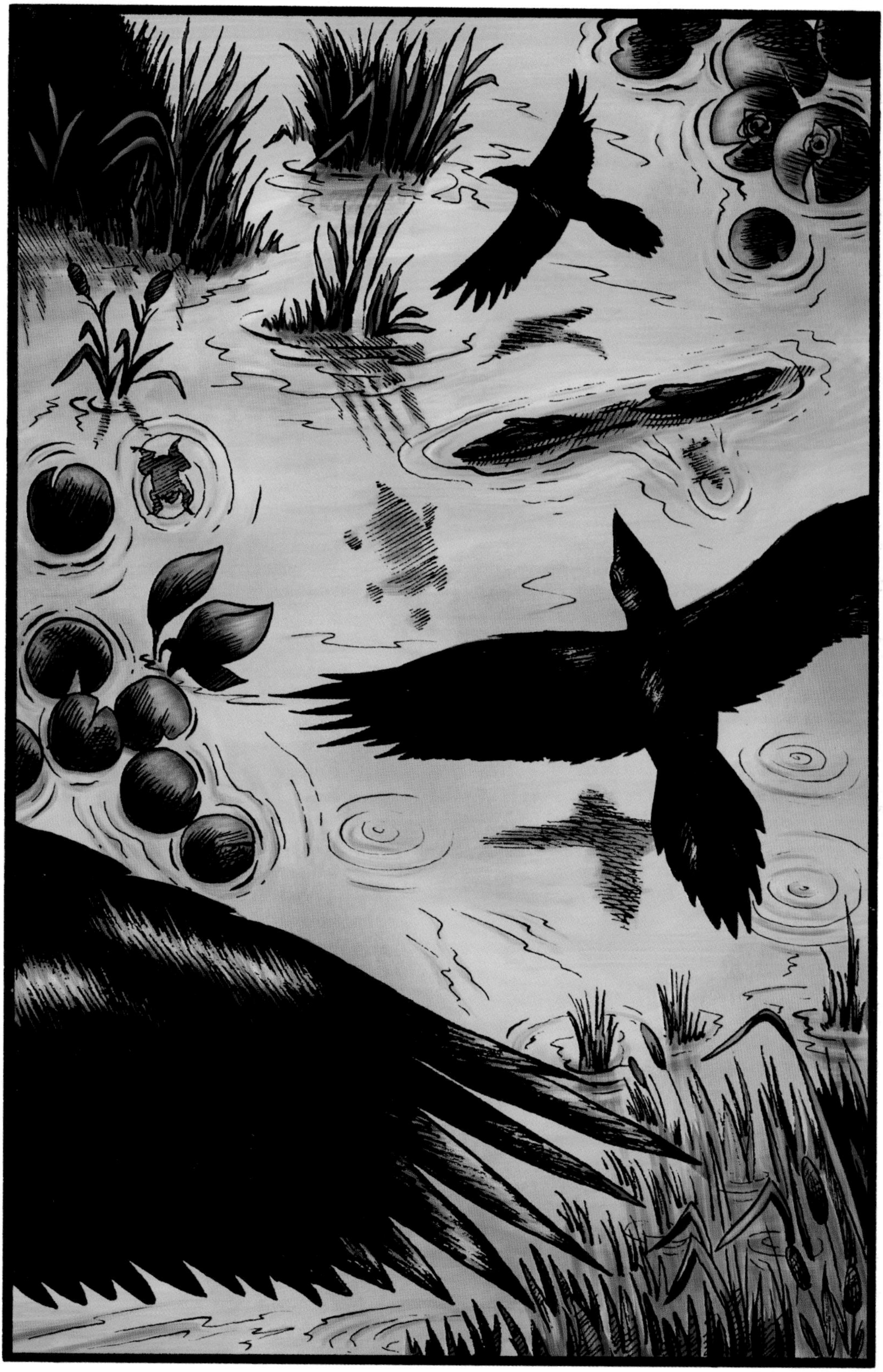

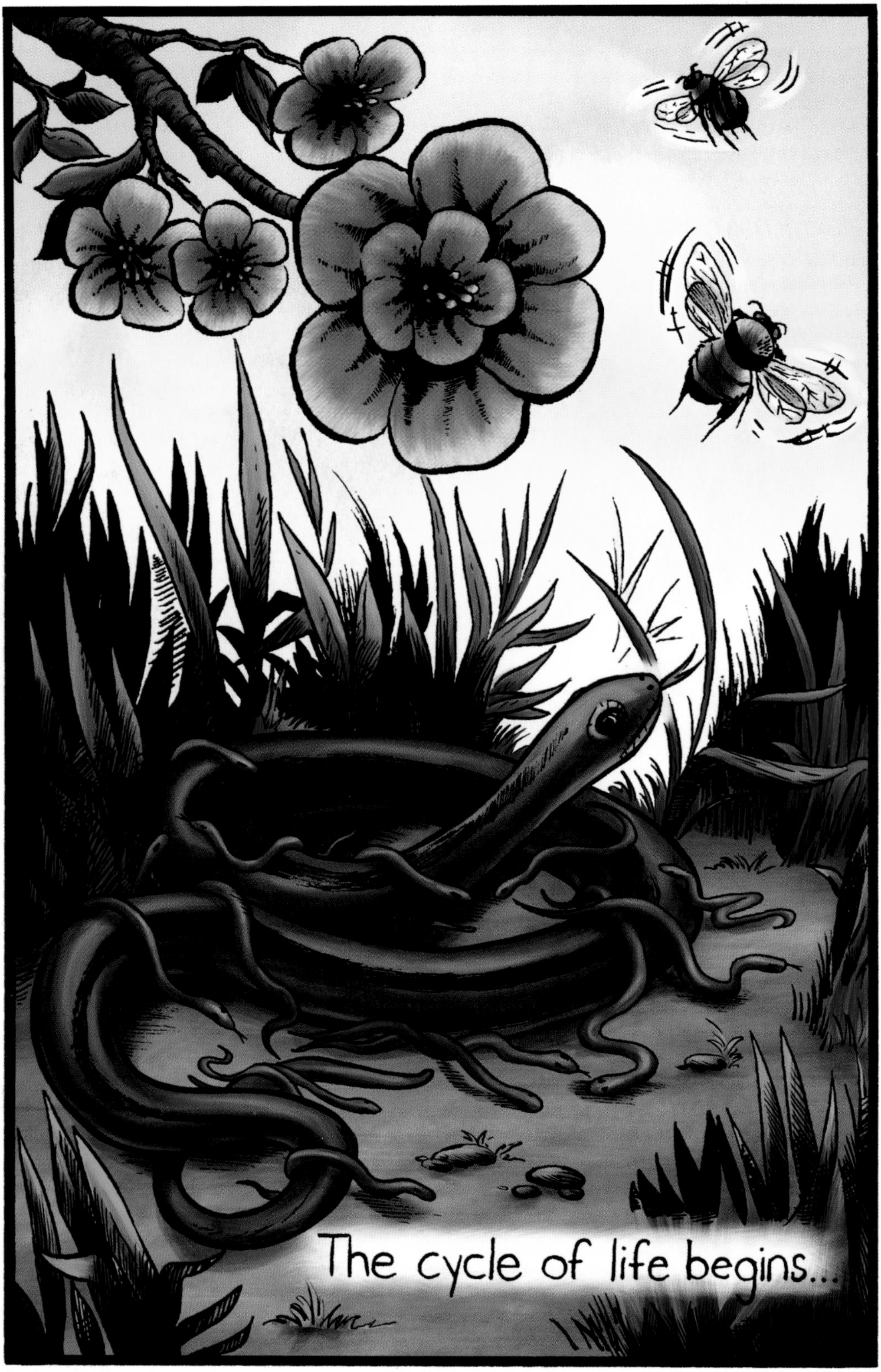
The cycle of life begins...

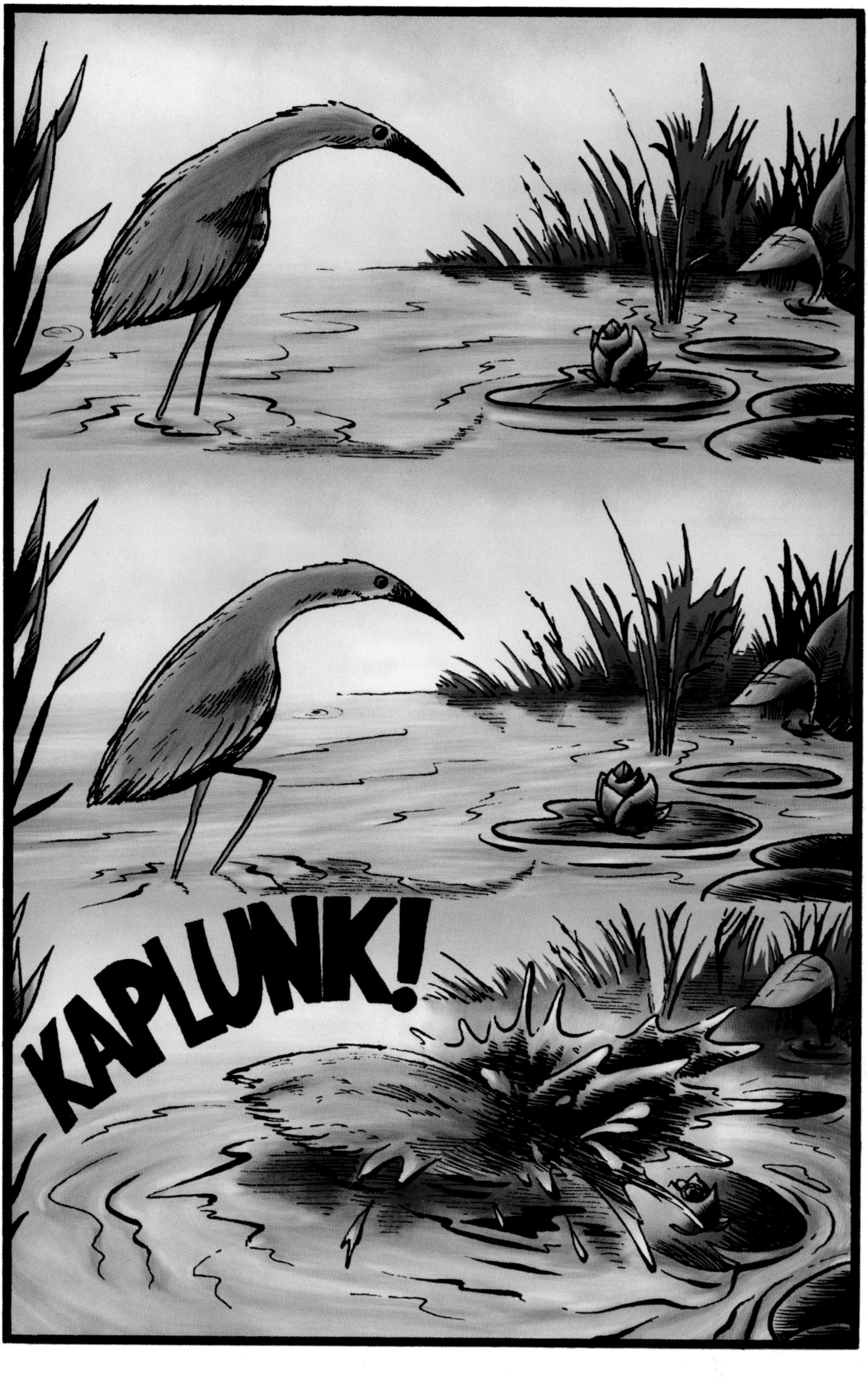
KAPLUNK!

...for most.

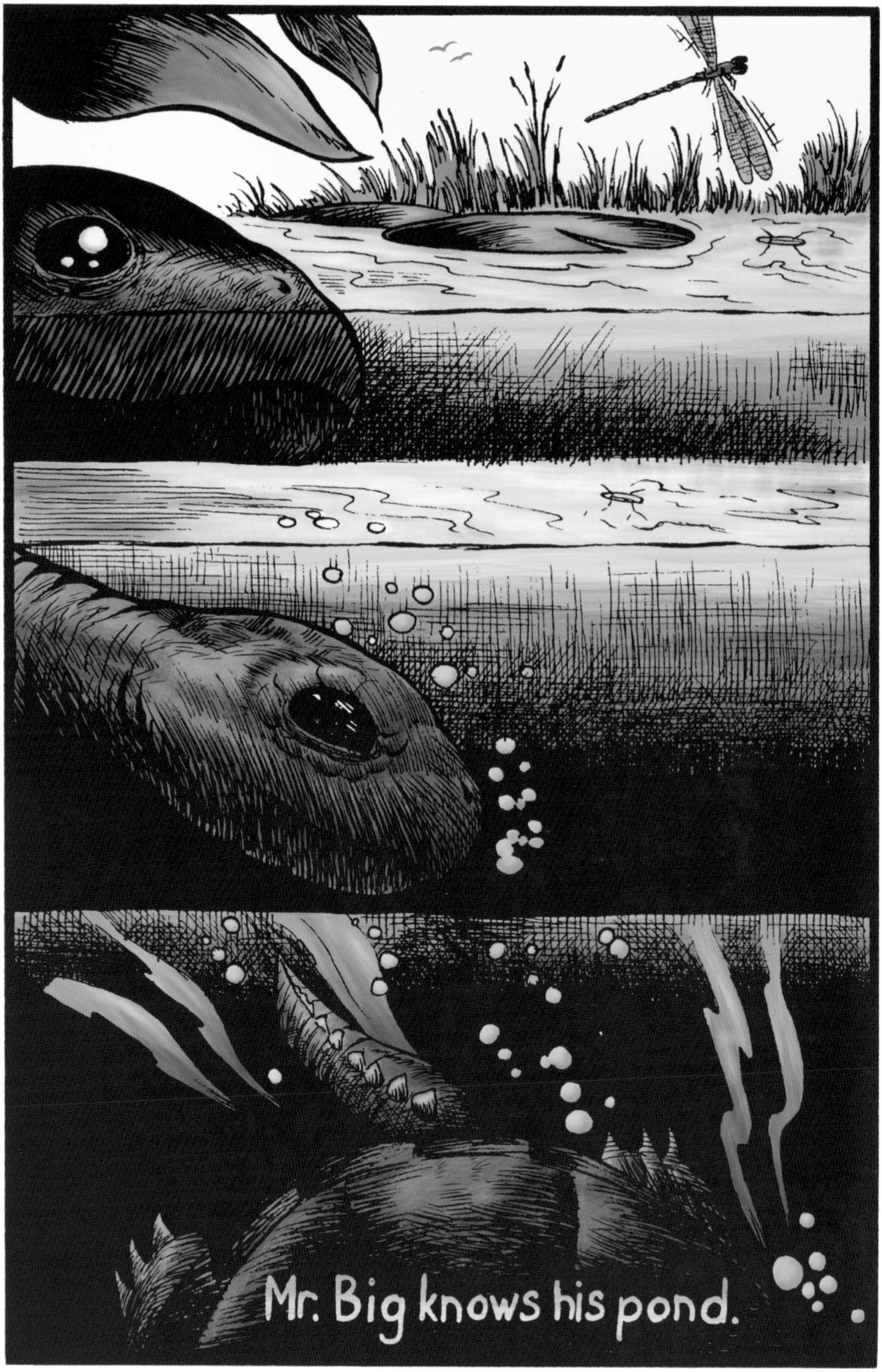
Mr. Big knows his pond.

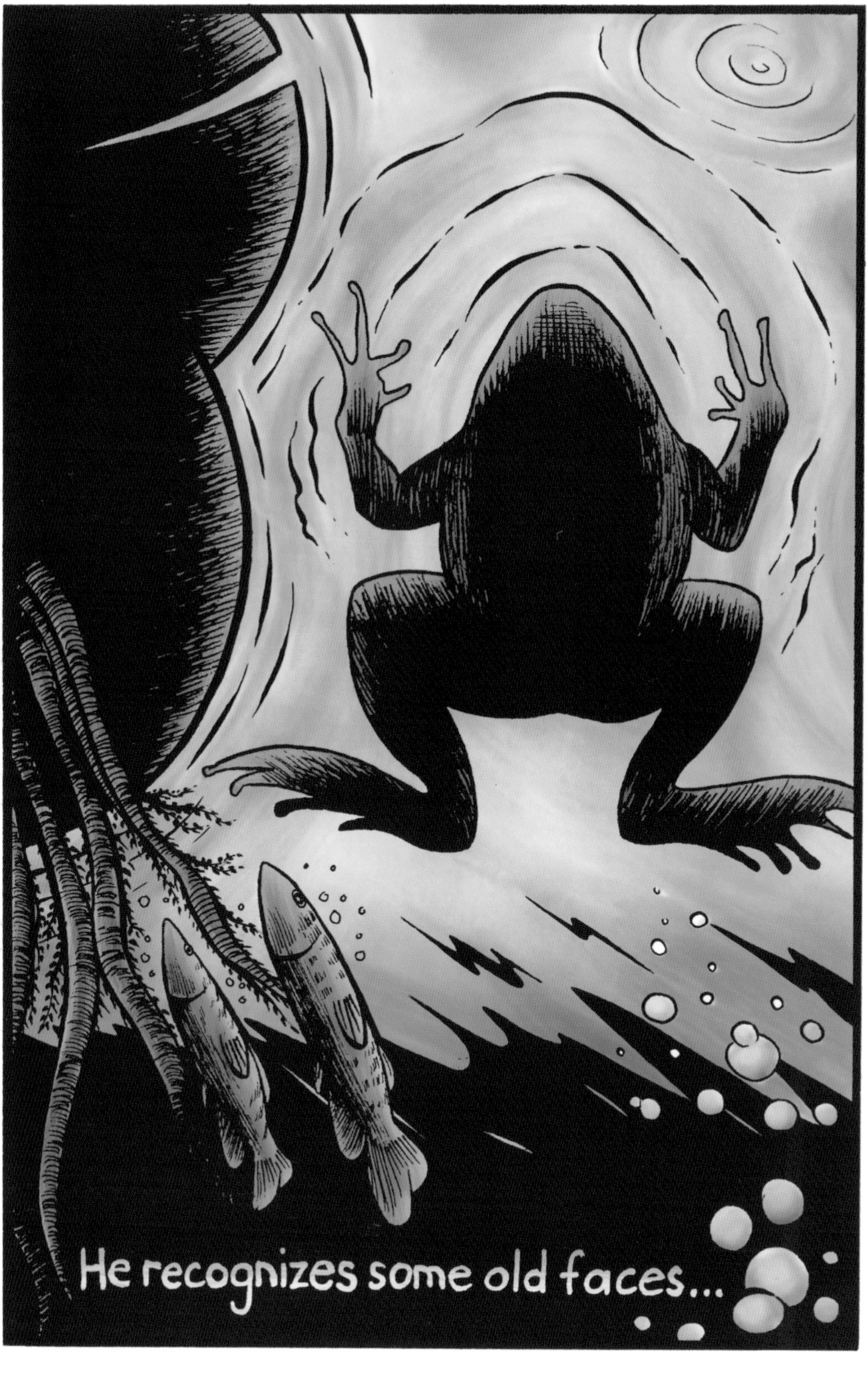
He recognizes some old faces...

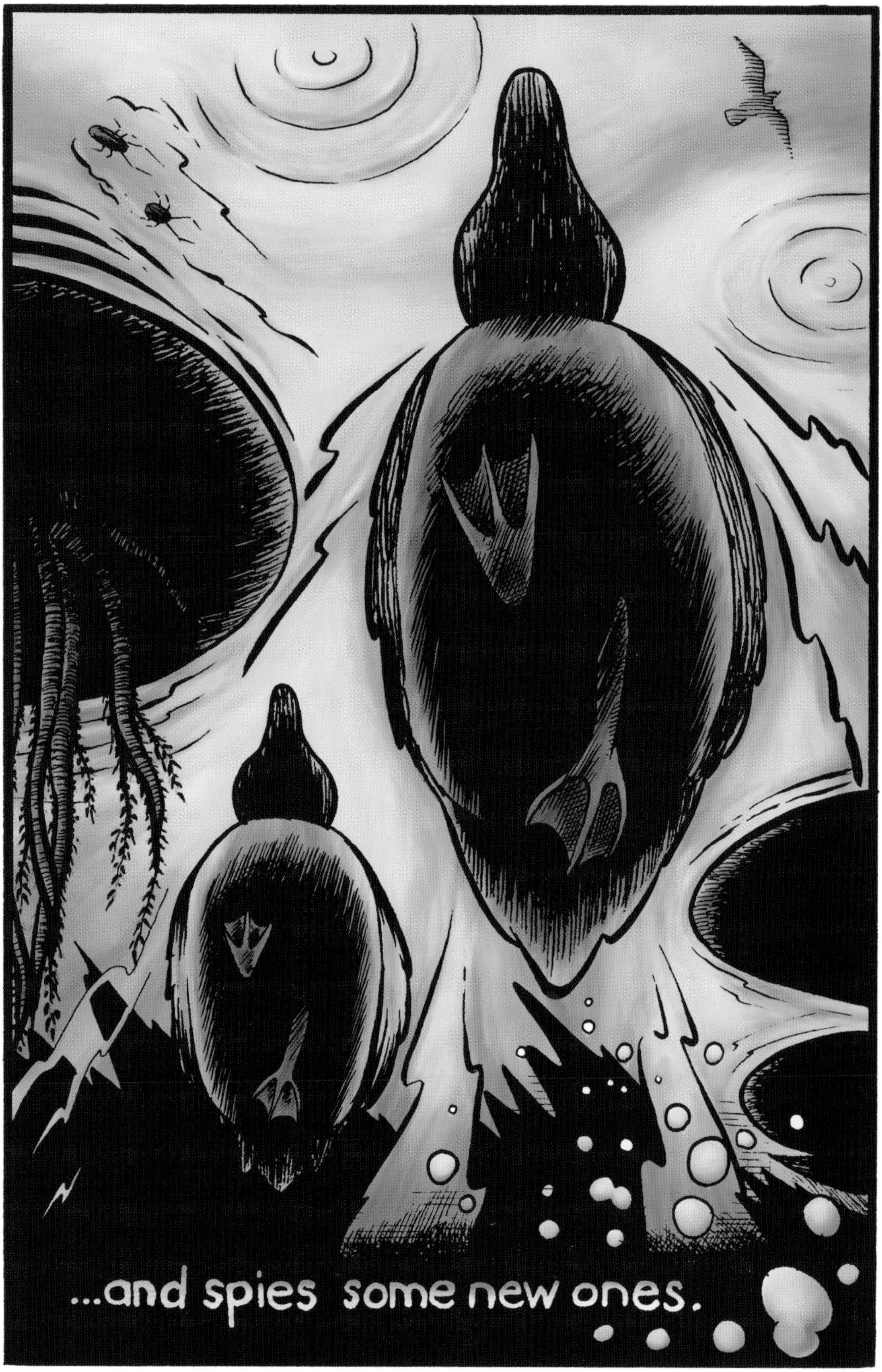
...and spies some new ones.

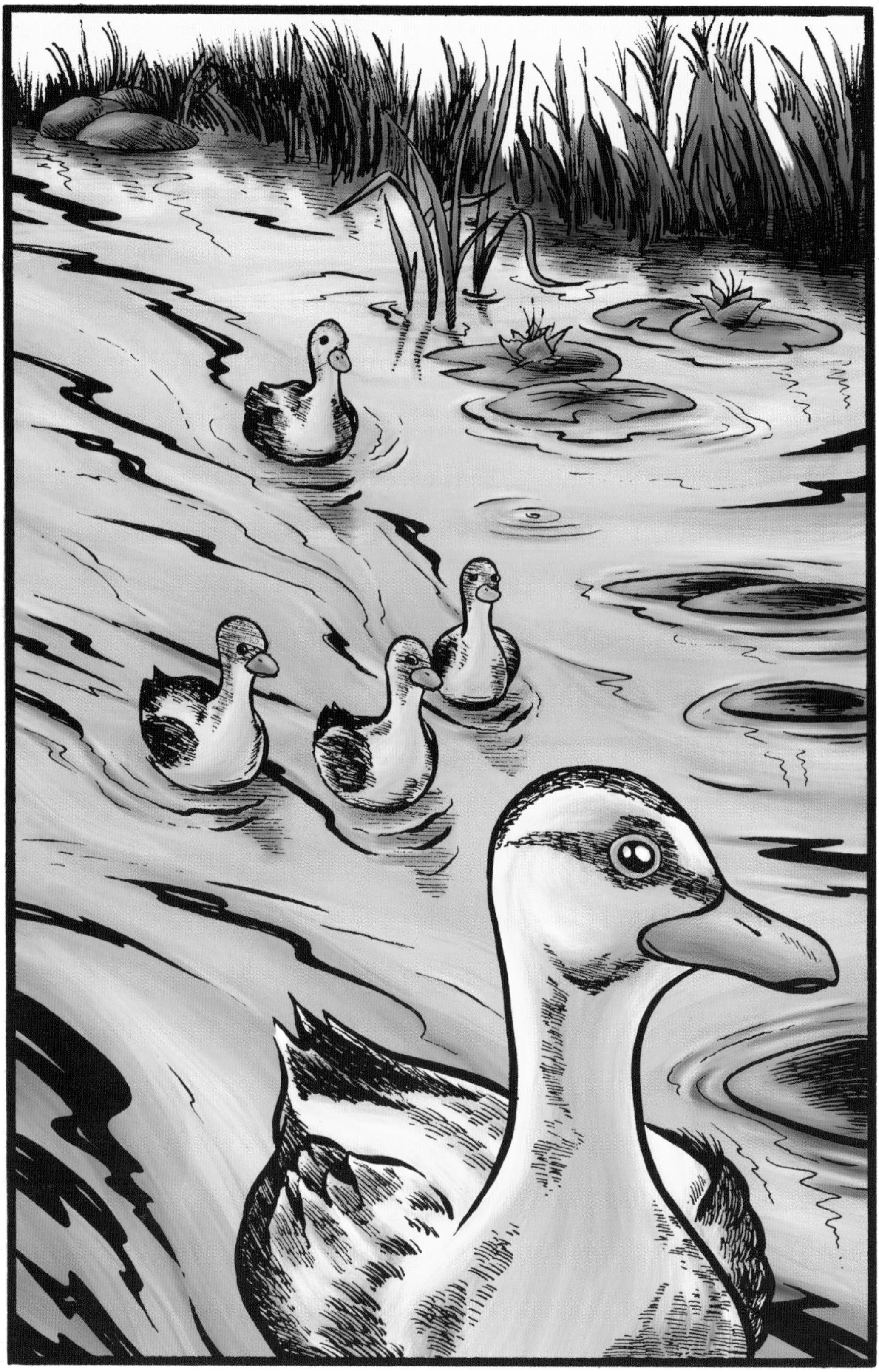

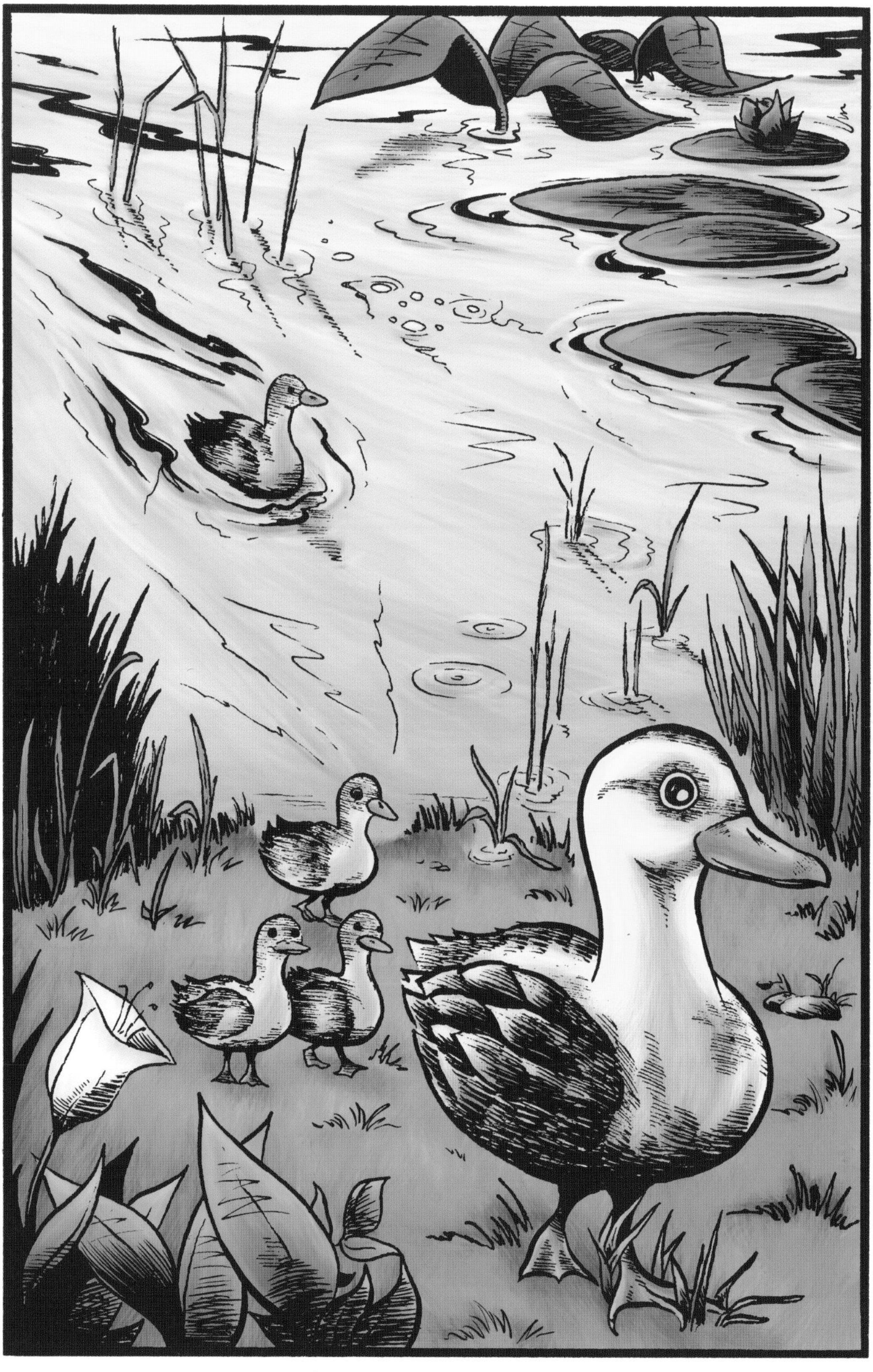

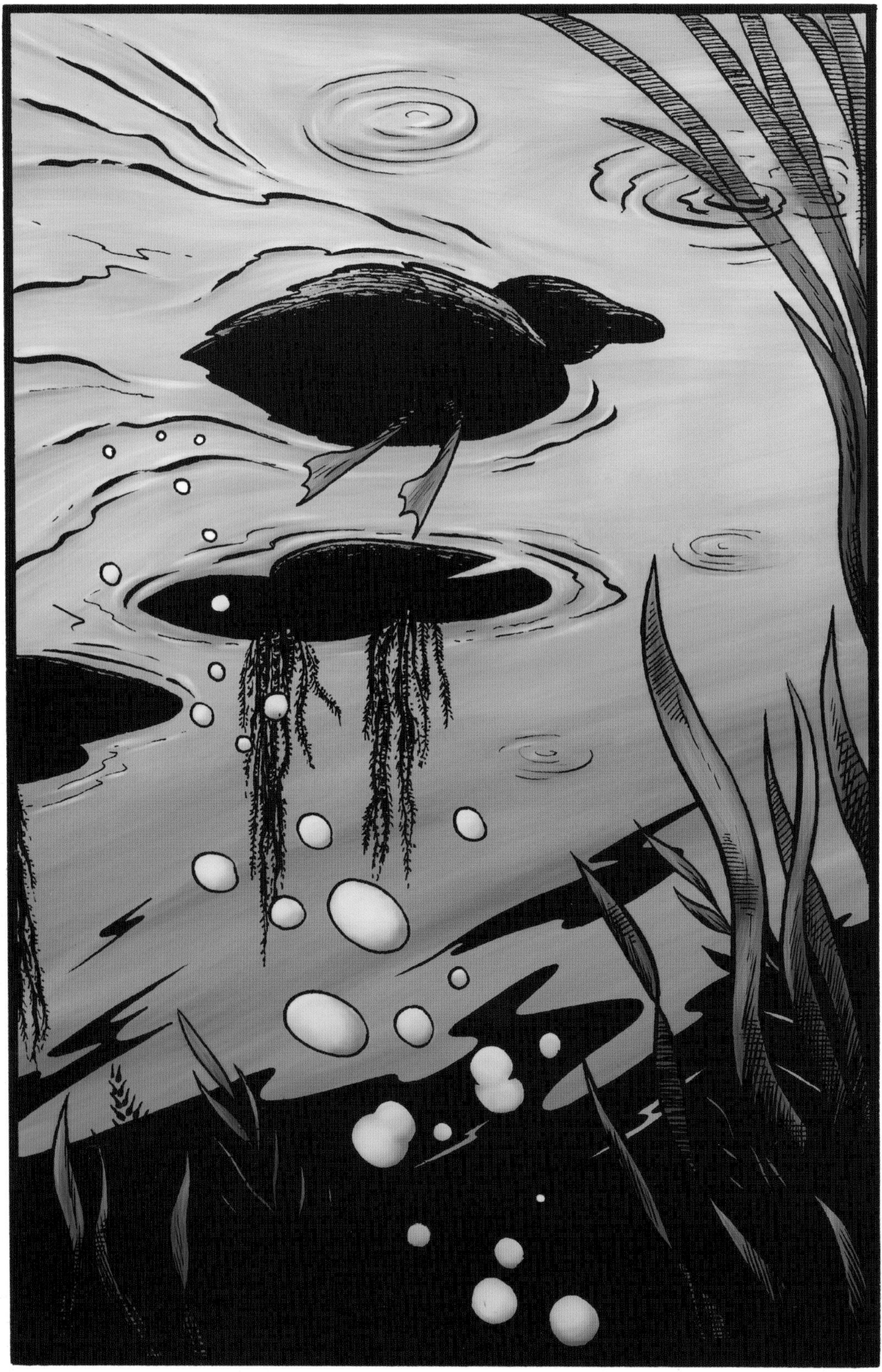

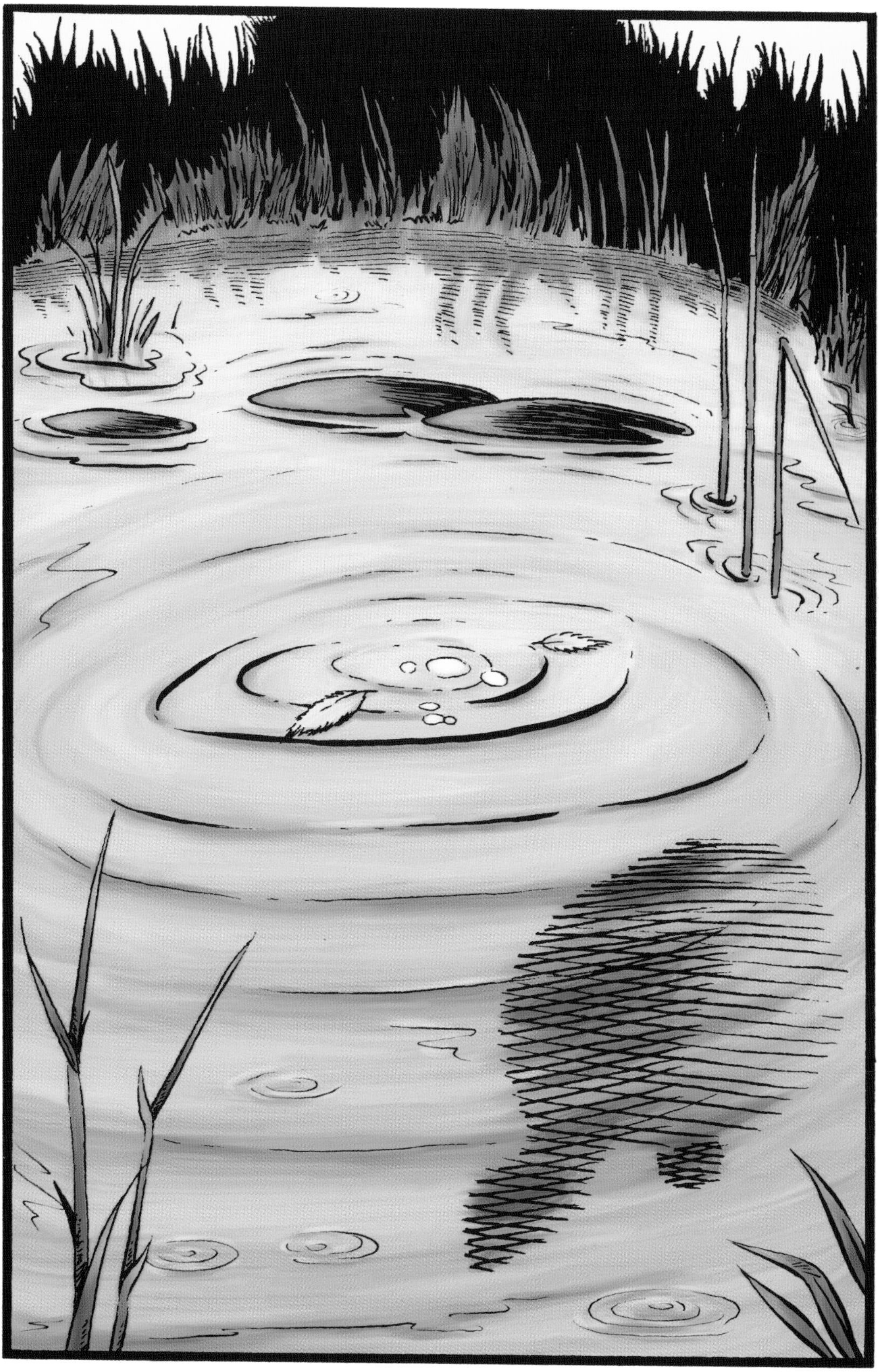

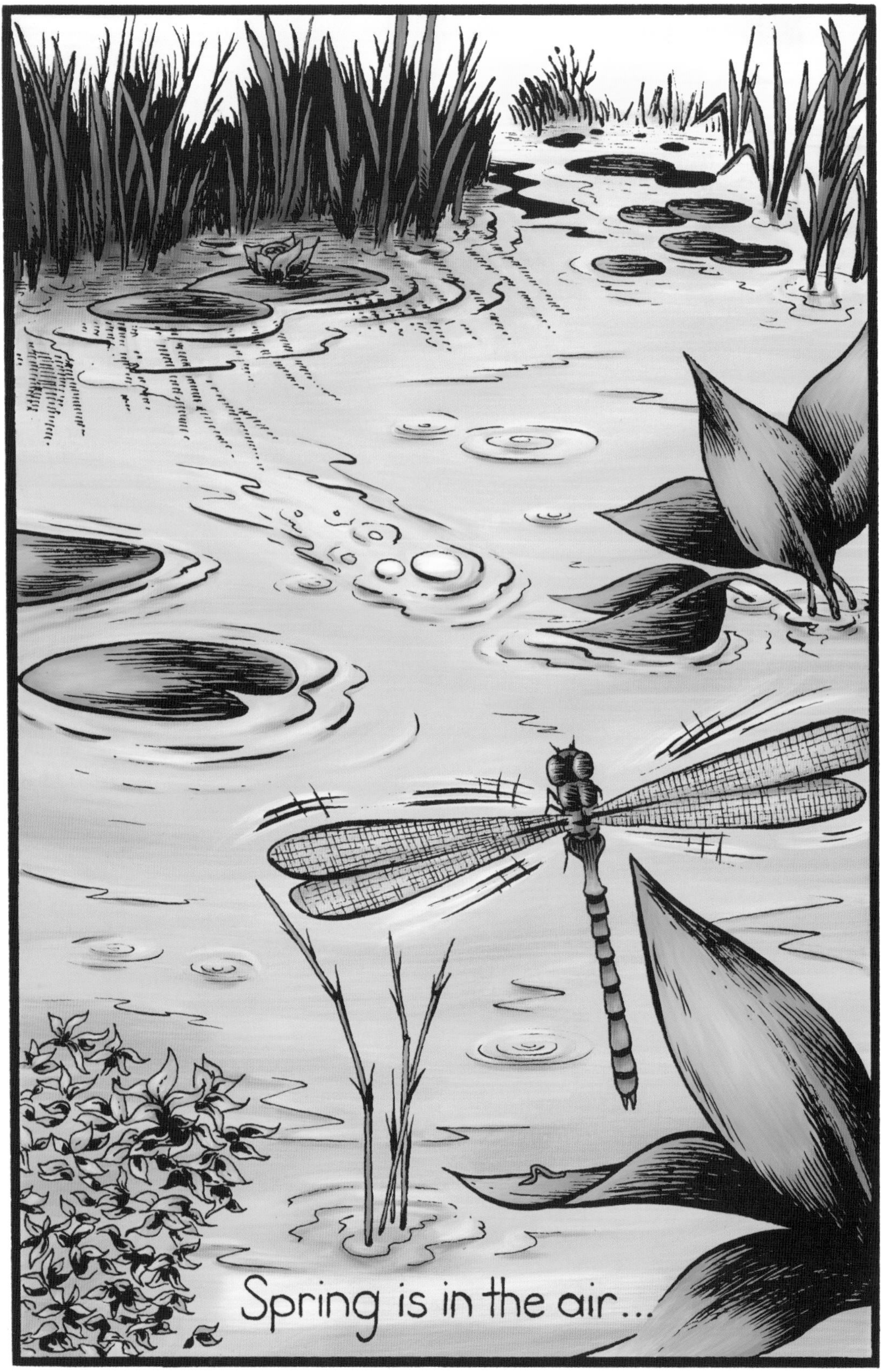
Spring is in the air...

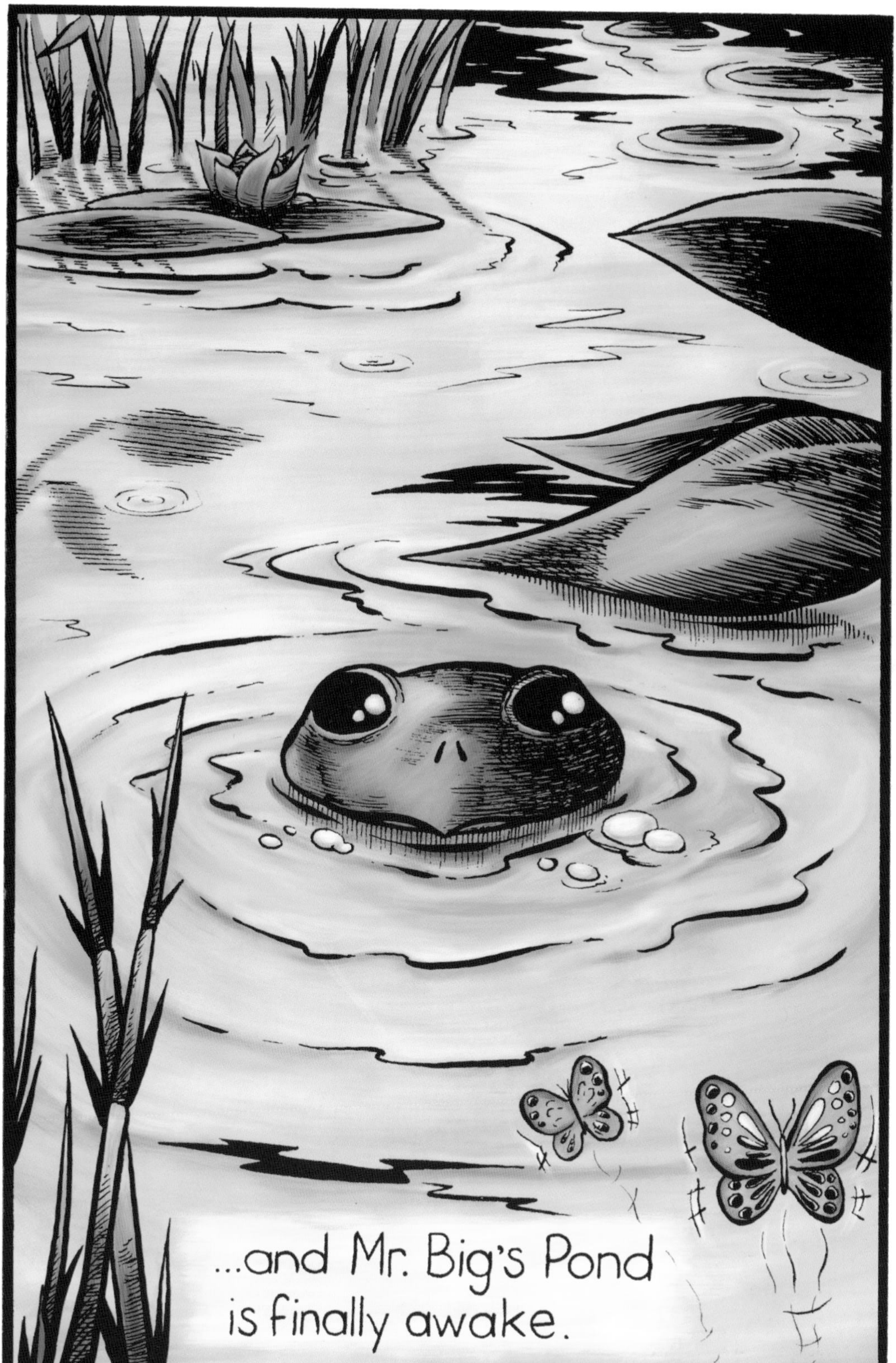
...and Mr. Big's Pond
is finally awake.

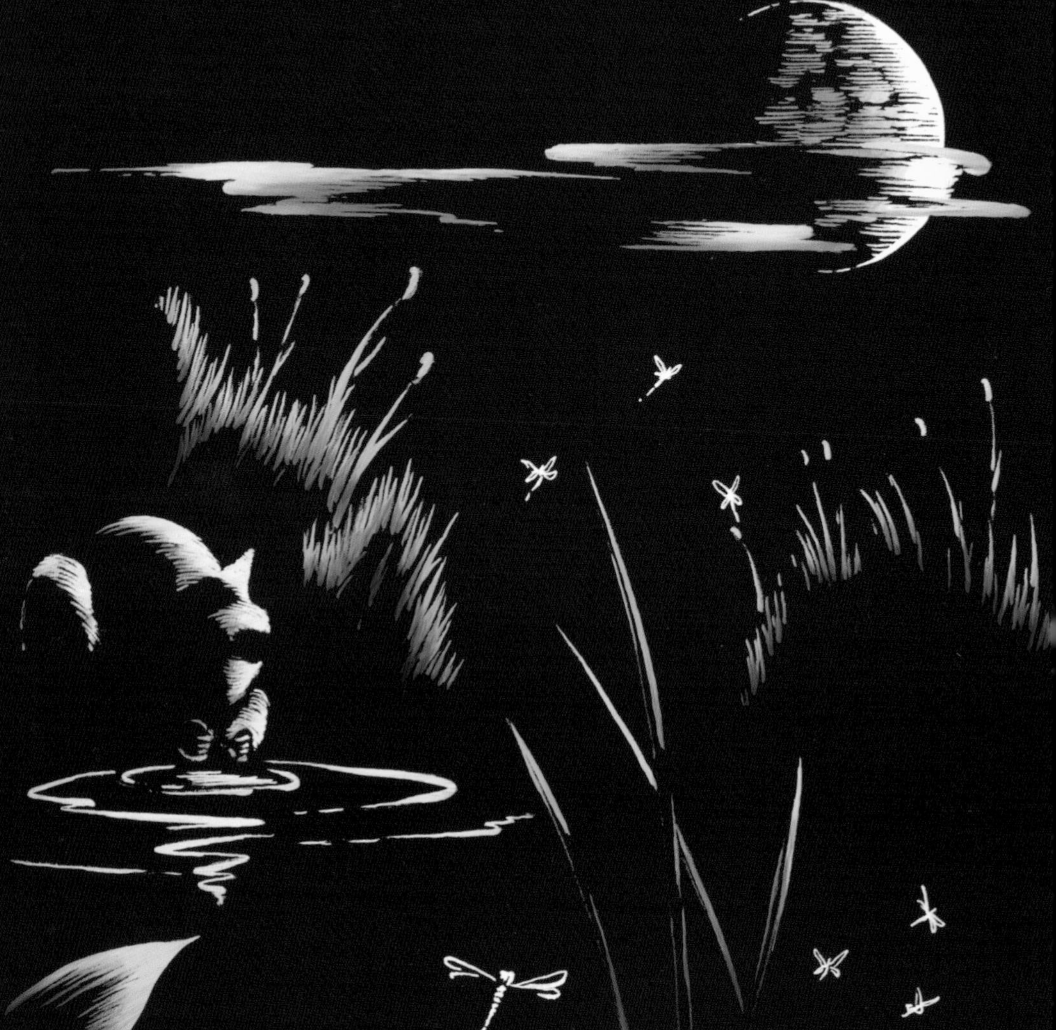

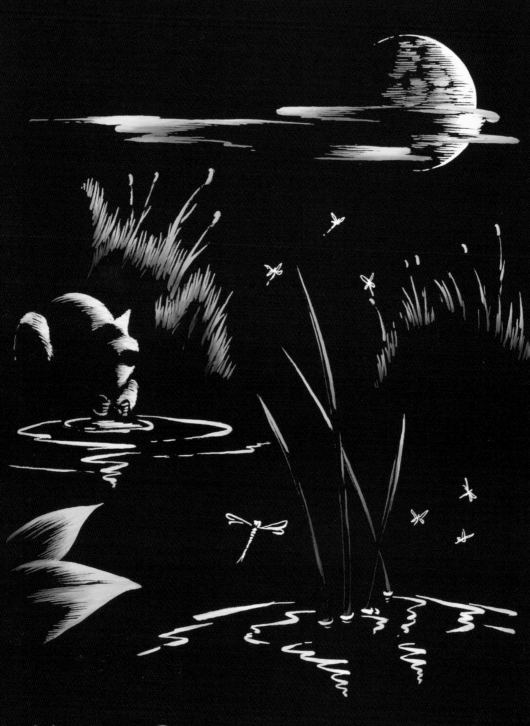

Mr. Big's Pond doesn't rest at night.

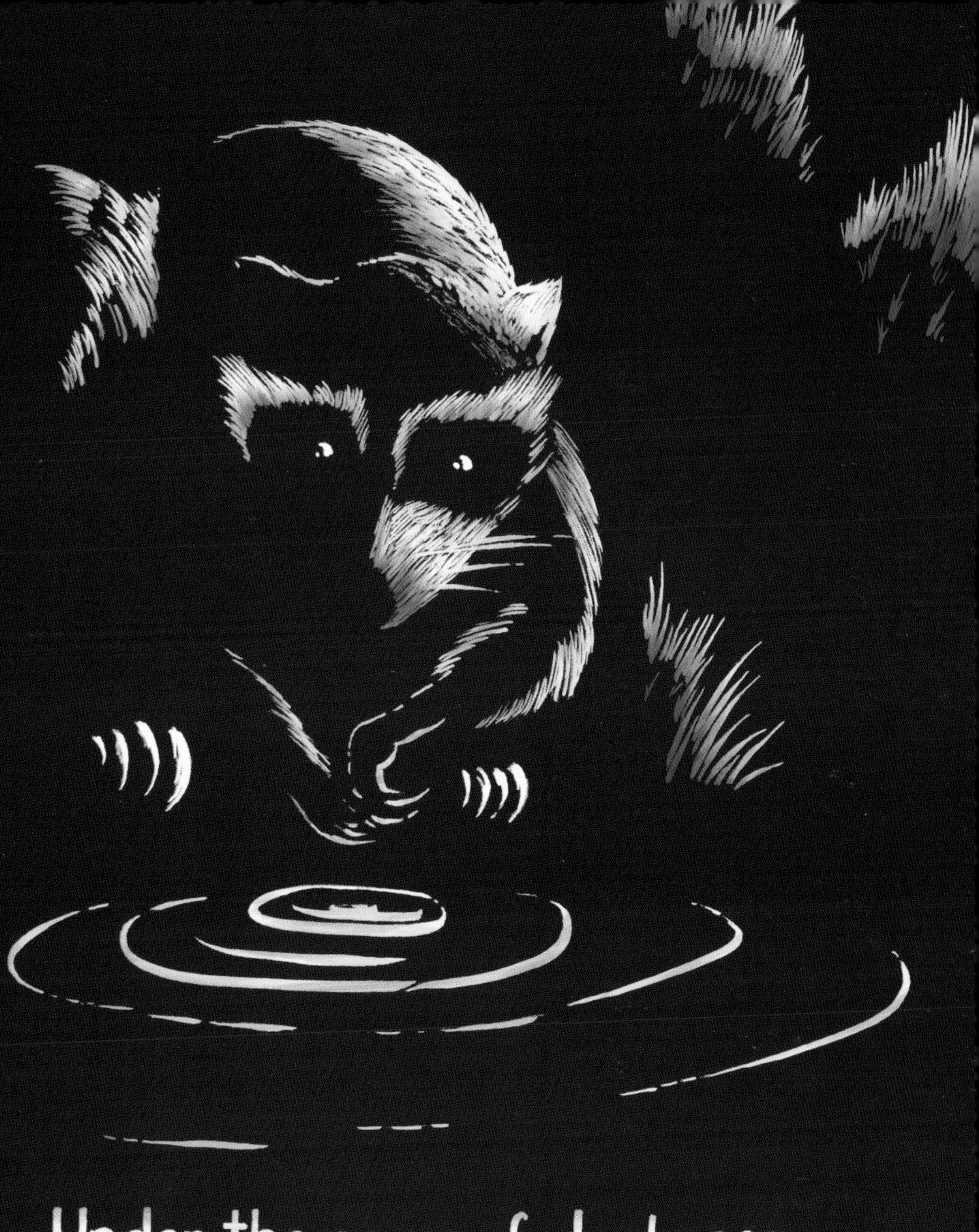

Under the cover of darkness,
things creep...

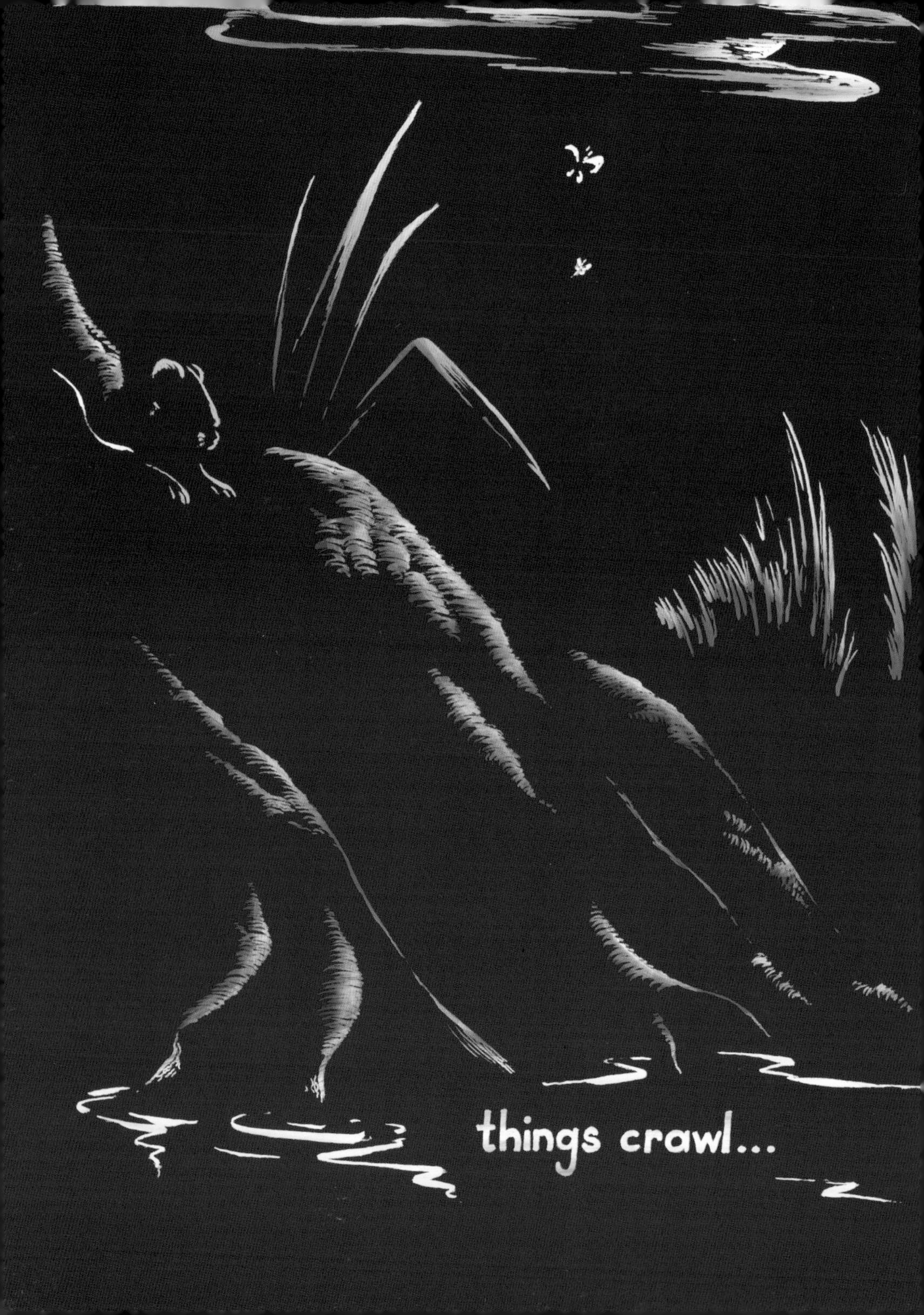

things crawl...

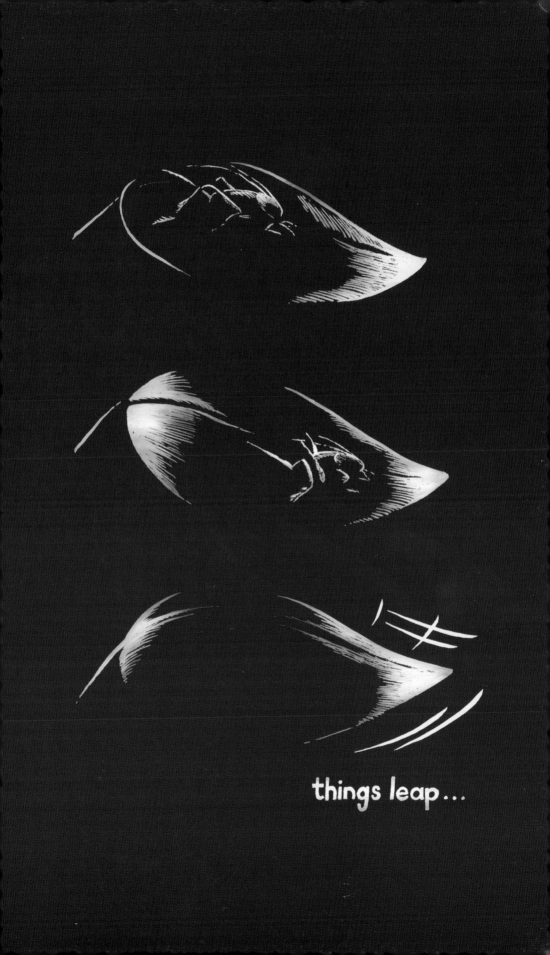

things leap...

and Mr. Big sees them all...

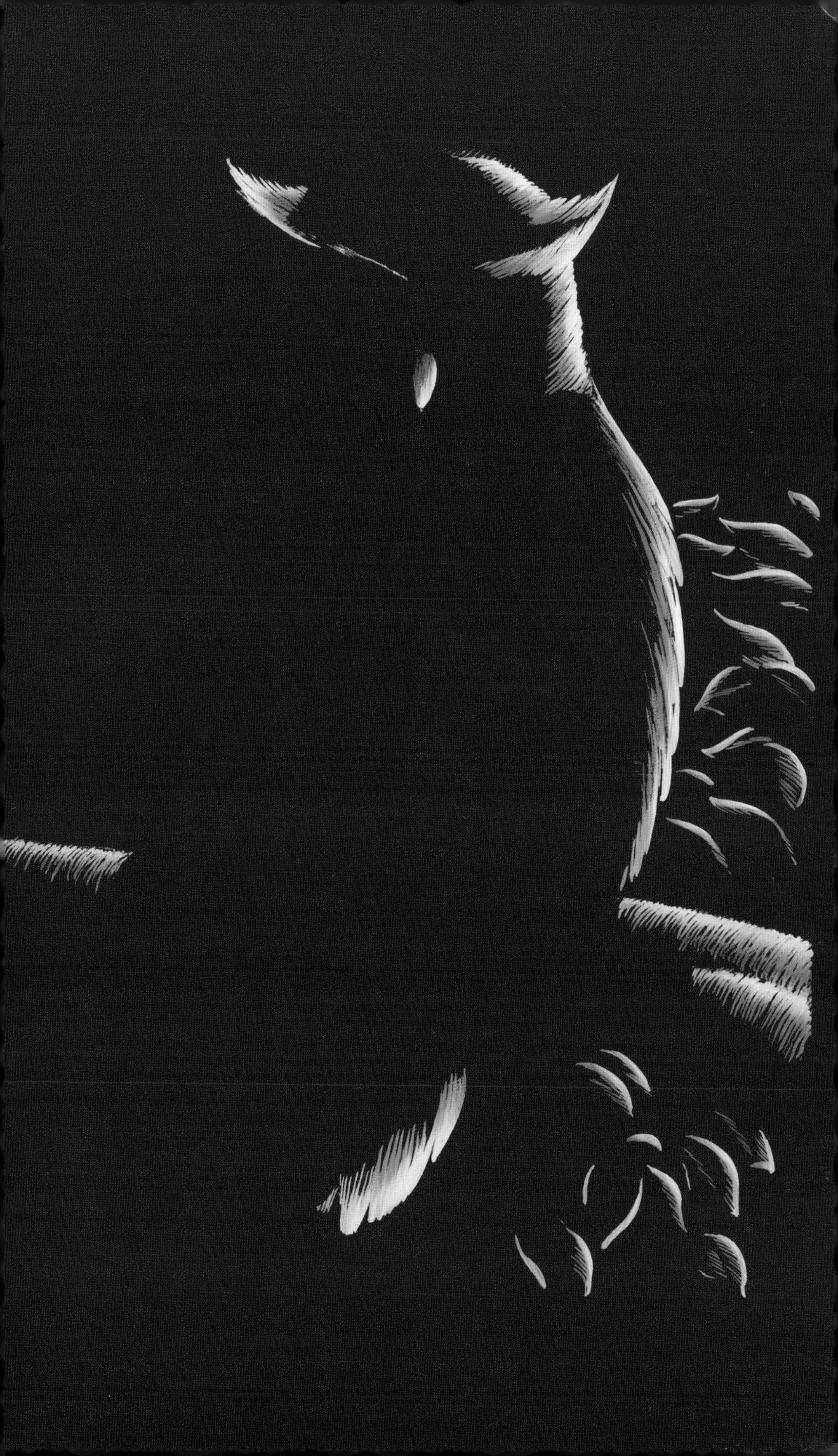

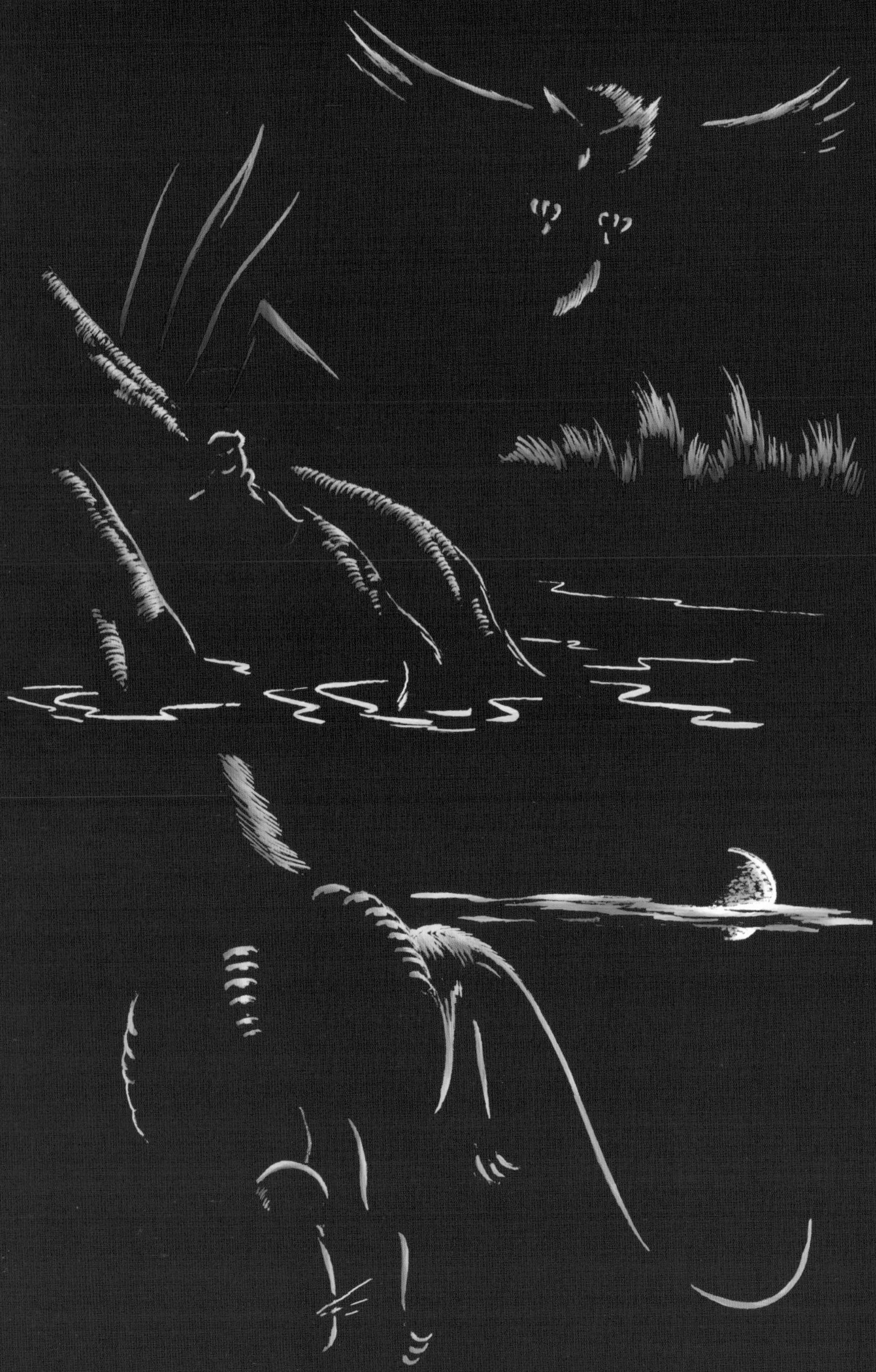

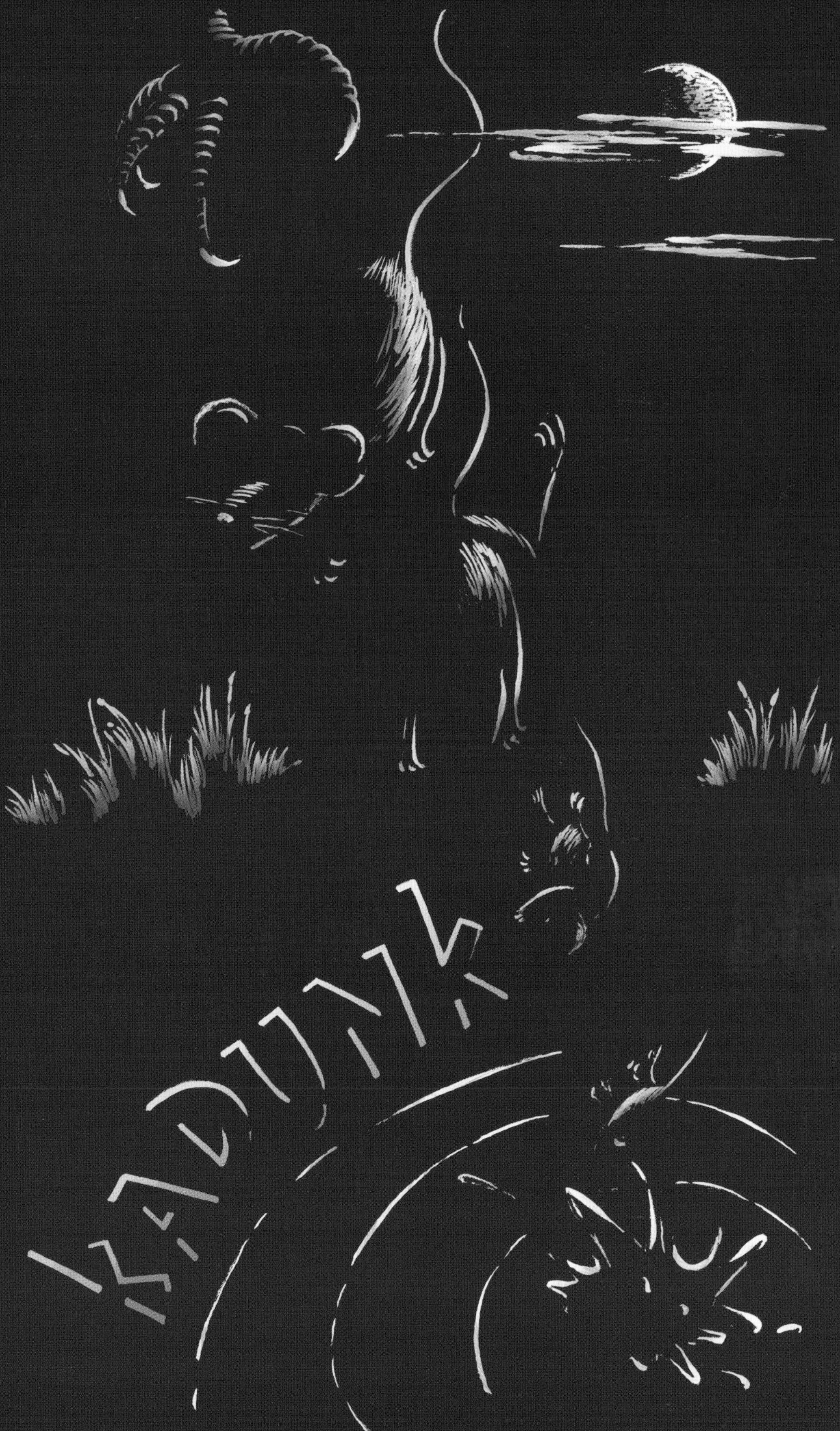
KA-DUNNK

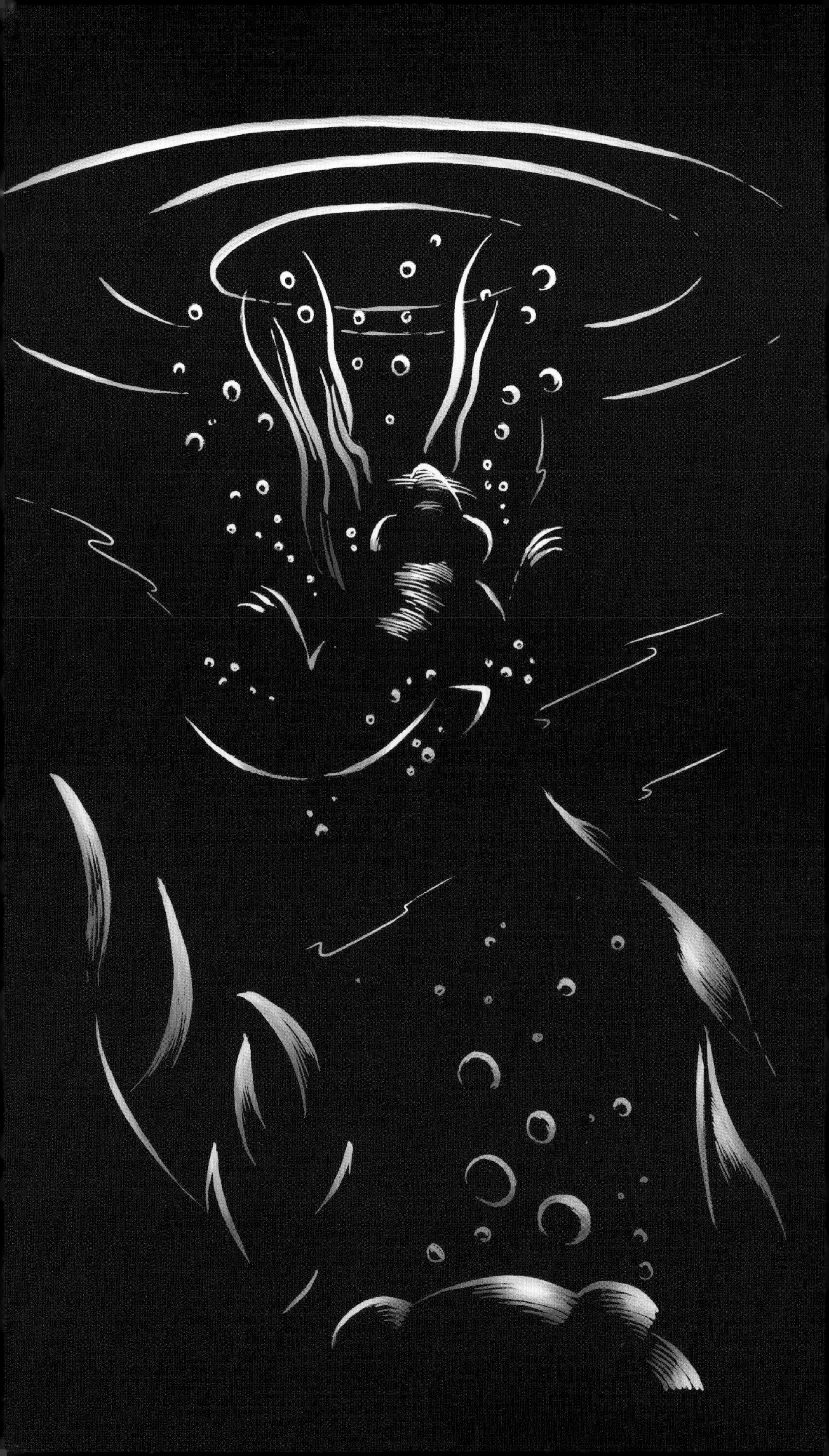

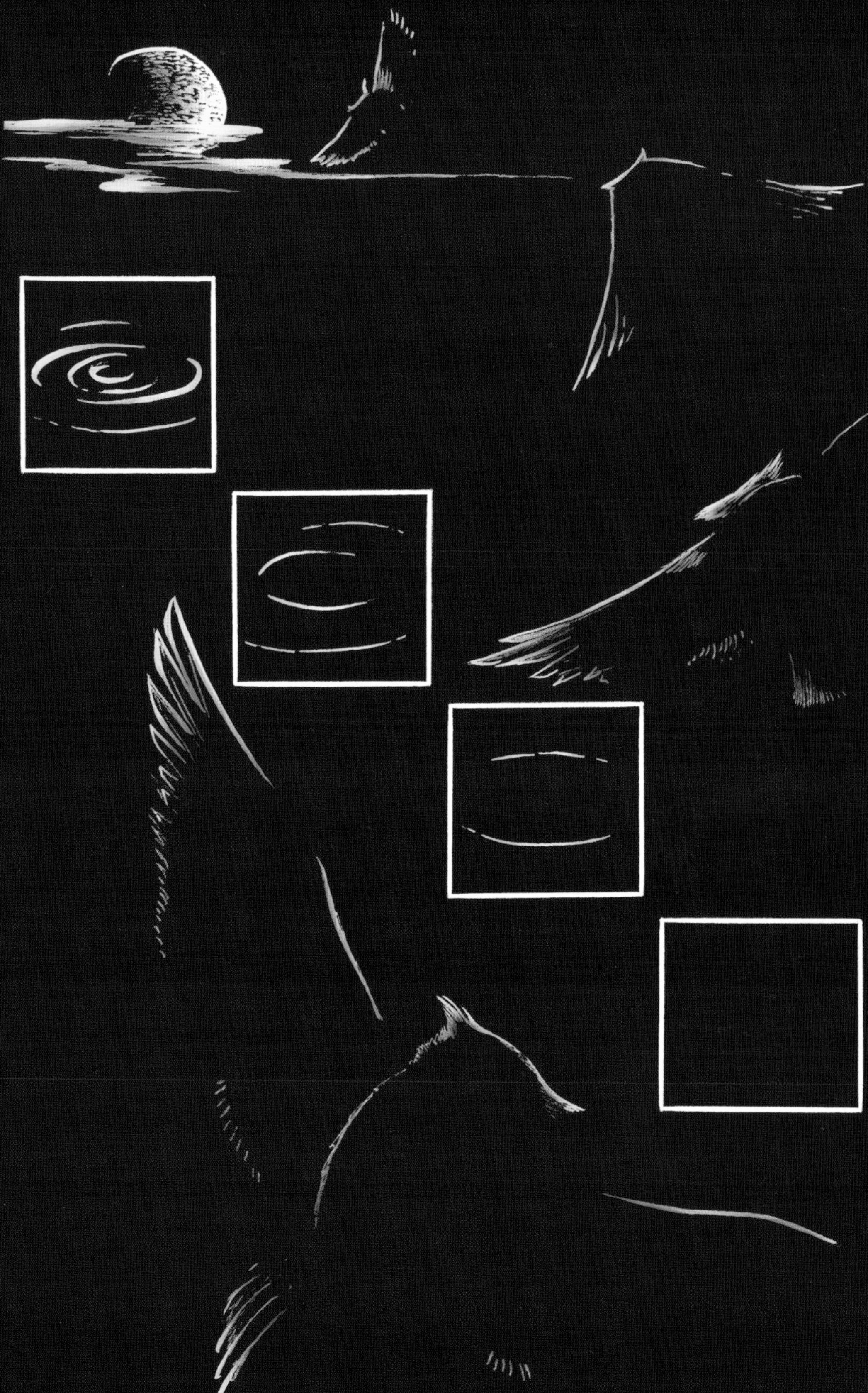

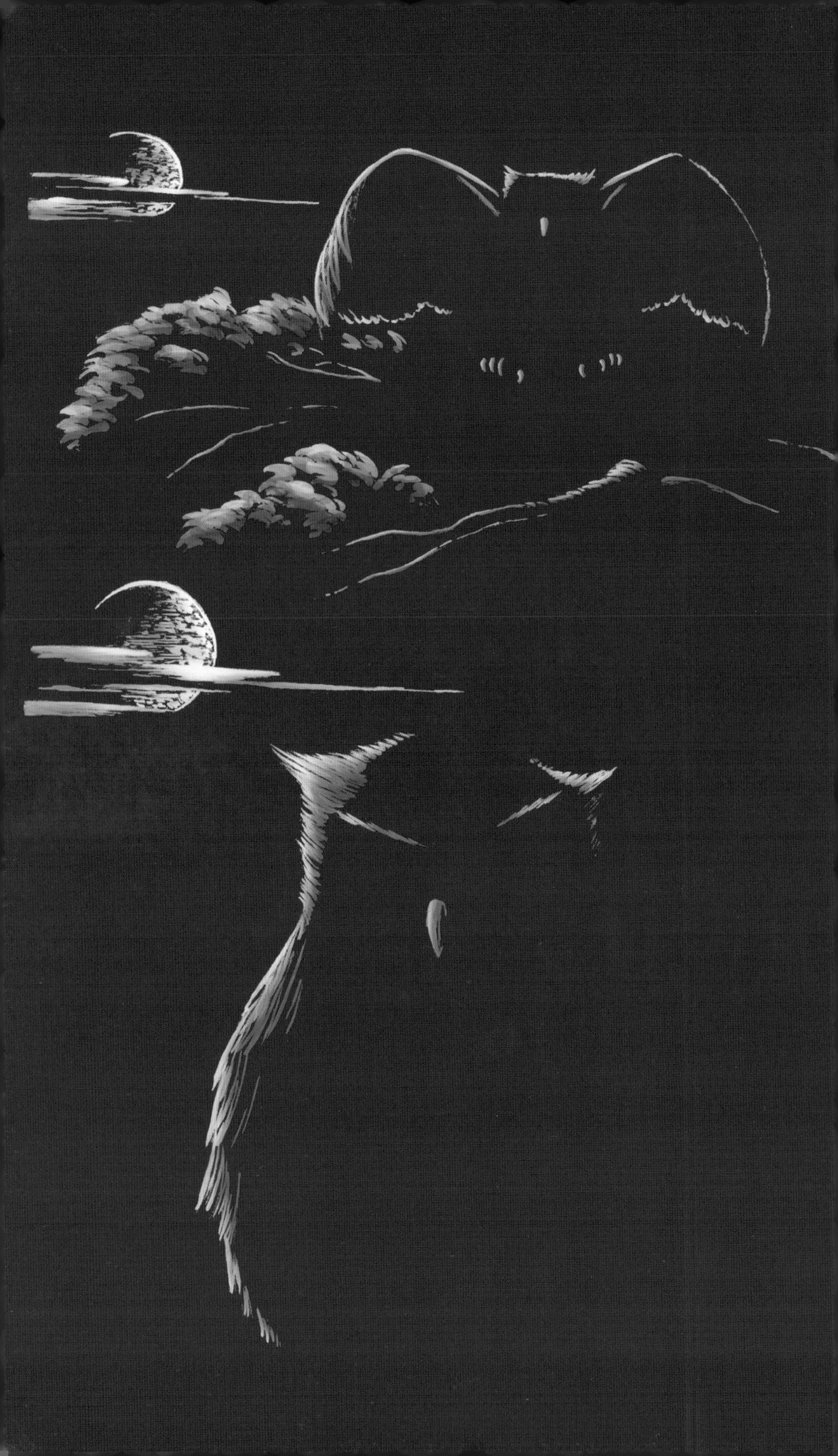

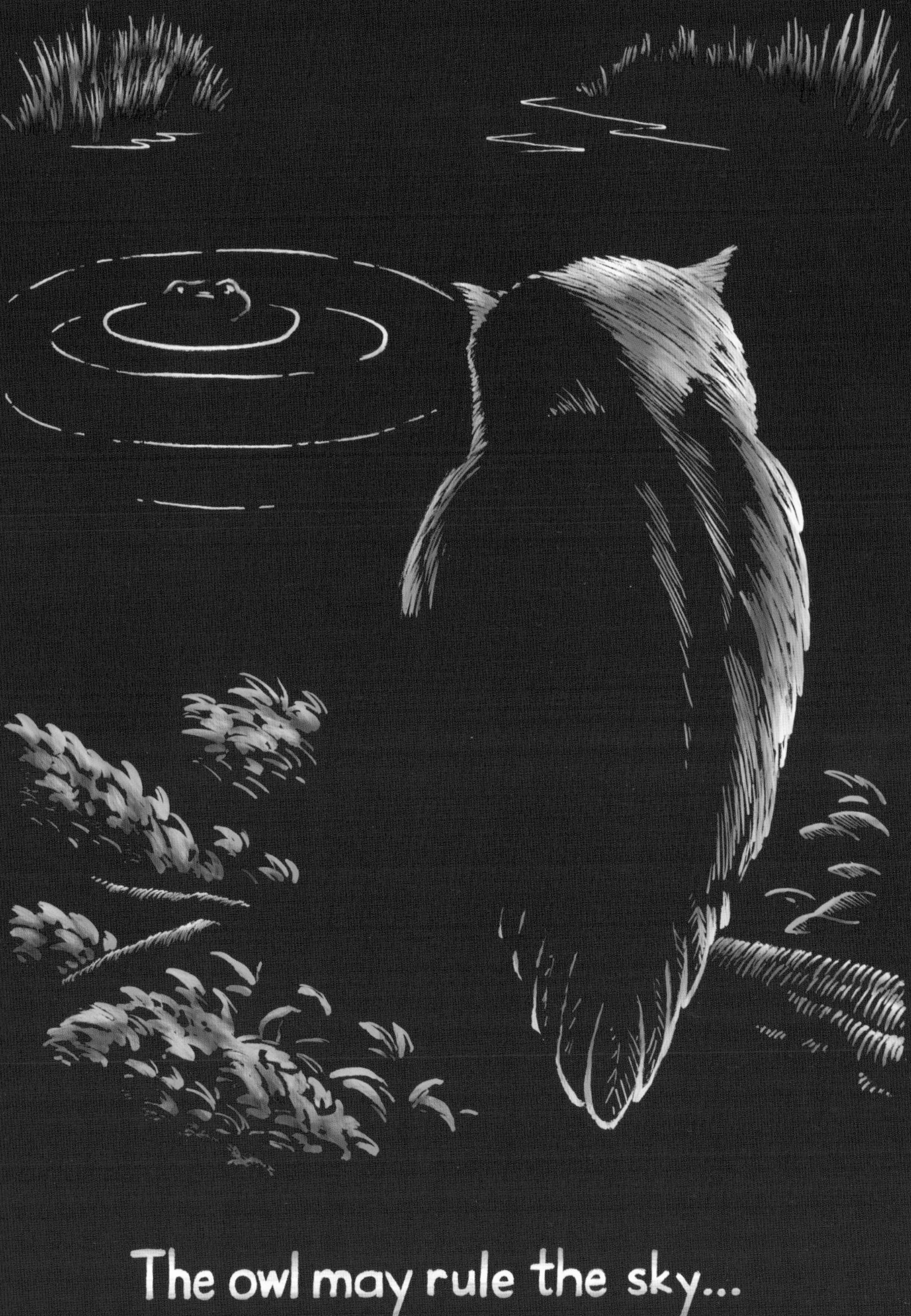

The owl may rule the sky...

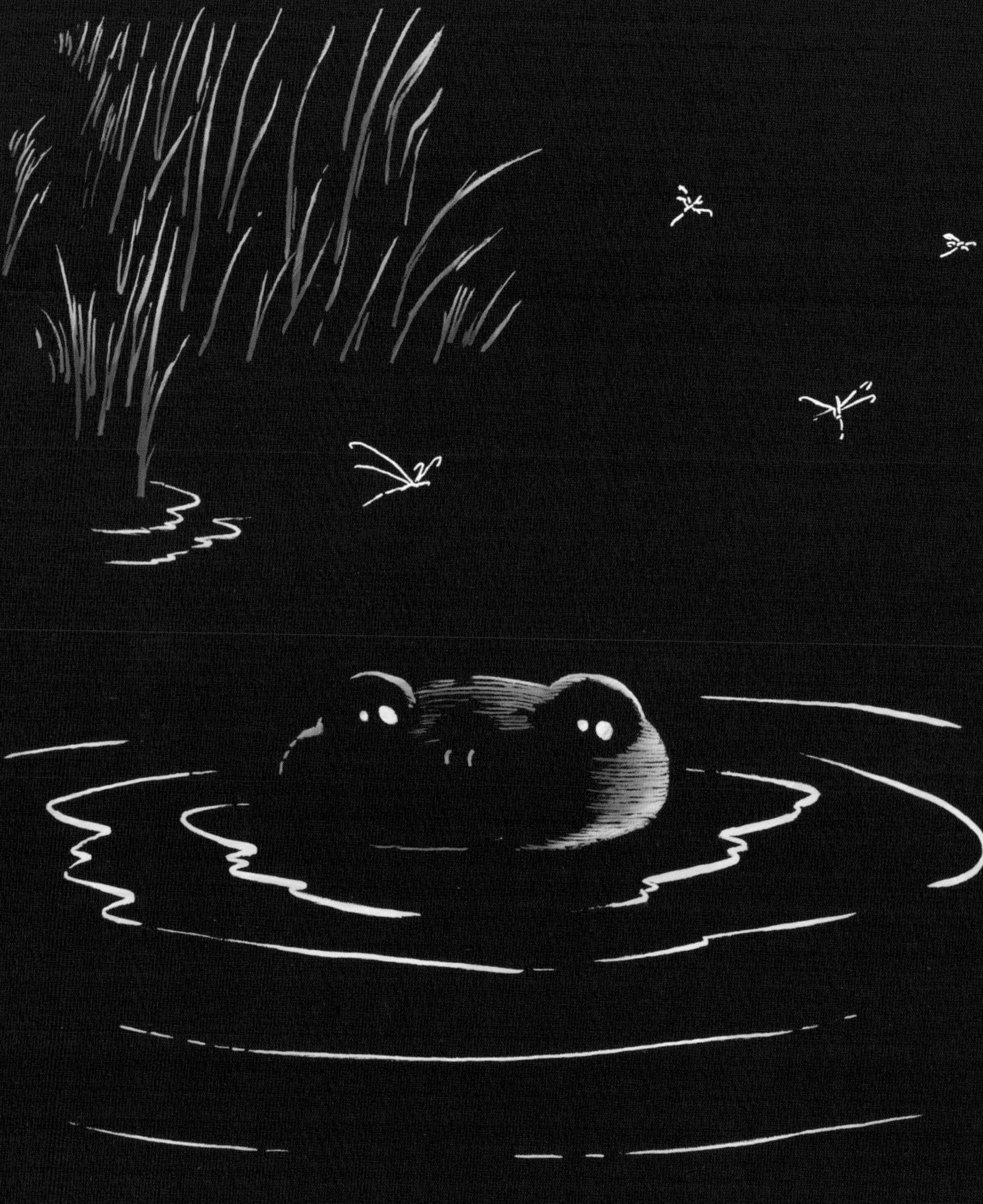

...but Mr. Big is king of the pond,
day and night.

And everyone knows this...

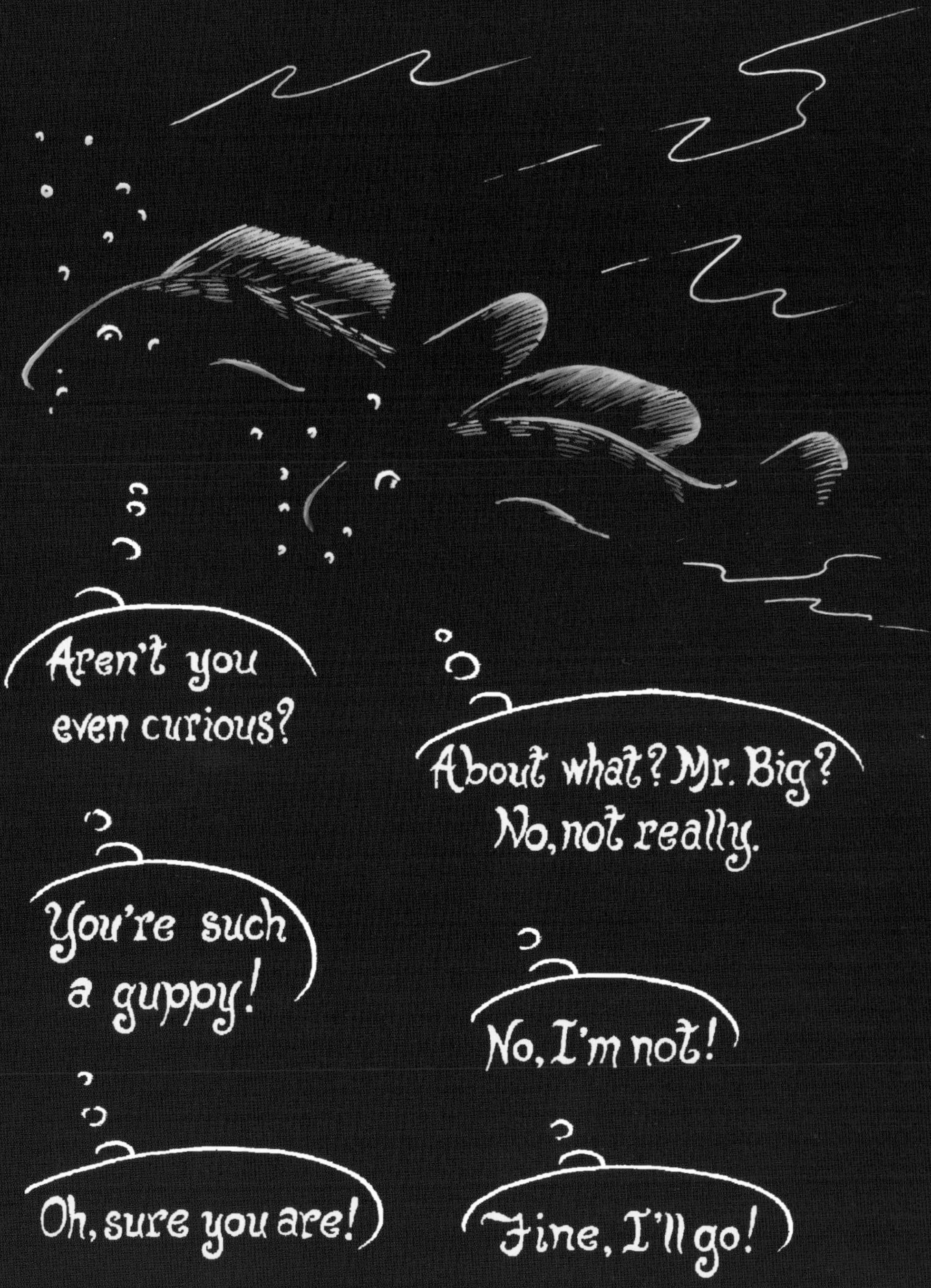
Aren't you even curious?
About what? Mr. Big? No, not really.
You're such a guppy!
No, I'm not!
Oh, sure you are!
Fine, I'll go!

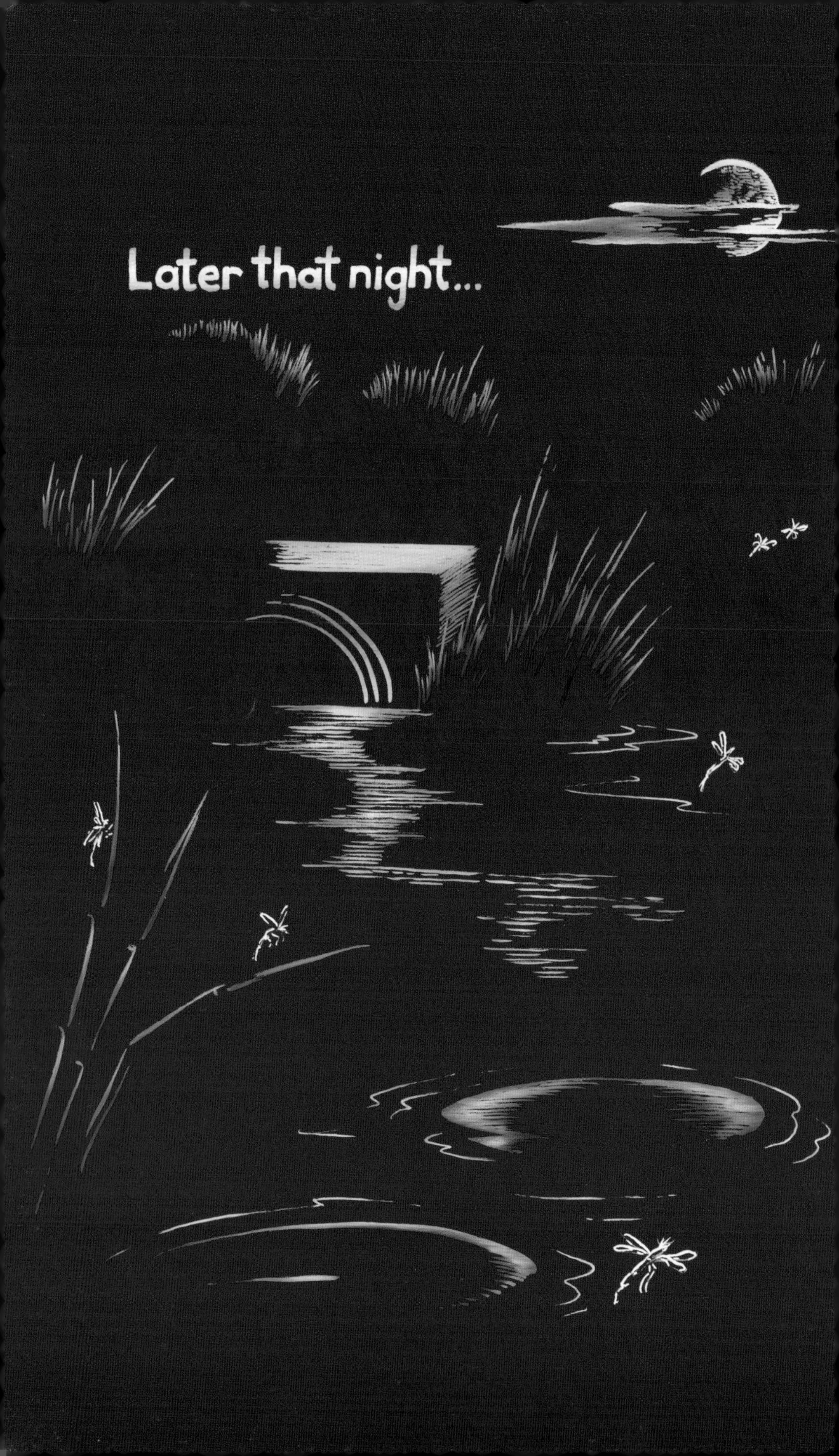
Later that night...

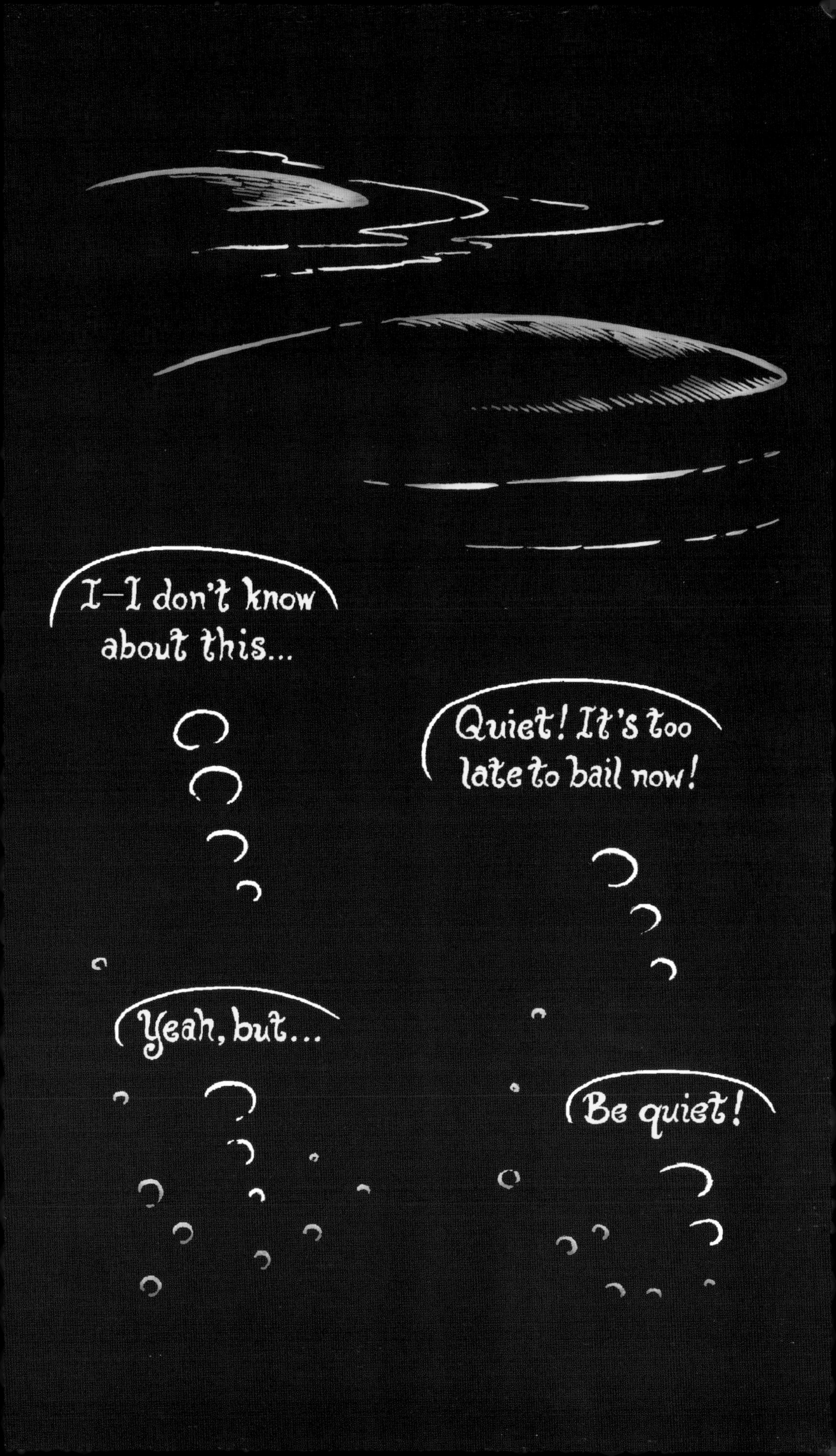
I—I don't know about this...
Quiet! It's too late to bail now!
Yeah, but...
Be quiet!

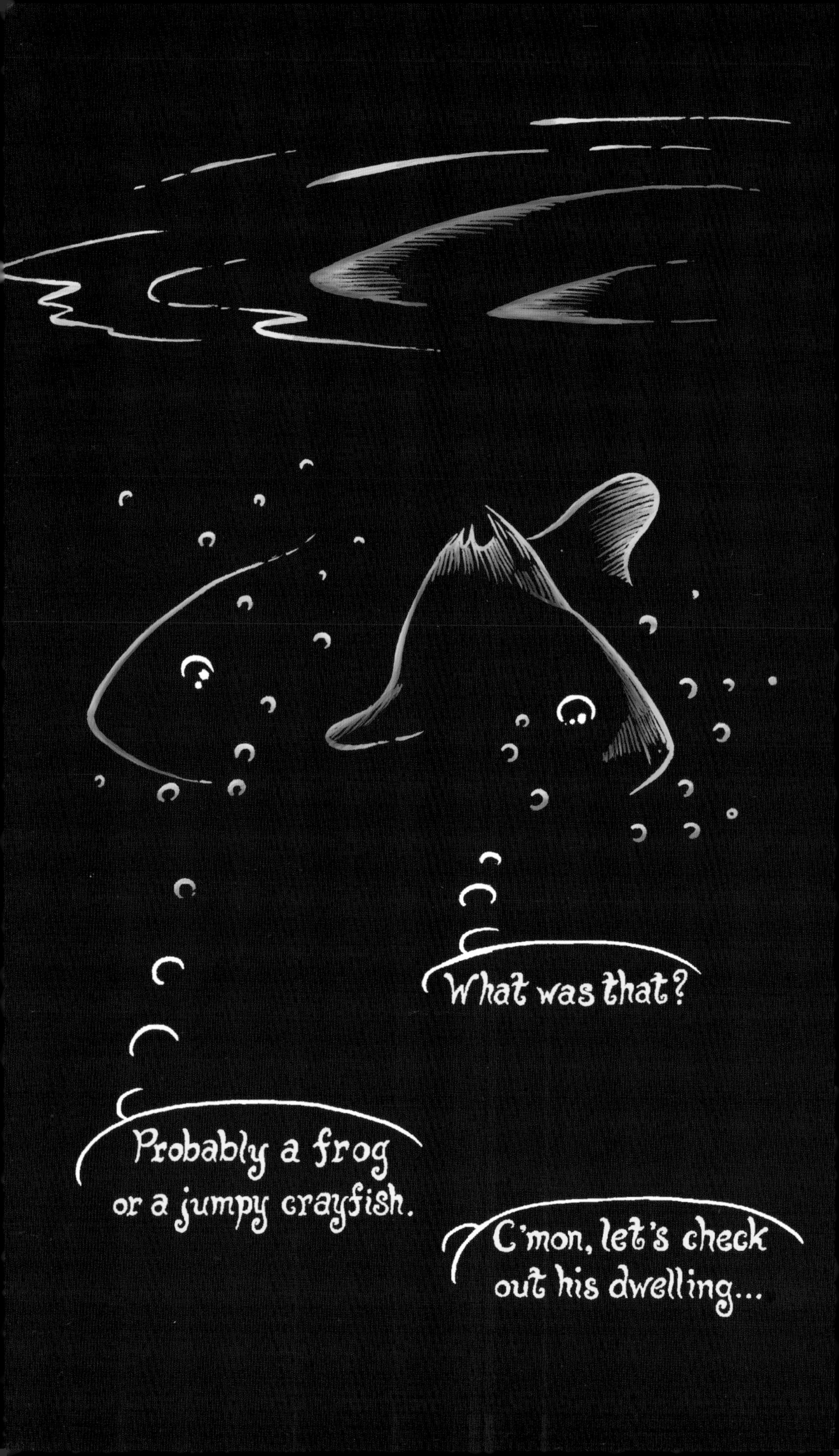
What was that?
Probably a frog or a jumpy crayfish.
C'mon, let's check out his dwelling...

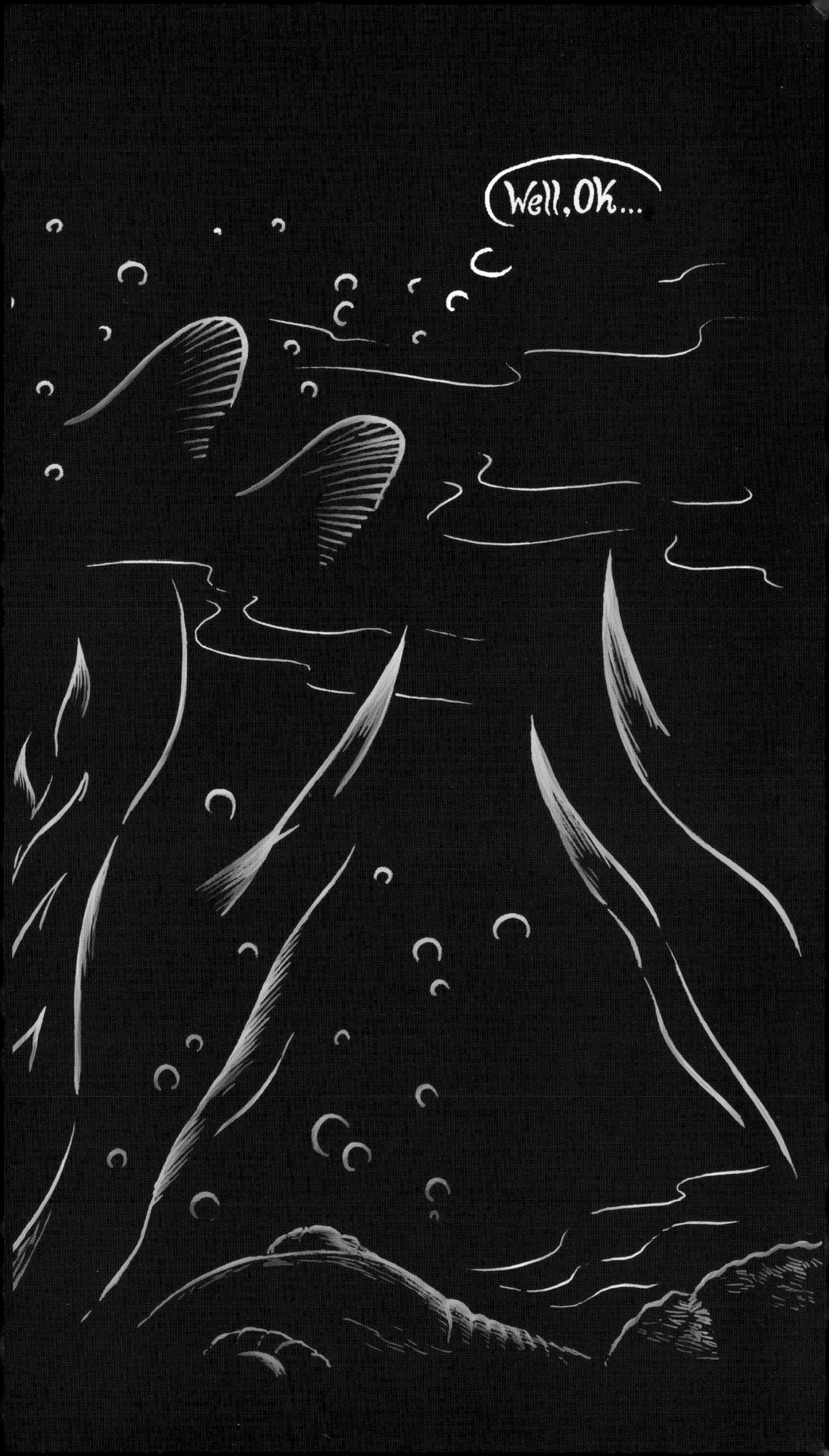
Well, OK...

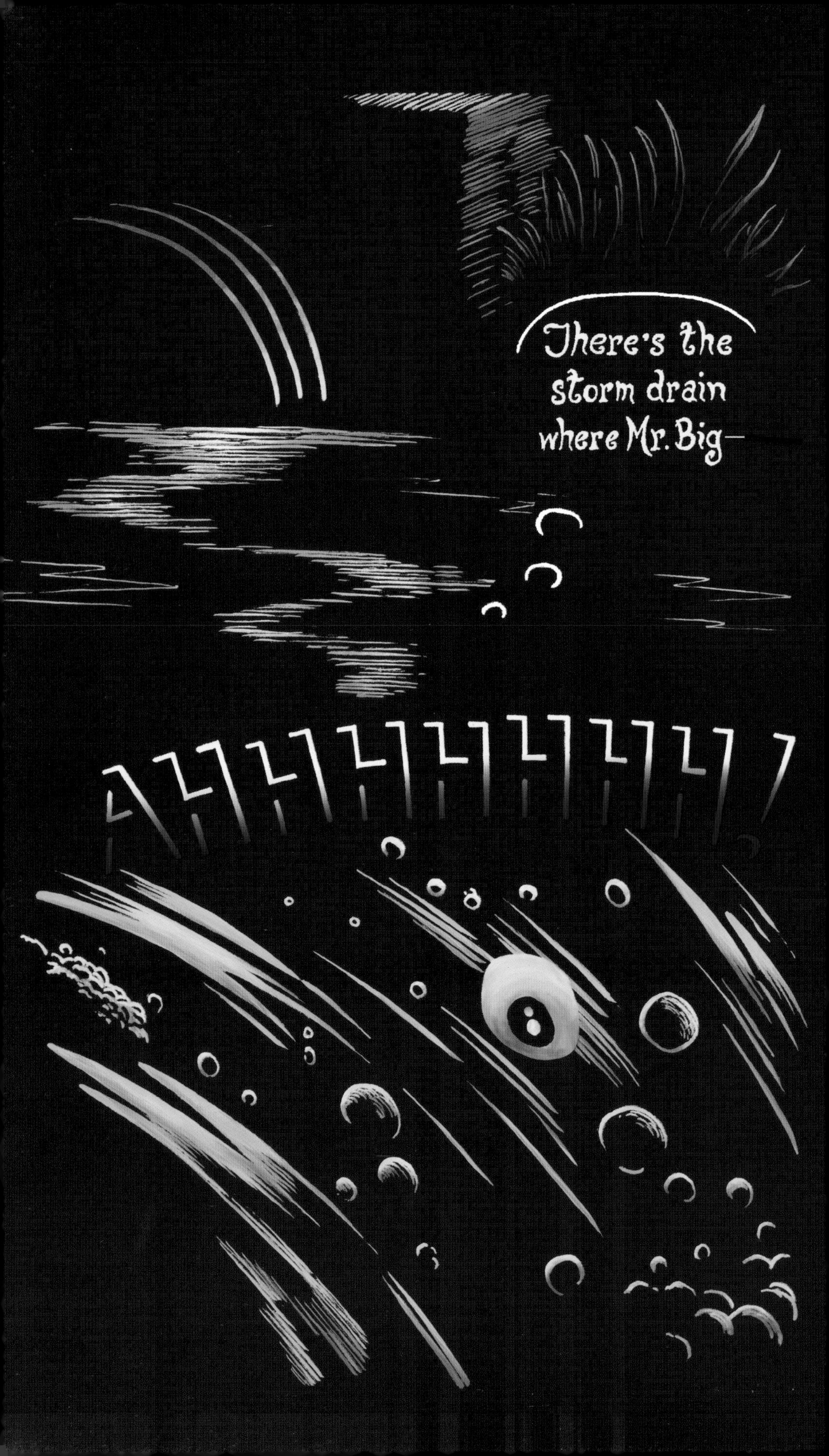
There's the storm drain where Mr. Big—
AHHHHHHHHHH!

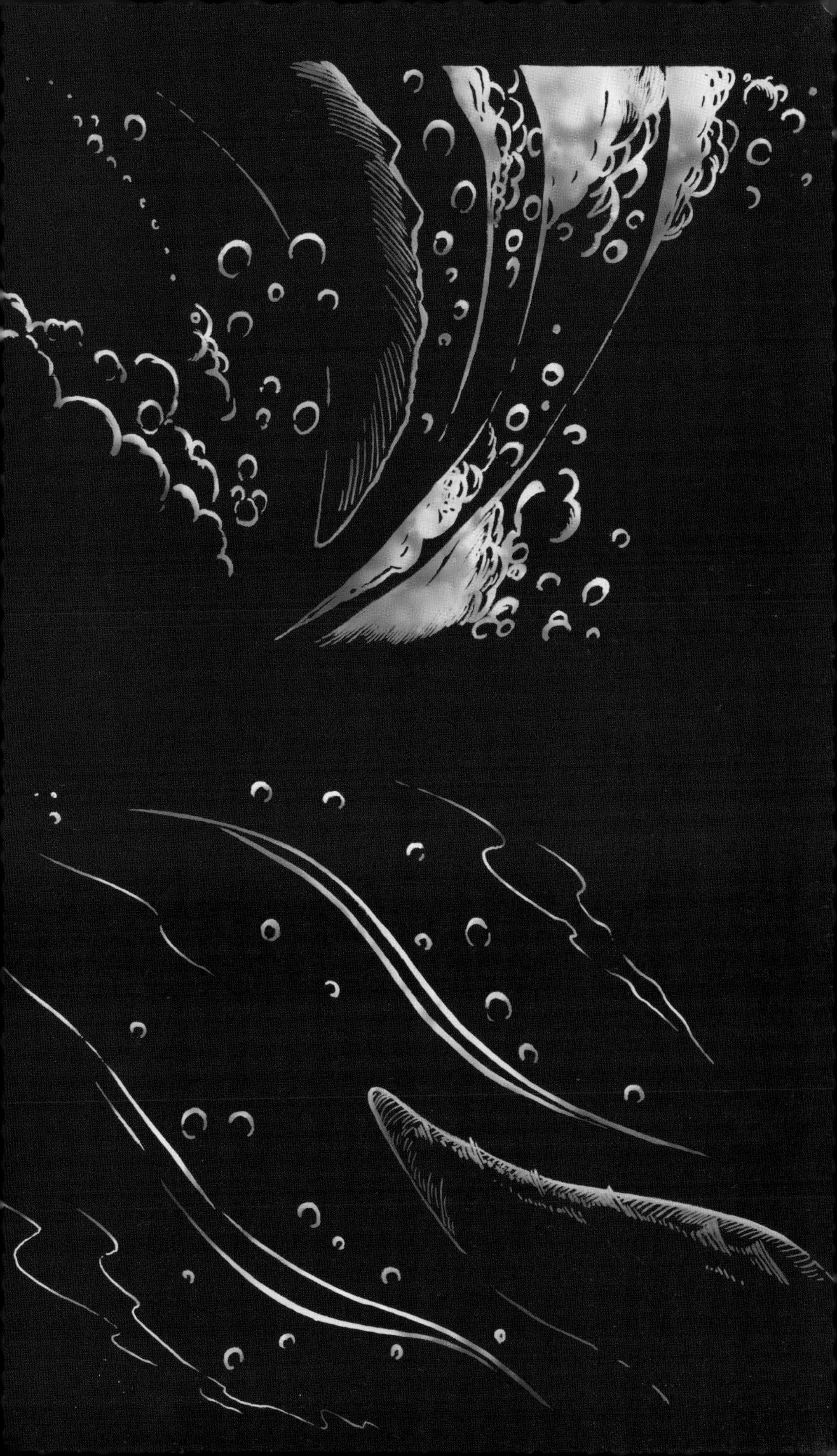

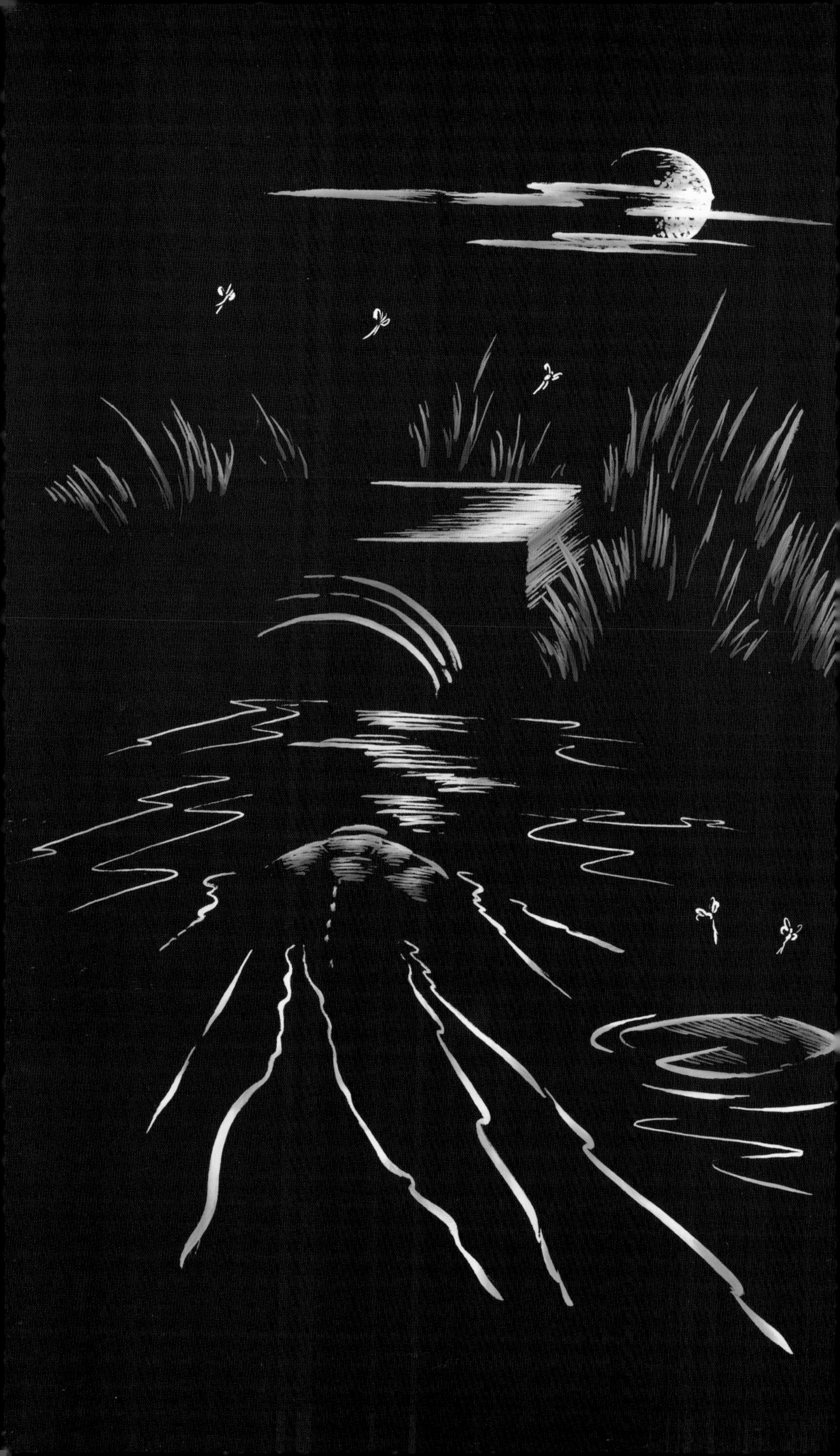

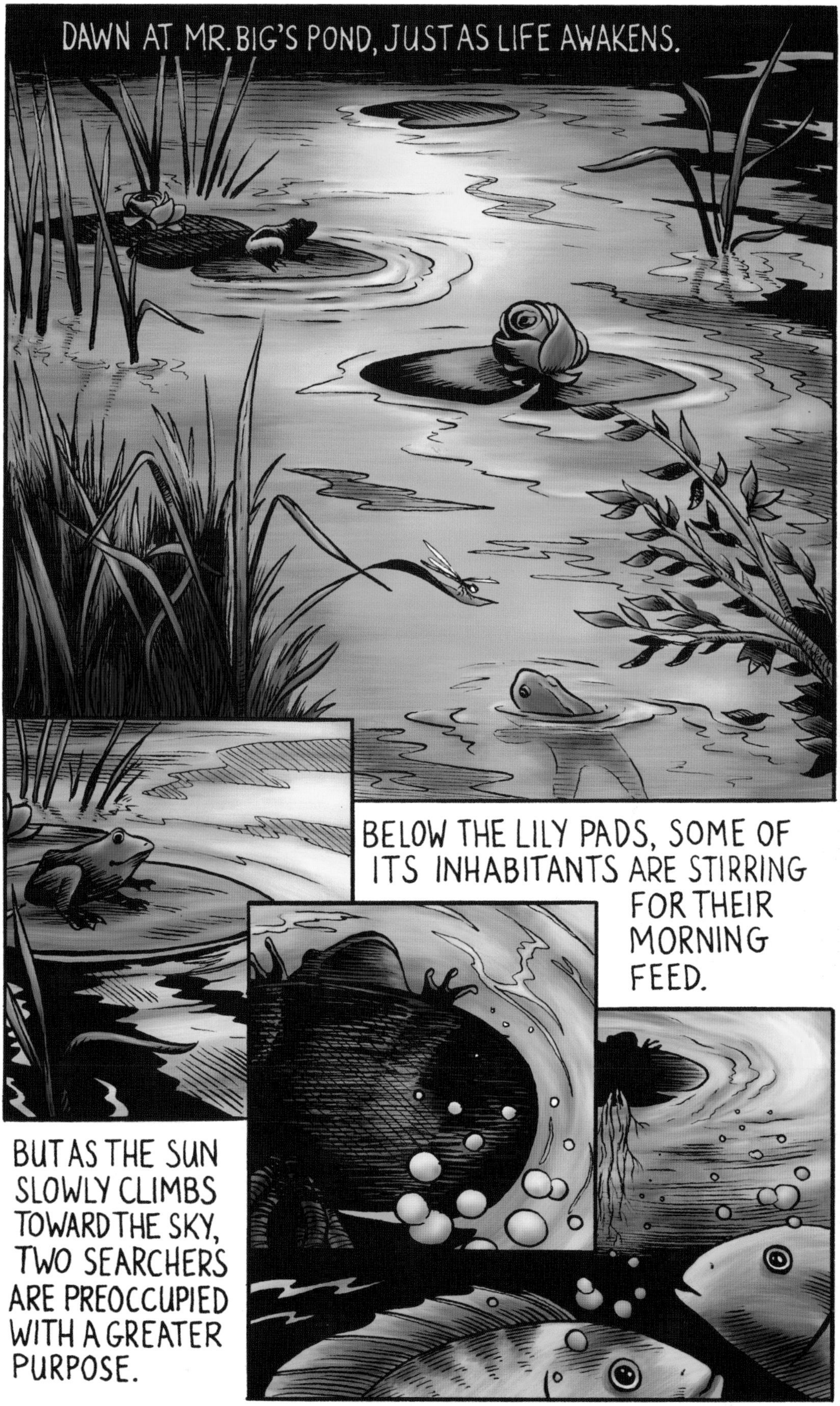
DAWN AT MR. BIG'S POND, JUST AS LIFE AWAKENS.
BELOW THE LILY PADS, SOME OF ITS INHABITANTS ARE STIRRING FOR THEIR MORNING FEED.
BUT AS THE SUN SLOWLY CLIMBS TOWARD THE SKY, TWO SEARCHERS ARE PREOCCUPIED WITH A GREATER PURPOSE.

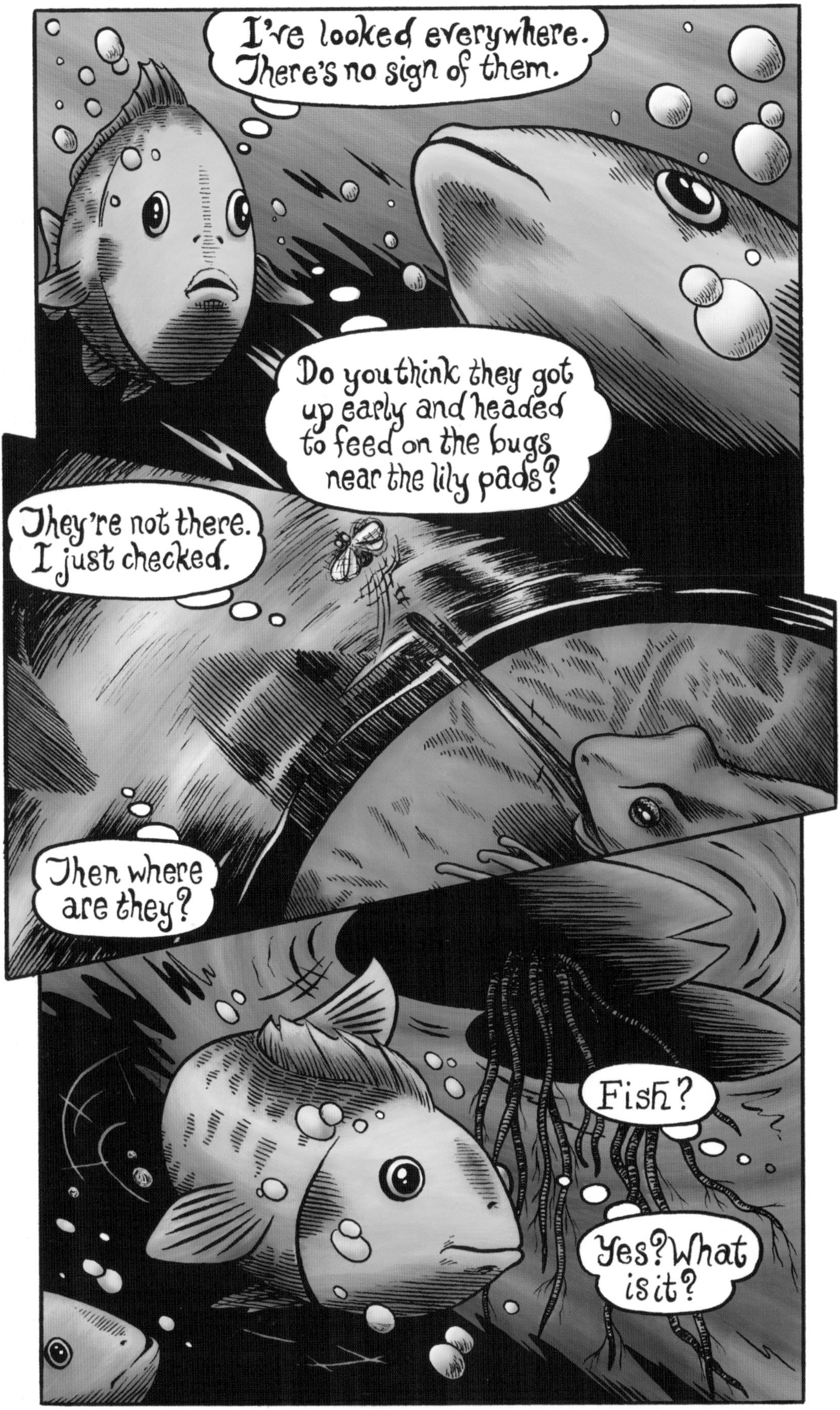
I've looked everywhere. There's no sign of them.
Do you think they got up early and headed to feed on the bugs near the lily pads?
They're not there. I just checked.
Then where are they?
Fish?
Yes? What is it?

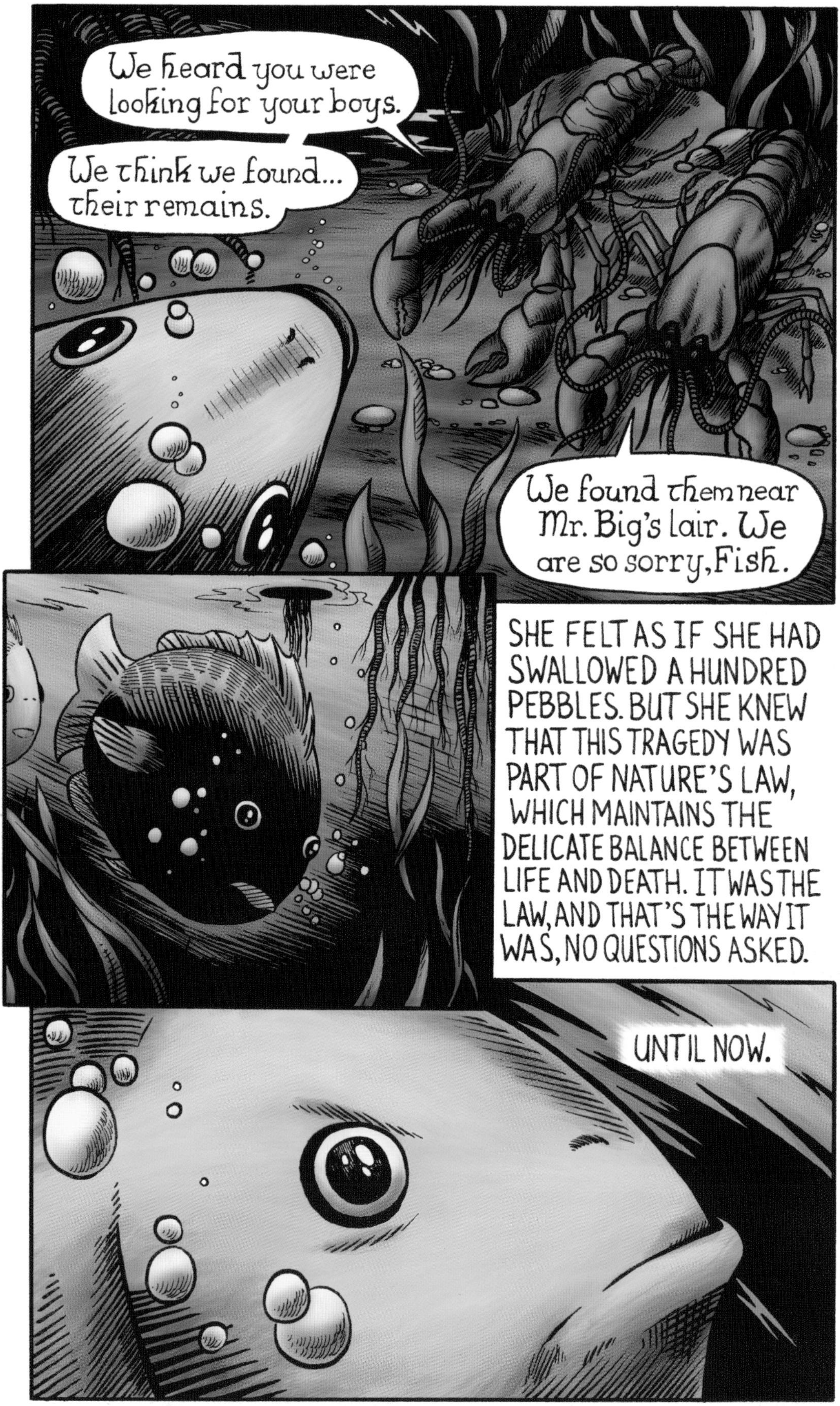
We heard you were looking for your boys.
We think we found... their remains.
We found them near Mr. Big's lair. We are so sorry, Fish.
SHE FELT AS IF SHE HAD SWALLOWED A HUNDRED PEBBLES. BUT SHE KNEW THAT THIS TRAGEDY WAS PART OF NATURE'S LAW, WHICH MAINTAINS THE DELICATE BALANCE BETWEEN LIFE AND DEATH. IT WAS THE LAW, AND THAT'S THE WAY IT WAS, NO QUESTIONS ASKED.
UNTIL NOW.

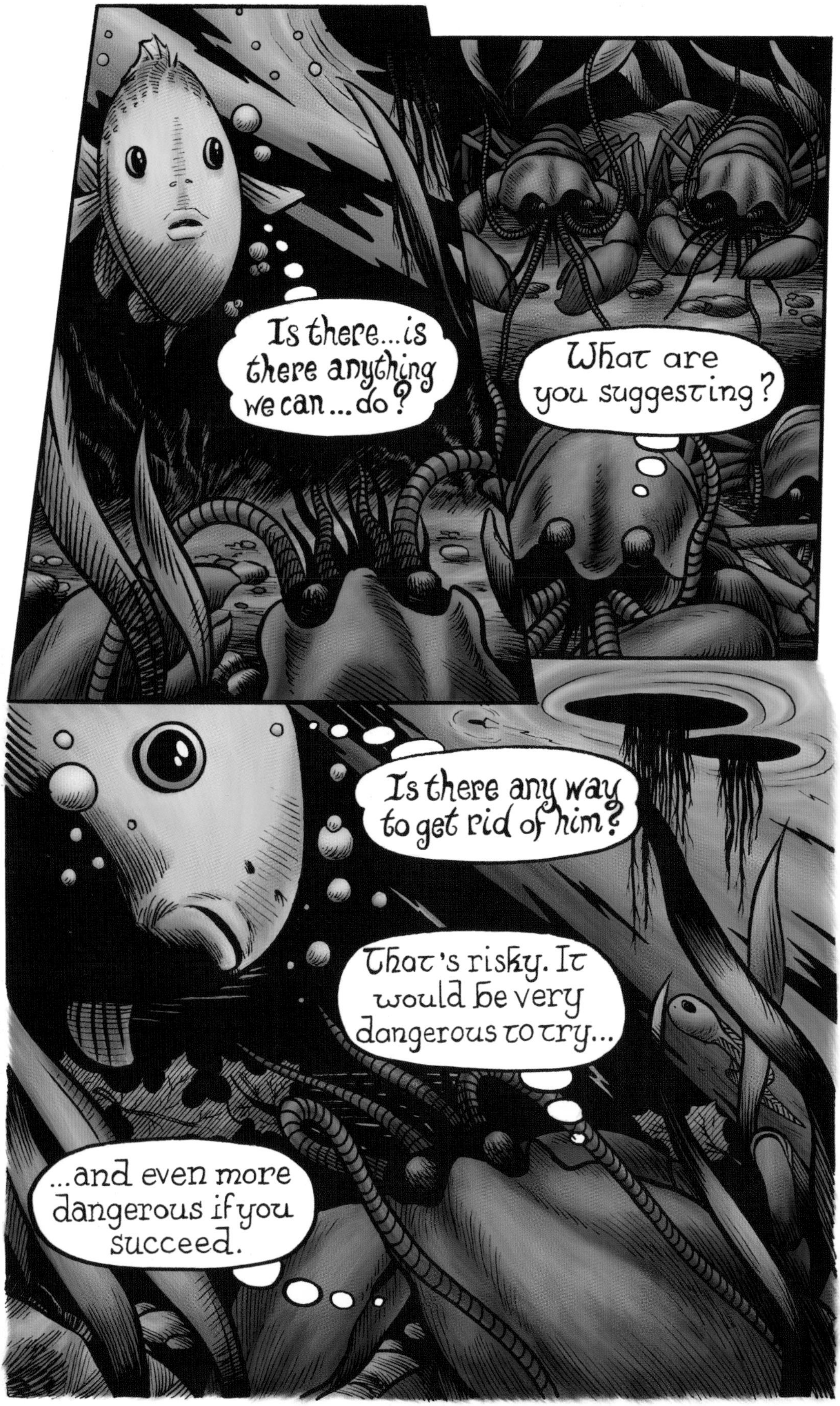
Is there...is there anything we can...do?
What are you suggesting?
Is there any way to get rid of him?
That's risky. It would be very dangerous to try...
...and even more dangerous if you succeed.

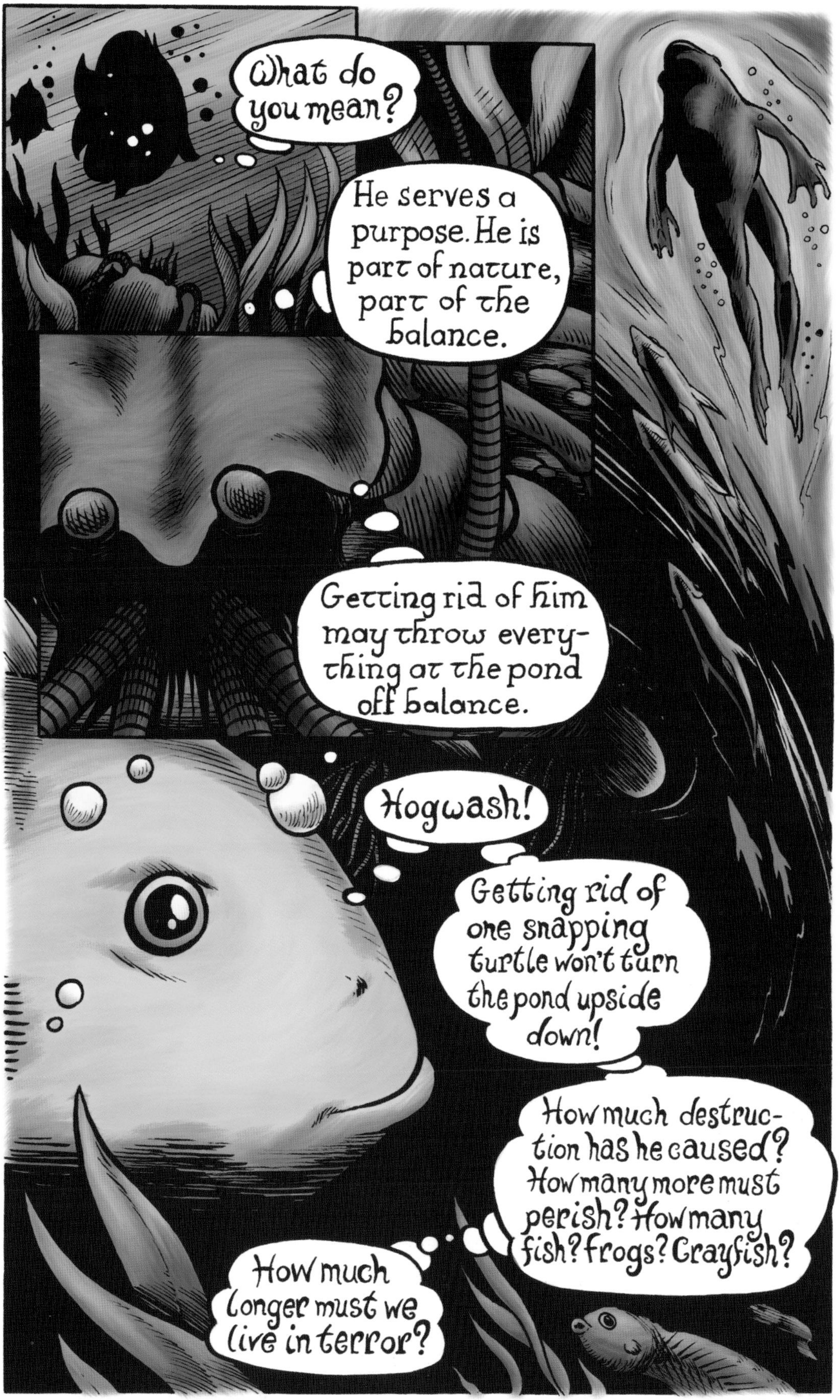
What do you mean?
He serves a purpose. He is part of nature, part of the balance.
Getting rid of him may throw everything at the pond off balance.
Hogwash!
Getting rid of one snapping turtle won't turn the pond upside down!
How much destruction has he caused? How many more must perish? How many fish? Frogs? Crayfish?
How much longer must we live in terror?

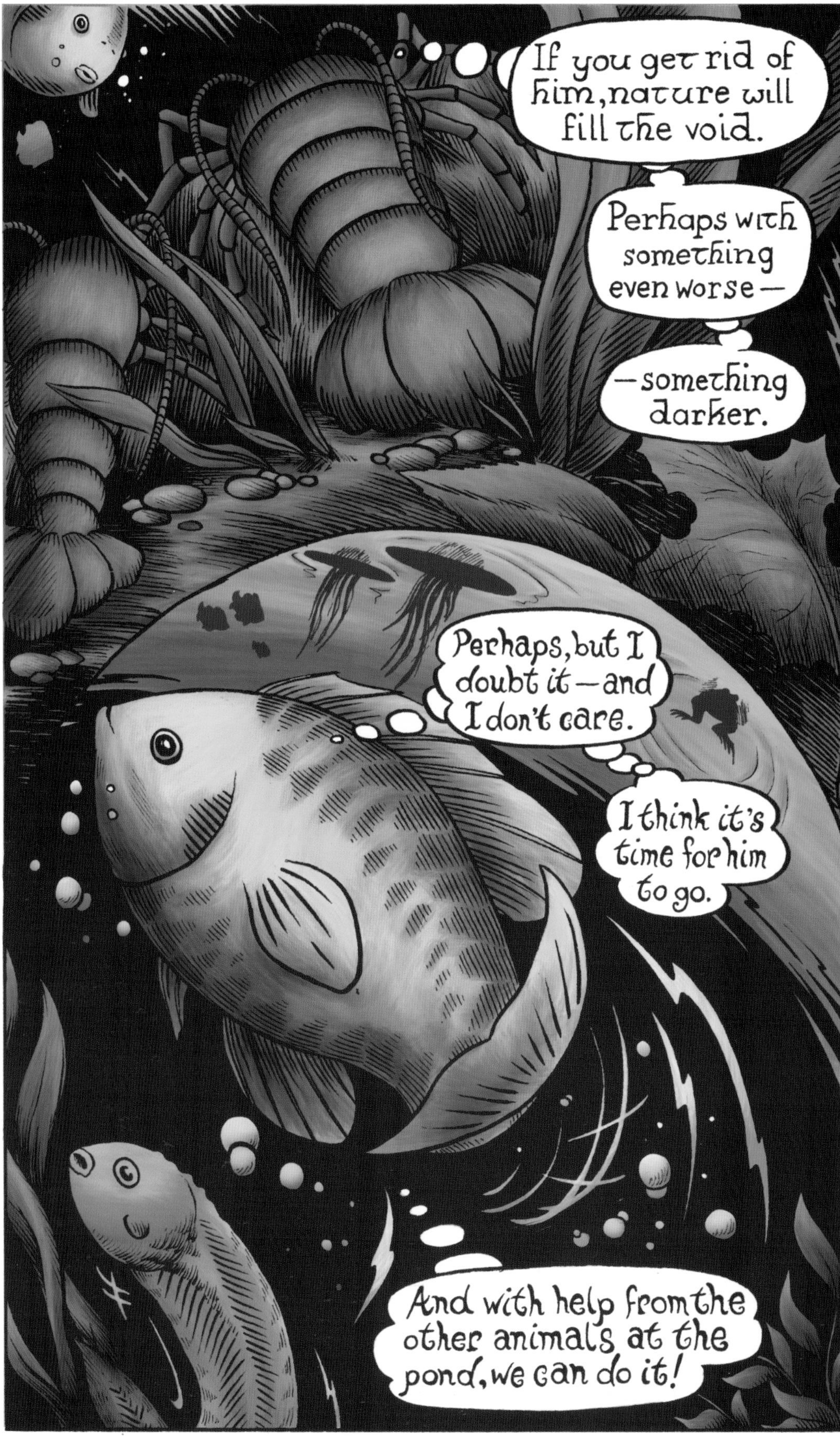
If you get rid of him, nature will fill the void.
Perhaps with something even worse—
—something darker.
Perhaps, but I doubt it—and I don't care.
I think it's time for him to go.
And with help from the other animals at the pond, we can do it!

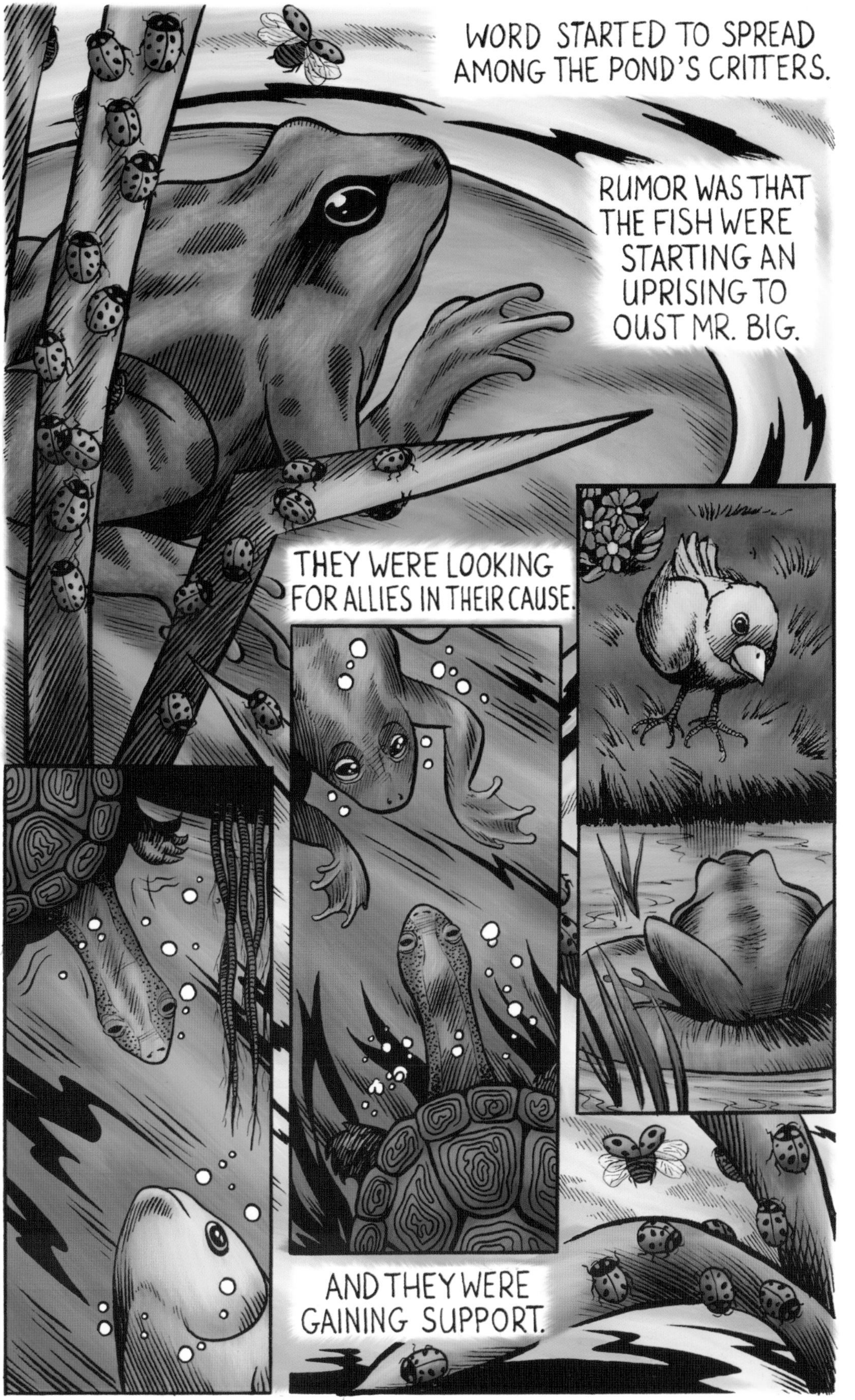
WORD STARTED TO SPREAD AMONG THE POND'S CRITTERS.
RUMOR WAS THAT THE FISH WERE STARTING AN UPRISING TO OUST MR. BIG.
THEY WERE LOOKING FOR ALLIES IN THEIR CAUSE.
AND THEY WERE GAINING SUPPORT.

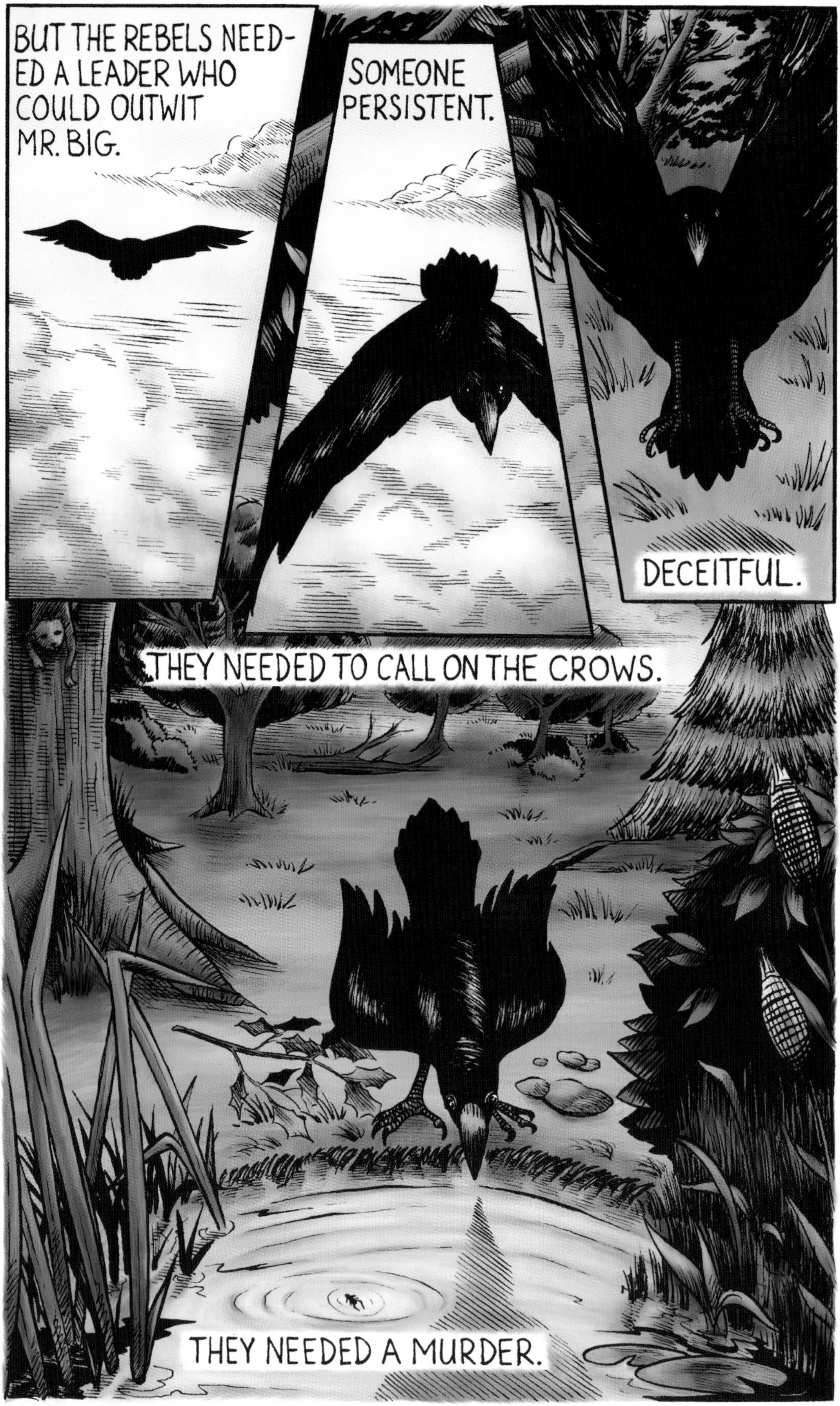

BUT THE REBELS NEEDED A LEADER WHO COULD OUTWIT MR. BIG.
SOMEONE PERSISTENT.
DECEITFUL.
THEY NEEDED TO CALL ON THE CROWS.
THEY NEEDED A MURDER.

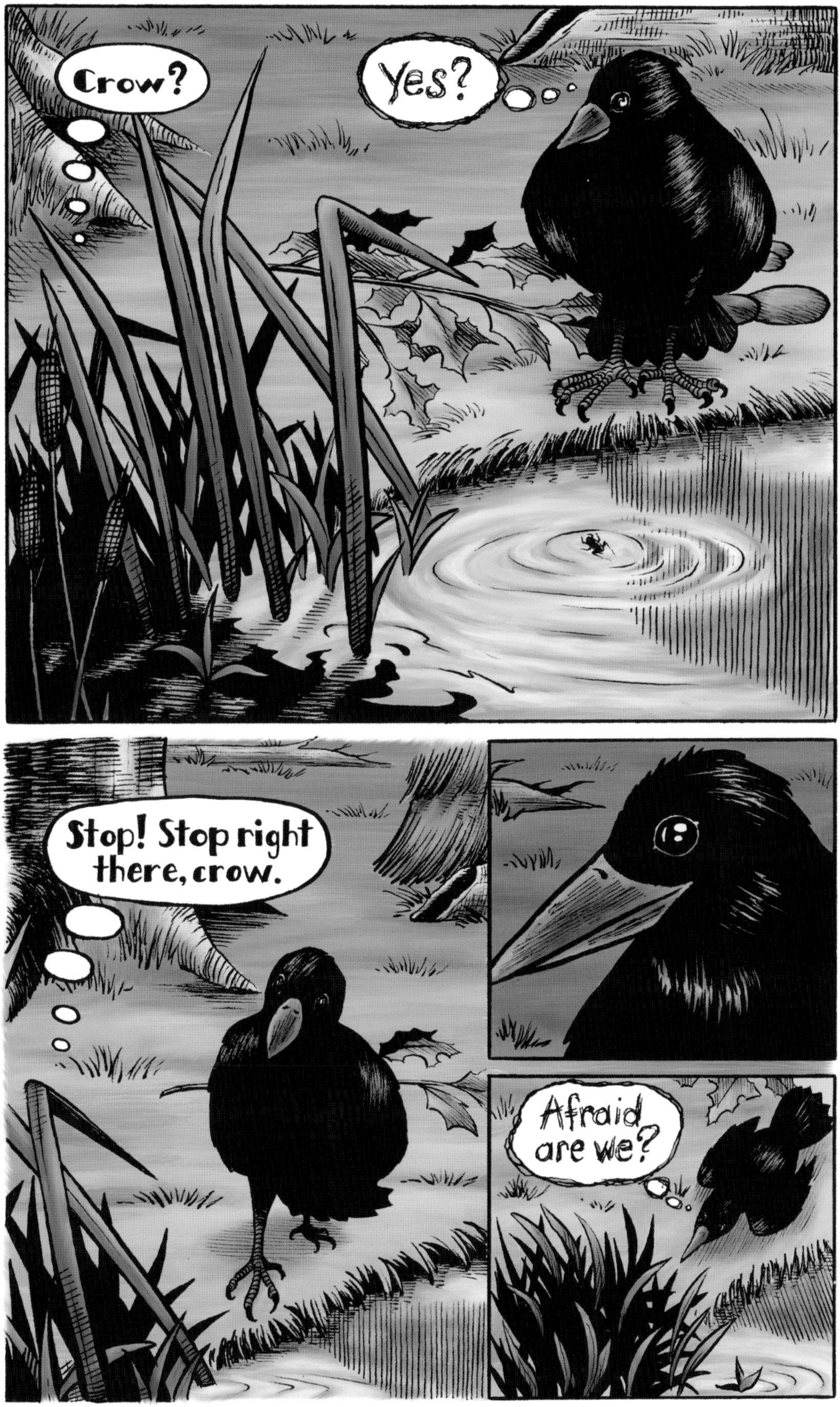
Crow?
Yes?
Stop! Stop right there, crow.
Afraid are we?

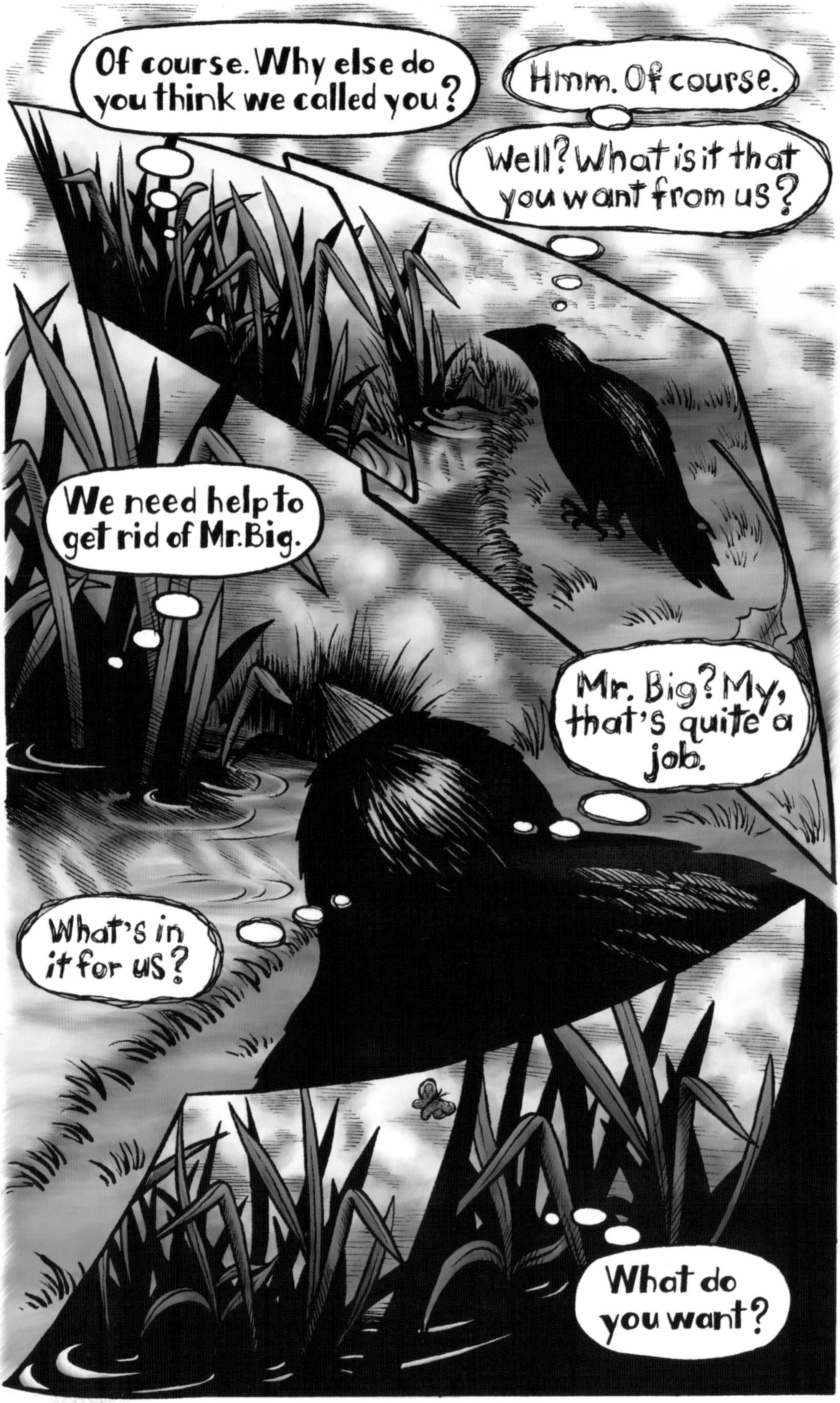
Of course. Why else do you think we called you?
Hmm. Of course.
Well? What is it that you want from us?
We need help to get rid of Mr. Big.
Mr. Big? My, that's quite a job.
What's in it for us?
What do you want?

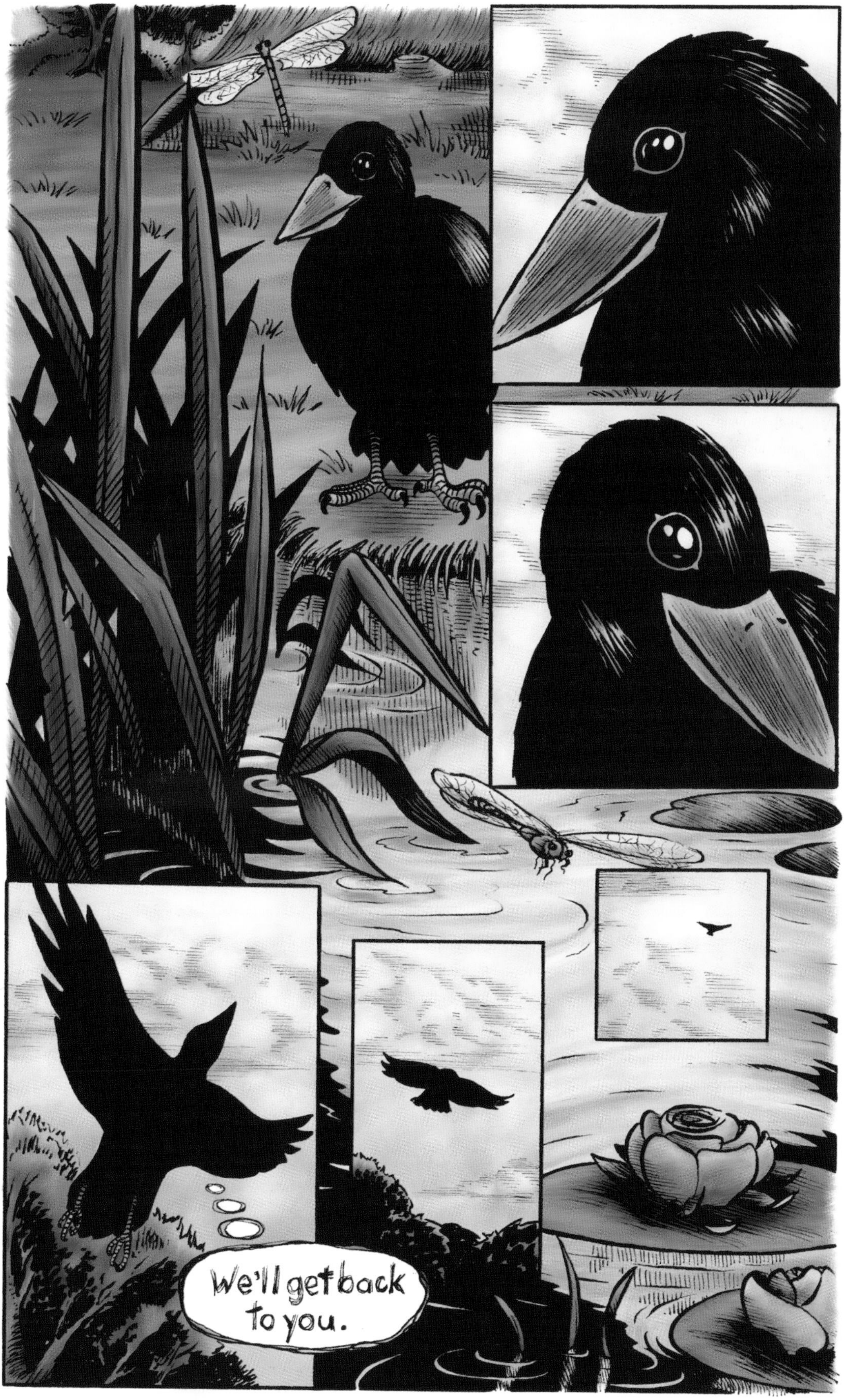
We'll get back to you.

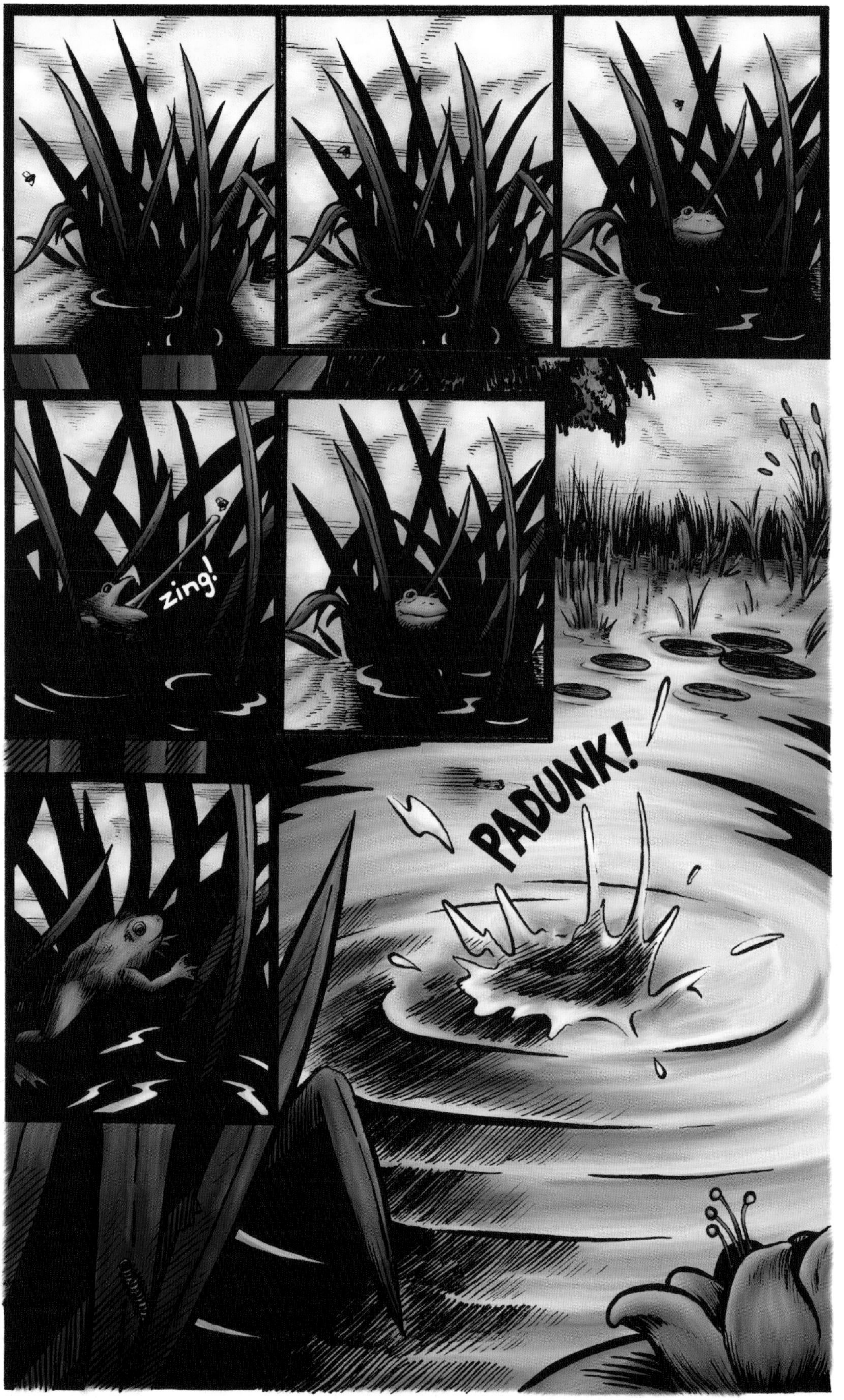
zing!
PADUNK!

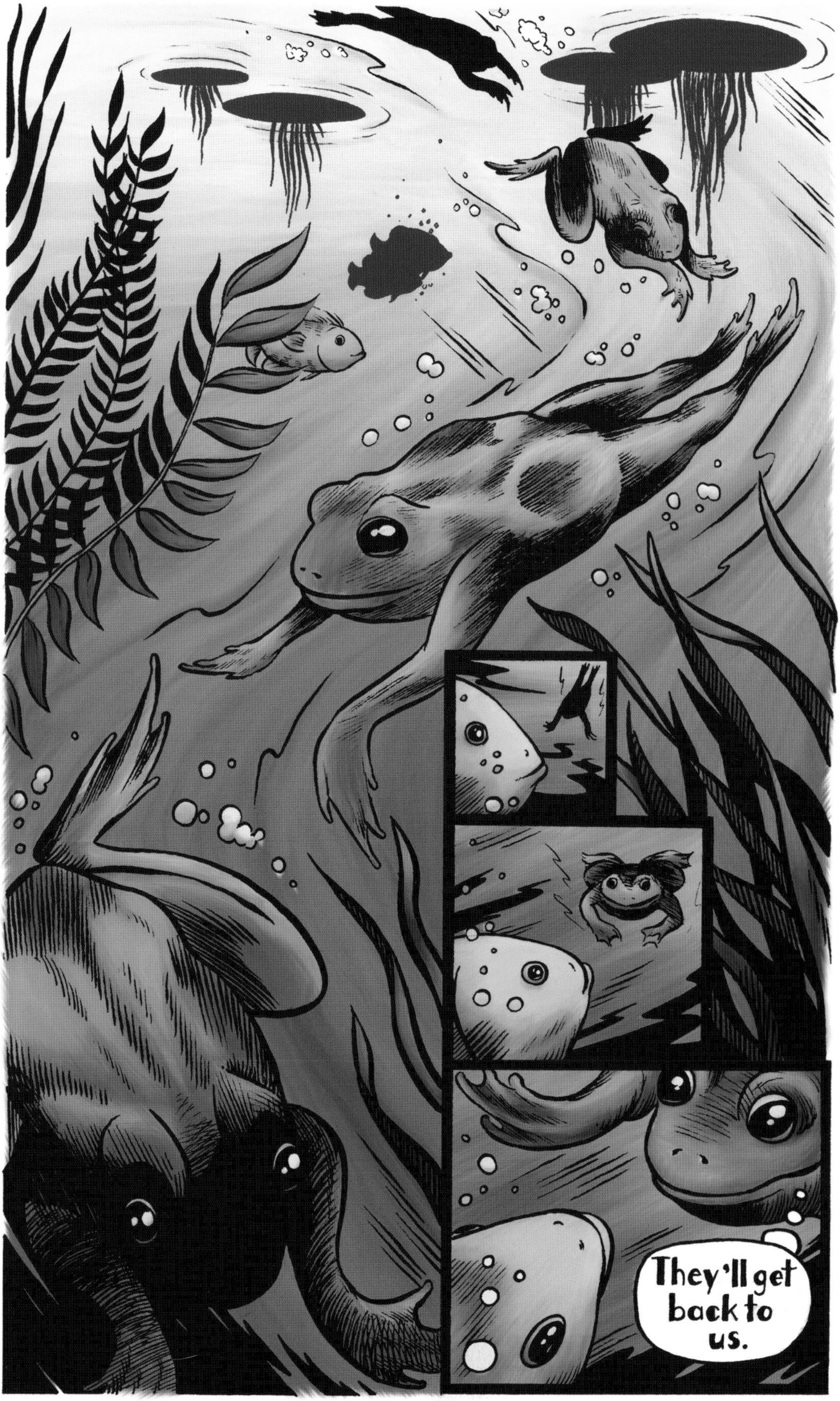
They'll get back to us.

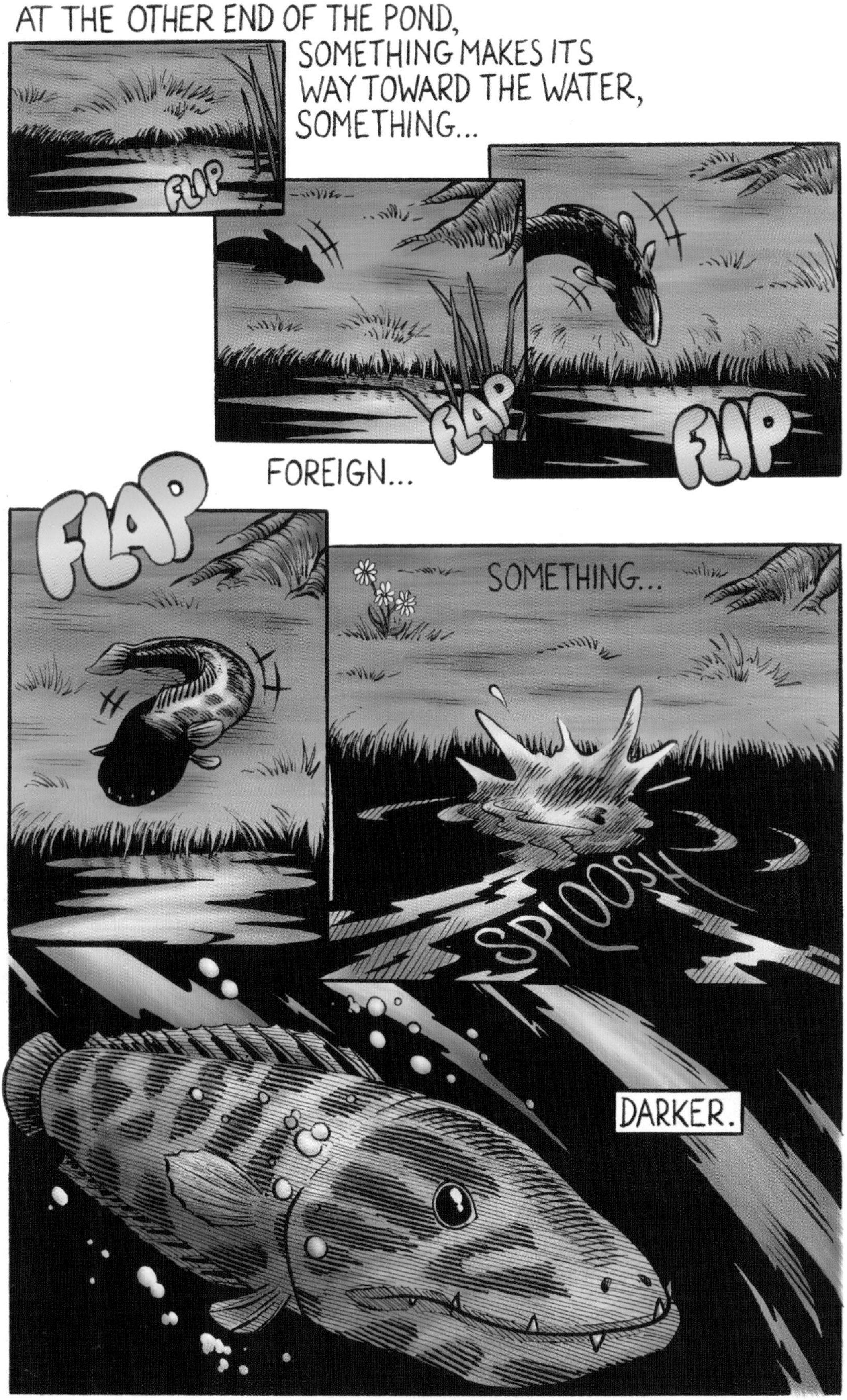
AT THE OTHER END OF THE POND,
SOMETHING MAKES ITS WAY TOWARD THE WATER, SOMETHING...
FLIP
FLAP
FLIP
FOREIGN...
FLAP
SOMETHING...
SPLOOSH
DARKER.

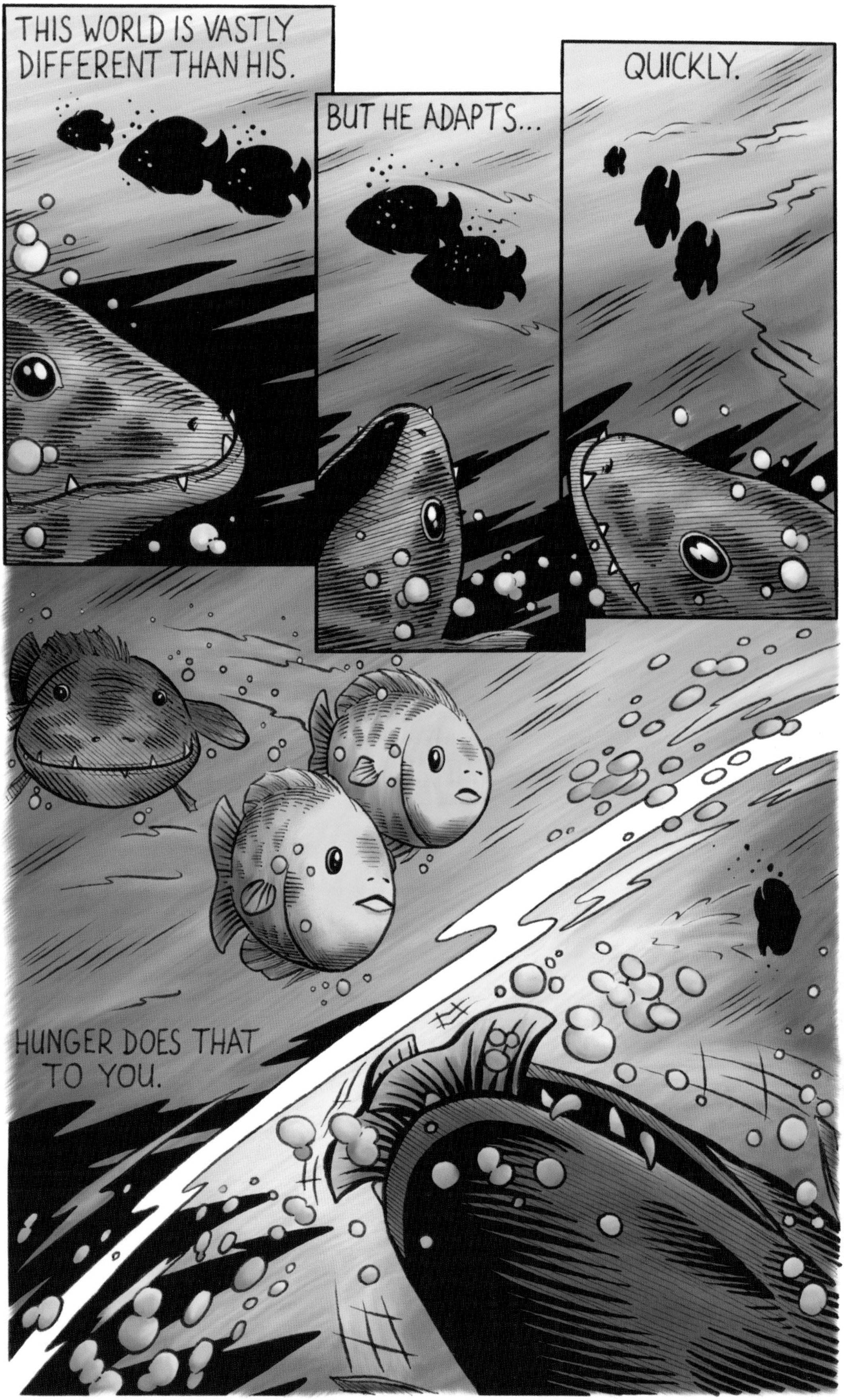
THIS WORLD IS VASTLY DIFFERENT THAN HIS.
BUT HE ADAPTS...
QUICKLY.
HUNGER DOES THAT TO YOU.

THE STRANGER IS NOT SATISFIED, NOT EVEN CLOSE.

HIS JOURNEY ACROSS LAND TO THIS LUSH POND TOOK MUCH STRENGTH AND STAMINA...

WHICH BUILT QUITE A FEROCIOUS APPETITE.

Mother Nature! What was that?!

SPLASH

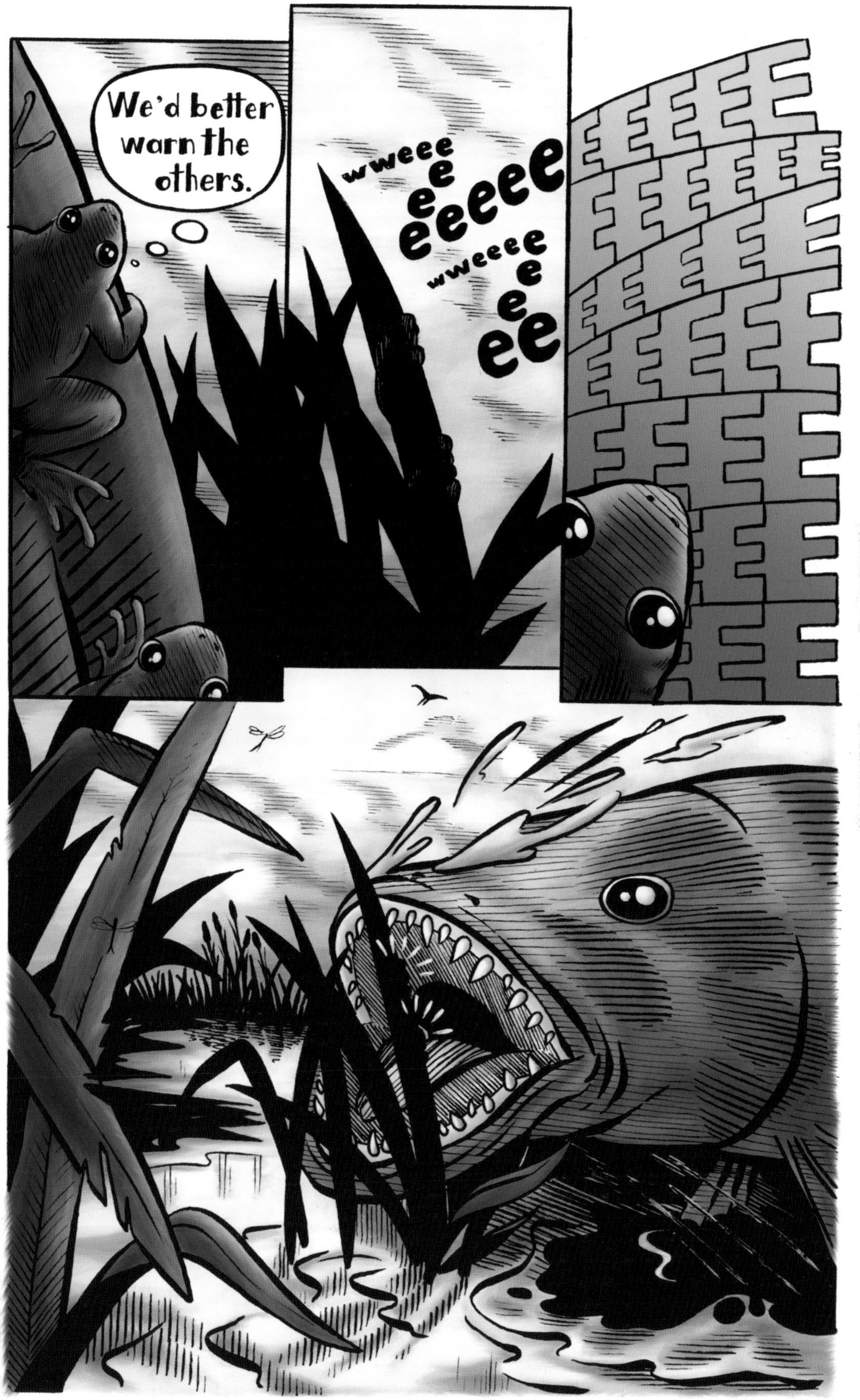
We'd better warn the others.
wweee e e eeeee
wweeee e e ee
EEEEEE

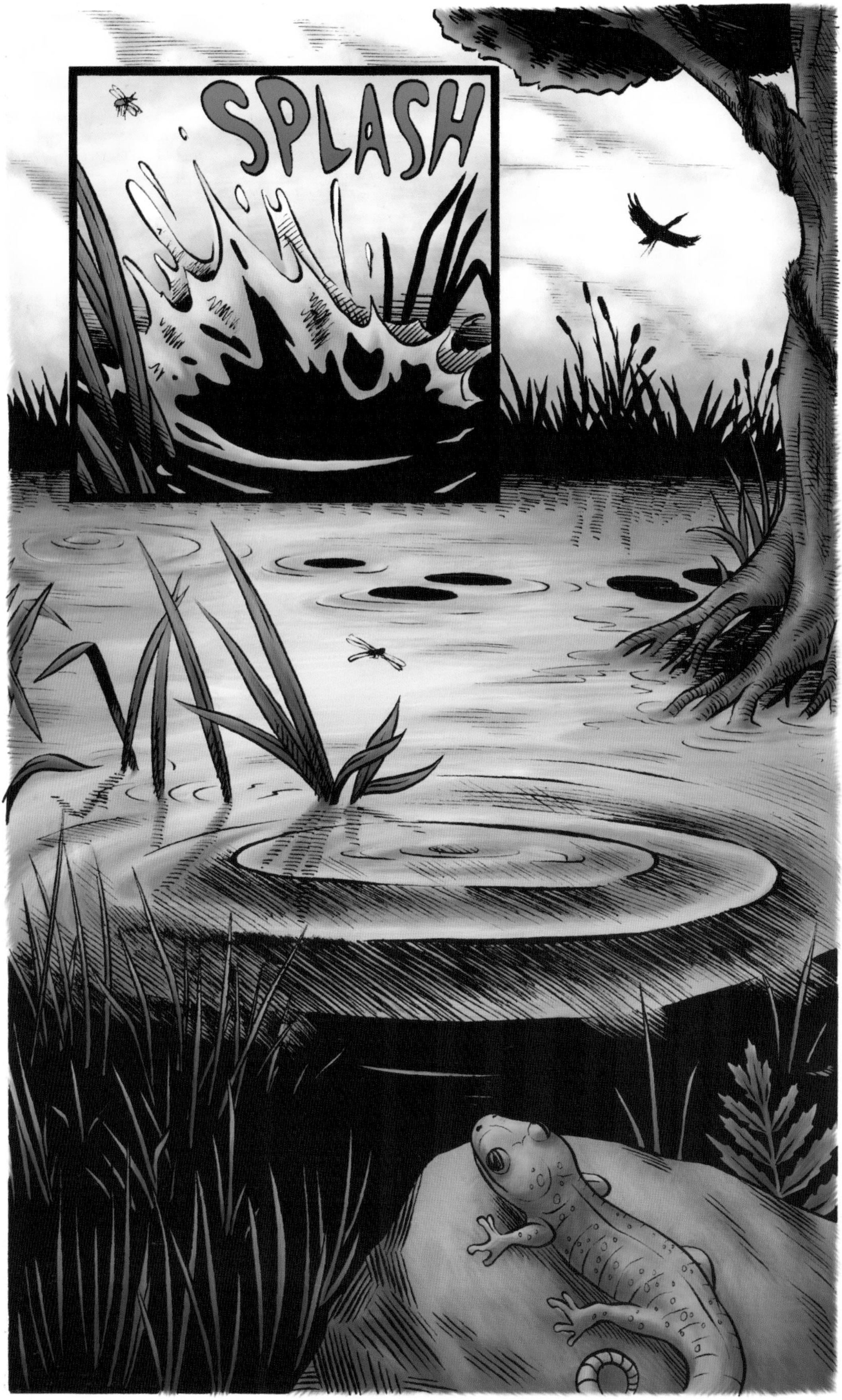
SPLASH

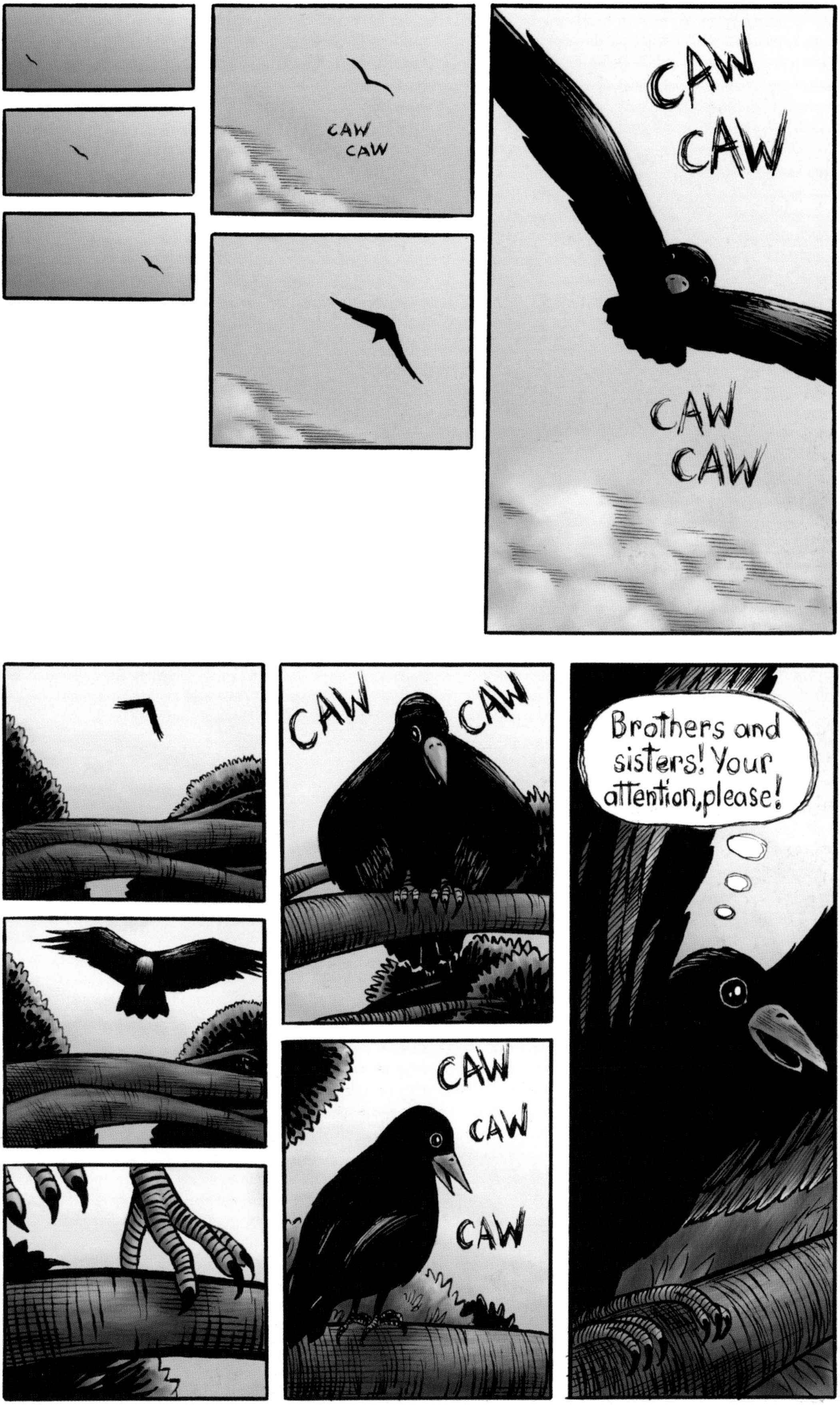
CAW
CAW
CAW
CAW
CAW
CAW
CAW
CAW
CAW
CAW
CAW
Brothers and sisters! Your attention, please!

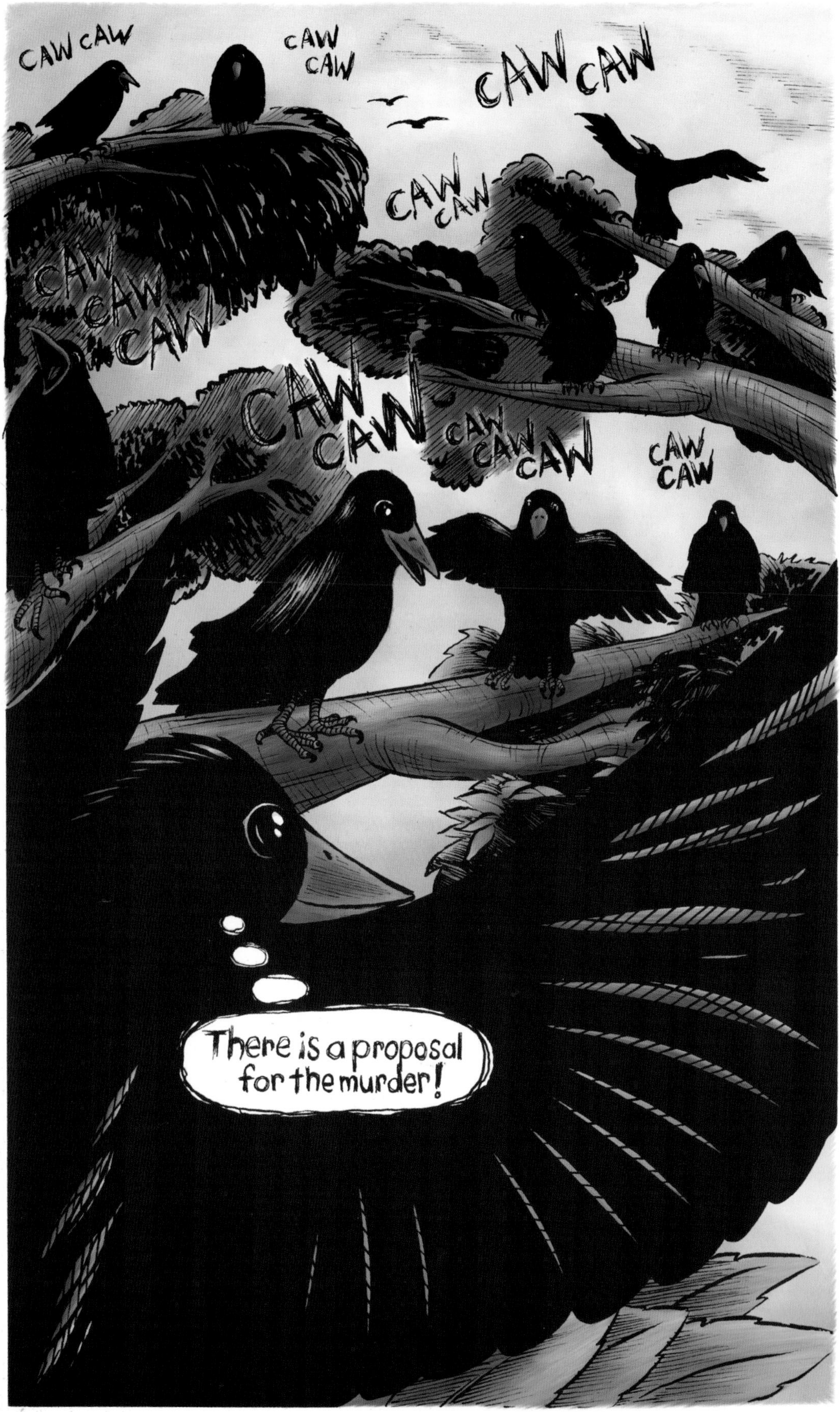
CAW CAW
CAW CAW
CAW CAW
CAW CAW
CAW CAW CAW
CAW CAW
CAW CAW CAW
CAW CAW
There is a proposal for the murder!

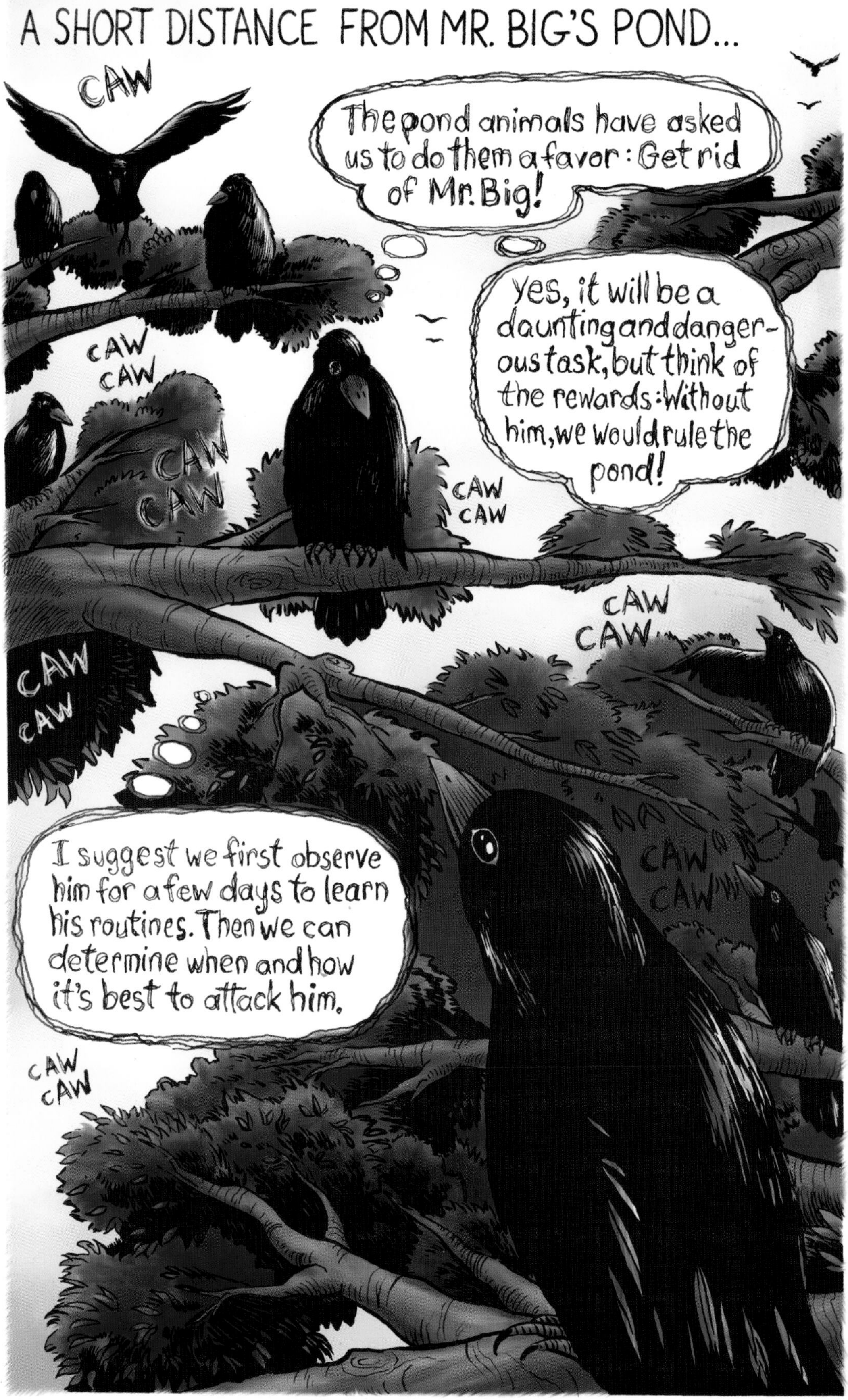
A SHORT DISTANCE FROM MR. BIG'S POND...
CAW
The pond animals have asked us to do them a favor: Get rid of Mr. Big!
CAW CAW
Yes, it will be a daunting and danger-ous task, but think of the rewards: Without him, we would rule the pond!
CAW CAW
CAW CAW
CAW CAW
CAW CAW
I suggest we first observe him for a few days to learn his routines. Then we can determine when and how it's best to attack him.
CAW CAW
CAW CAW

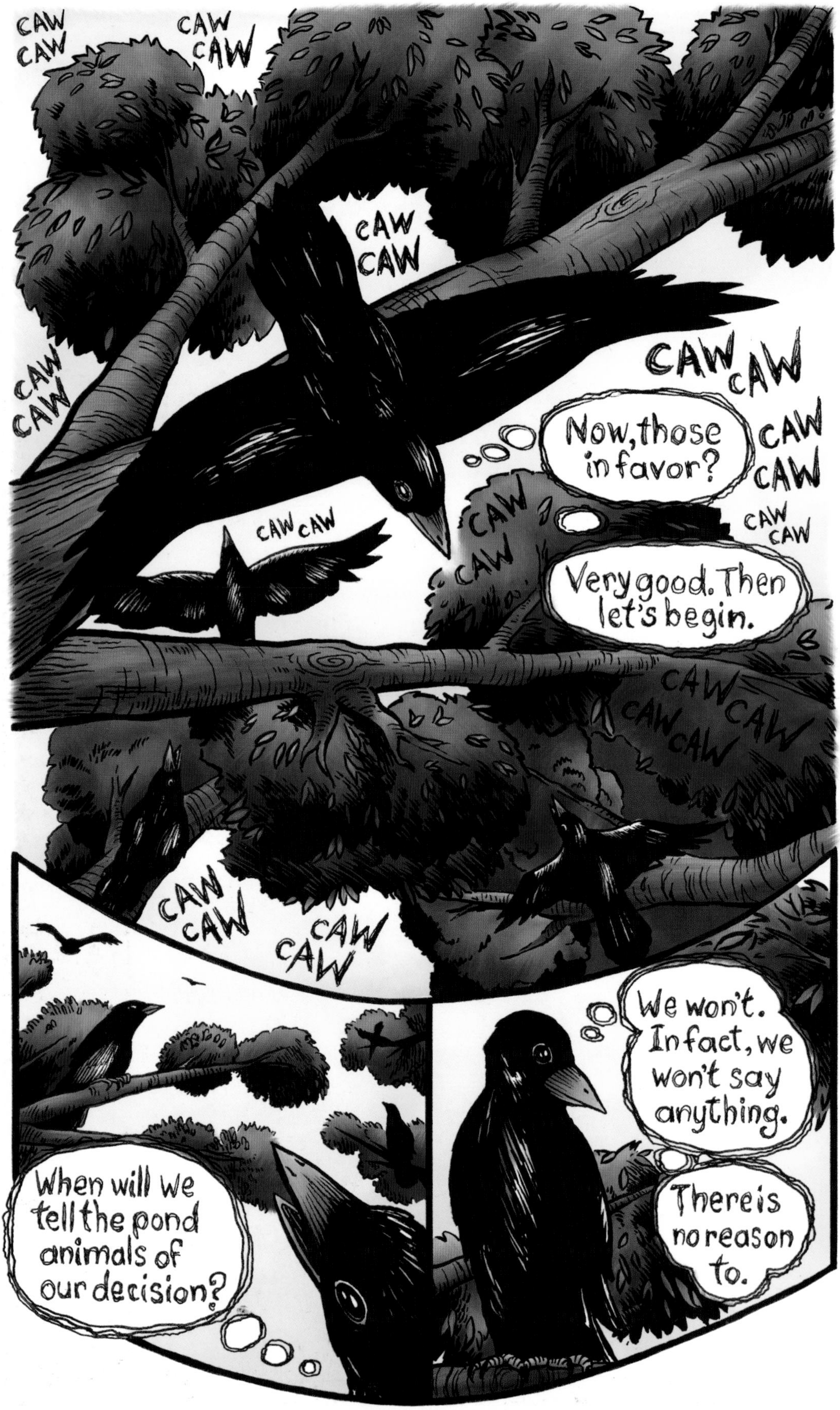
CAW CAW
CAW CAW
CAW CAW
CAW CAW
CAW CAW
Now, those in favor?
CAW CAW
CAW CAW
CAW CAW
CAW CAW
Very good. Then let's begin.
CAW CAW CAW CAW
CAW CAW
CAW CAW
When will we tell the pond animals of our decision?
We won't. In fact, we won't say anything.
There is no reason to.

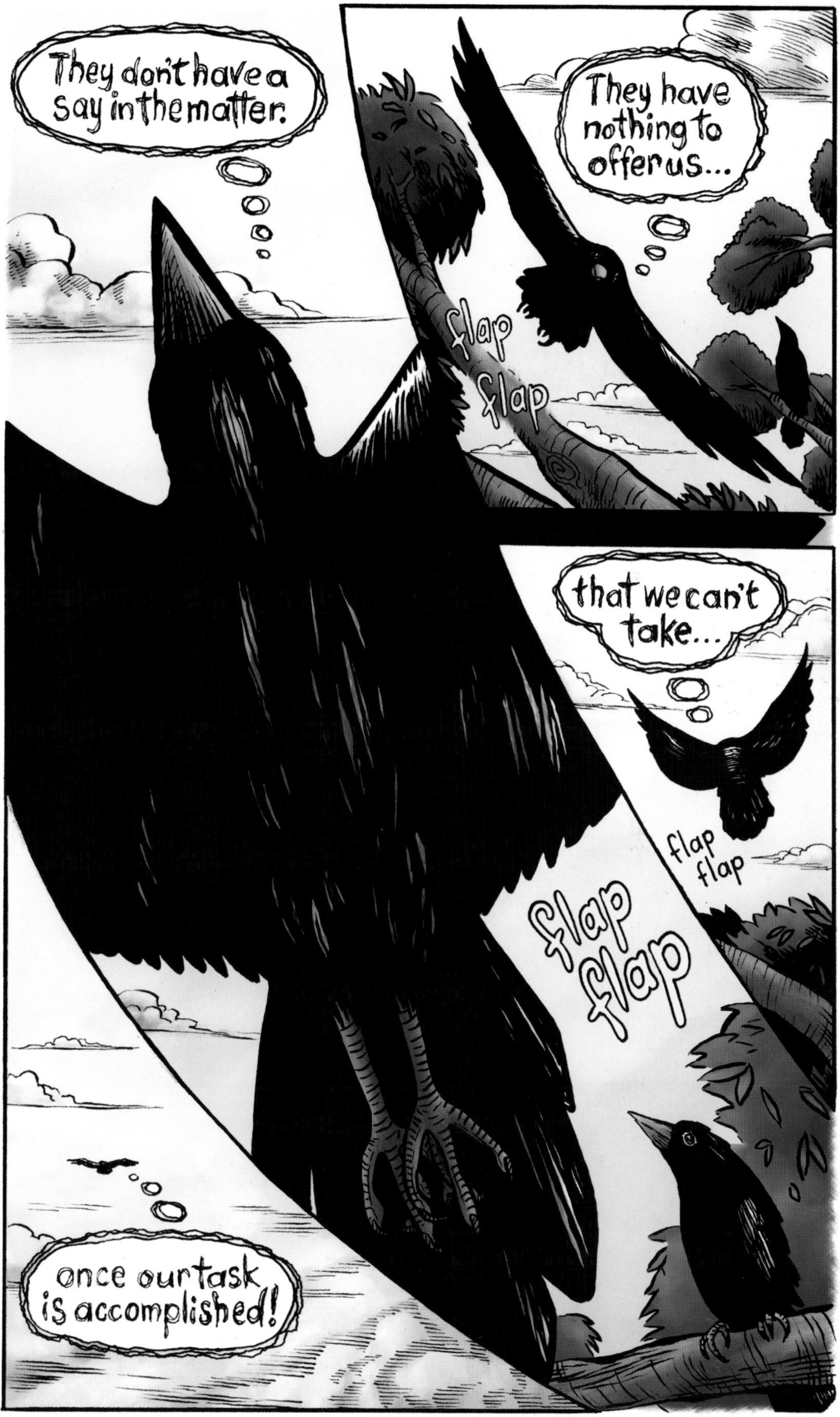
They don't have a say in the matter.
They have nothing to offer us...
flap
flap
that we can't take...
flap
flap
flap
flap
once our task is accomplished!

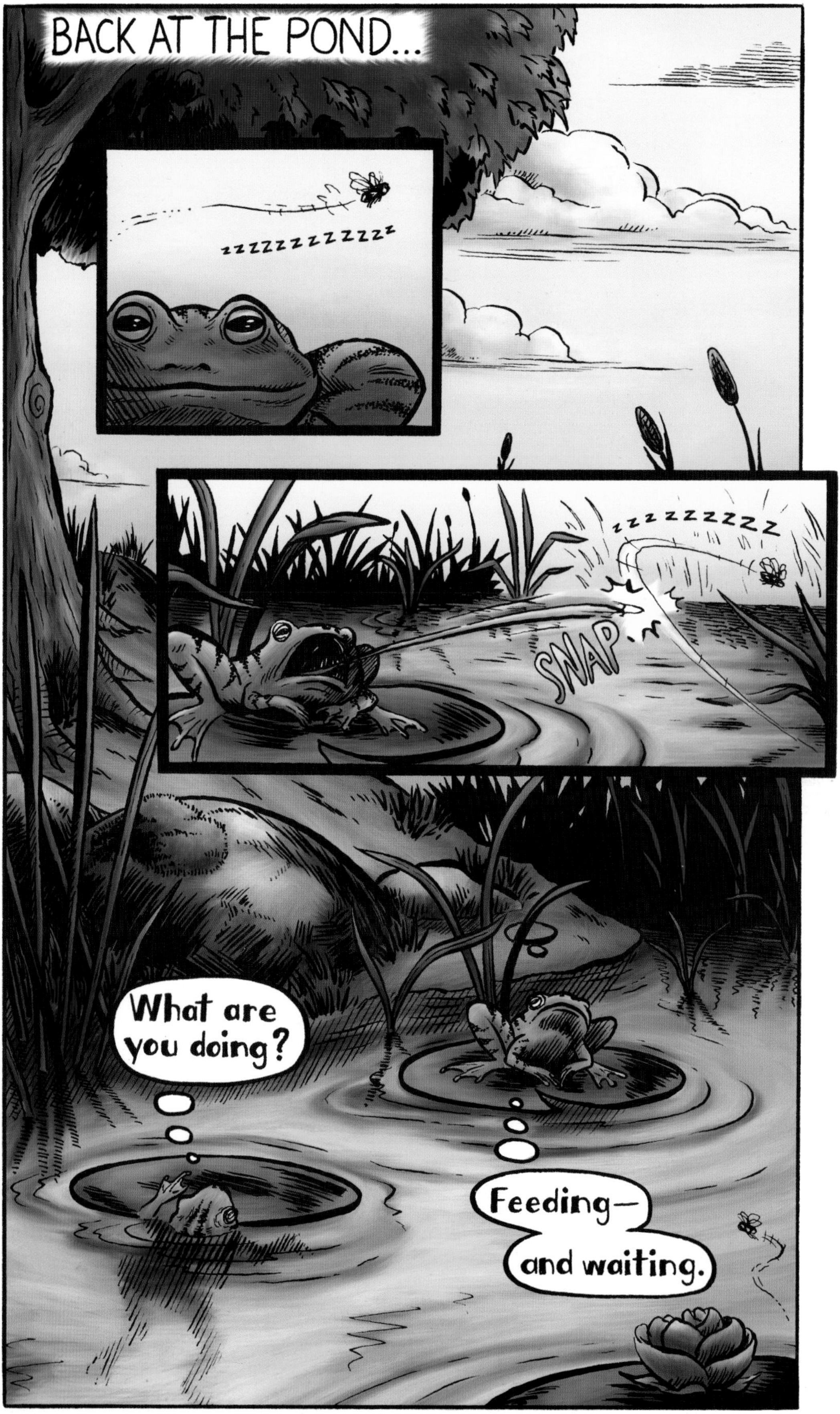
BACK AT THE POND...
zzzzzzzzzzzz
zzzzzzzzz
SNAP
What are you doing?
Feeding—
and waiting.

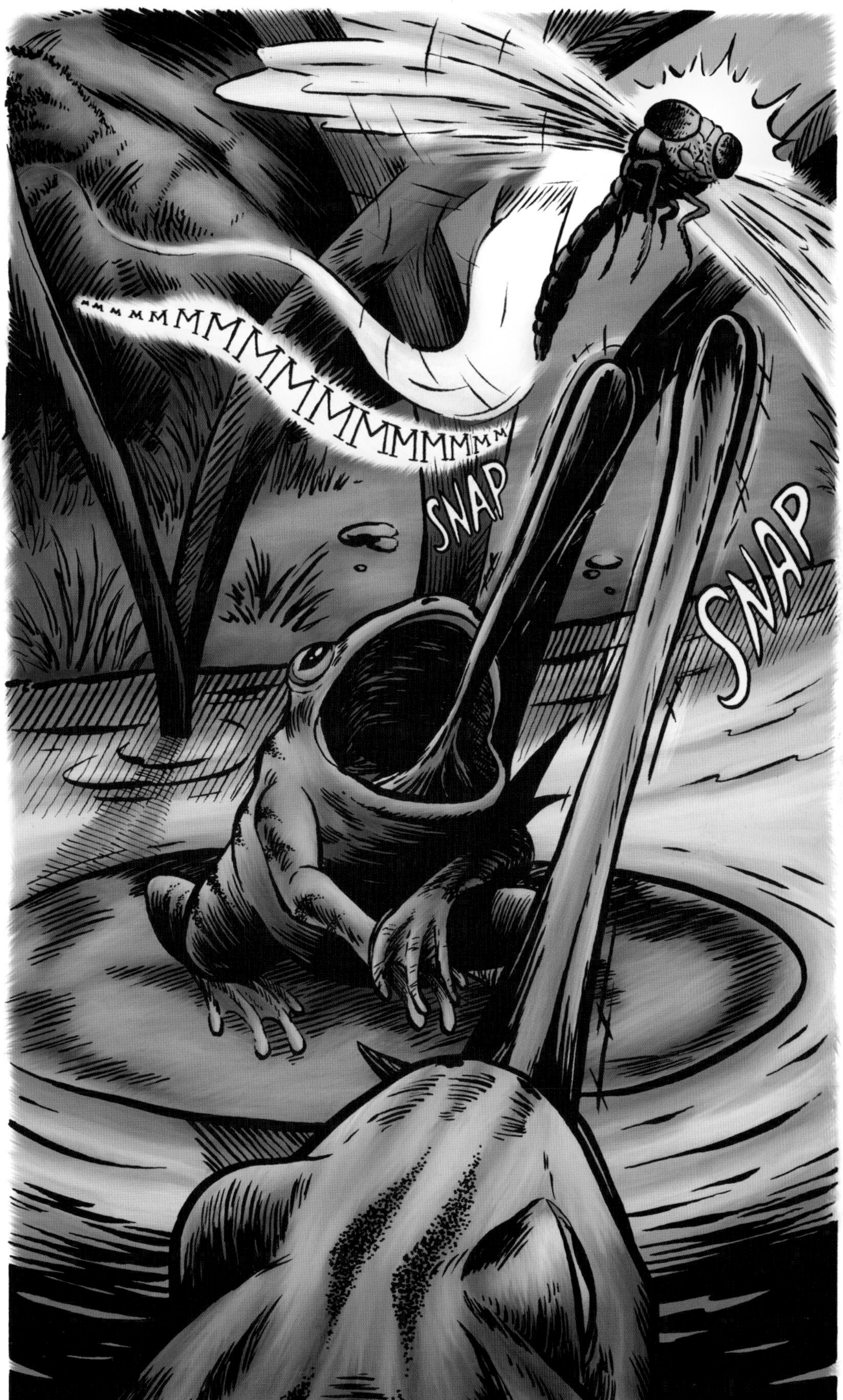

mmmmMMMMMMMMMMMmm
SNAP
SNAP

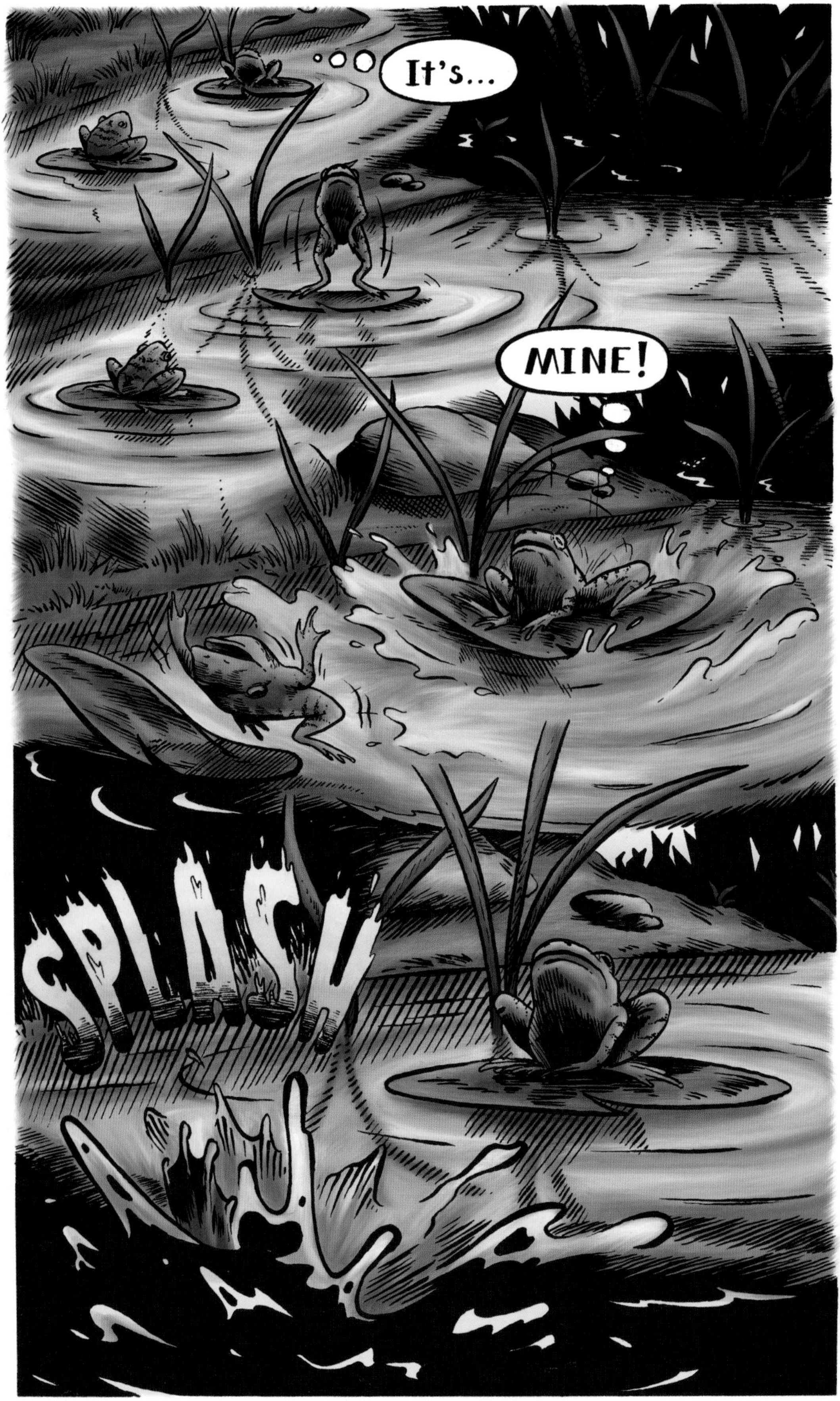
It's...
MINE!
SPLASH

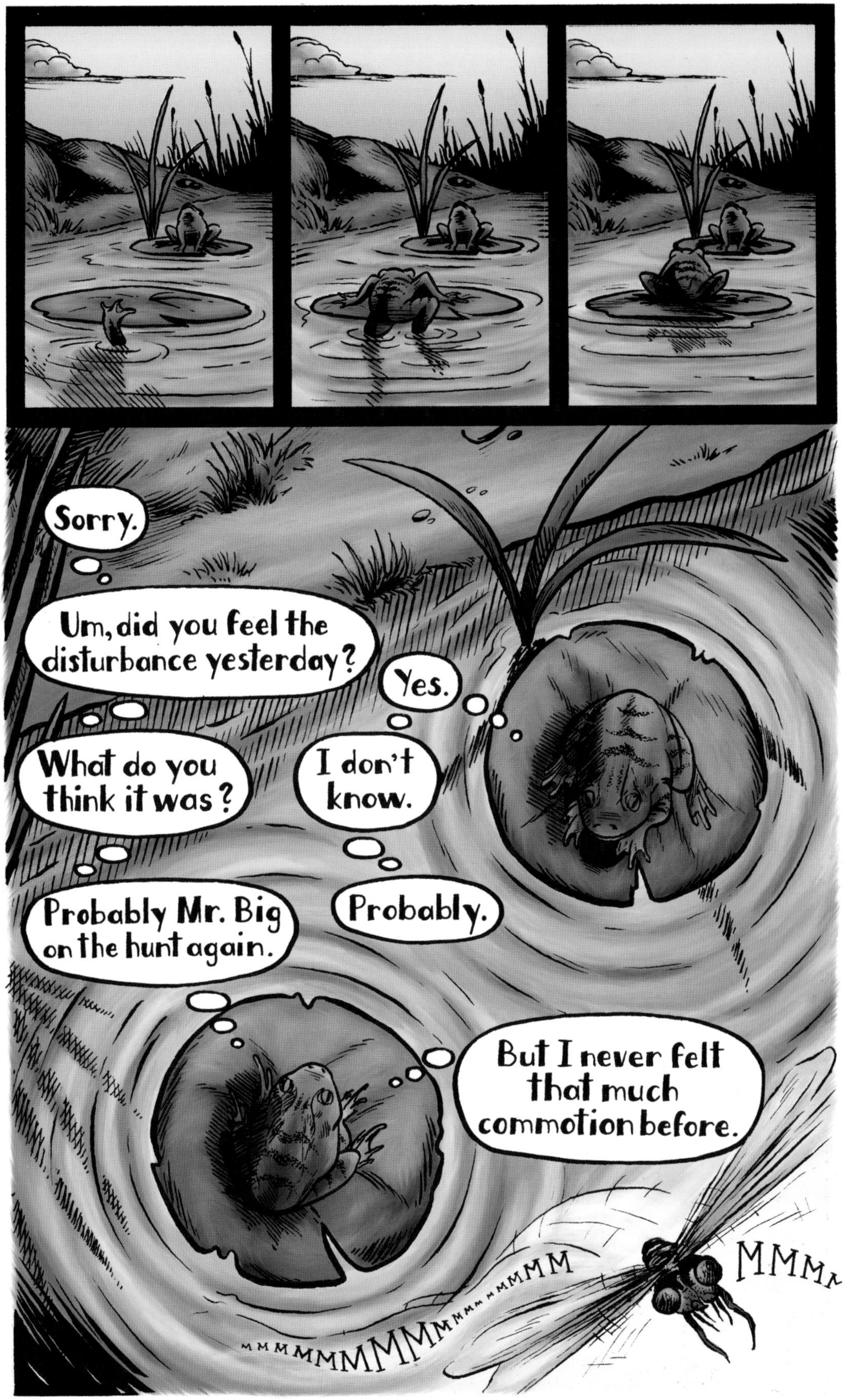
Sorry.
Um, did you feel the disturbance yesterday?
Yes.
What do you think it was?
I don't know.
Probably Mr. Big on the hunt again.
Probably.
But I never felt that much commotion before.
MMMMMMMMMMMMMMMMMMMMM
MMMM

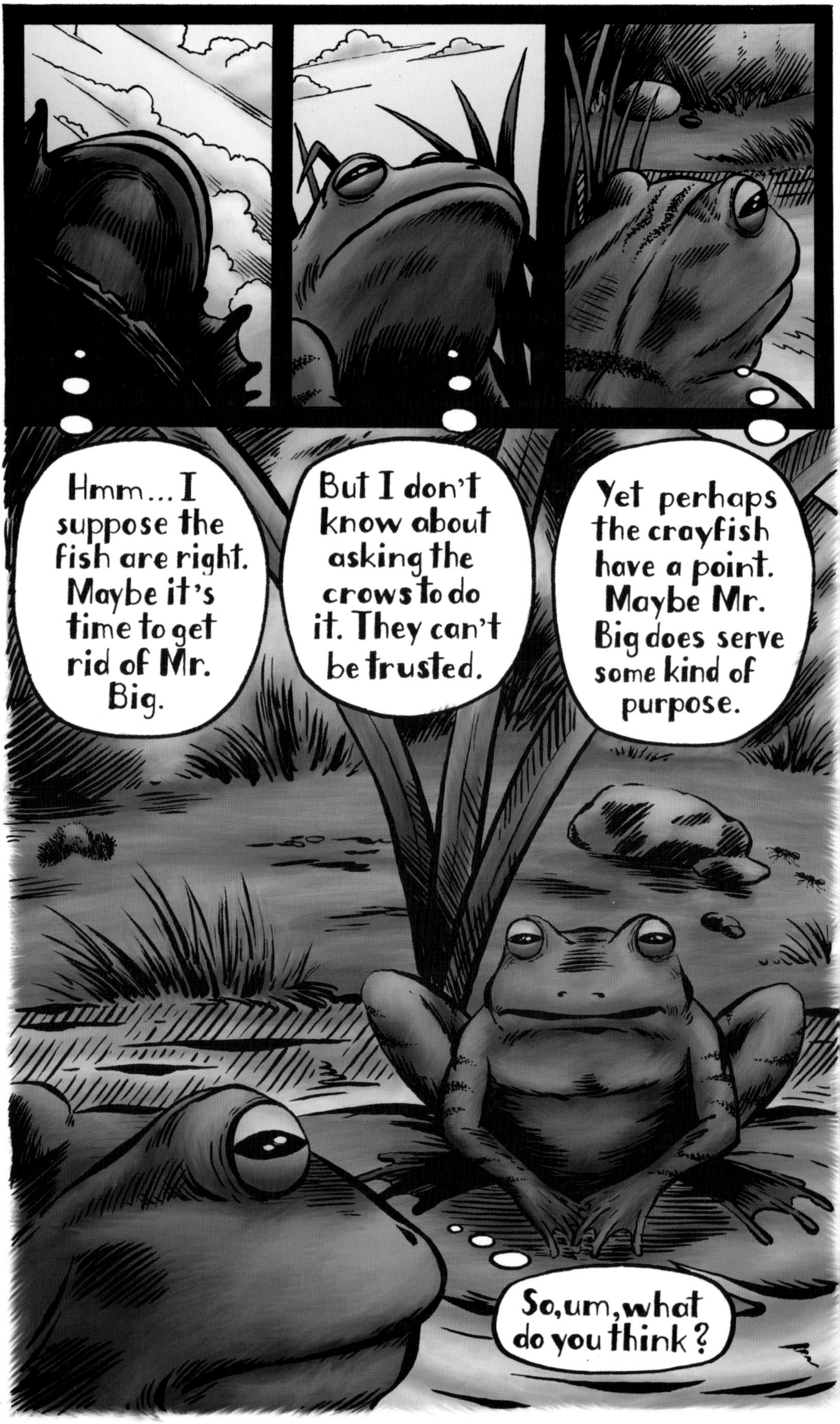
Hmm... I suppose the fish are right. Maybe it's time to get rid of Mr. Big.
But I don't know about asking the crows to do it. They can't be trusted.
Yet perhaps the crayfish have a point. Maybe Mr. Big does serve some kind of purpose.
So, um, what do you think?

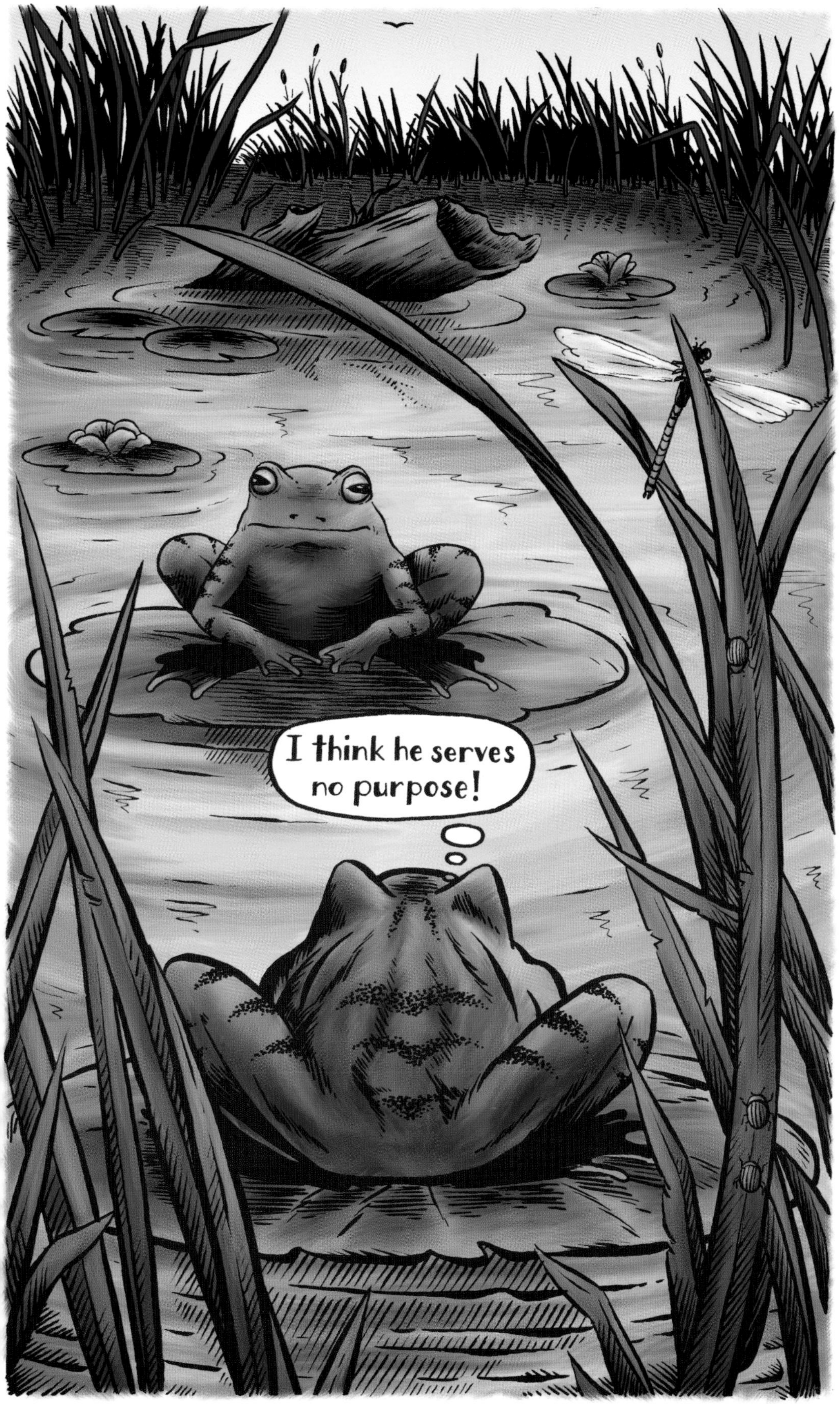
I think he serves no purpose!

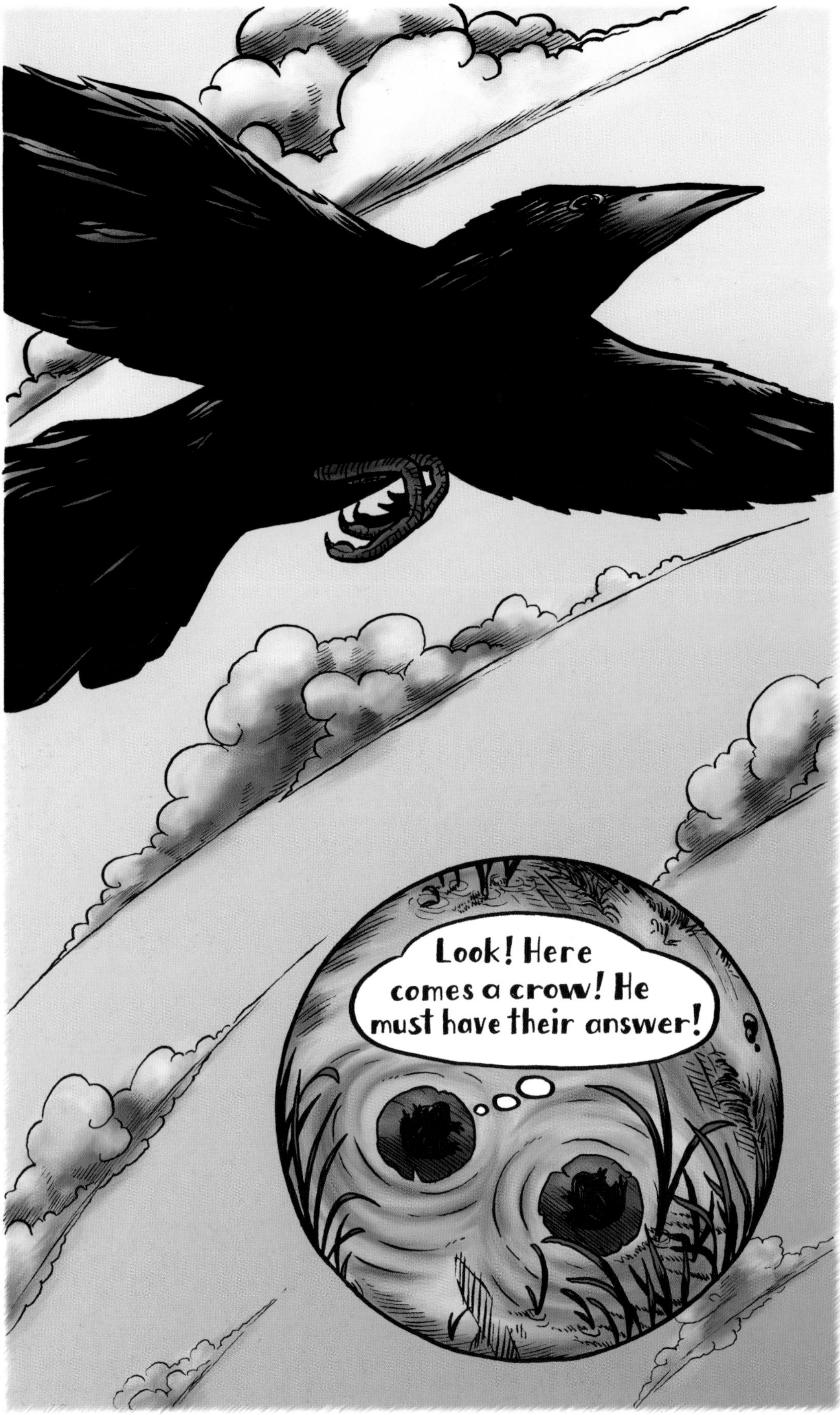
Look! Here comes a crow! He must have their answer!

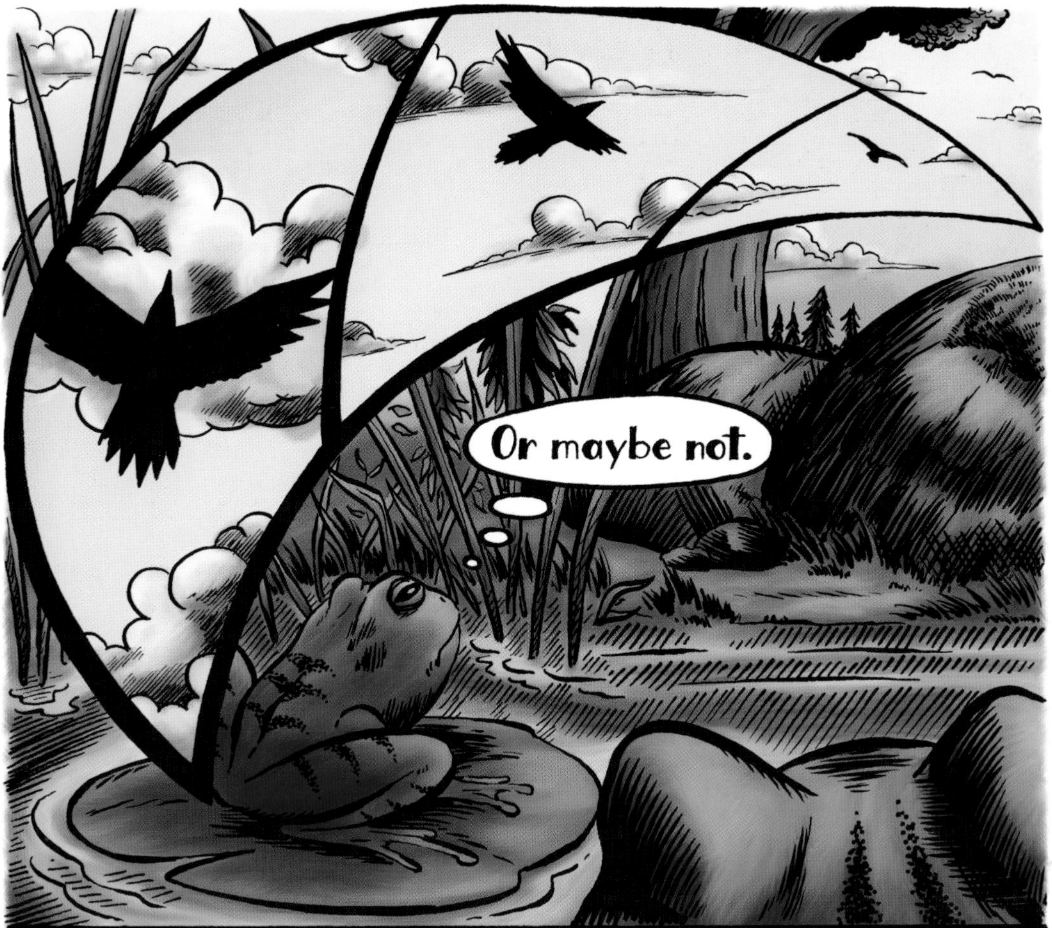
Or maybe not.

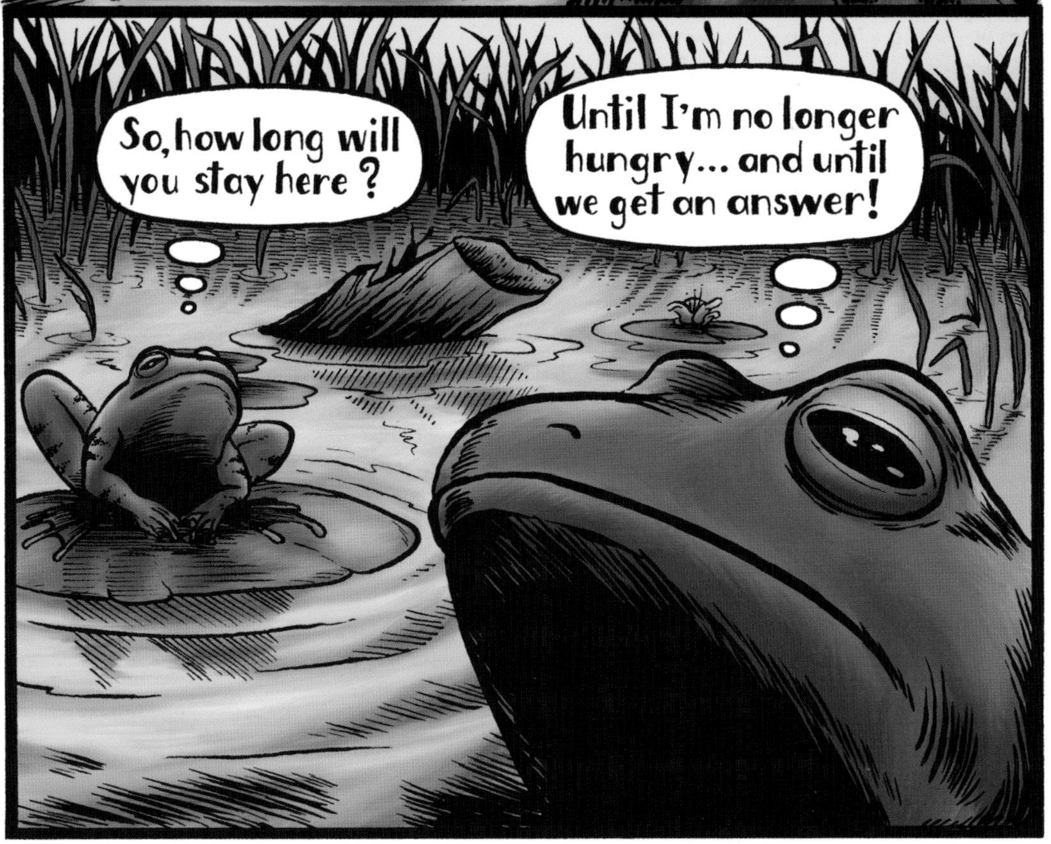
So, how long will you stay here?
Until I'm no longer hungry... and until we get an answer!

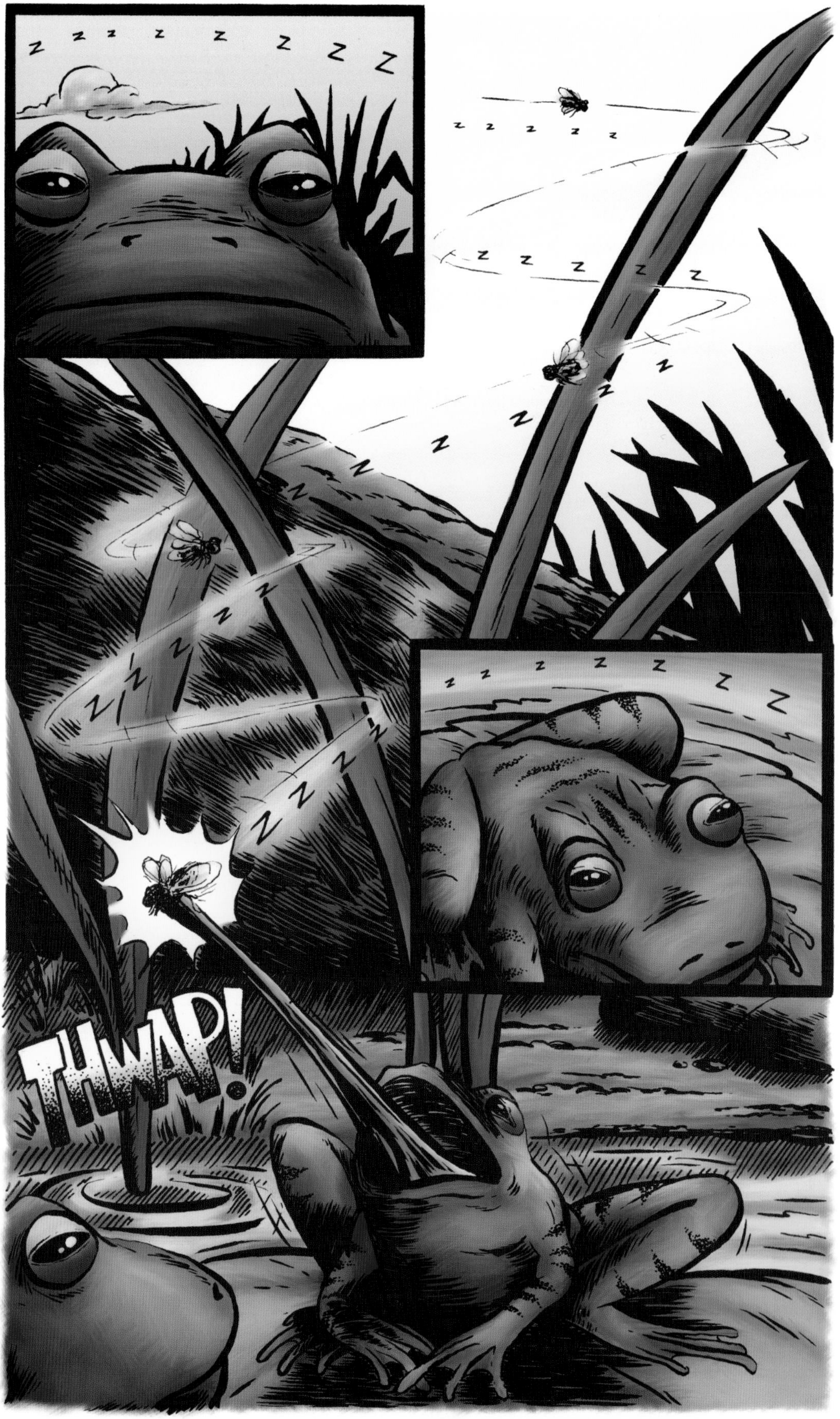
z z z z z z z Z
z z z z z
Z Z Z Z Z
Z Z Z Z Z Z Z
z z z z z z Z Z
THWAP!

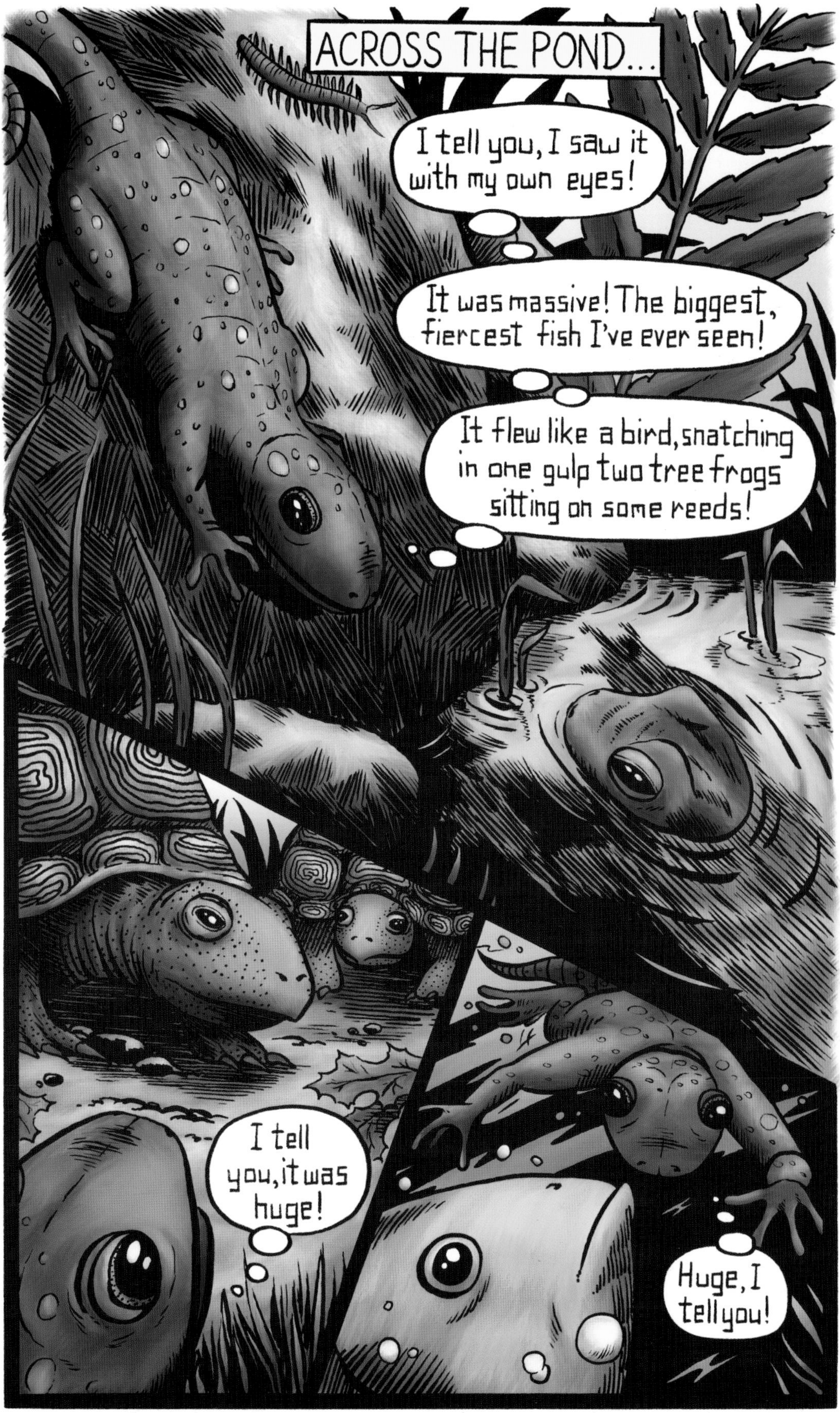
ACROSS THE POND...
I tell you, I saw it with my own eyes!
It was massive! The biggest, fiercest fish I've ever seen!
It flew like a bird, snatching in one gulp two tree frogs sitting on some reeds!
I tell you, it was huge!
Huge, I tell you!

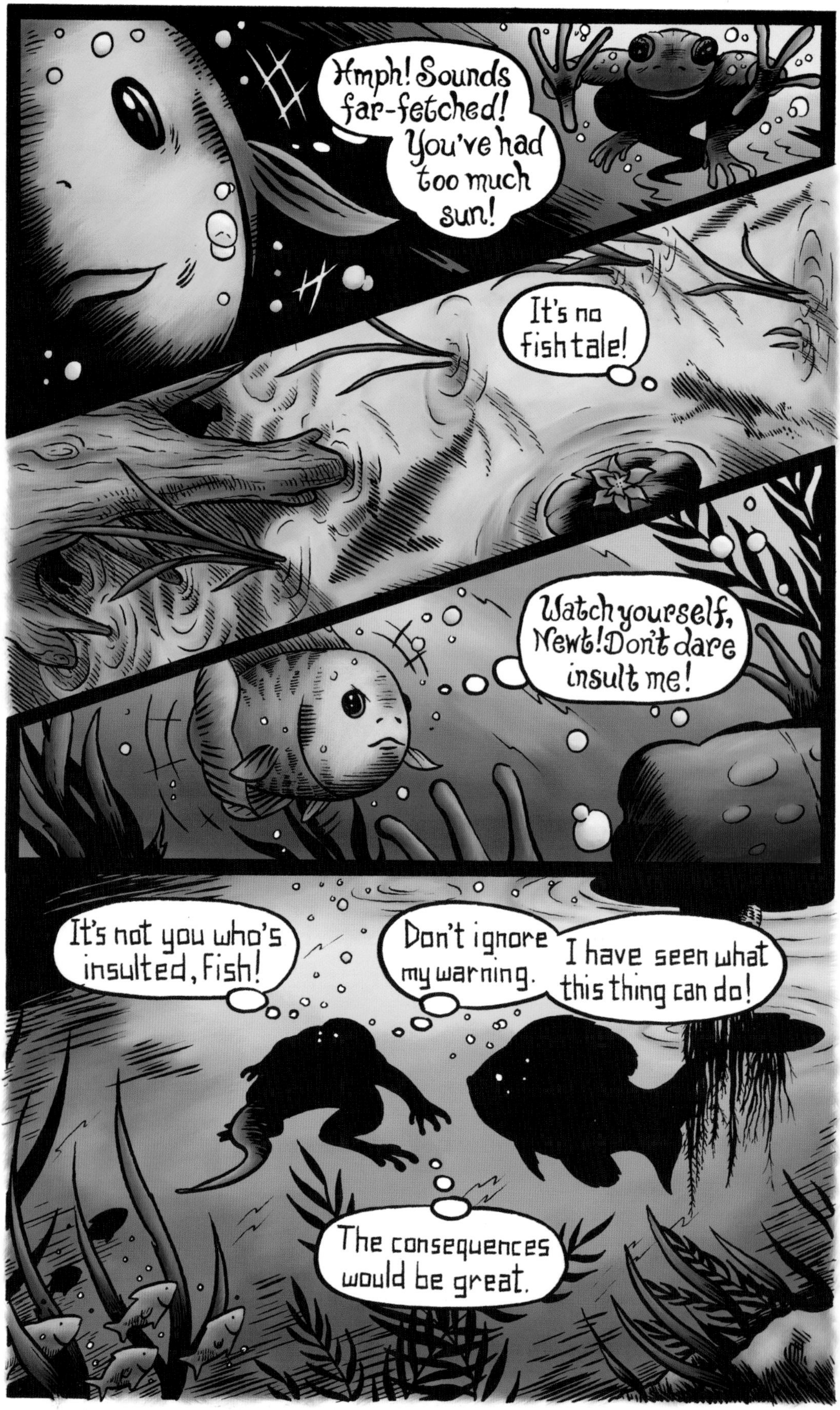
Hmph! Sounds far-fetched! You've had too much sun!
It's no fish tale!
Watch yourself, Newt! Don't dare insult me!
It's not you who's insulted, Fish!
Don't ignore my warning.
I have seen what this thing can do!
The consequences would be great.

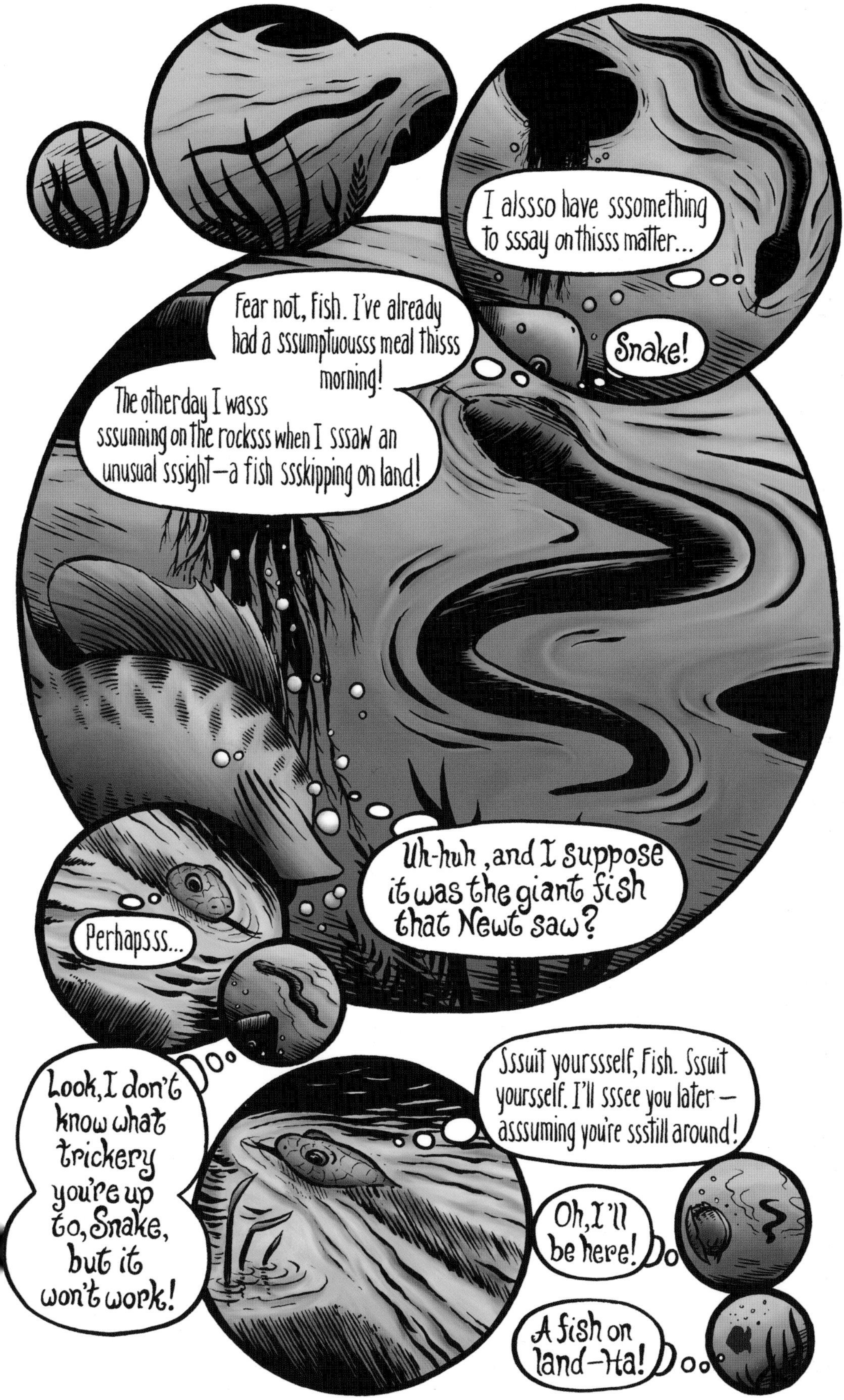
I alsssso have sssomething to sssay on thisss matter...
Snake!
Fear not, Fish. I've already had a sssumptuousss meal thisss morning!
The other day I wasss sssunning on the rocksss when I sssaw an unusual sssight—a fish ssskipping on land!
Uh-huh, and I suppose it was the giant fish that Newt saw?
Perhapsss...
Look, I don't know what trickery you're up to, Snake, but it won't work!
Sssuit yourssself, Fish. Sssuit yoursself. I'll sssee you later—asssuming you're ssstill around!
Oh, I'll be here!
A fish on land—Ha!

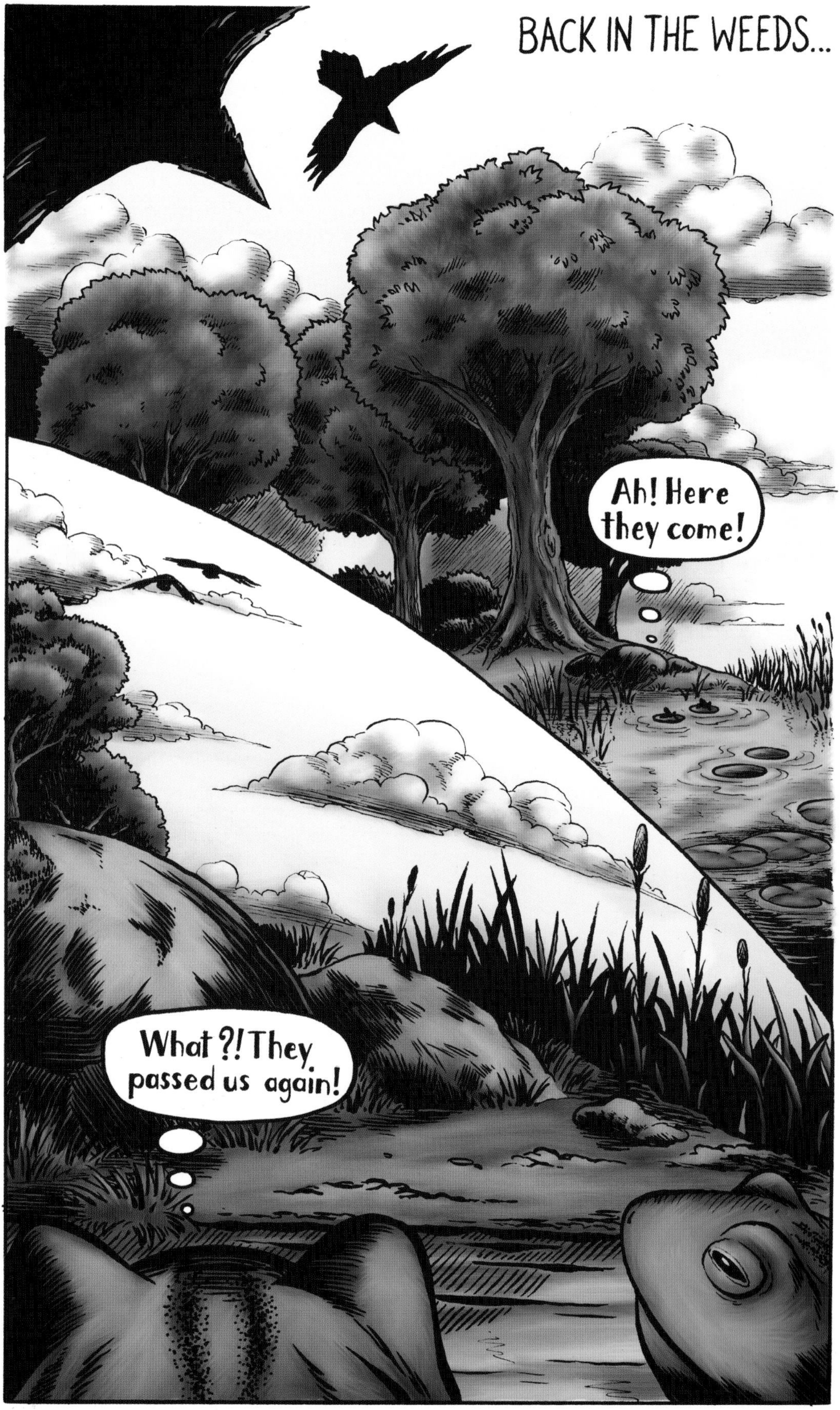
BACK IN THE WEEDS...
Ah! Here they come!
What ?! They passed us again!

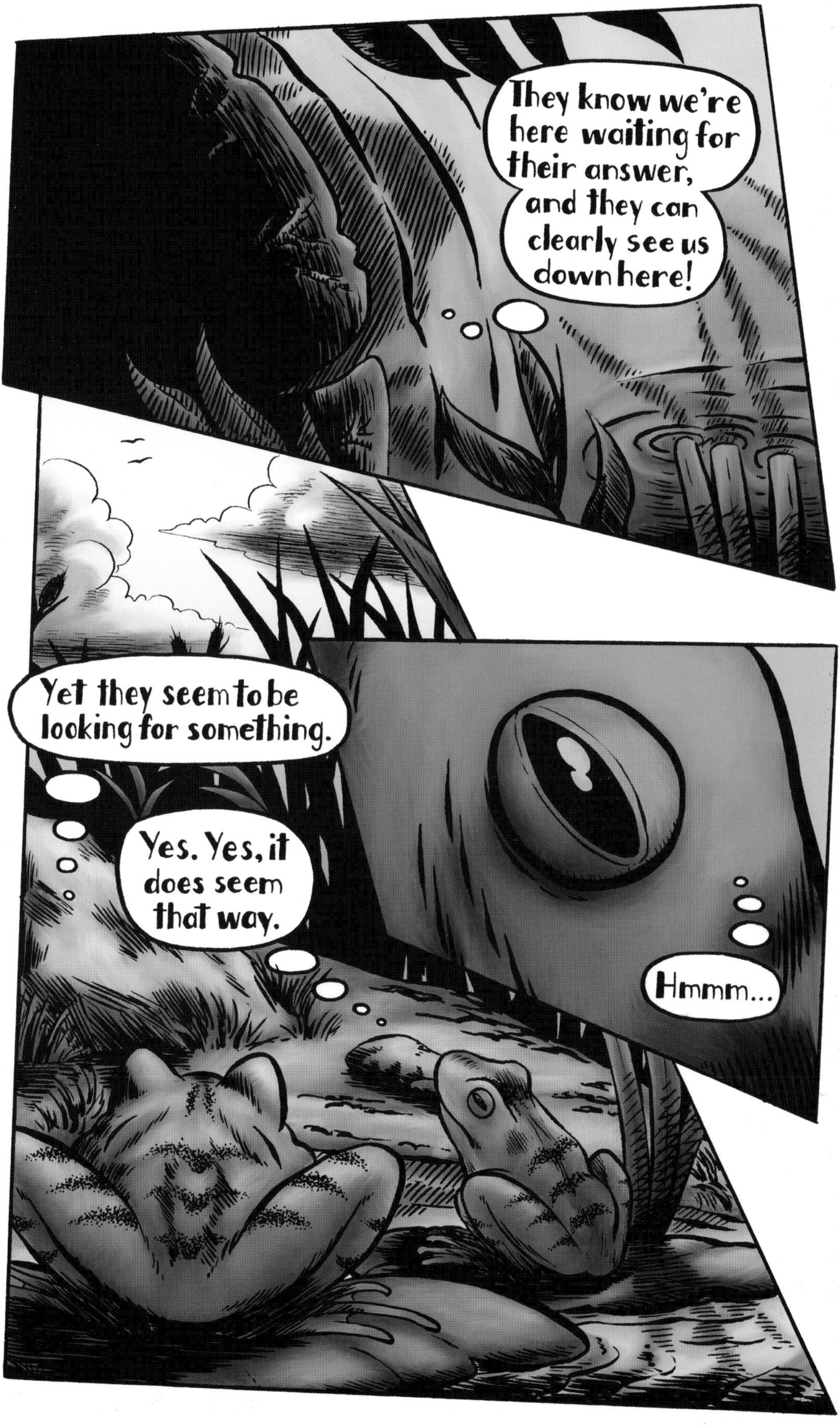
They know we're here waiting for their answer, and they can clearly see us down here!
Yet they seem to be looking for something.
Yes. Yes, it does seem that way.
Hmmm...

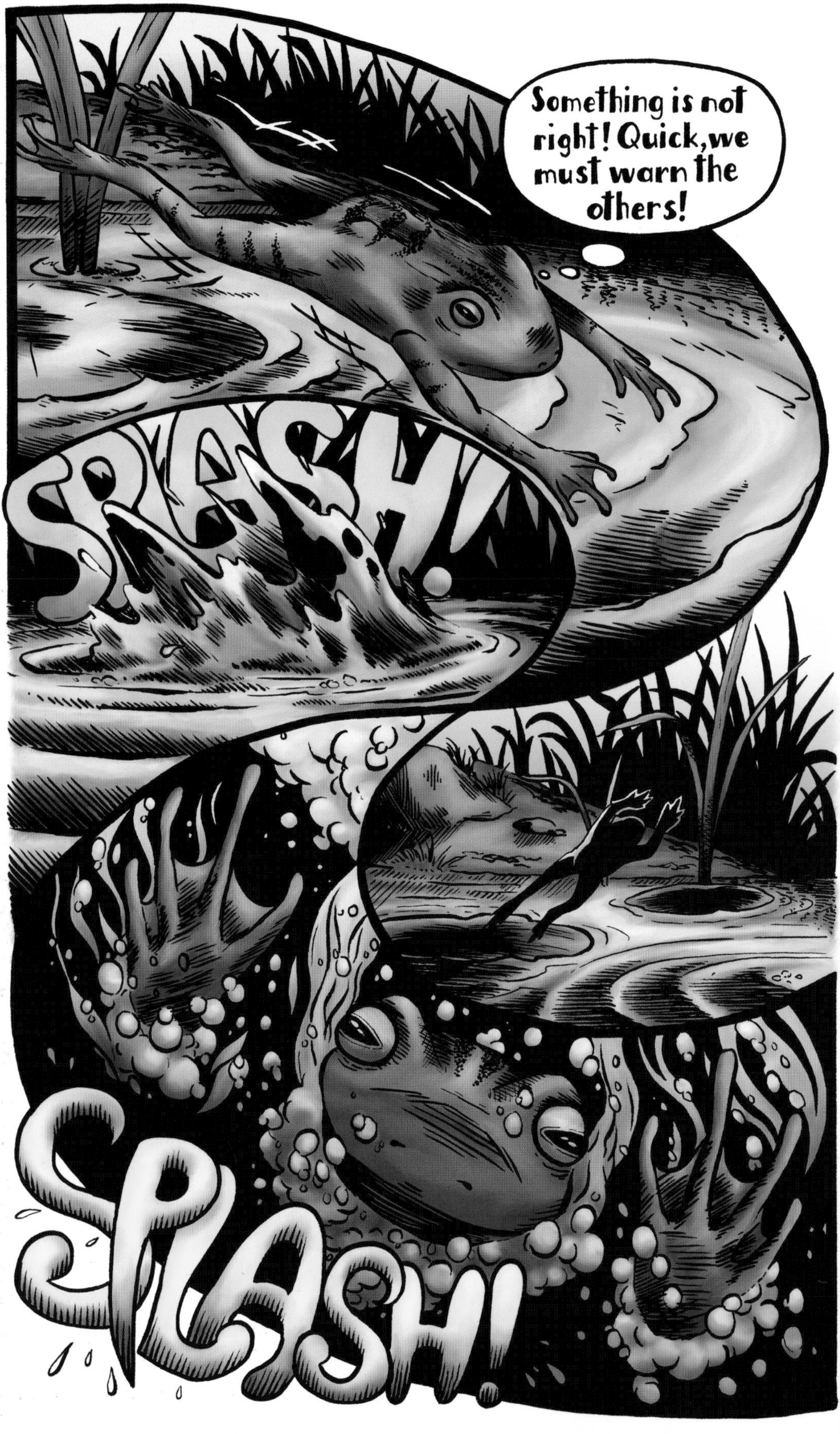
Something is not right! Quick, we must warn the others!
SPLASH!
SPLASH!

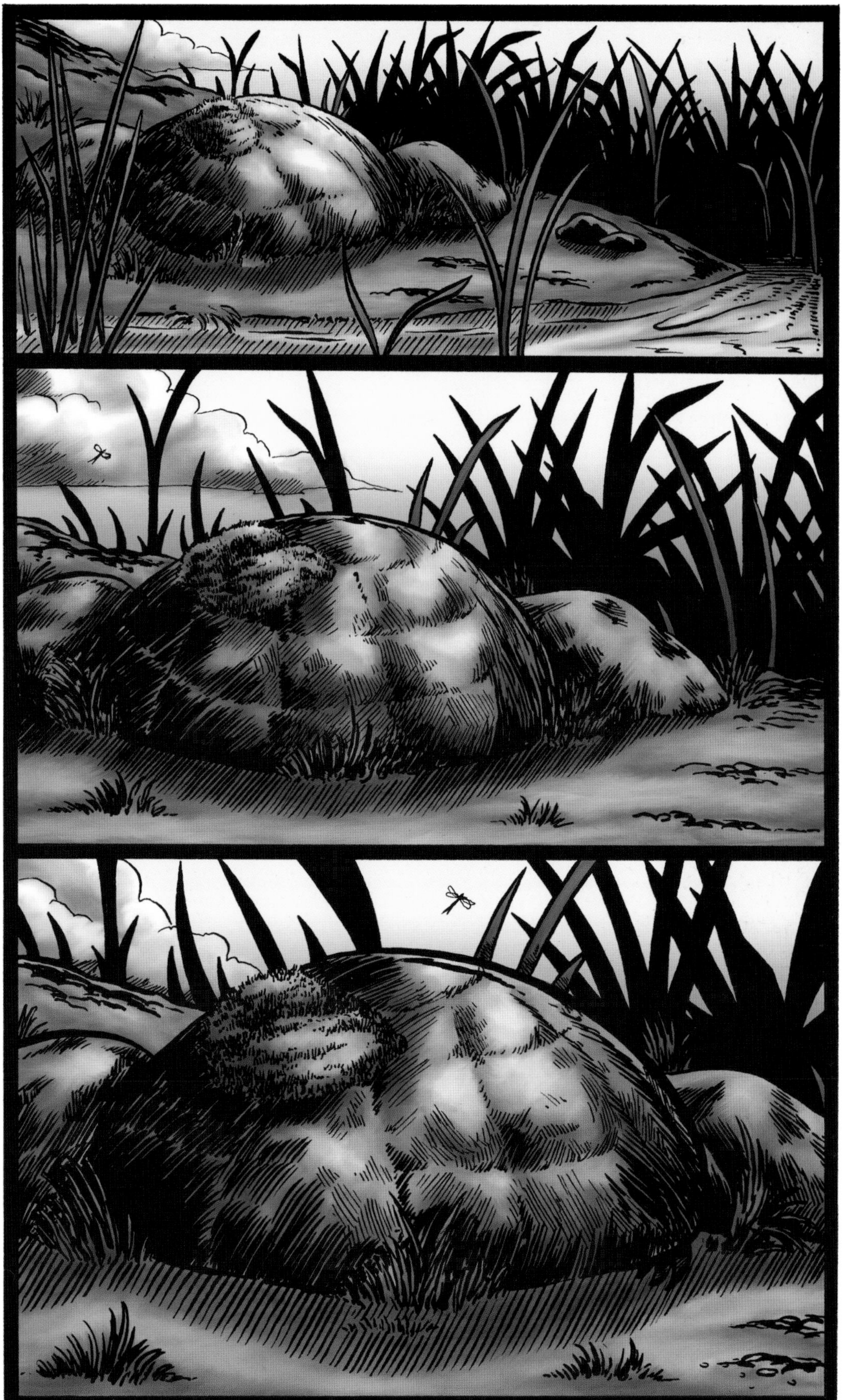

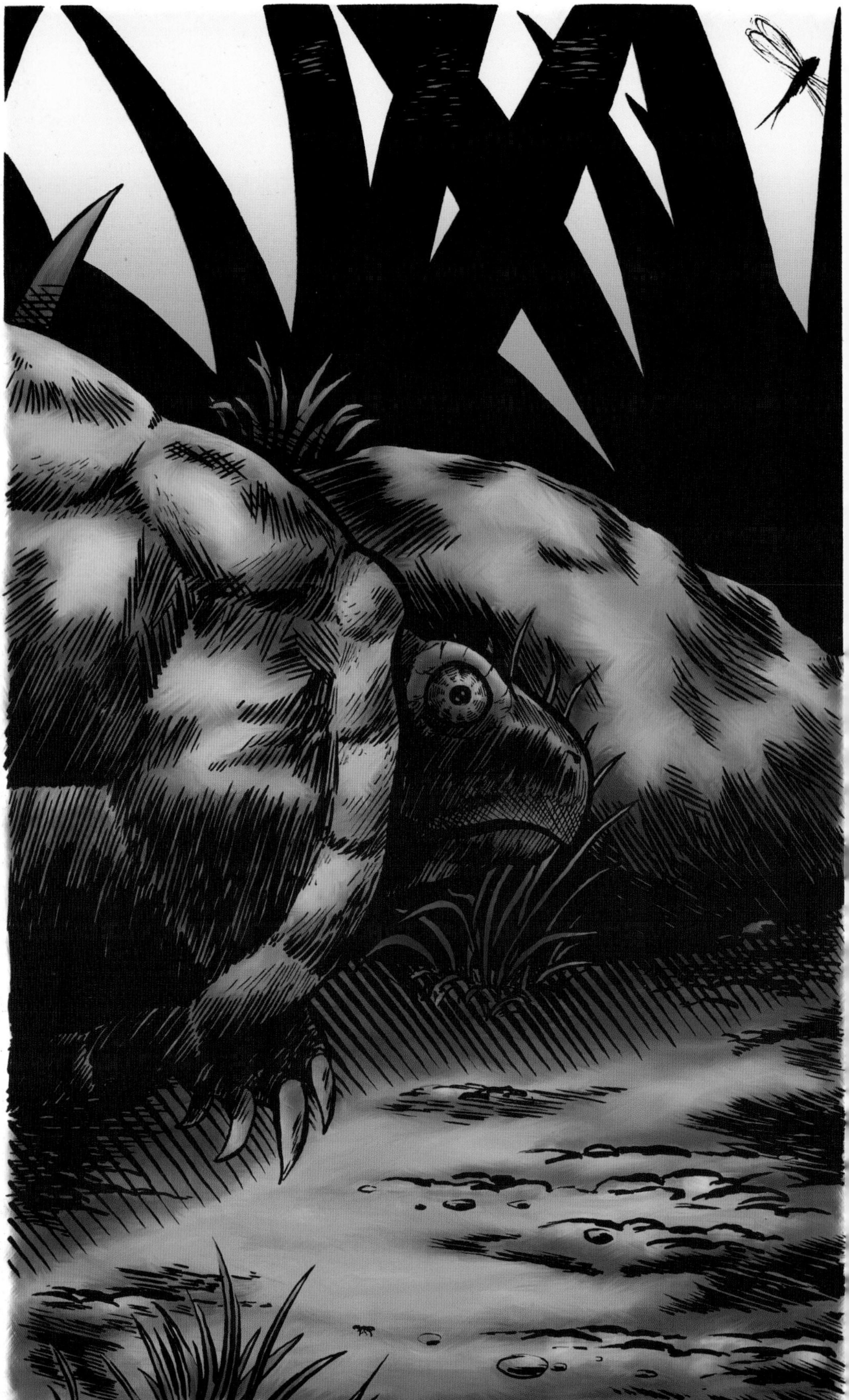

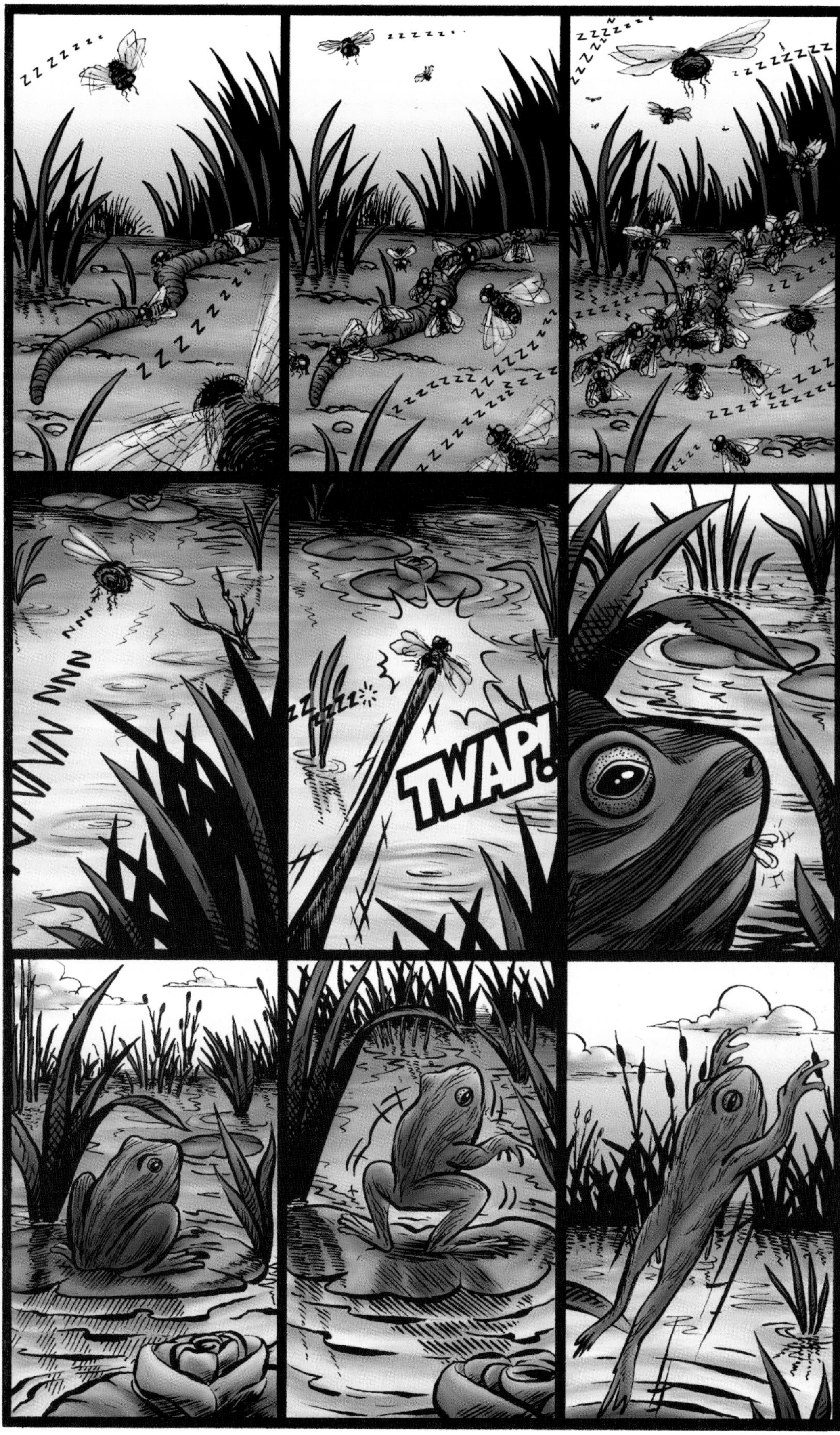
TWAP!

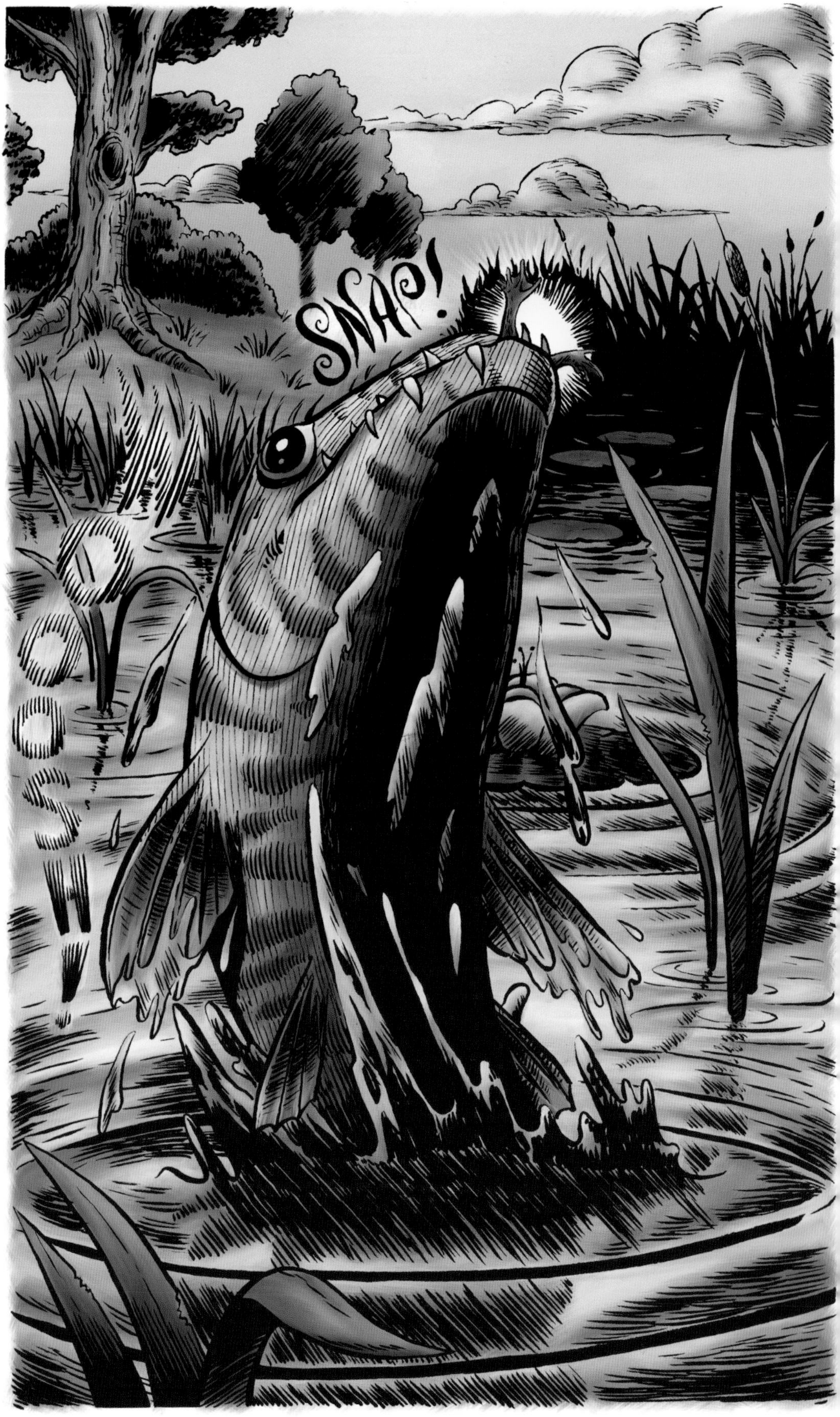
SNAP!

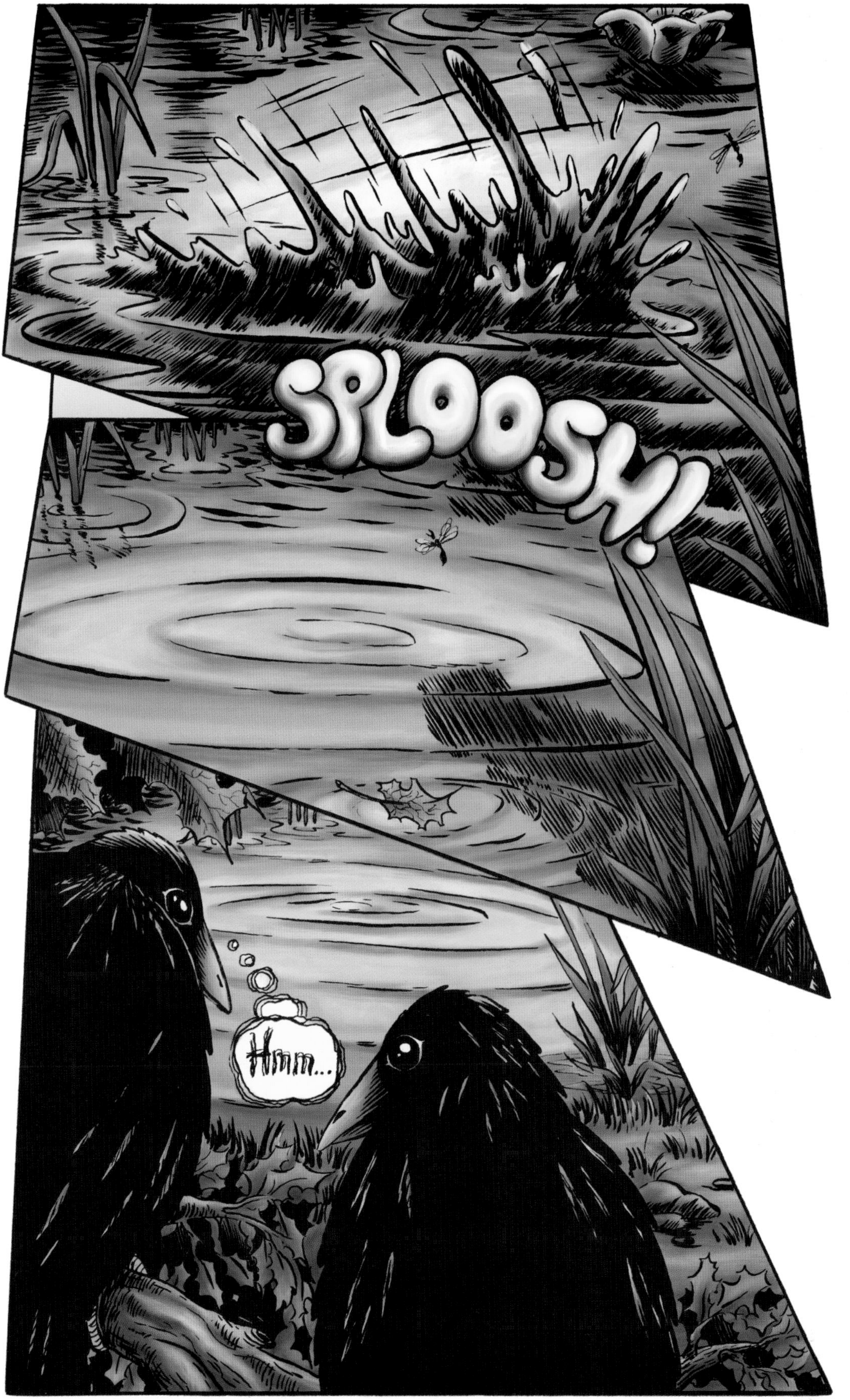
SPLOOSH!
Hmm...

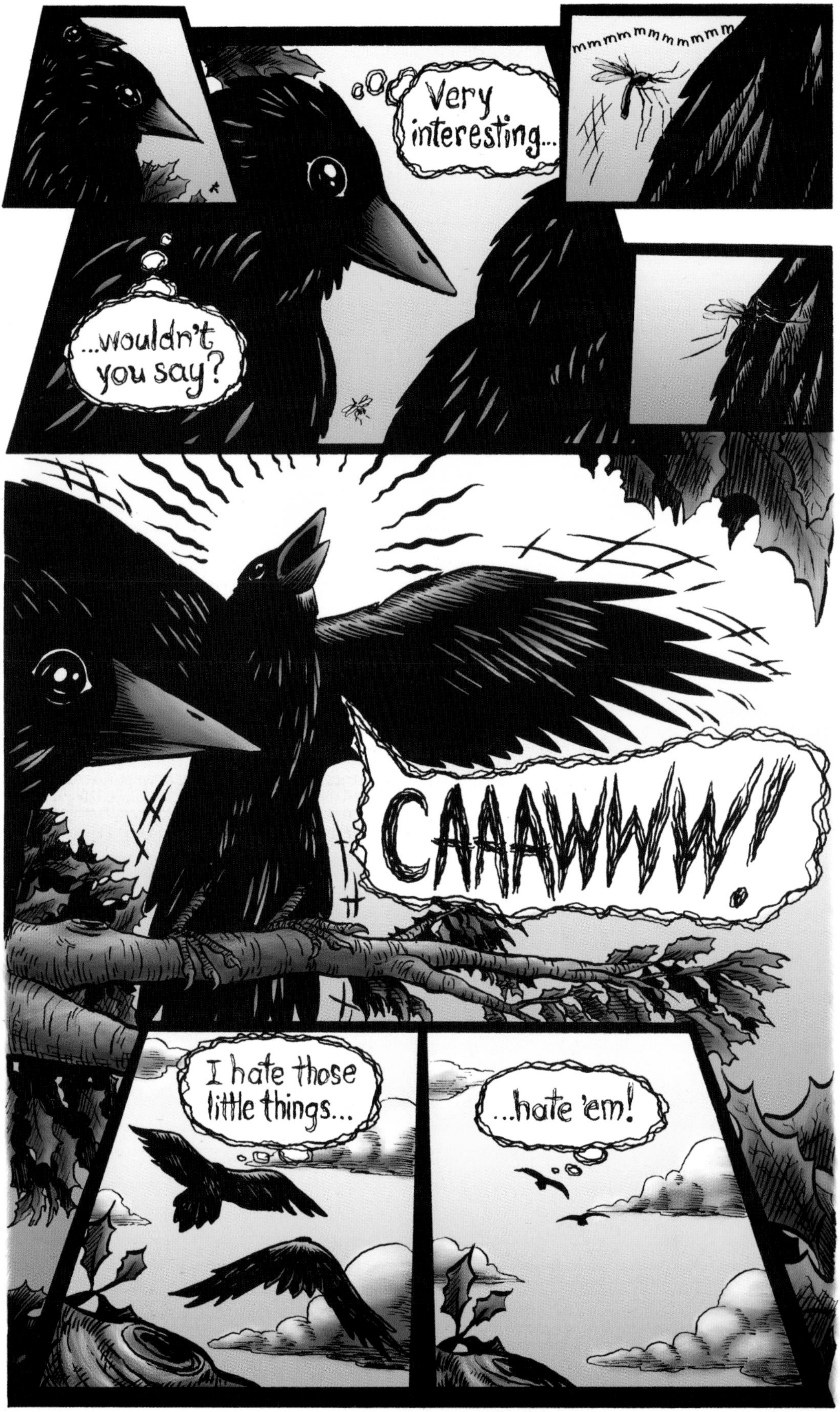
Very interesting...
mmmmmmmmmmmmm
...wouldn't you say?
CAAWWW!
I hate those little things...
...hate 'em!

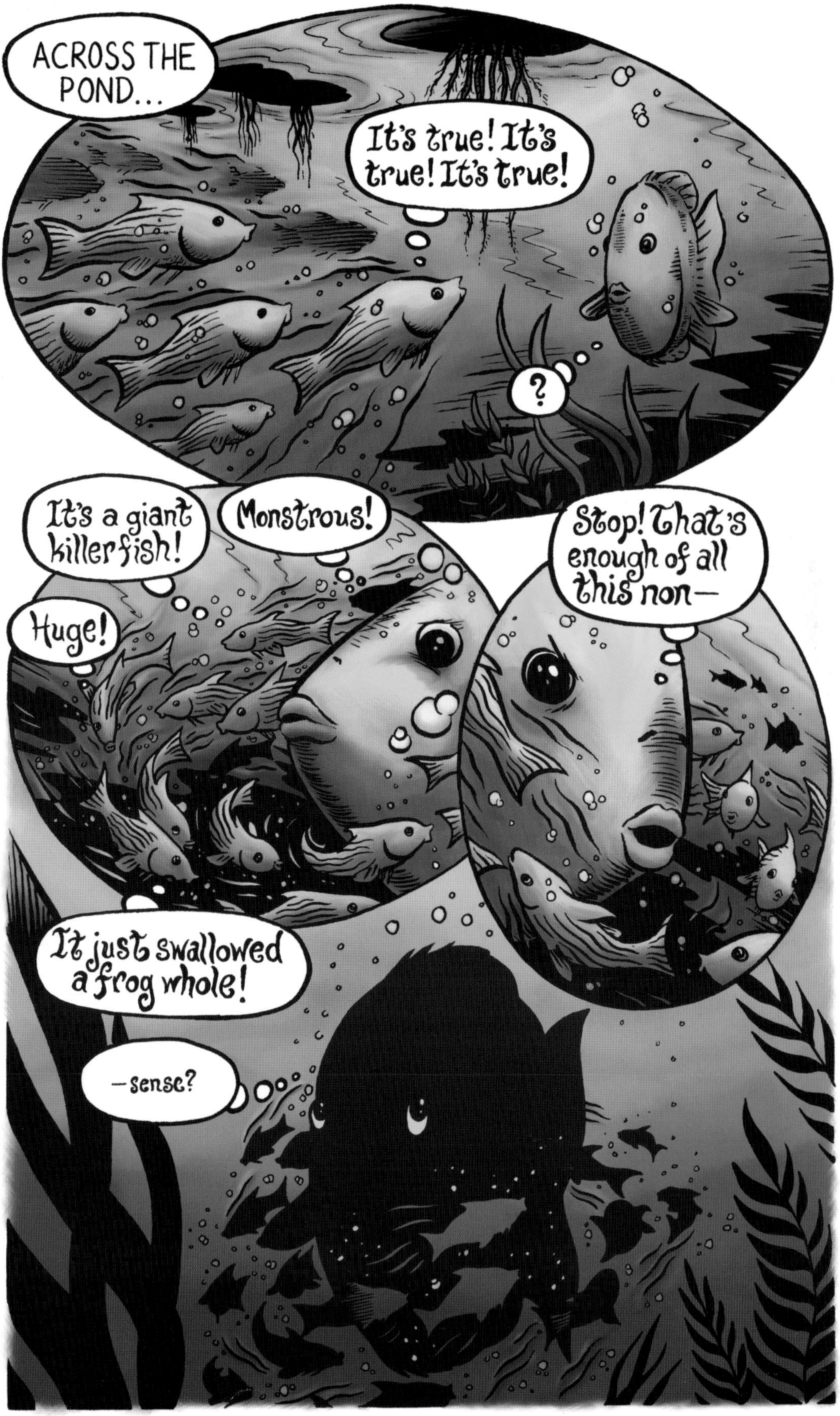
ACROSS THE POND...
It's true! It's true! It's true! It's true!
?
It's a giant killer fish!
Monstrous!
Huge!
Stop! That's enough of all this non—
It just swallowed a frog whole!
—sense?

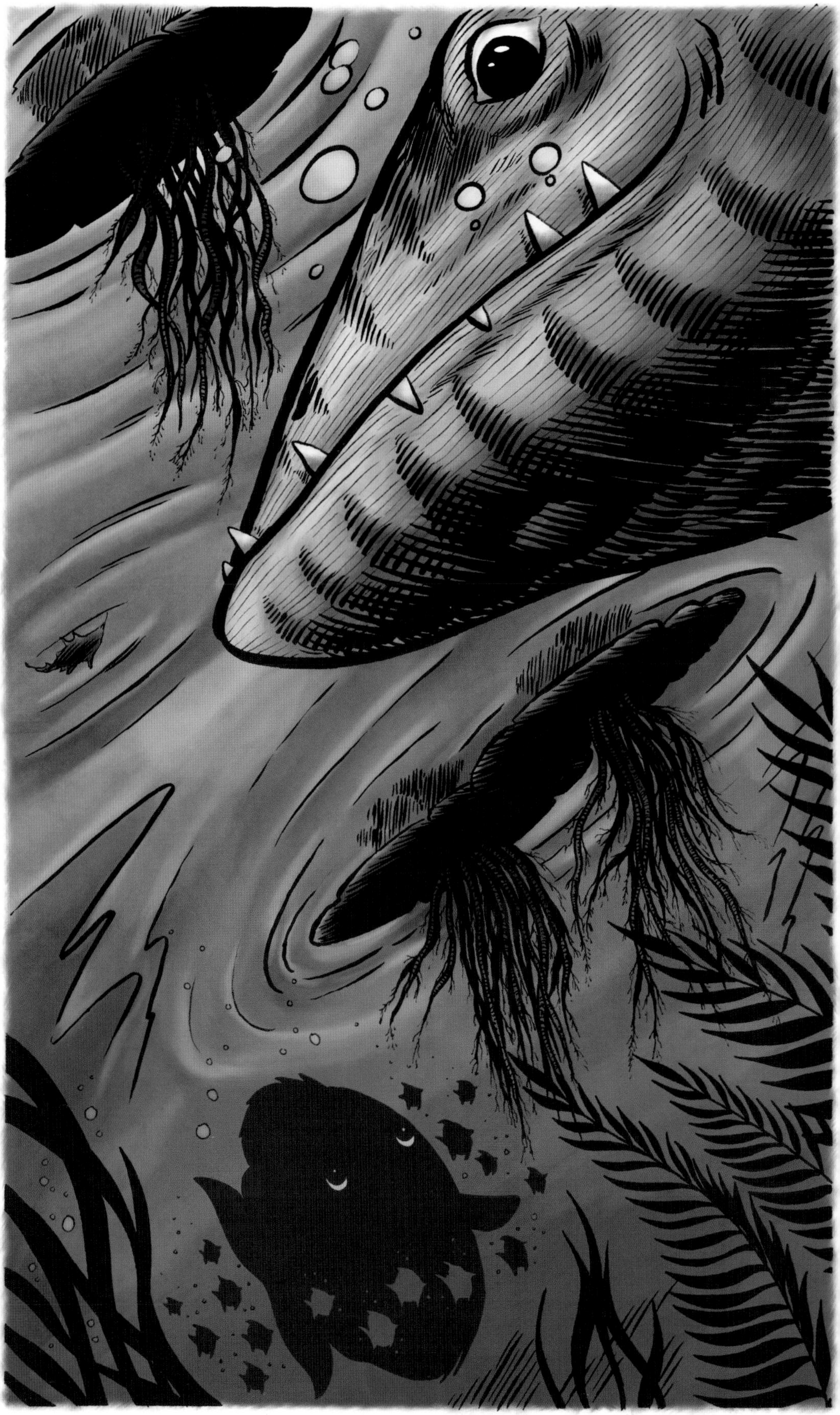

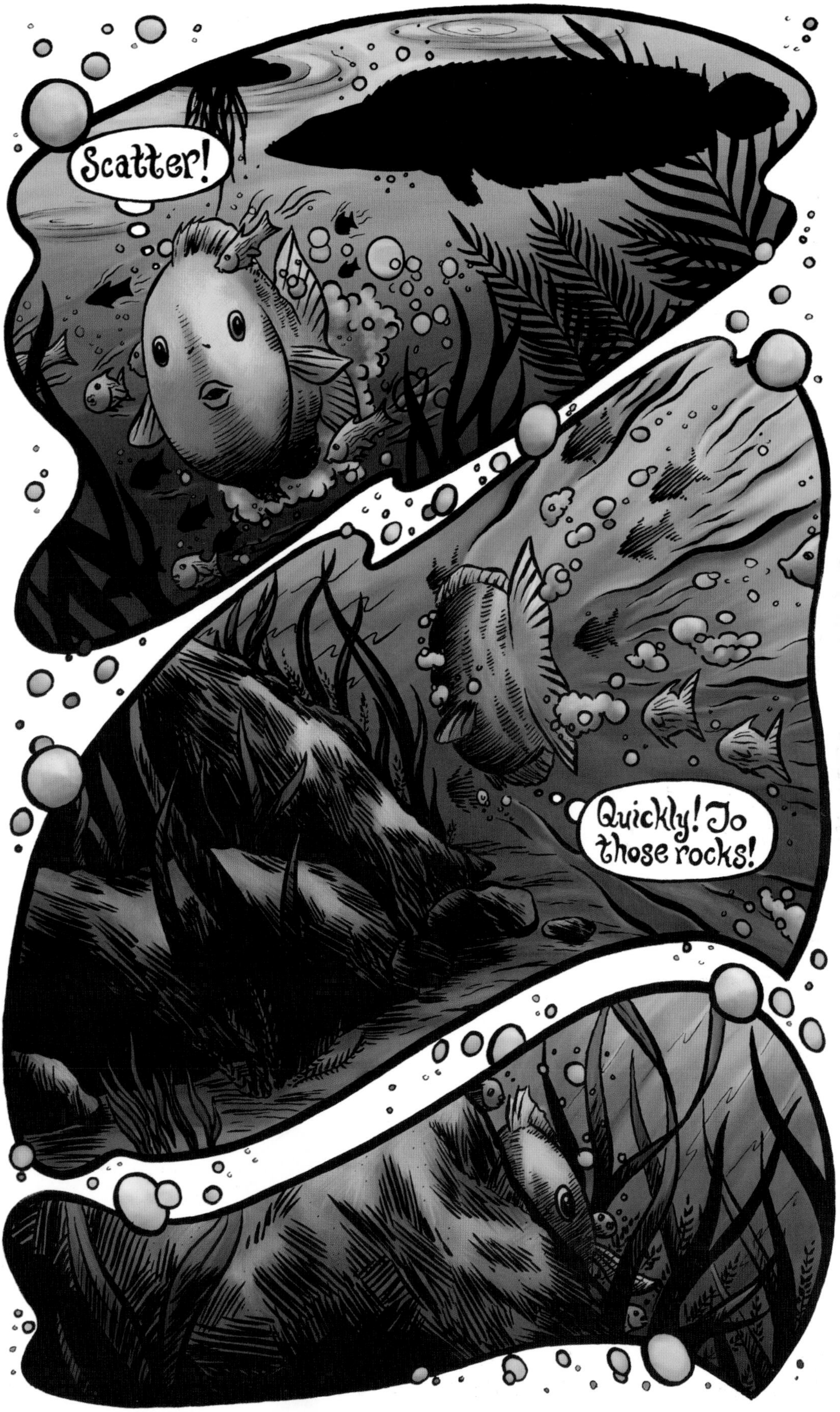
Scatter!
Quickly! To those rocks!

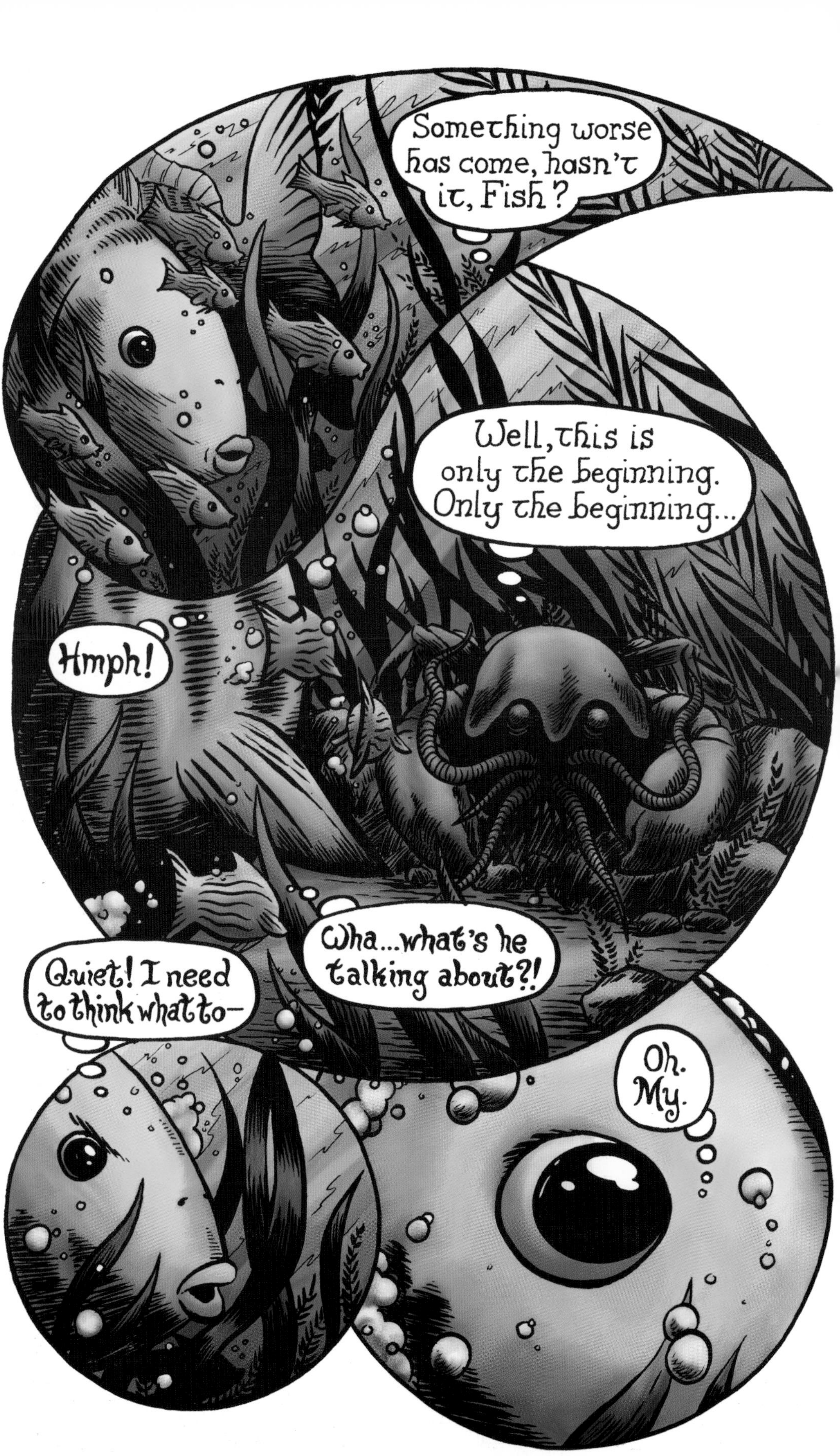
Something worse has come, hasn't it, Fish?
Well, this is only the beginning. Only the beginning...
Hmph!
Wha...what's he talking about?!
Quiet! I need to think what to-
Oh. My.

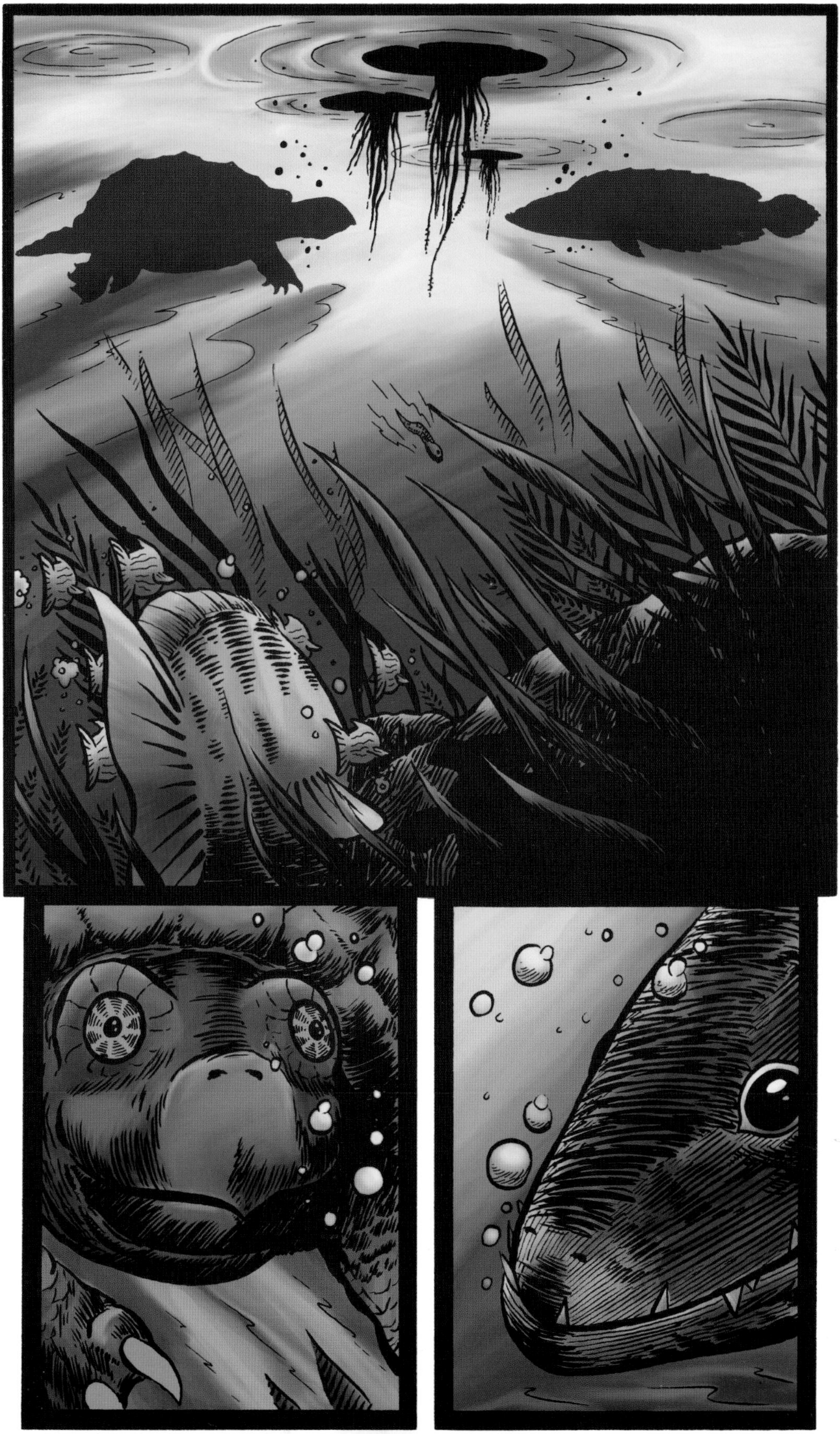

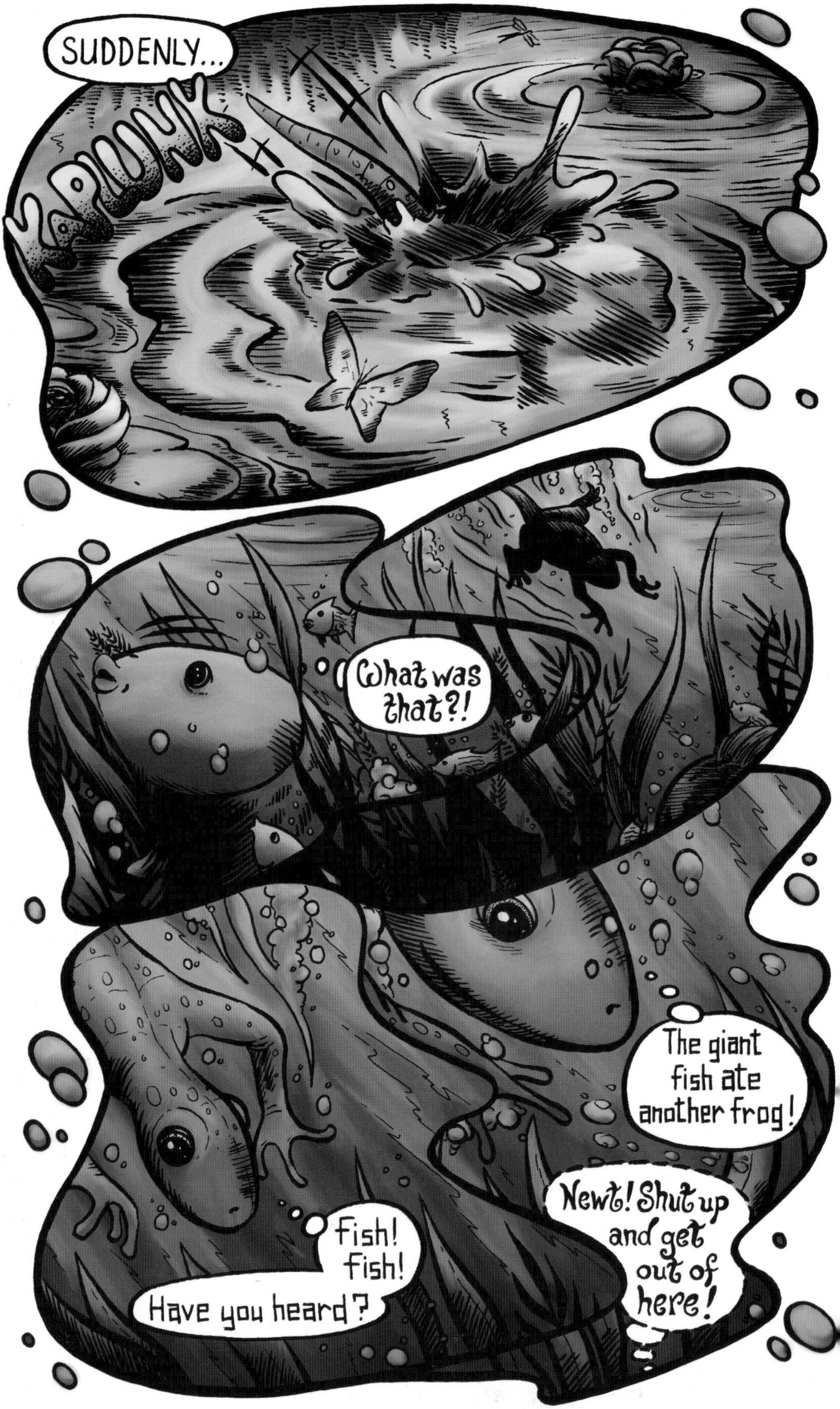
SUDDENLY...
SPLUNK!!
What was that?!
The giant fish ate another frog!
Fish! Fish! Have you heard?
Newt! Shut up and get out of here!

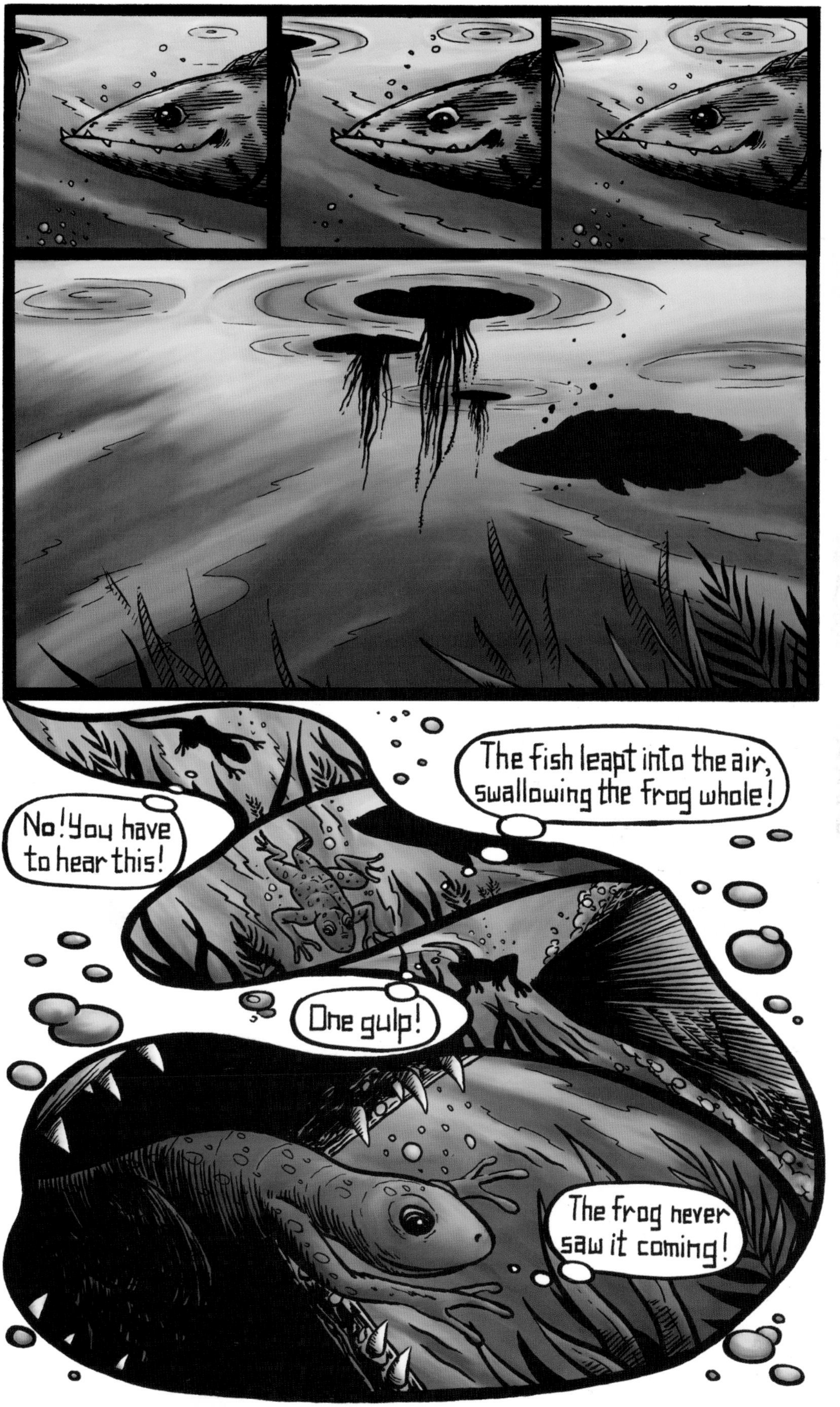
No! You have to hear this!
The fish leapt into the air, swallowing the frog whole!
One gulp!
The frog never saw it coming!

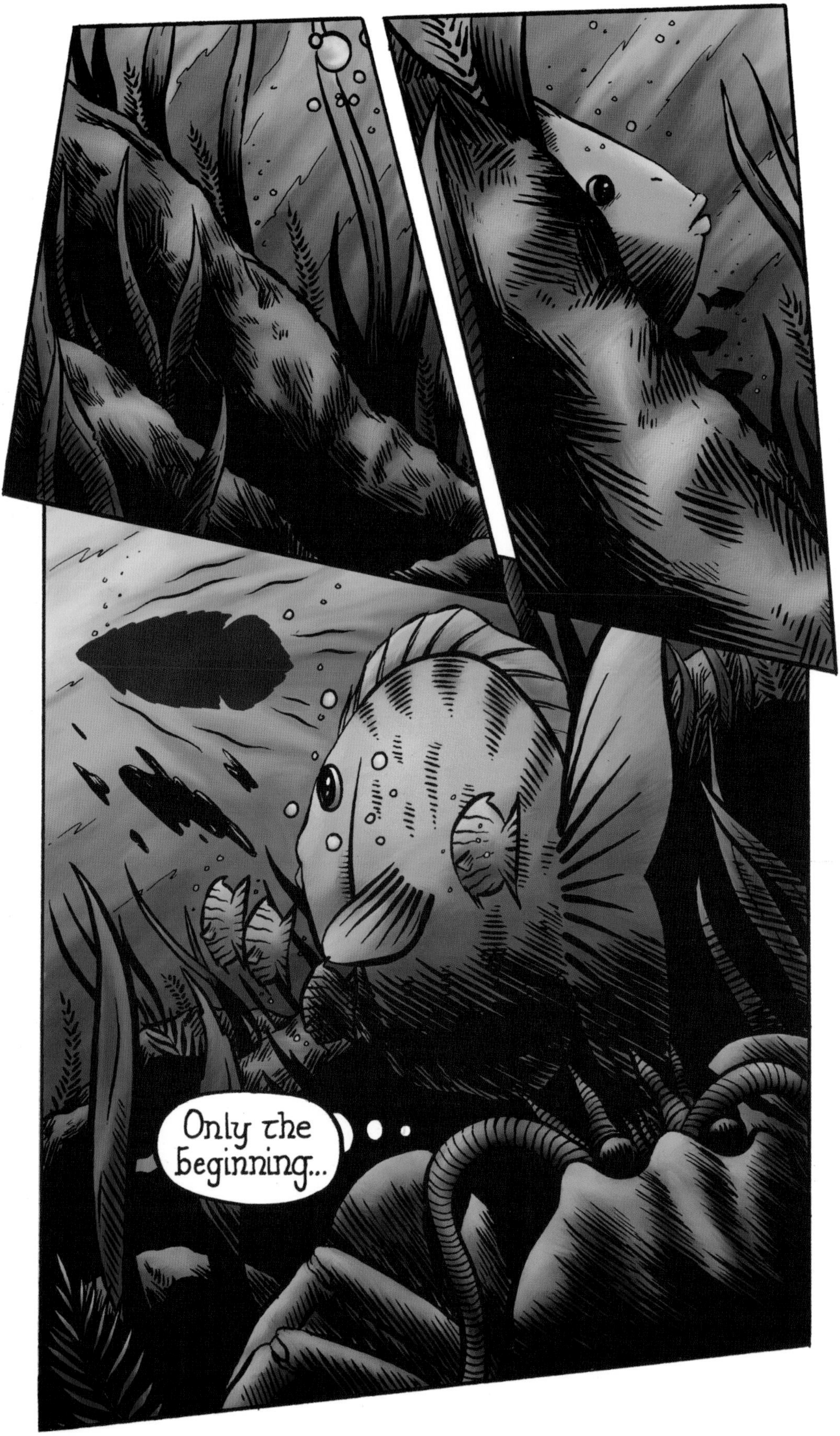
Only the beginning...

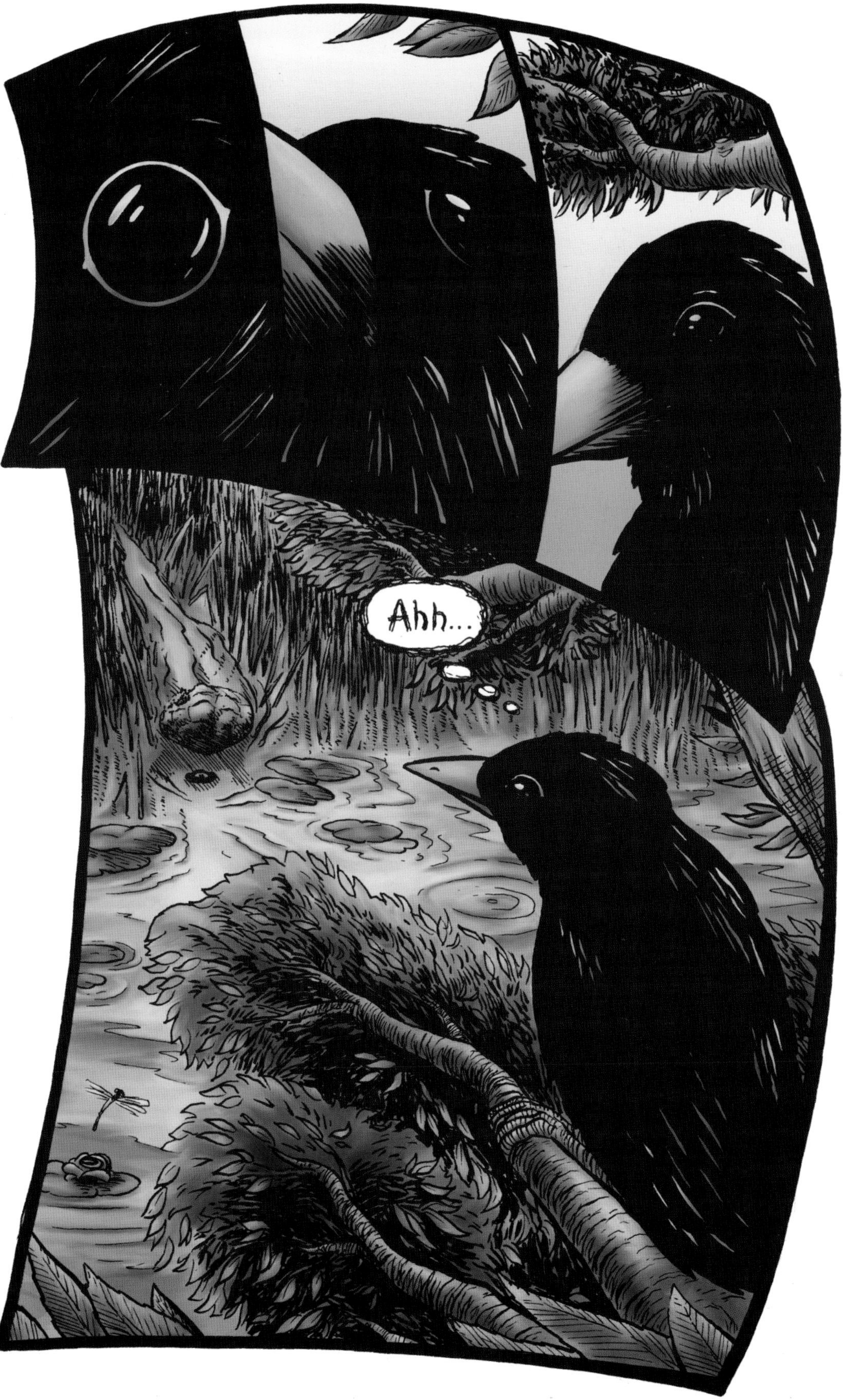
Ahh...

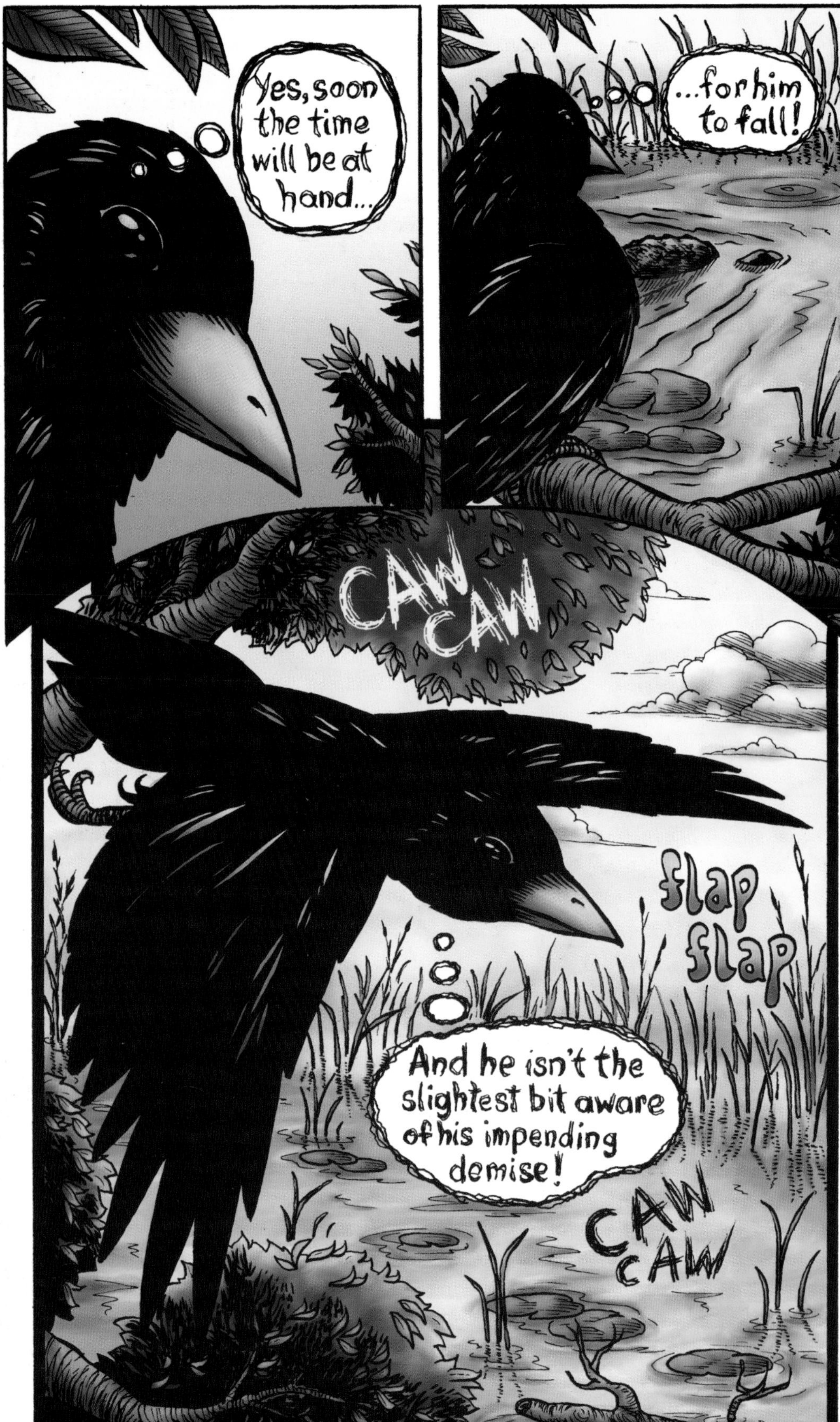
Yes, soon the time will be at hand...
...for him to fall!
CAW CAW
flap flap
And he isn't the slightest bit aware of his impending demise!
CAW CAW

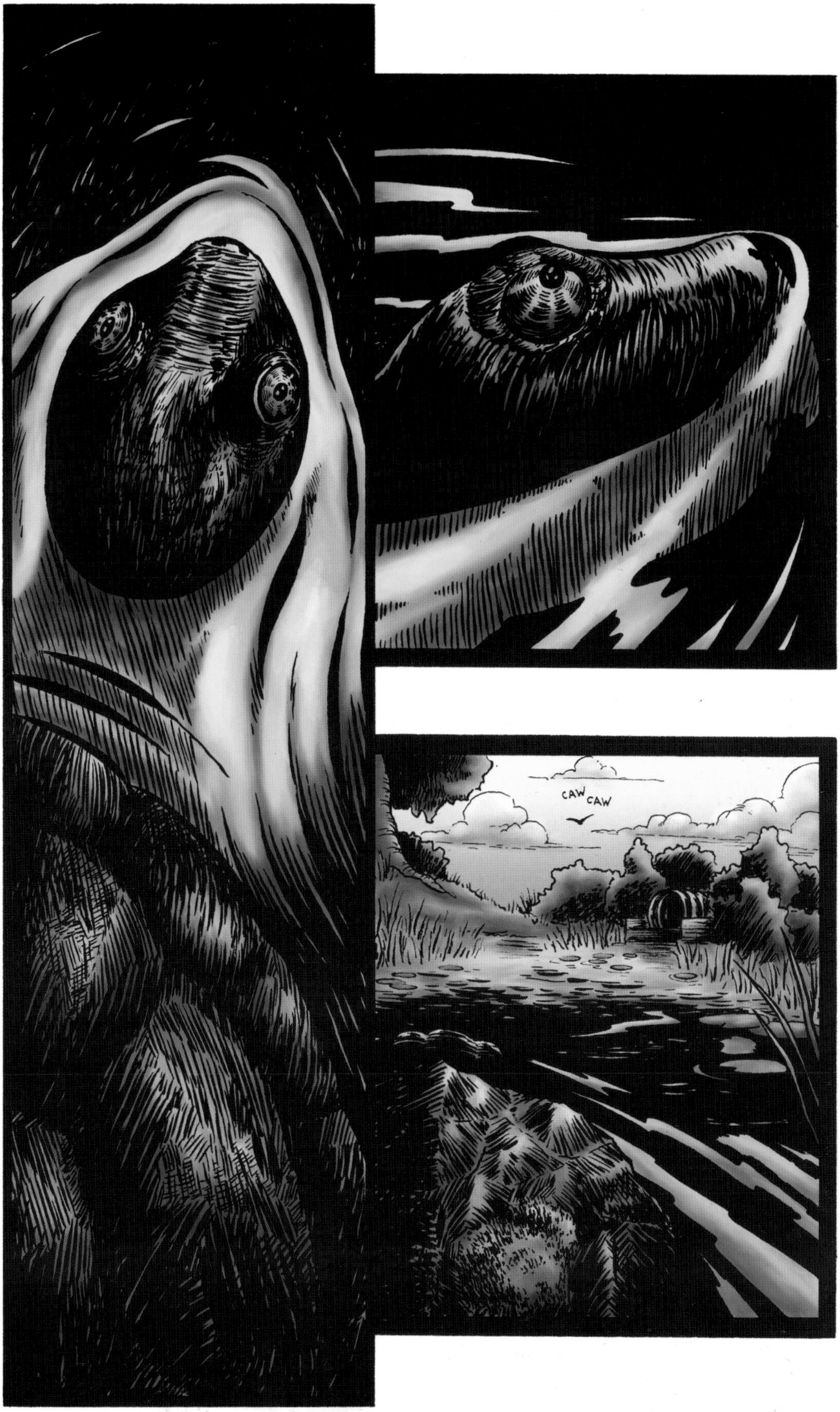
CAW CAW

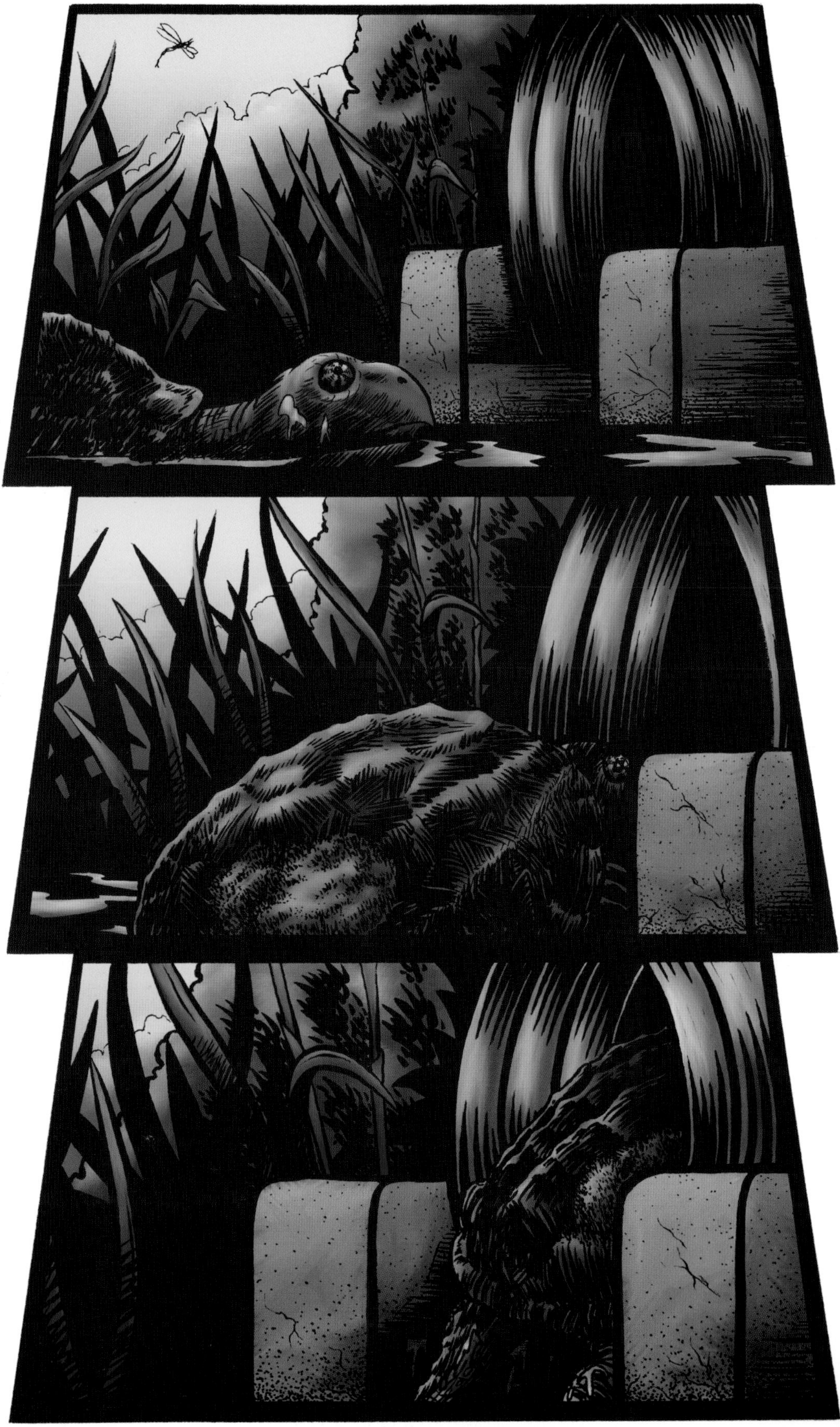

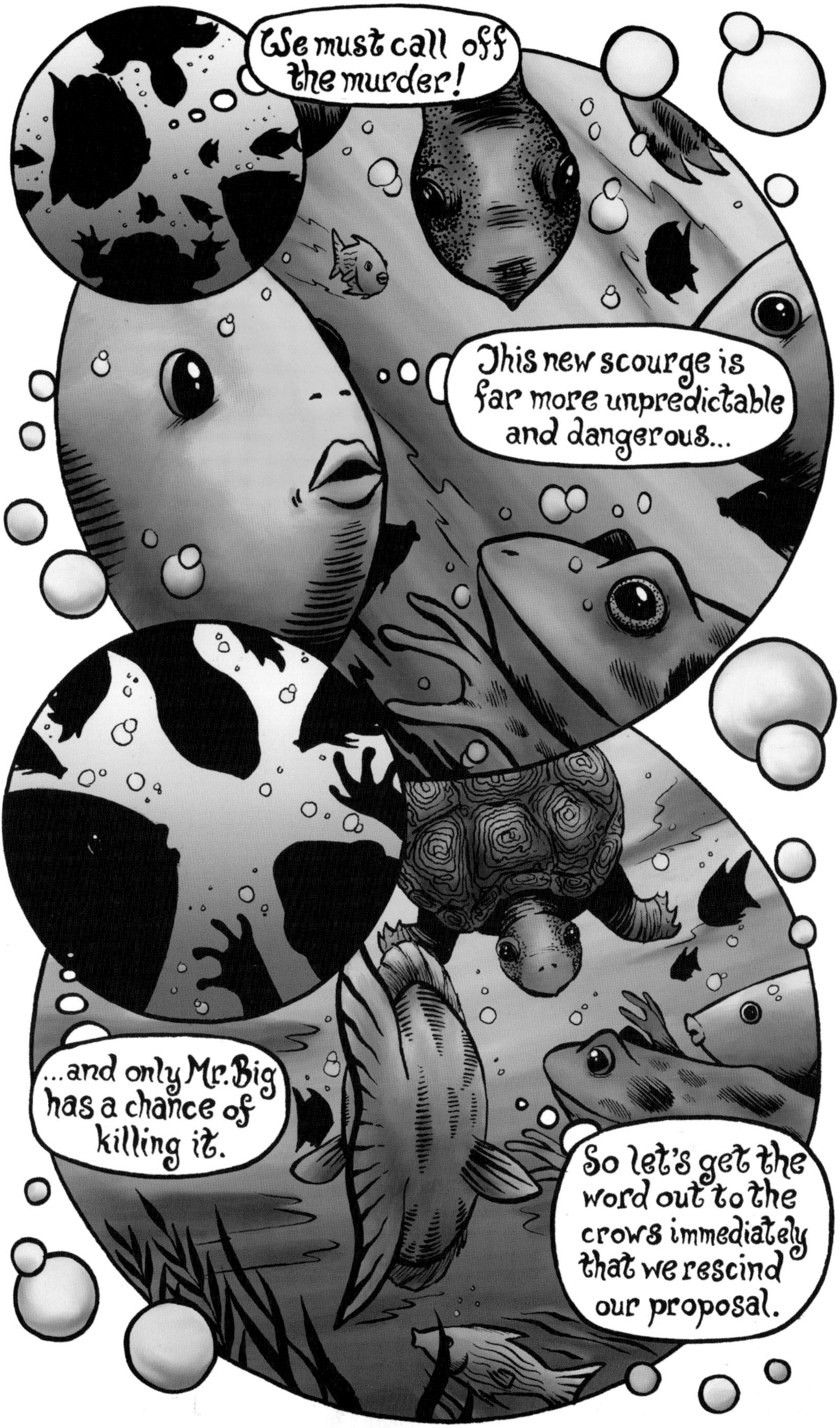
We must call off the murder!
This new scourge is far more unpredictable and dangerous...
...and only Mr. Big has a chance of killing it.
So let's get the word out to the crows immediately that we rescind our proposal.

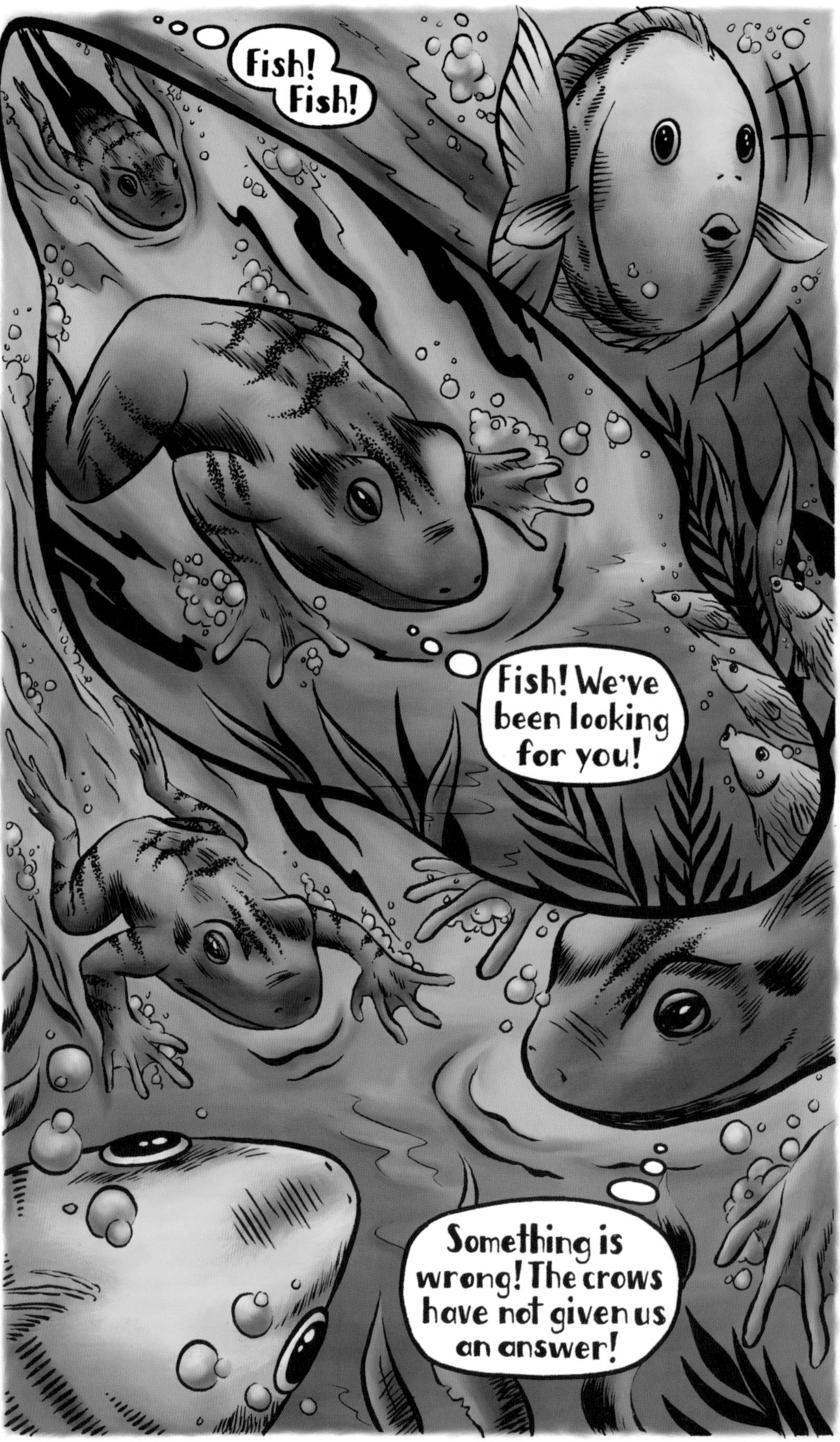
Fish! Fish!
Fish! We've been looking for you!
Something is wrong! The crows have not given us an answer!

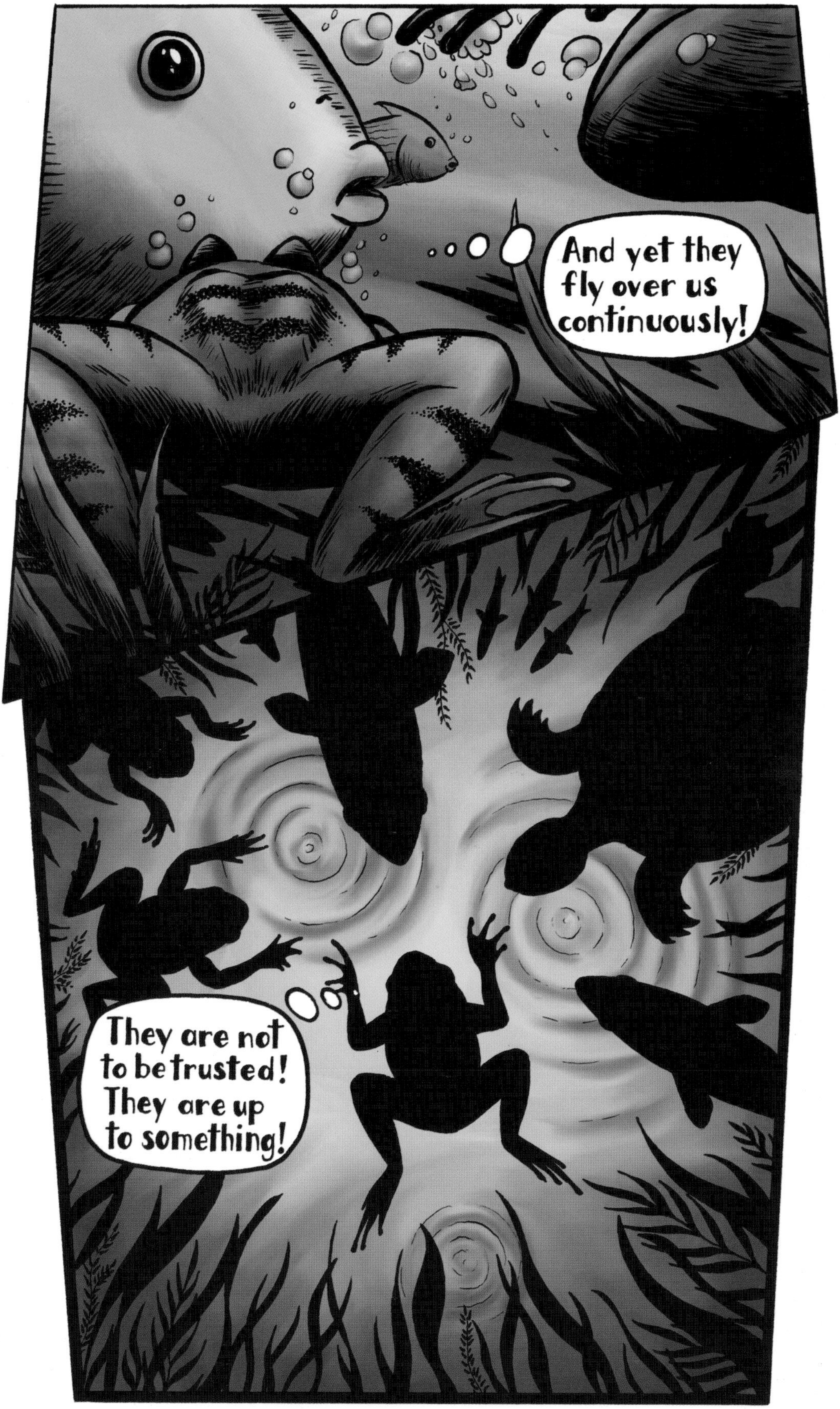
And yet they fly over us continuously!
They are not to be trusted! They are up to something!

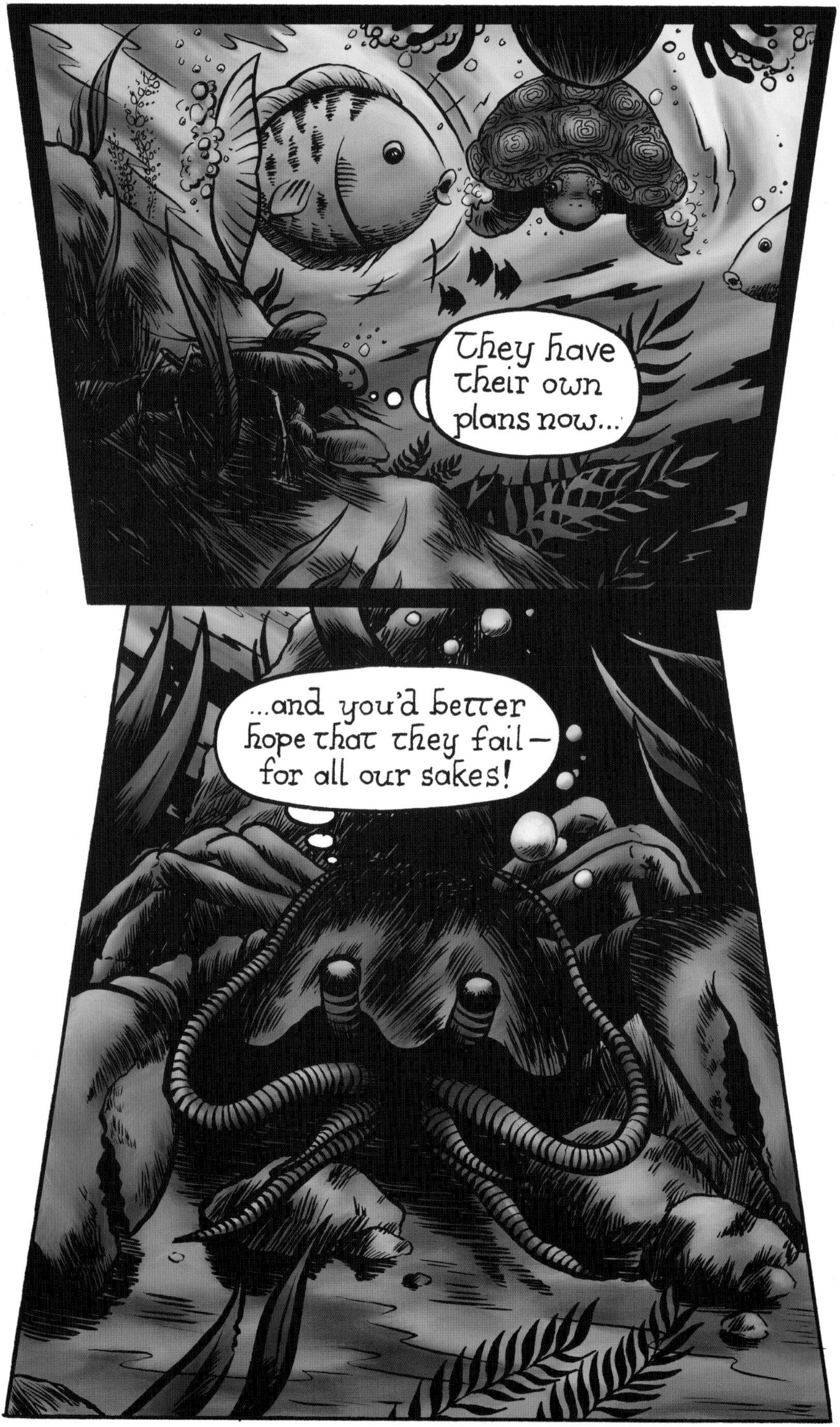
They have their own plans now...
...and you'd better hope that they fail—for all our sakes!

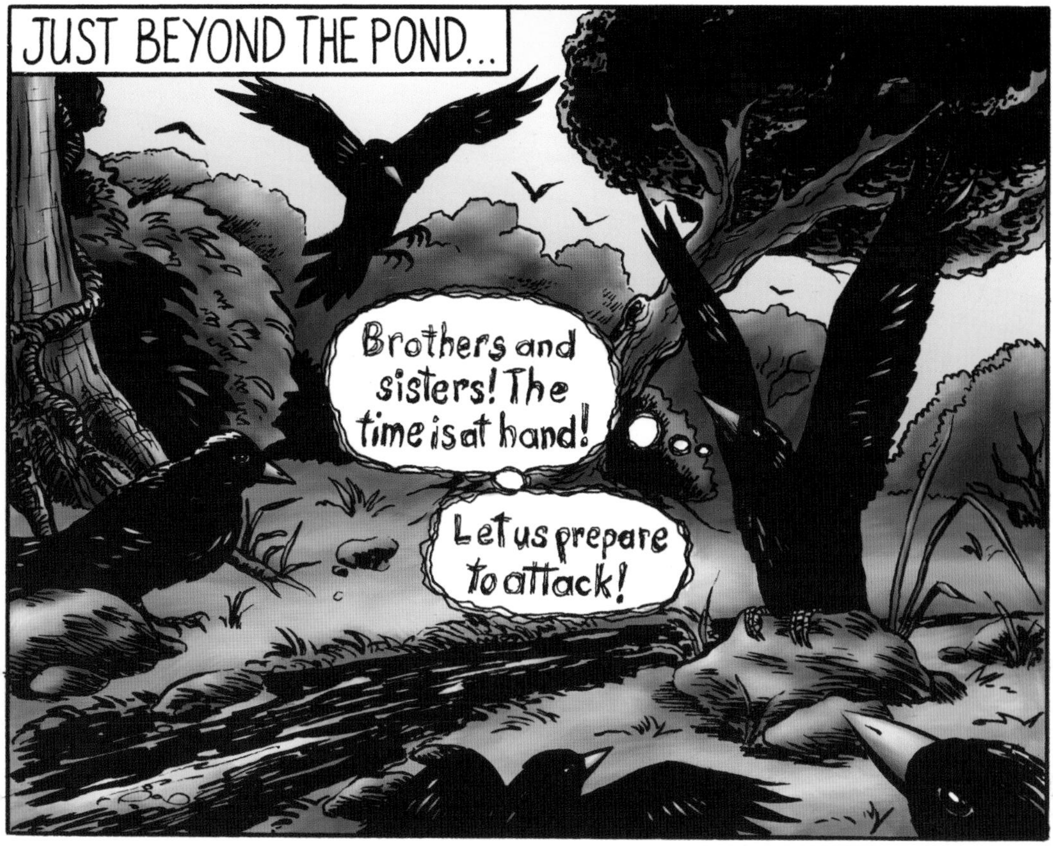
JUST BEYOND THE POND...
Brothers and sisters! The time is at hand!
Let us prepare to attack!

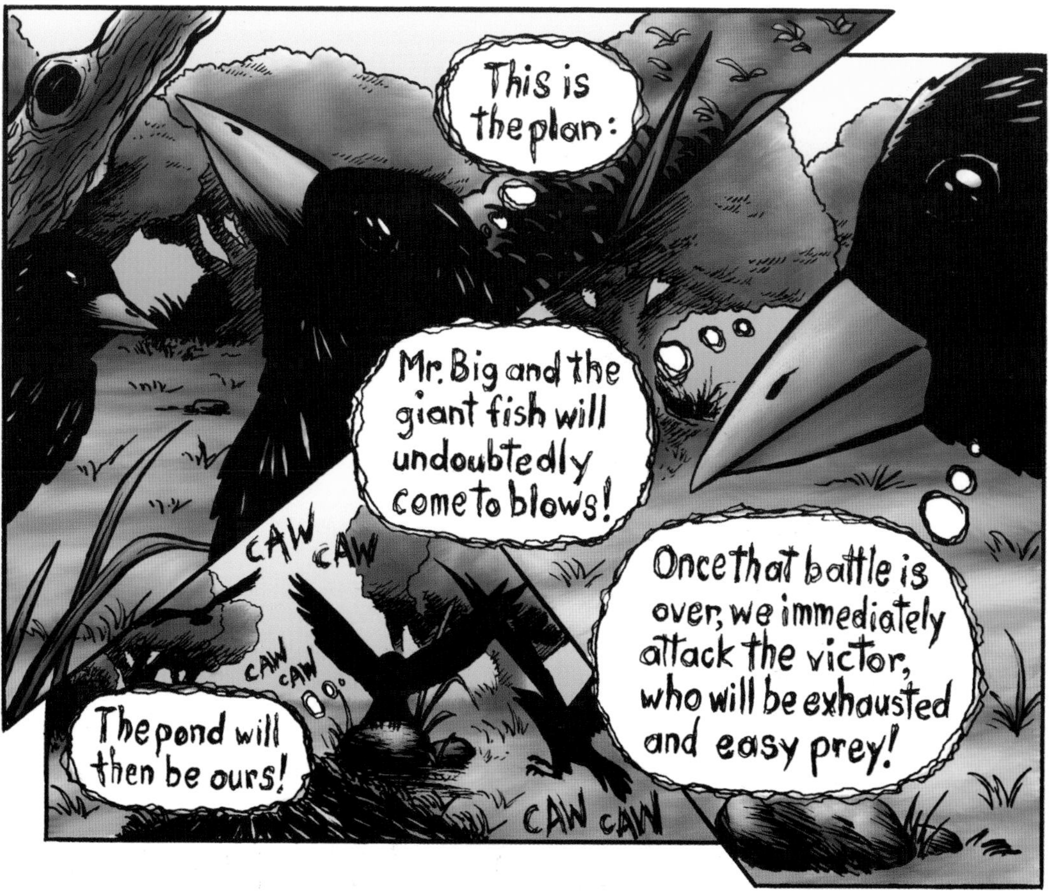
This is the plan:
Mr. Big and the giant fish will undoubtedly come to blows!
CAW CAW
CAW CAW
Once that battle is over, we immediately attack the victor, who will be exhausted and easy prey!
The pond will then be ours!
CAW CAW

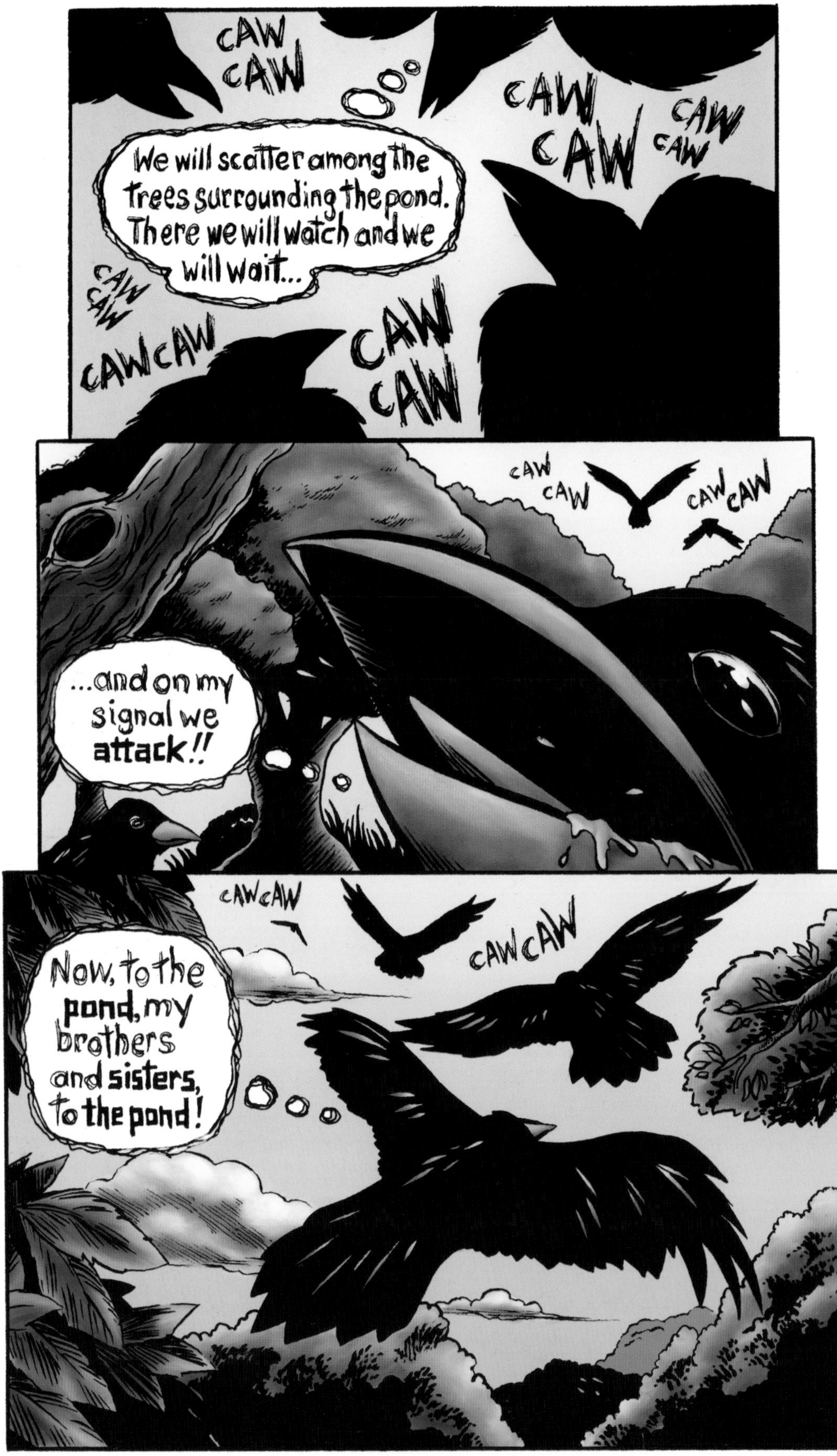

CAW CAW
CAW CAW
CAW CAW
We will scatter among the trees surrounding the pond. There we will watch and we will wait...
CAW CAW
CAWCAW
CAW CAW
CAW CAW
CAW CAW
...and on my signal we **attack**!!
CAWCAW
CAWCAW
Now, to the **pond**, my brothers and **sisters**, to the **pond**!

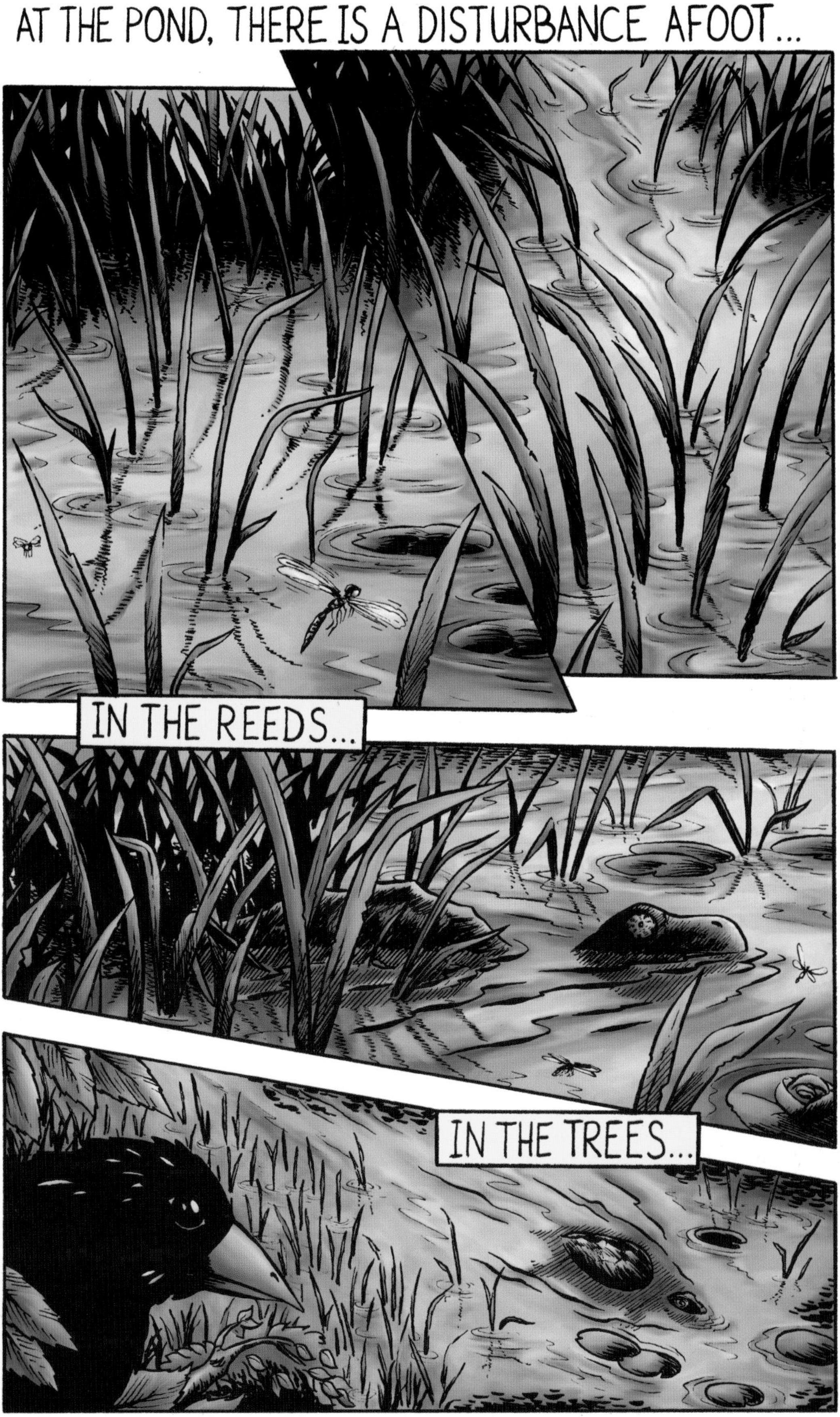
AT THE POND, THERE IS A DISTURBANCE AFOOT...
IN THE REEDS...
IN THE TREES...

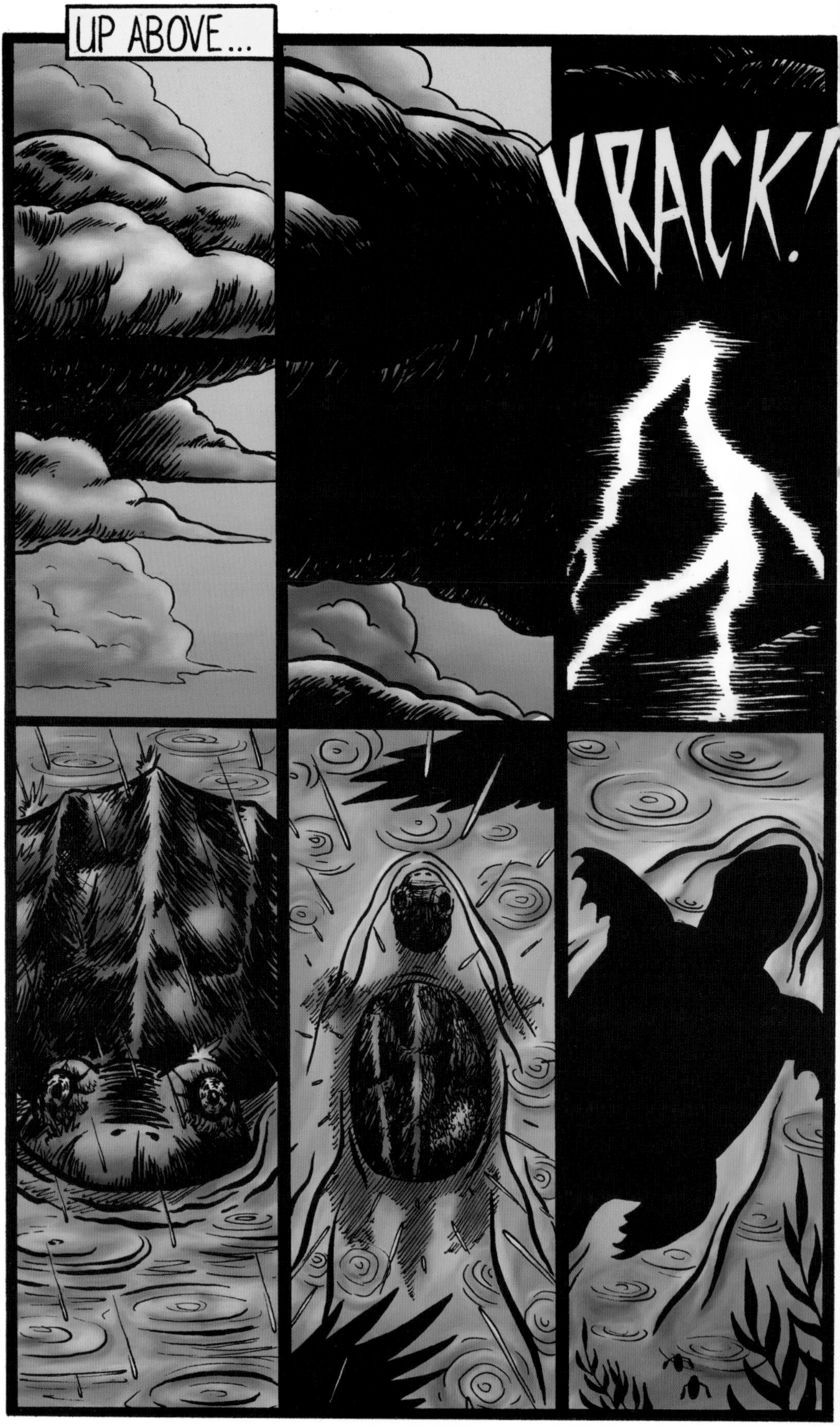
UP ABOVE...
KRACK!

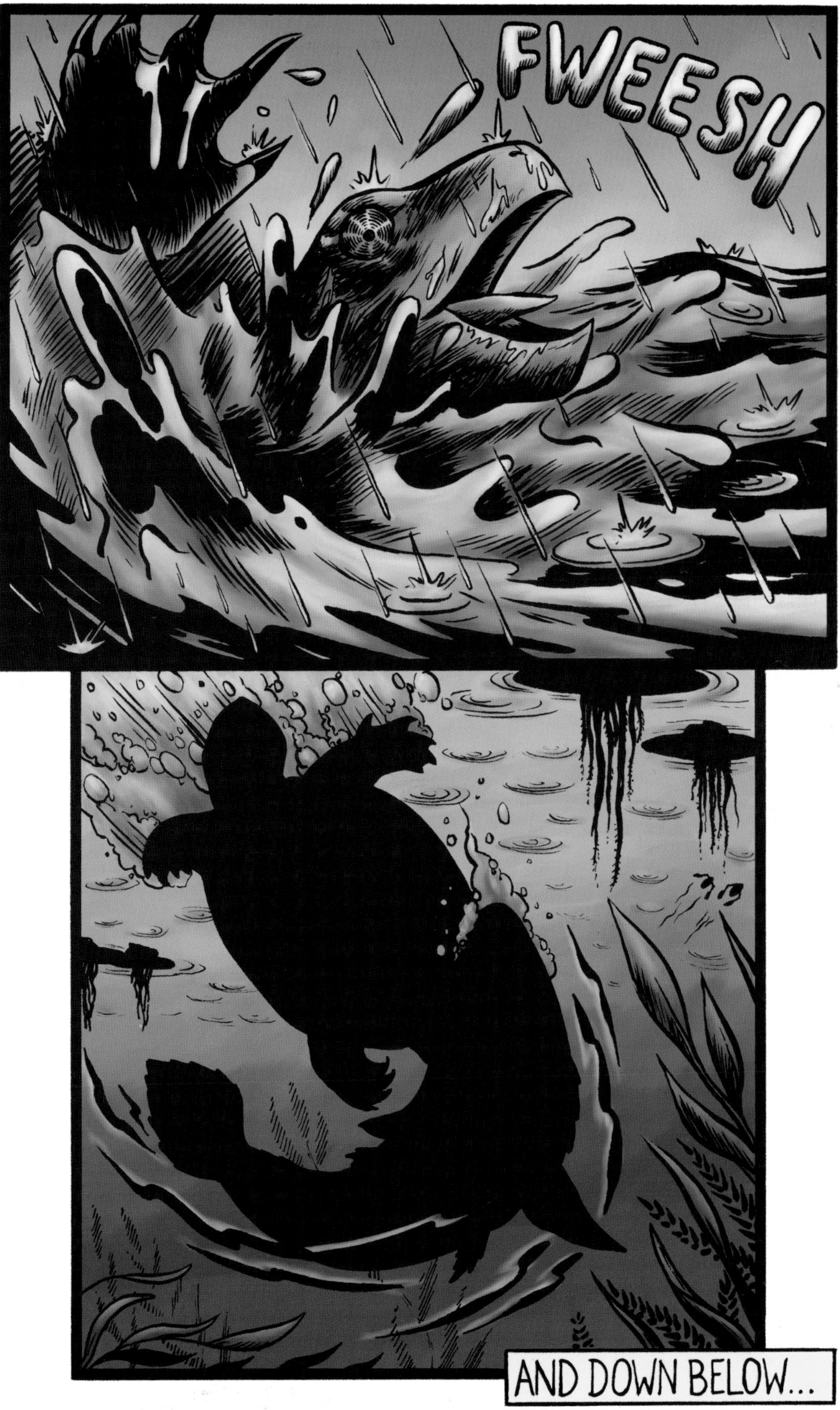
FWEESH
AND DOWN BELOW...

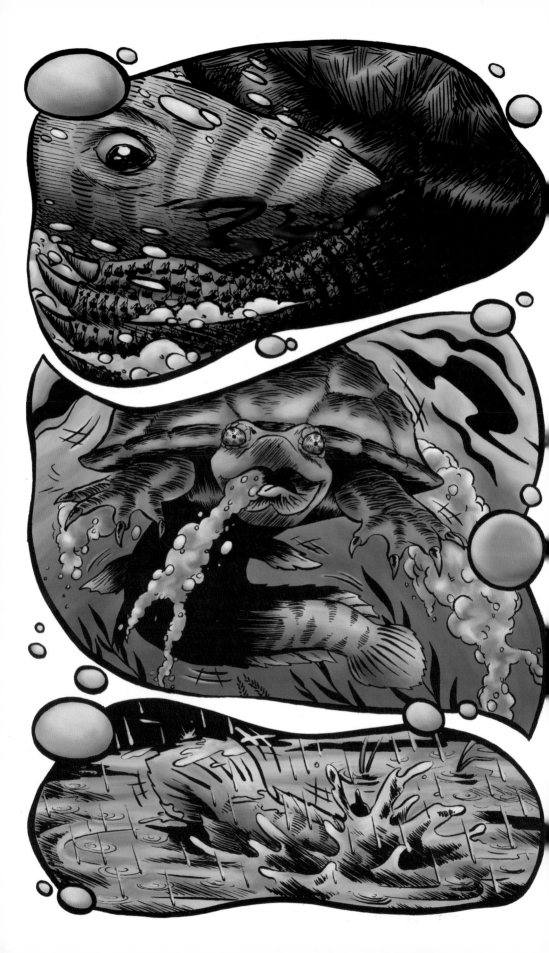

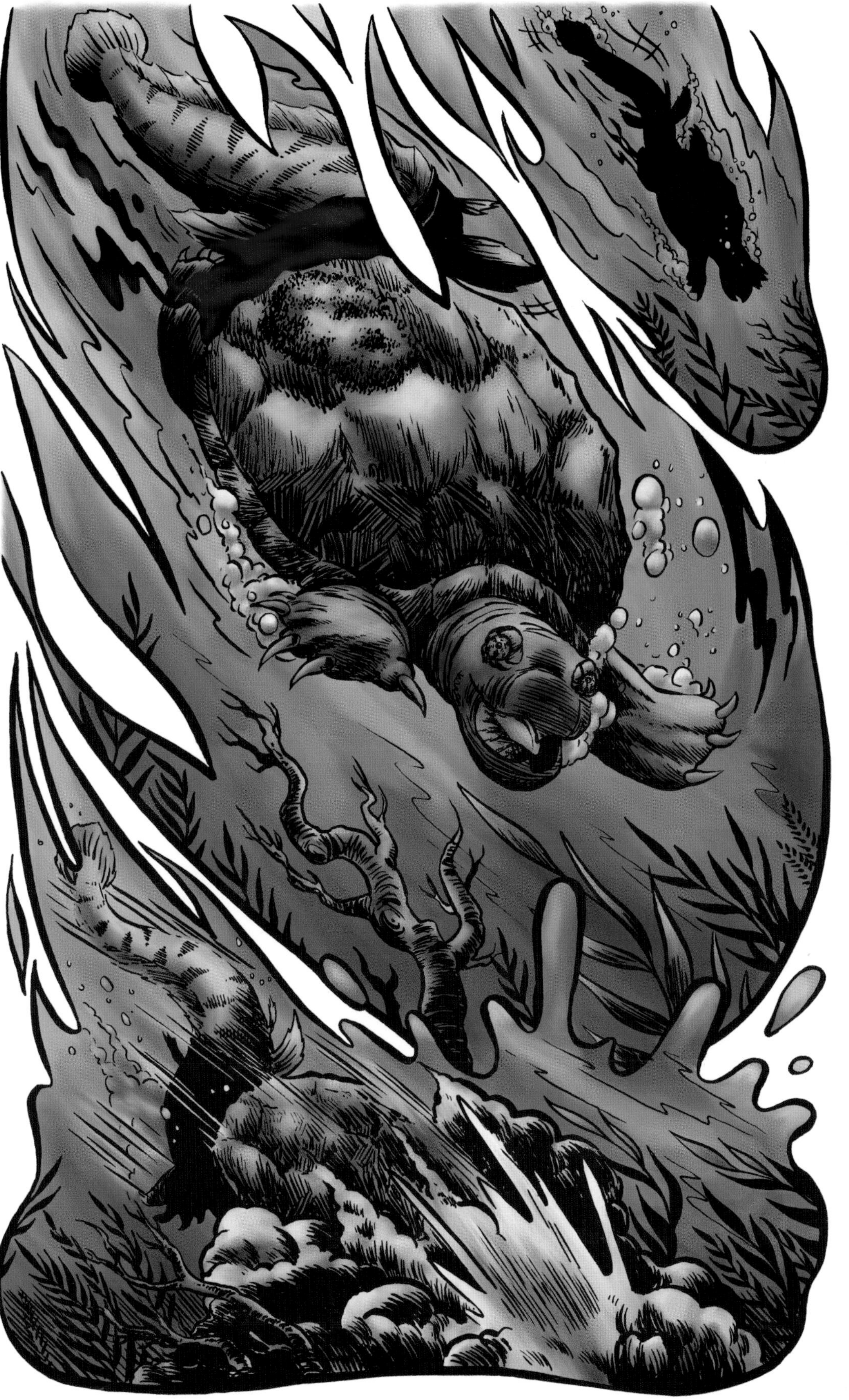

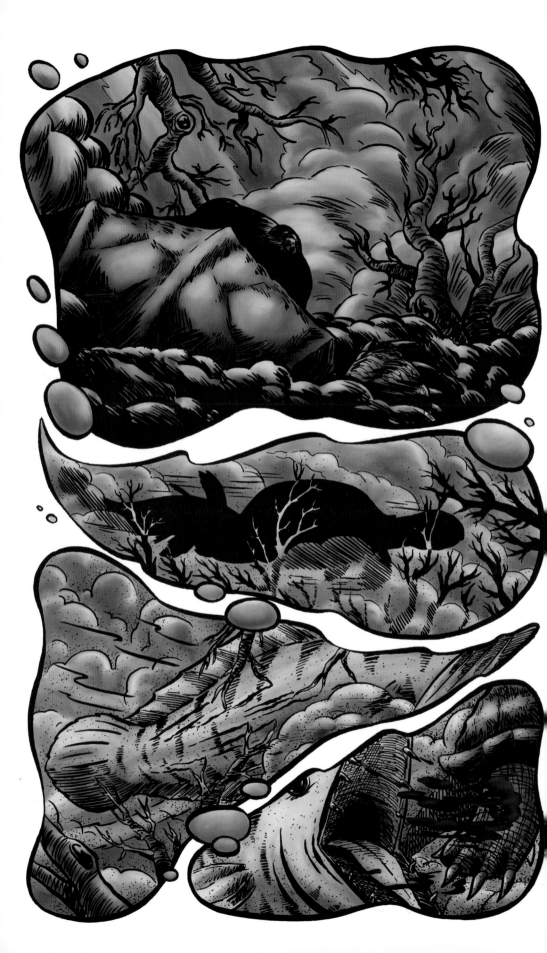

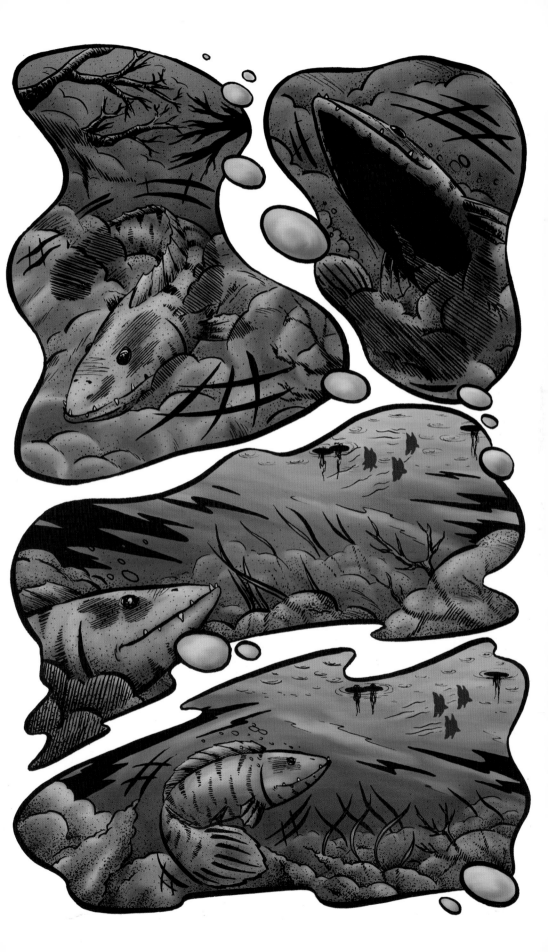

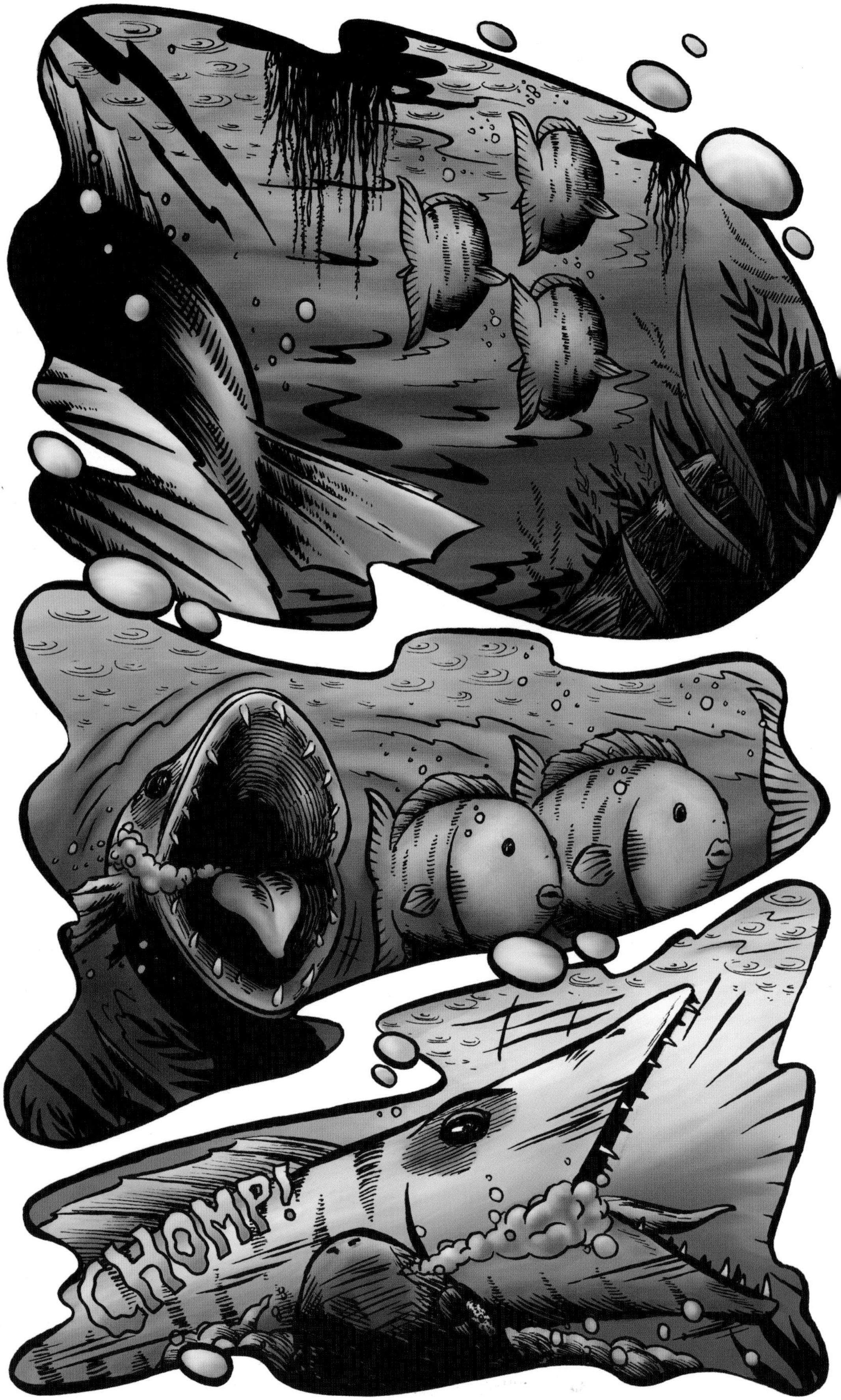
CHOMP!

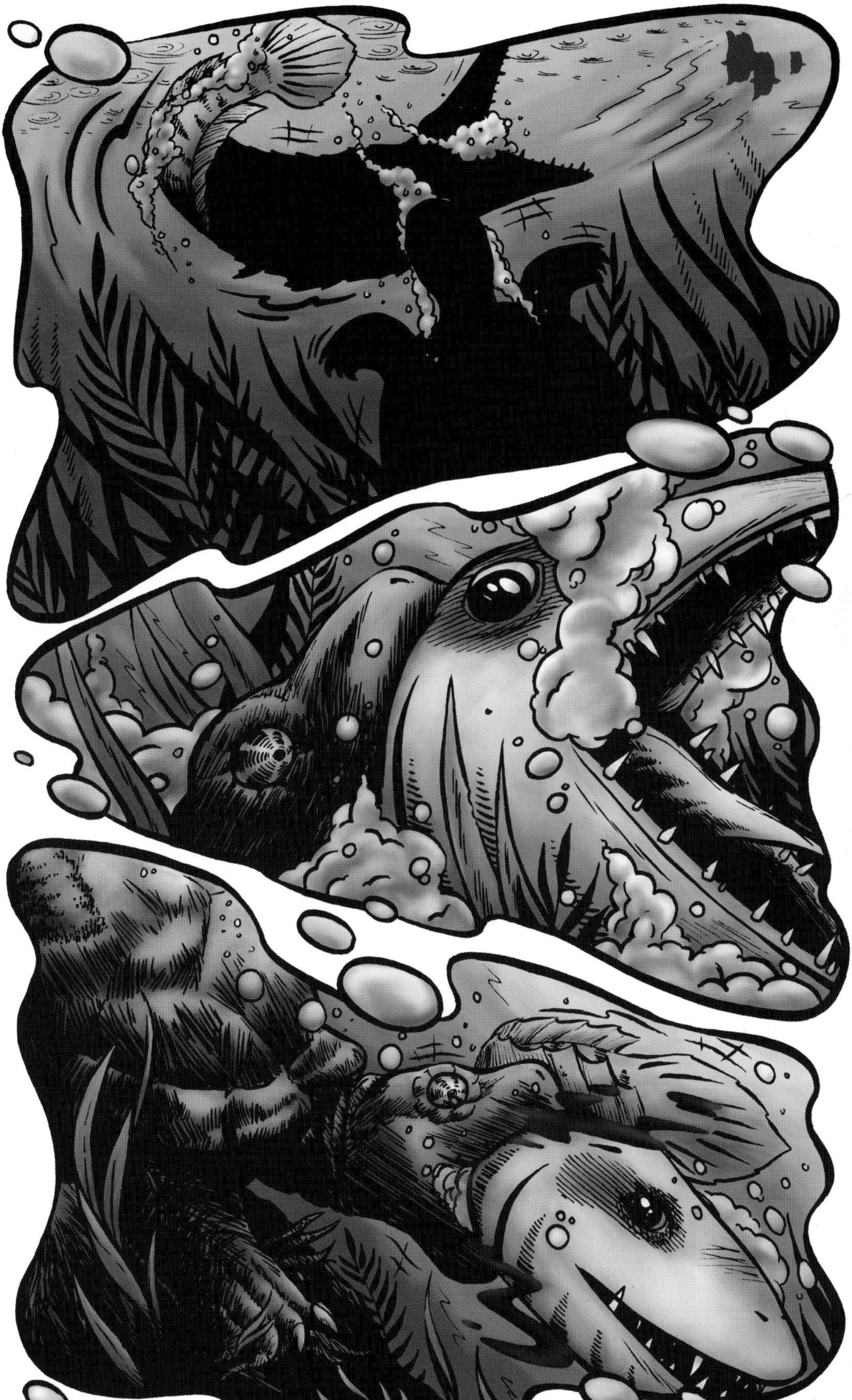

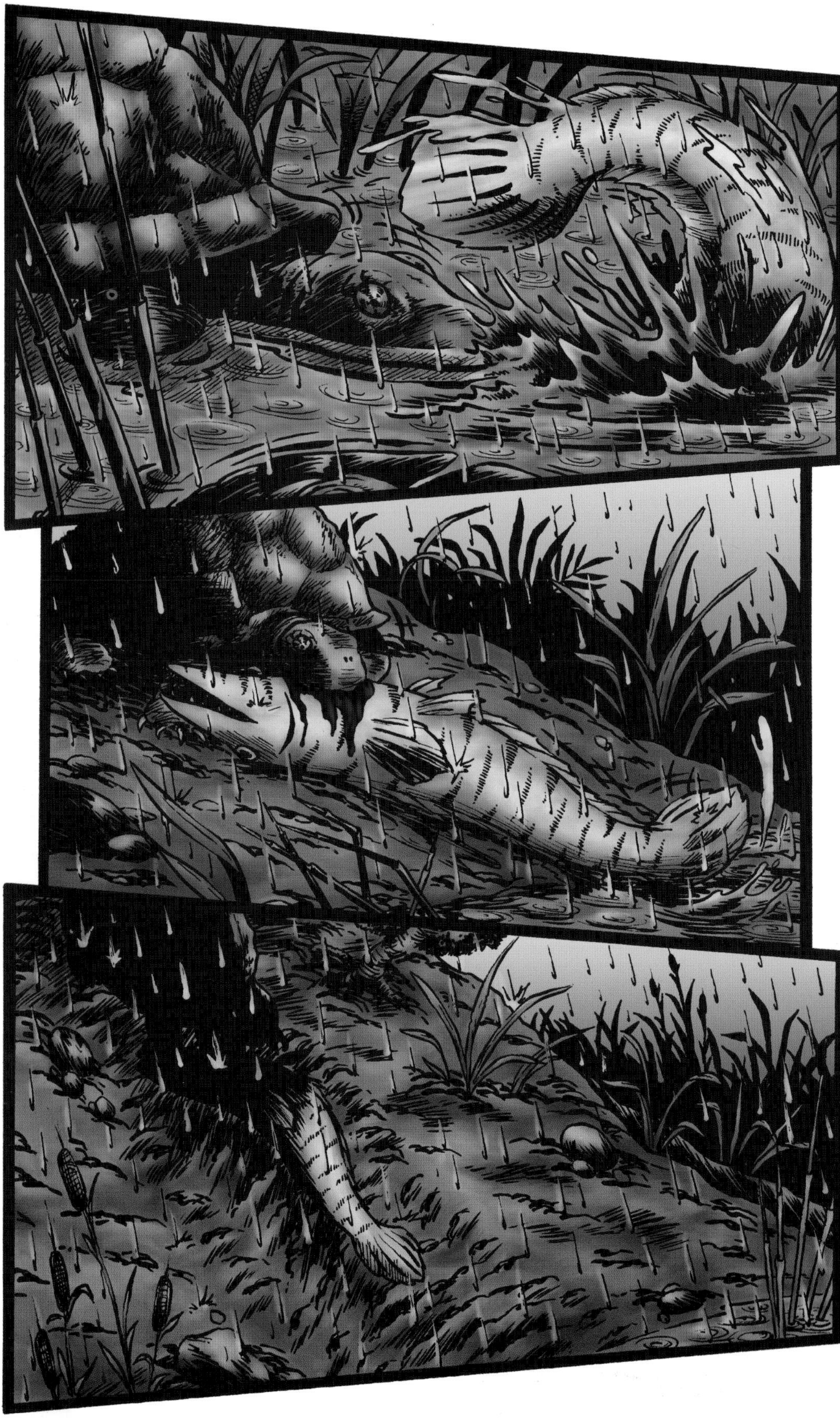

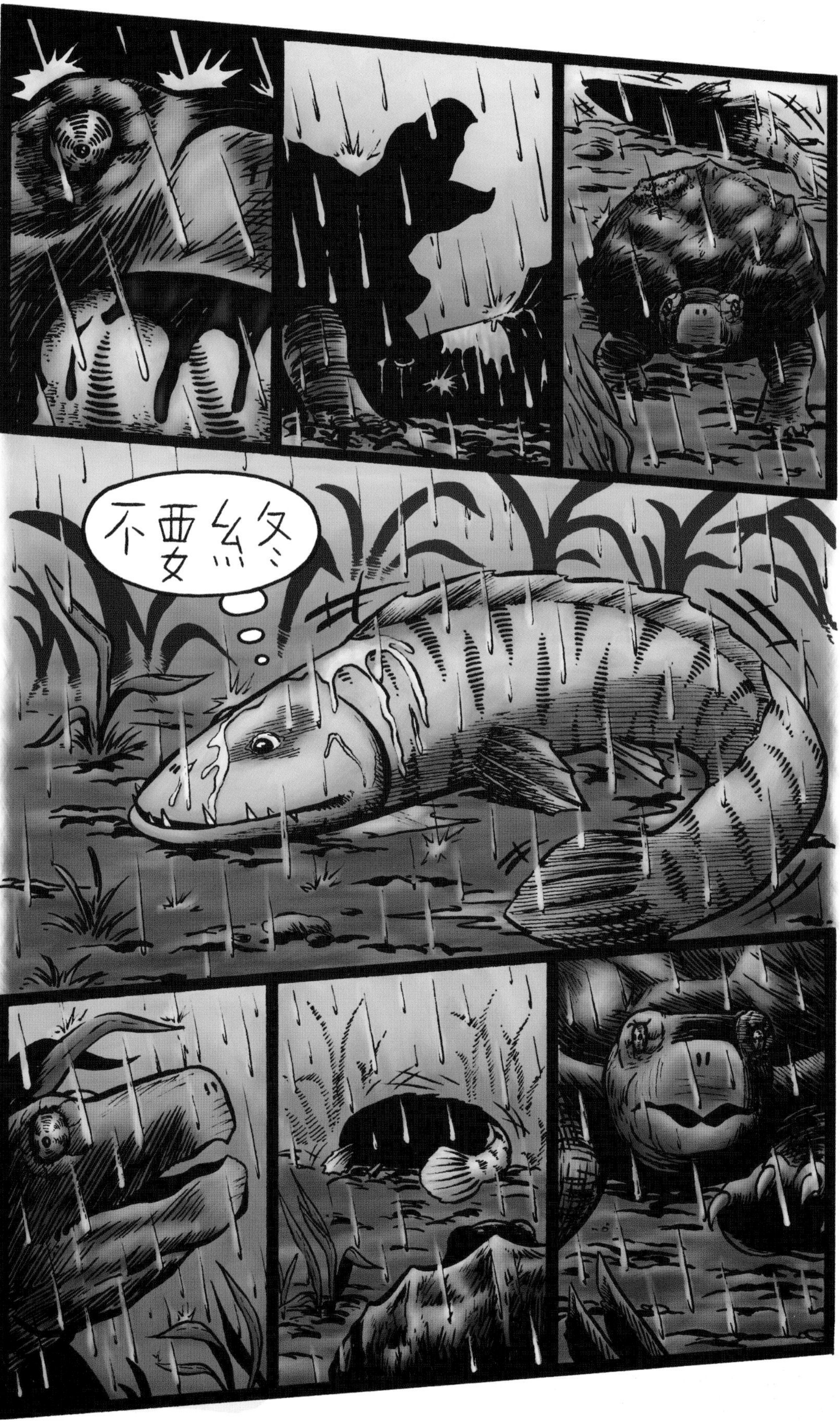
不要終

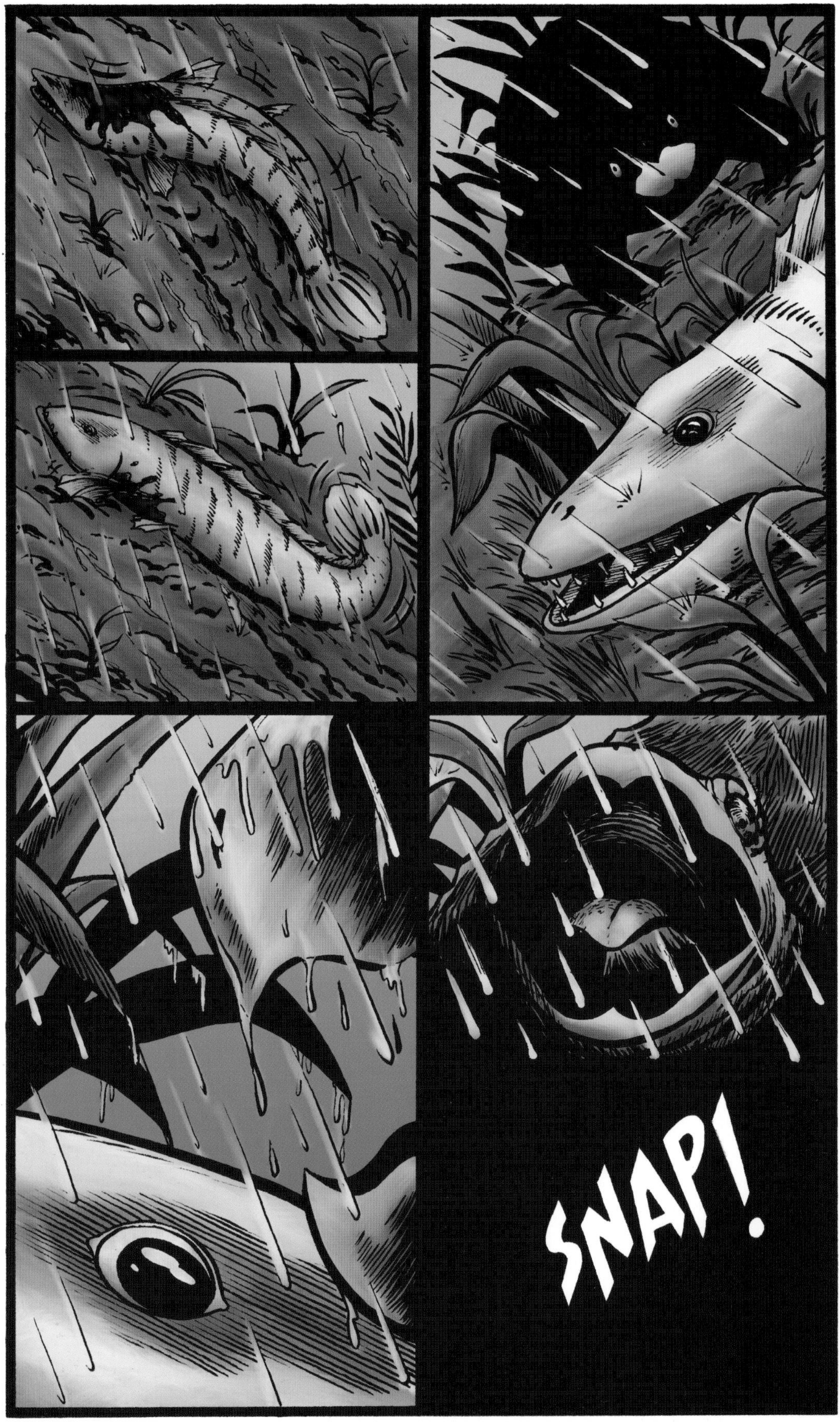
SNAP!

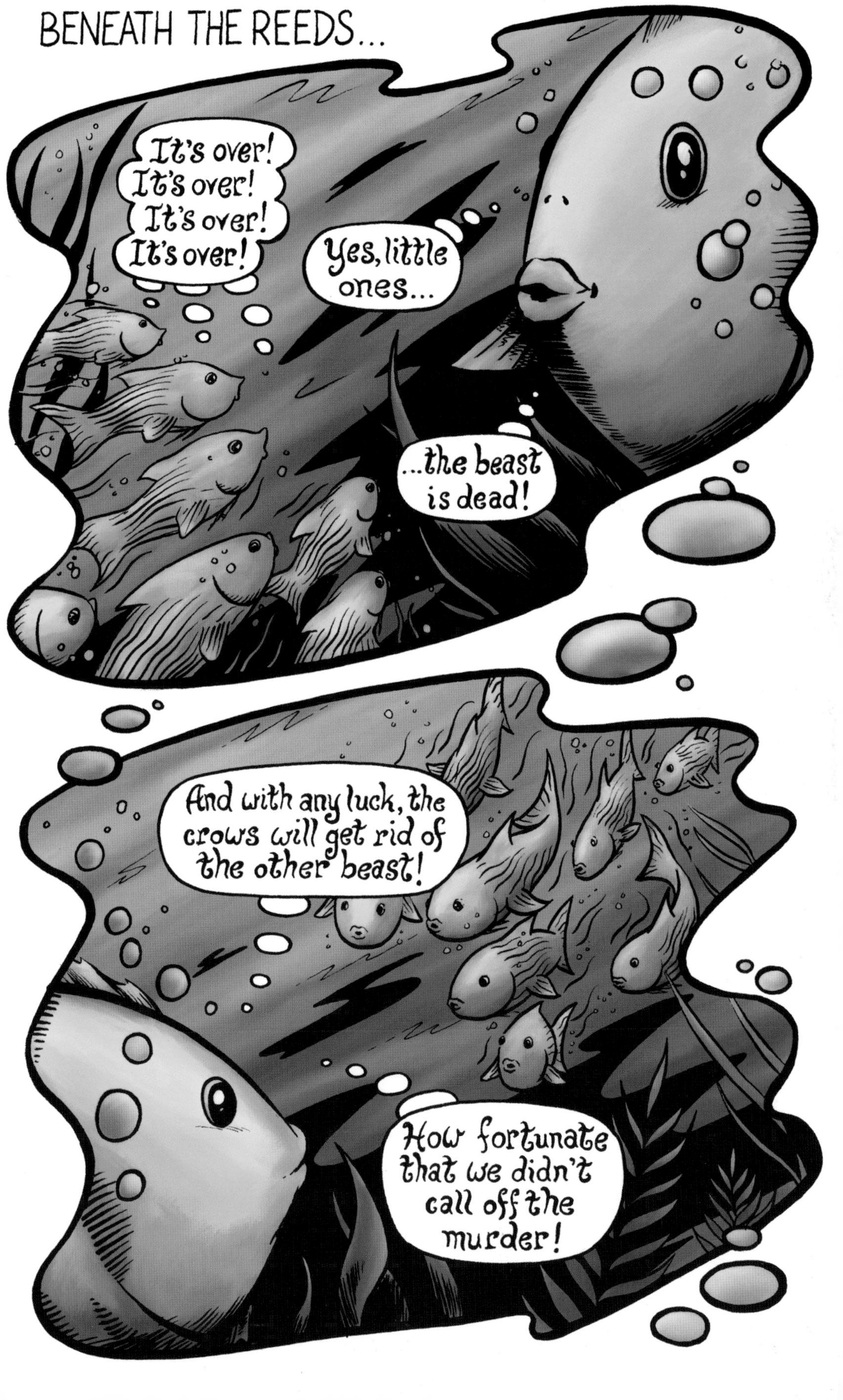
BENEATH THE REEDS...
It's over! It's over! It's over! It's over!
Yes, little ones...
...the beast is dead!
And with any luck, the crows will get rid of the other beast!
How fortunate that we didn't call off the murder!

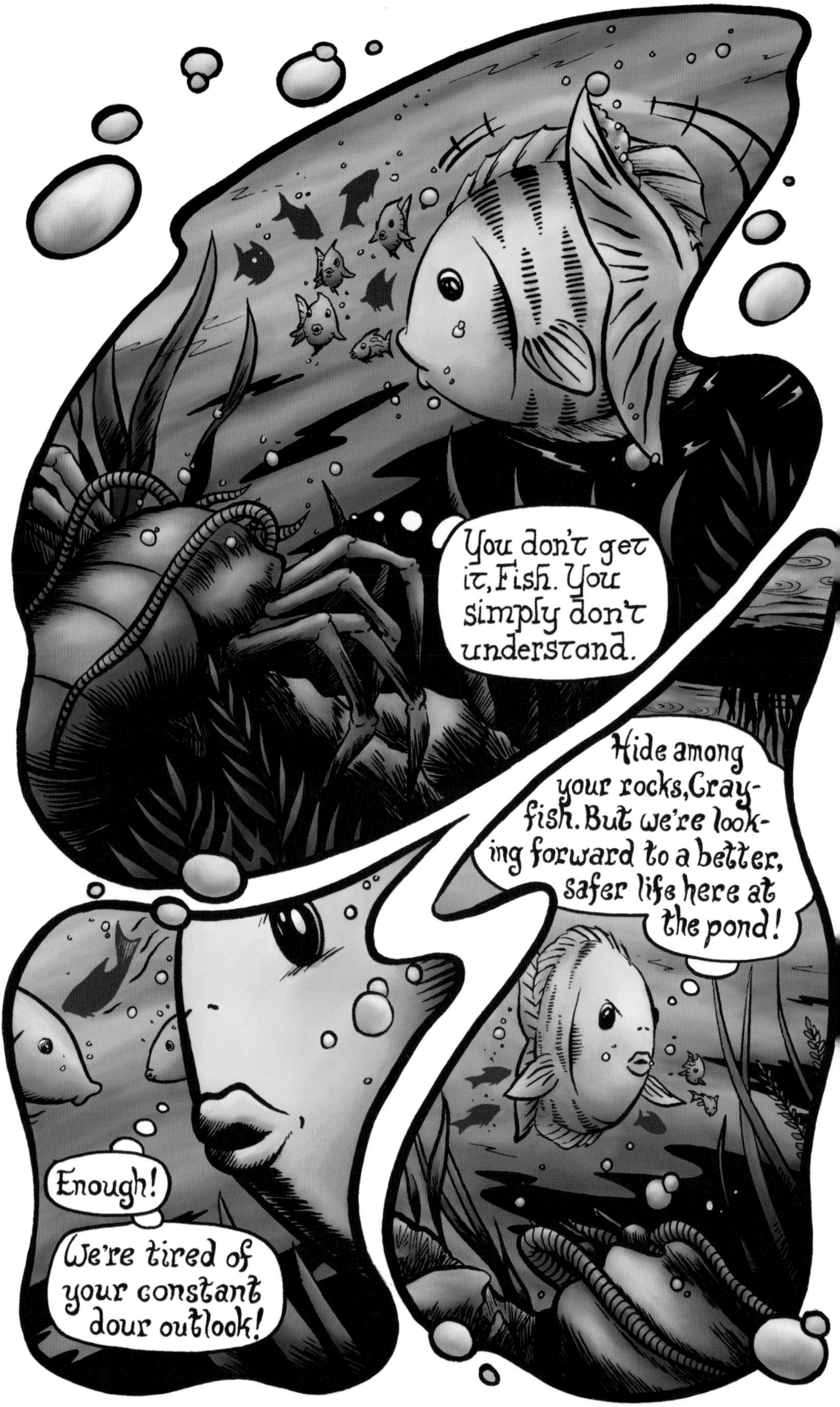
You don't get it, Fish. You simply don't understand.
Hide among your rocks, Crayfish. But we're looking forward to a better, safer life here at the pond!
Enough!
We're tired of your constant dour outlook!

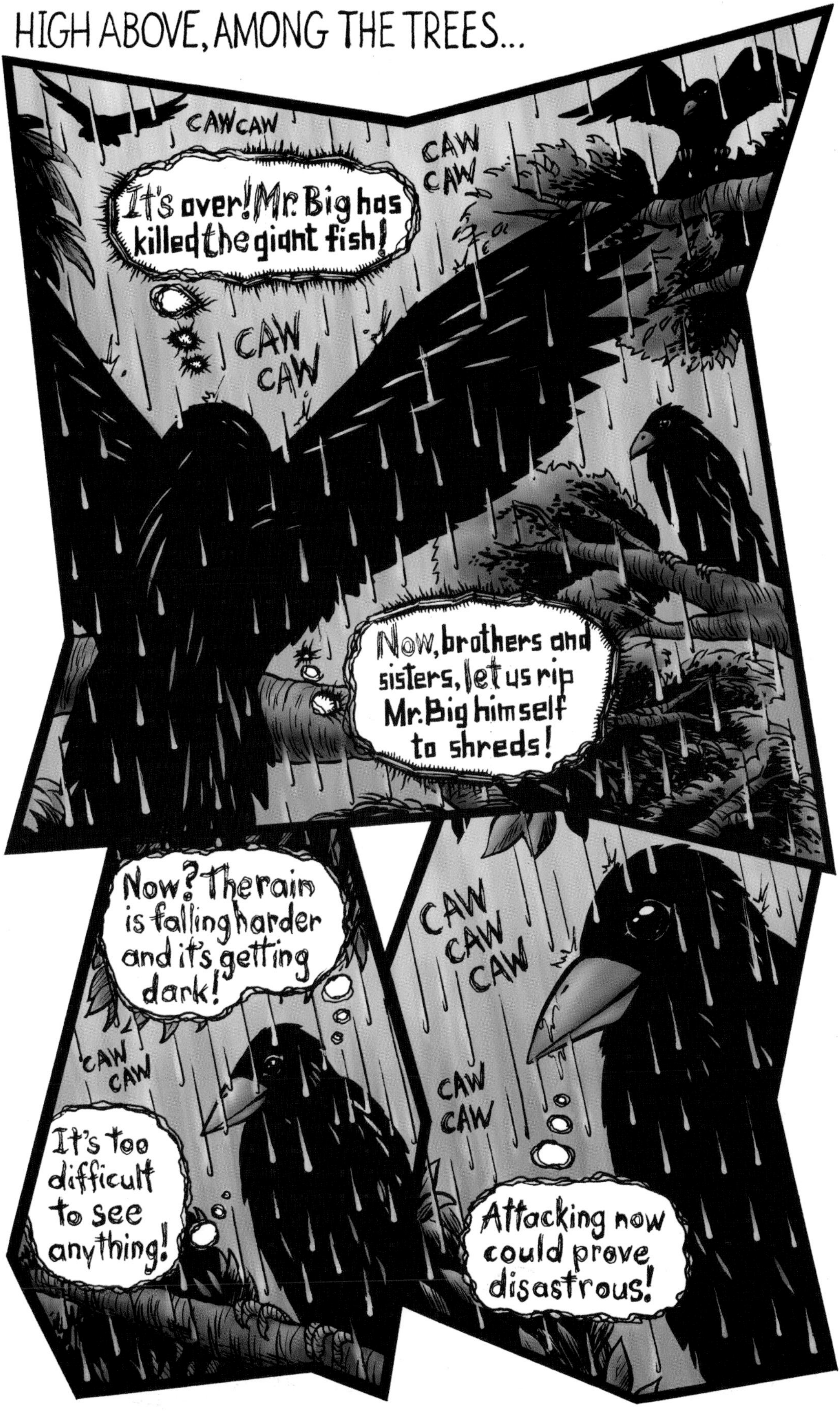
HIGH ABOVE, AMONG THE TREES...
CAWCAW
CAW CAW
It's over! Mr. Big has killed the giant fish!
CAW CAW
Now, brothers and sisters, let us rip Mr. Big himself to shreds!
Now? The rain is falling harder and it's getting dark!
CAW CAW
It's too difficult to see anything!
CAW CAW CAW
CAW CAW
Attacking now could prove disastrous!

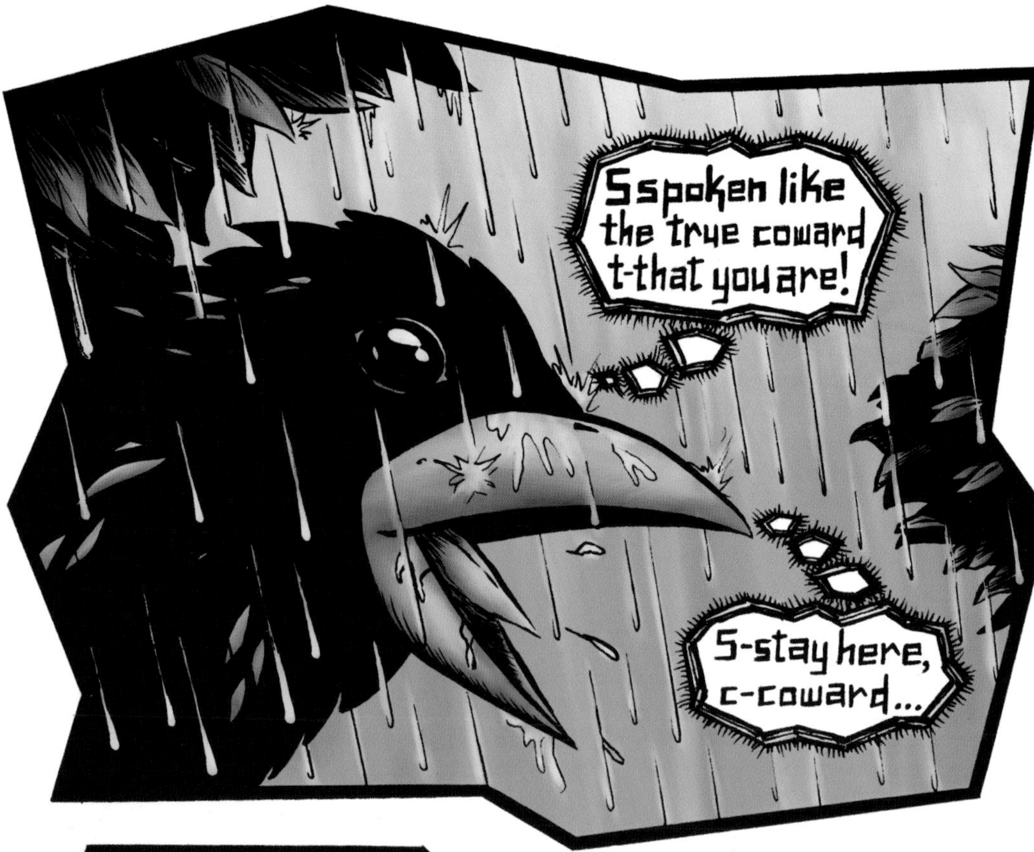
Sspoken like the true coward t-that you are!
S-stay here, c-coward...

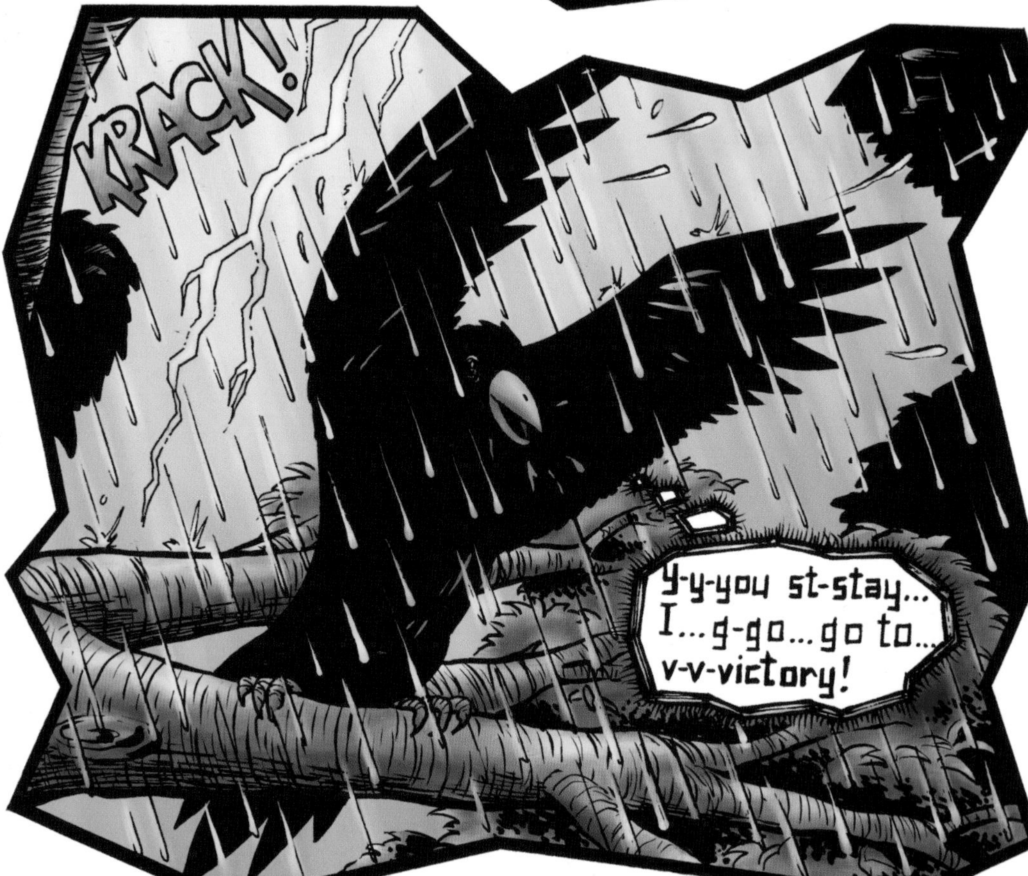
KRACK!
Y-y-you st-stay... I... g-go... go to... v-v-victory!

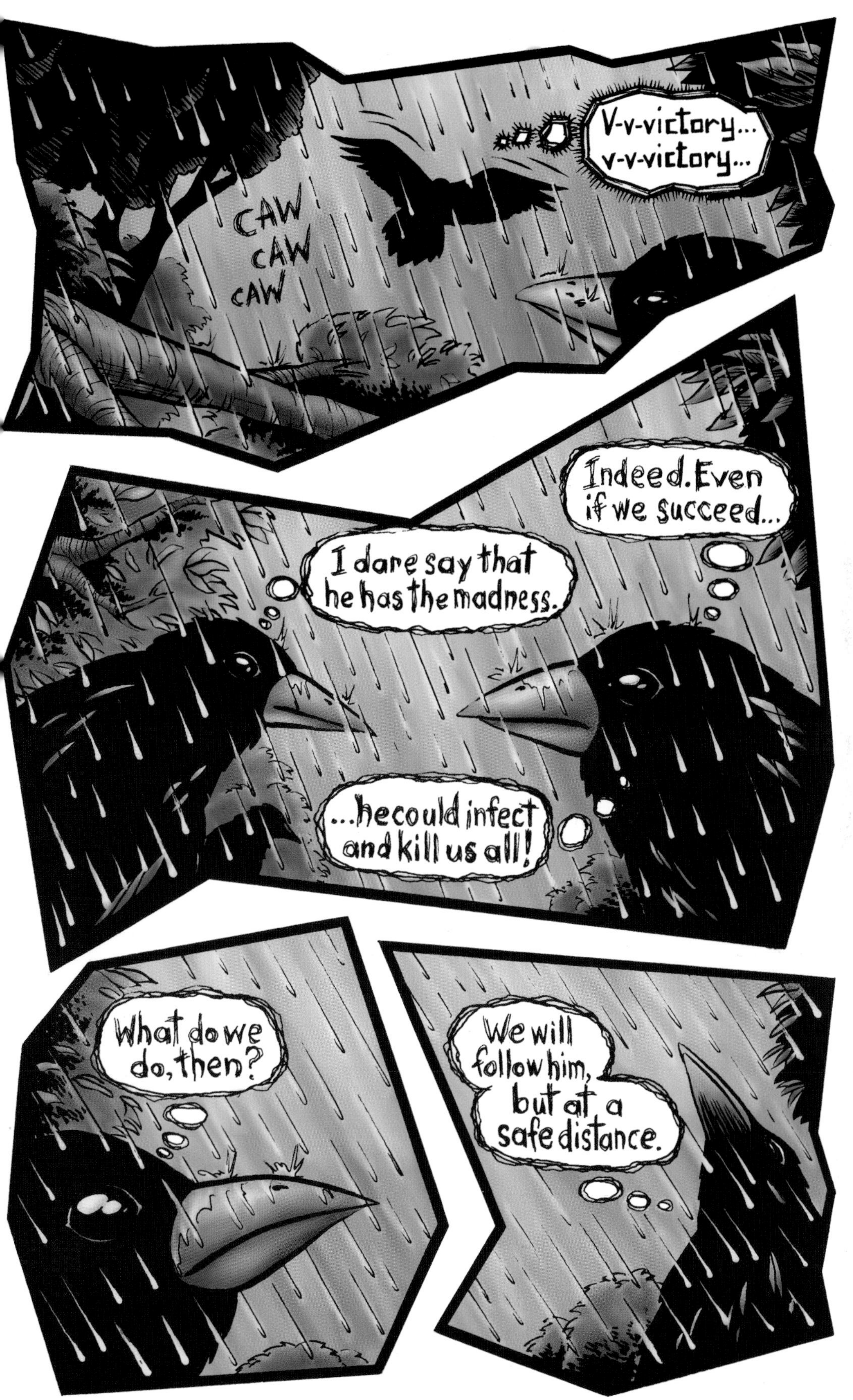
V-v-victory... v-v-victory...
CAW CAW CAW
I dare say that he has the madness.
Indeed. Even if we succeed...
...he could infect and kill us all!
What do we do, then?
We will follow him, but at a safe distance.

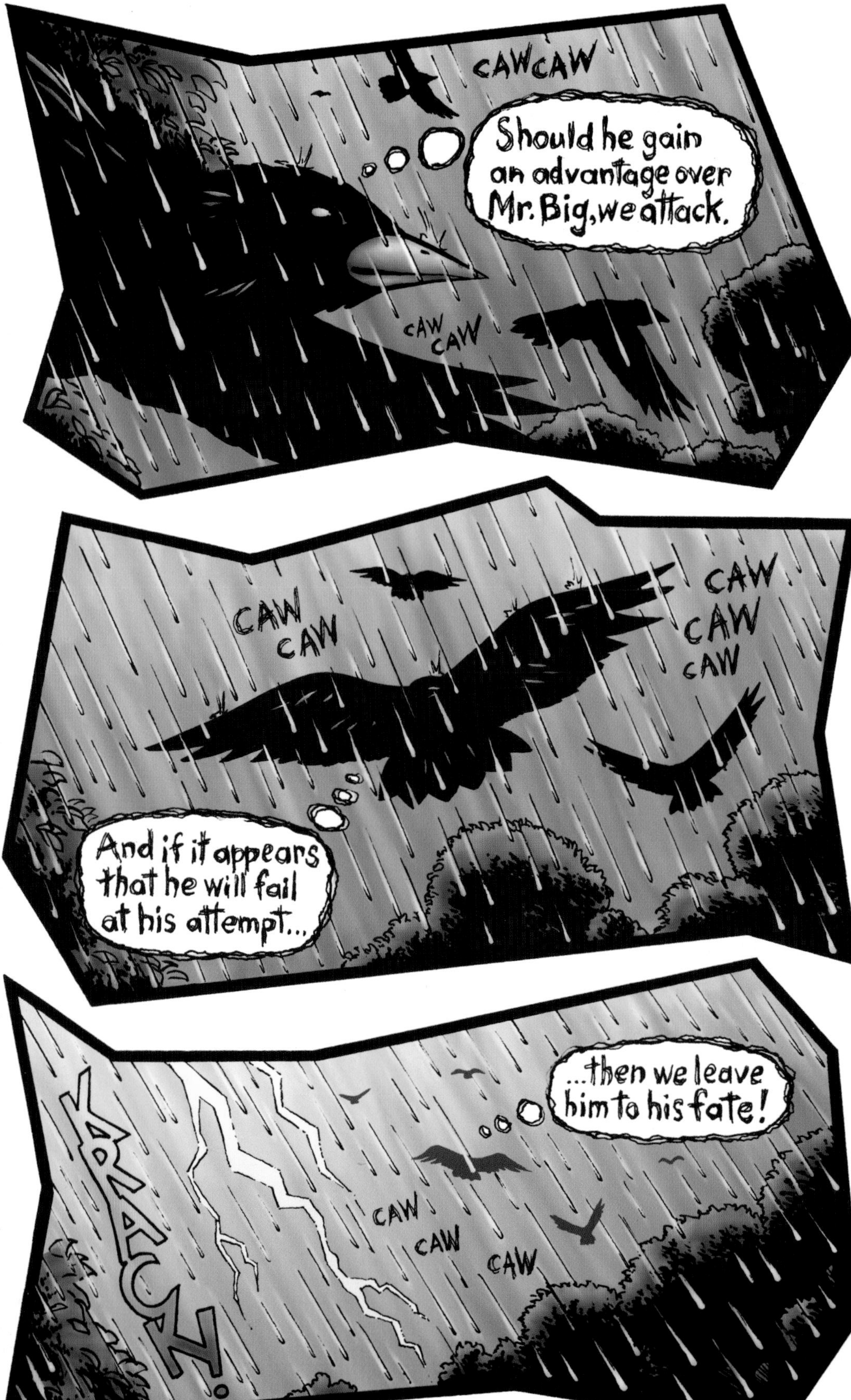
CAW CAW
Should he gain an advantage over Mr. Big, we attack.
CAW CAW
CAW CAW
CAW CAW CAW
And if it appears that he will fail at his attempt...
KRAACK!
...then we leave him to his fate!
CAW CAW CAW

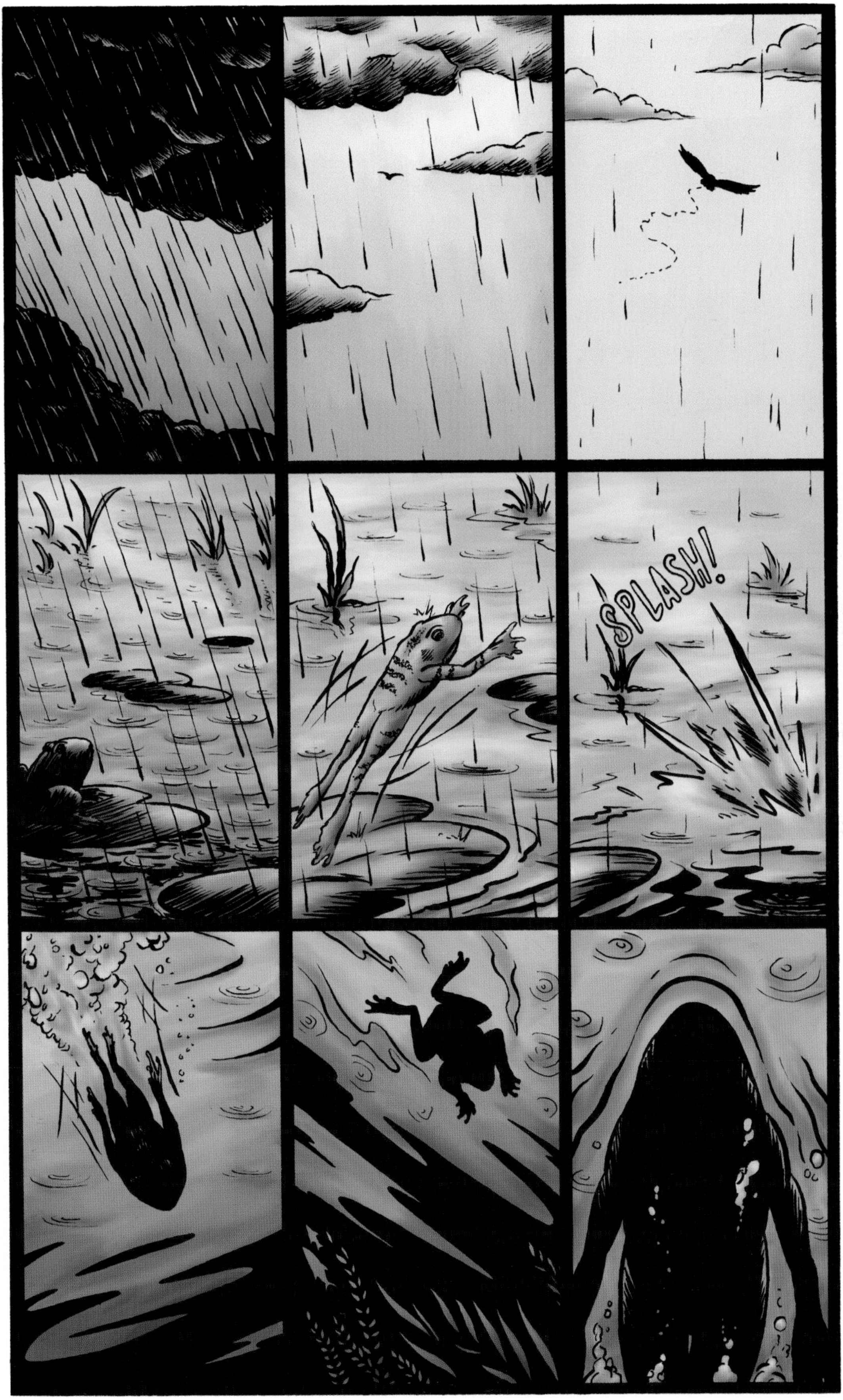
SPLASH!

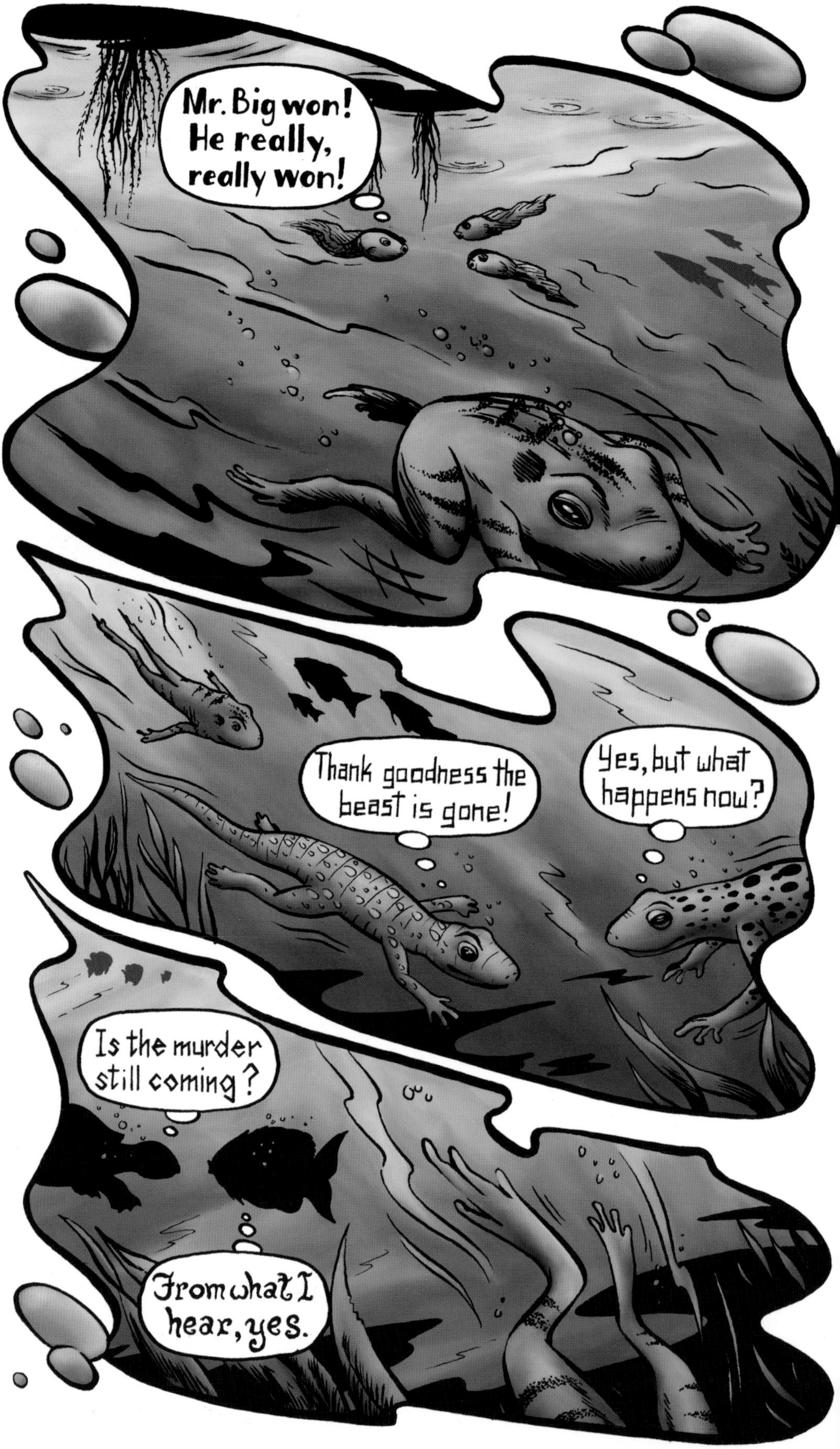
Mr. Big won! He really, really won!
Thank goodness the beast is gone!
Yes, but what happens now?
Is the murder still coming?
From what I hear, yes.

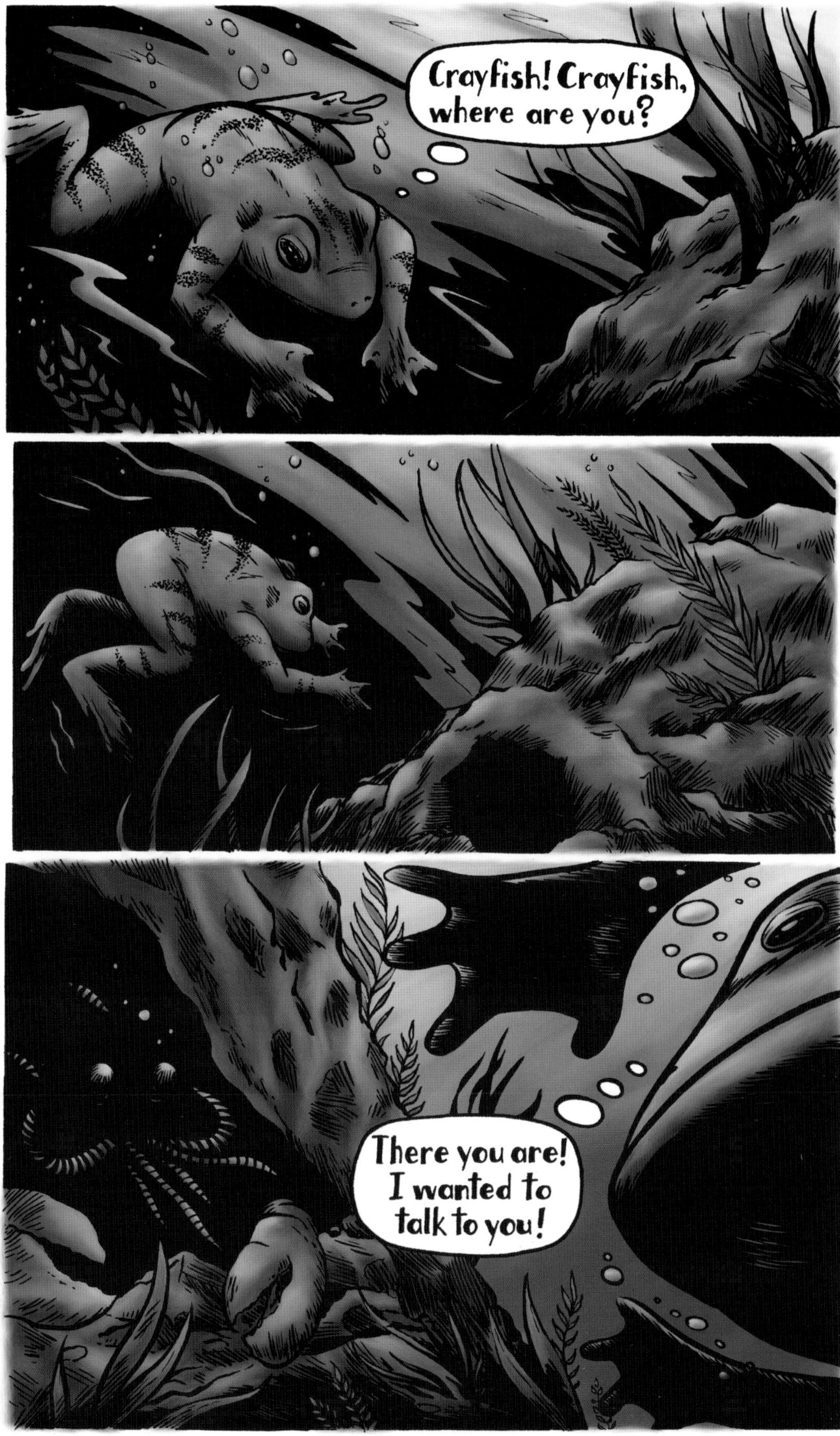
Crayfish! Crayfish, where are you?
There you are! I wanted to talk to you!

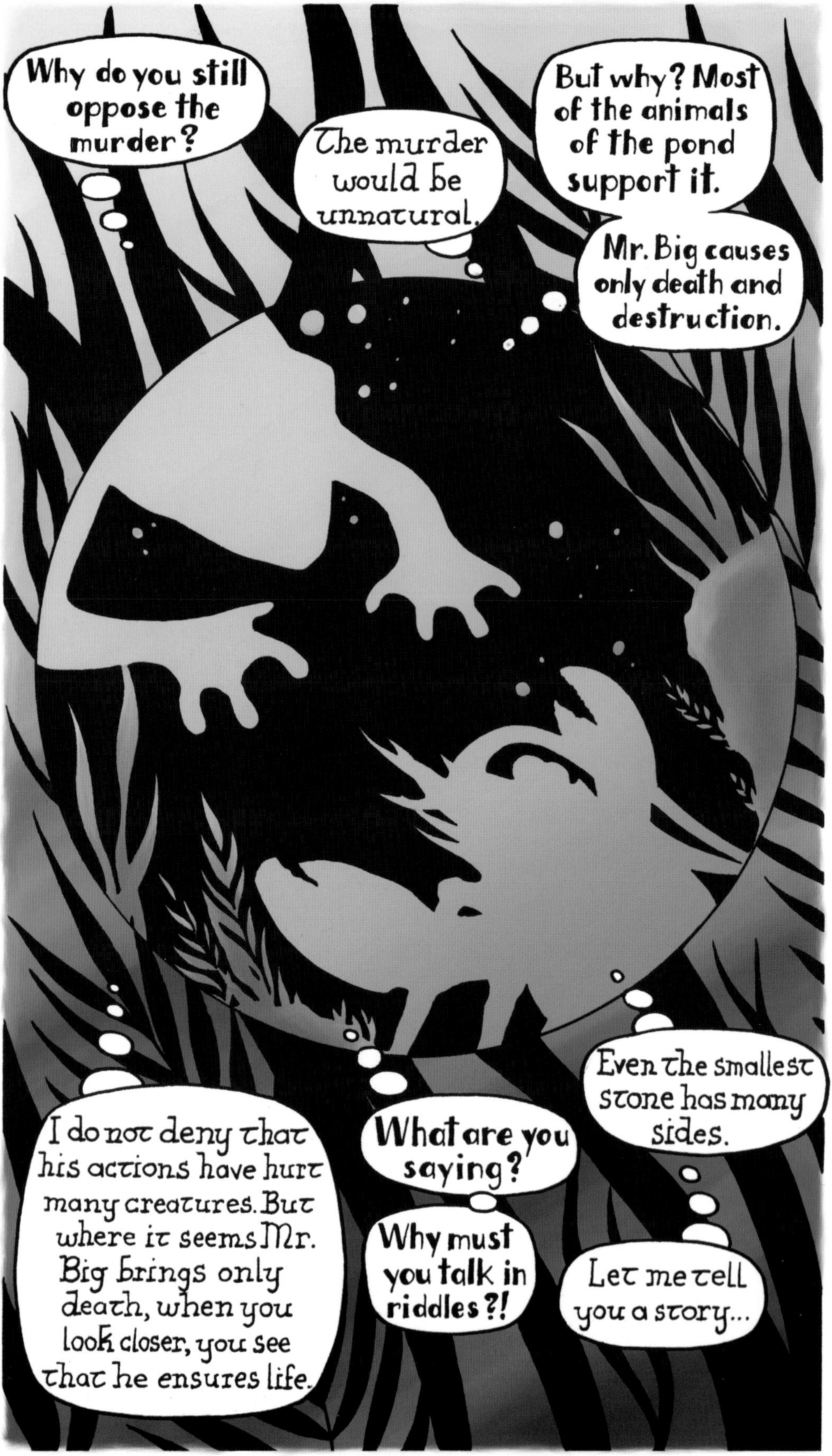
Why do you still oppose the murder?
The murder would be unnatural.
But why? Most of the animals of the pond support it.
Mr. Big causes only death and destruction.
I do not deny that his actions have hurt many creatures. But where it seems Mr. Big brings only death, when you look closer, you see that he ensures life.
What are you saying?
Why must you talk in riddles?!
Even the smallest stone has many sides.
Let me tell you a story...

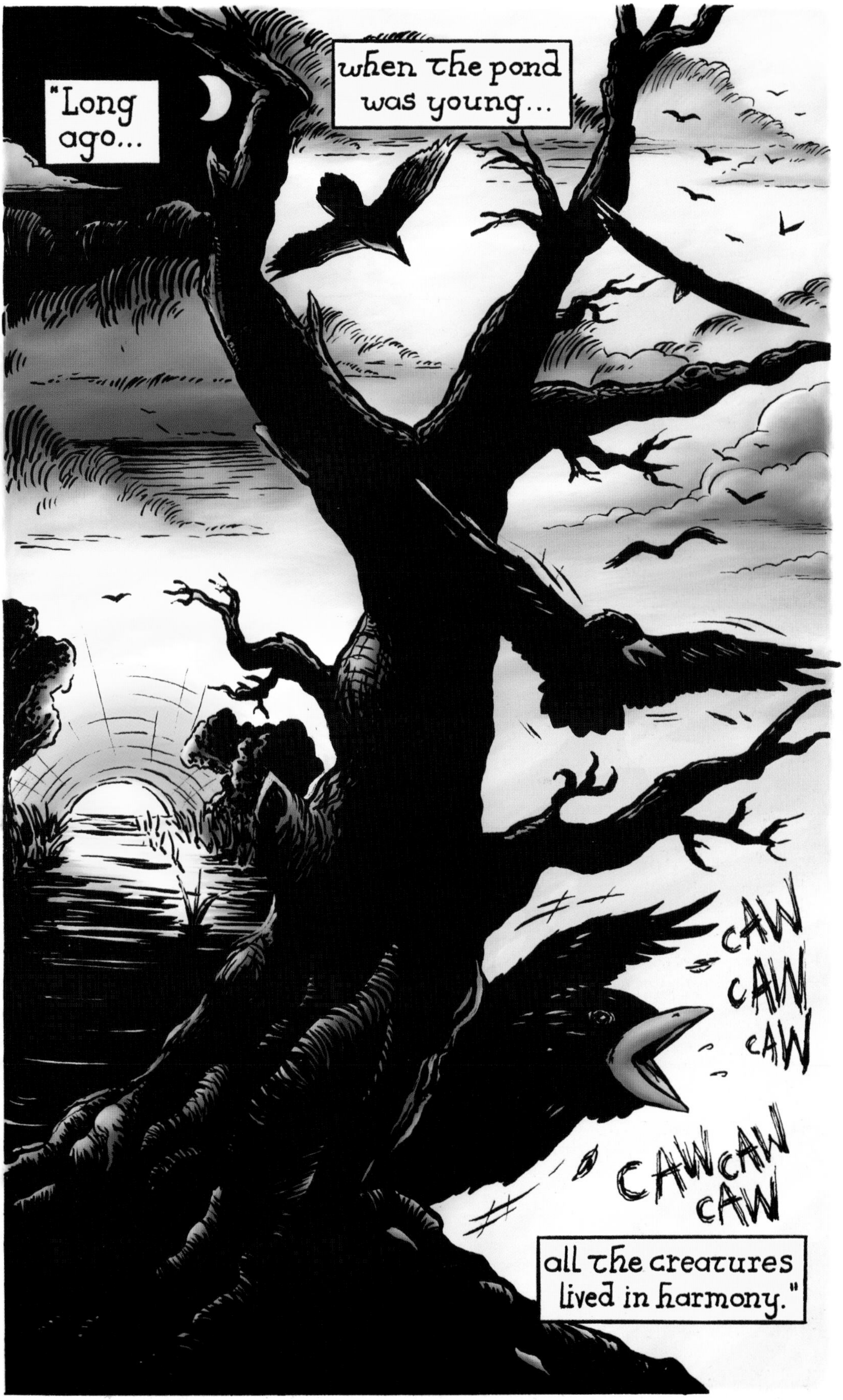
"Long ago...
when the pond was young...
CAW CAW CAW
CAWCAW CAW
all the creatures lived in harmony."

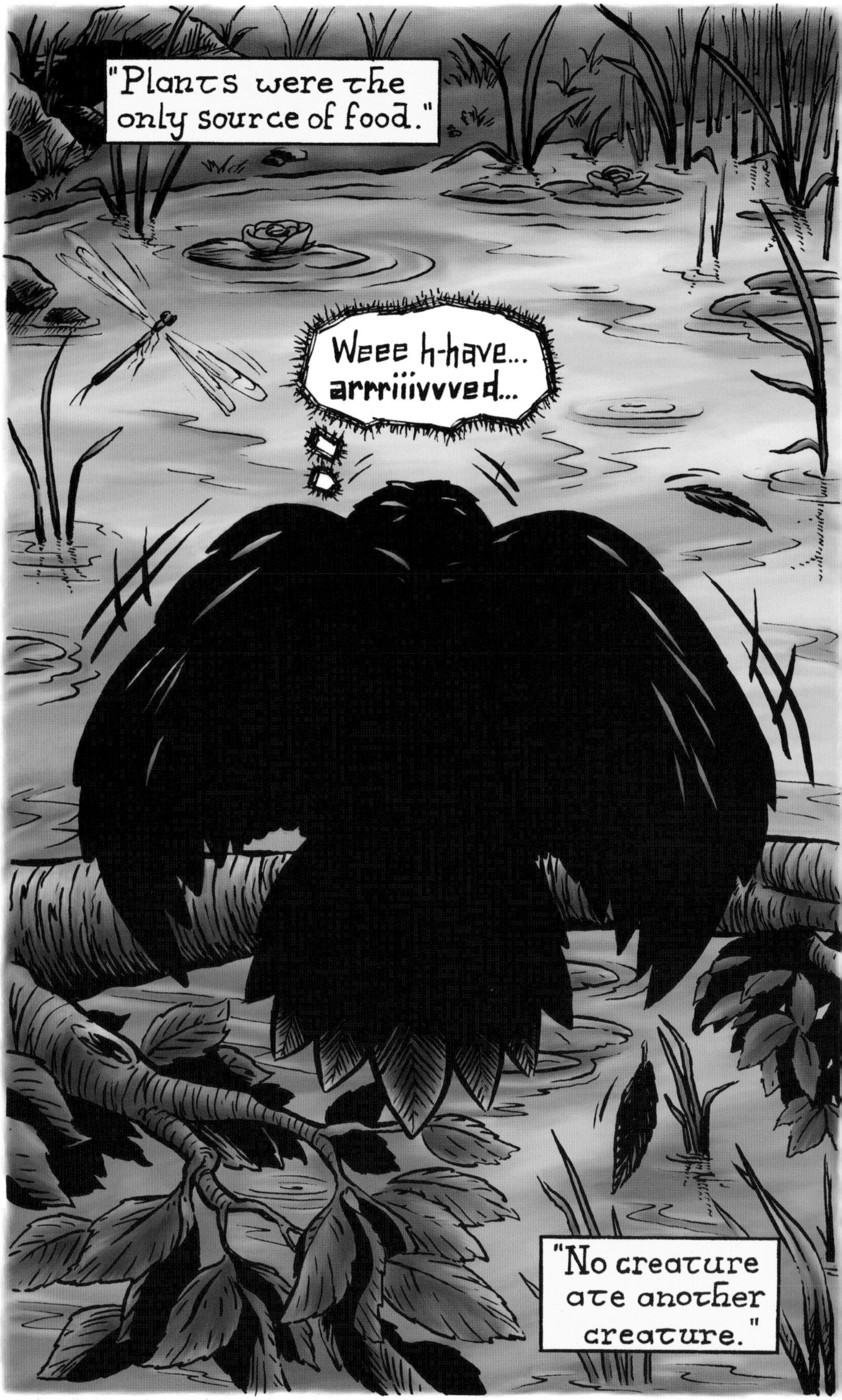
"Plants were the only source of food."
Weee h-have... arrriiivvved...
"No creature ate another creature."

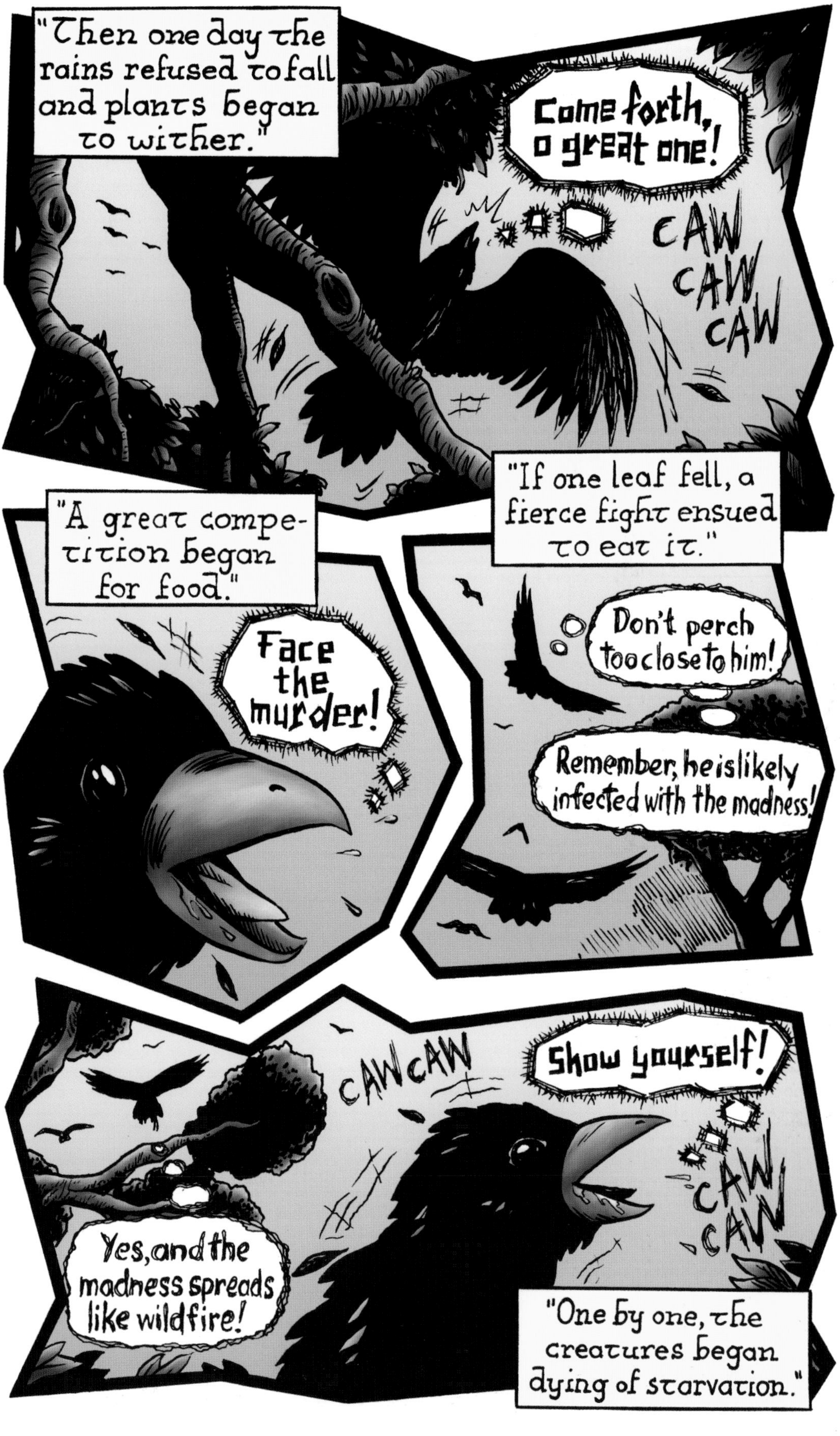
"Then one day the rains refused to fall and plants began to wither."
Come forth, o great one!
CAW CAW CAW
"A great competition began for food."
Face the murder!
"If one leaf fell, a fierce fight ensued to eat it."
Don't perch too close to him!
Remember, he is likely infected with the madness!
CAW CAW
Show yourself!
CAW CAW
Yes, and the madness spreads like wildfire!
"One by one, the creatures began dying of starvation."

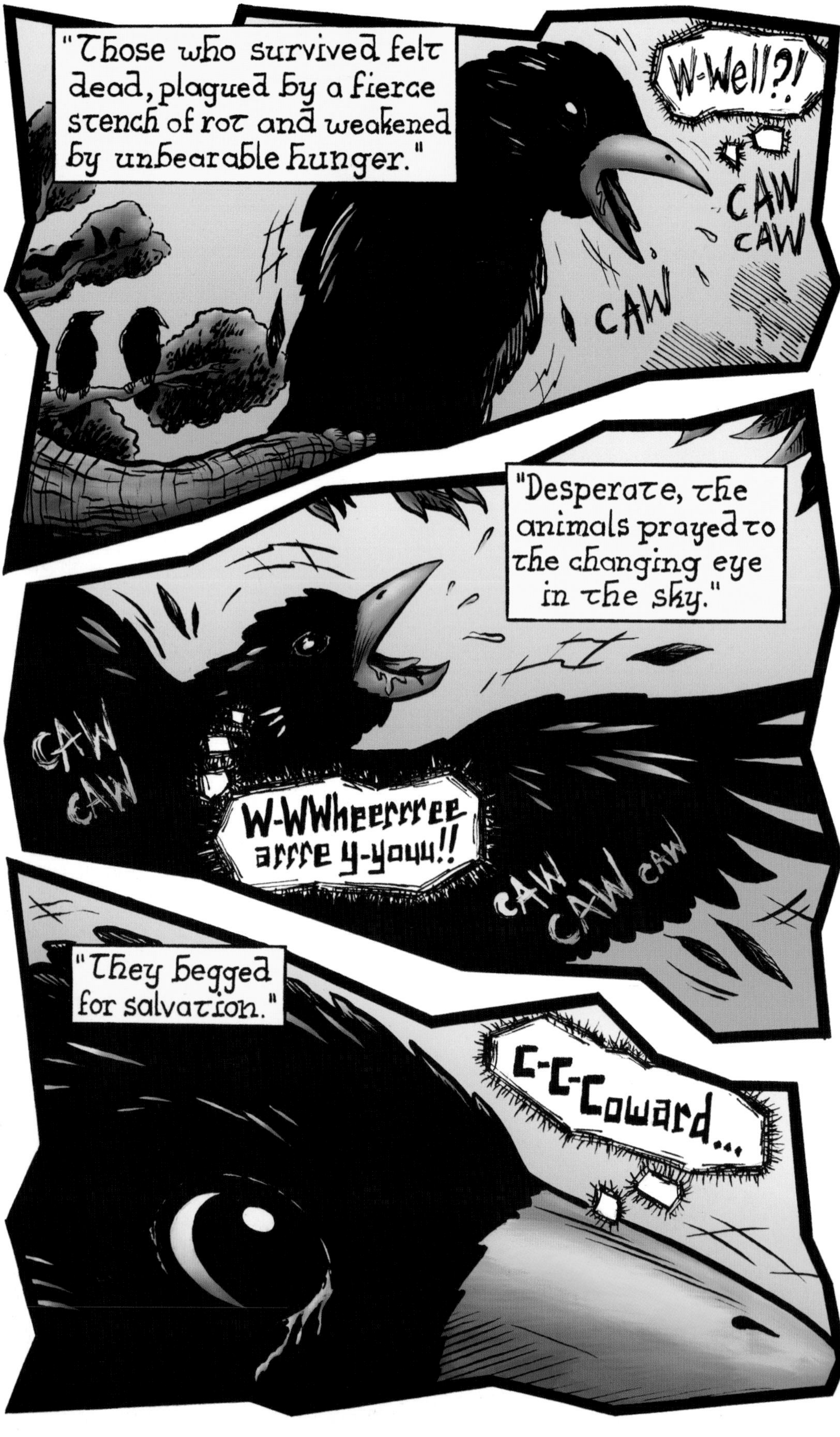
"Those who survived felt dead, plagued by a fierce stench of rot and weakened by unbearable hunger."
W-Well?!
CAW
CAW
CAW
"Desperate, the animals prayed to the changing eye in the sky."
CAW
CAW
W-WWheerrree arrre y-youu!!
CAW
CAW
CAW
"They begged for salvation."
C-C-Coward...

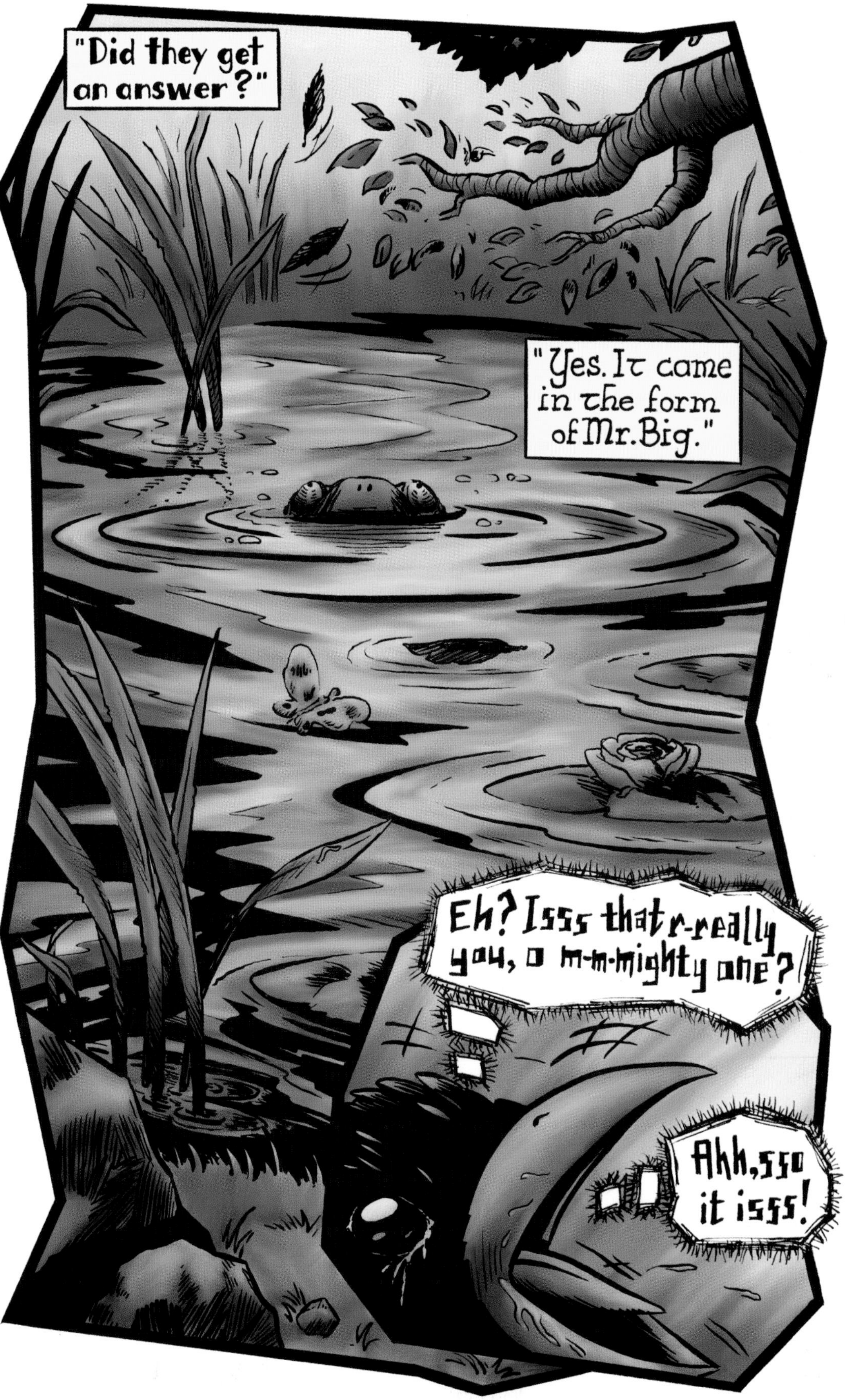
"Did they get an answer?"
"Yes. It came in the form of Mr. Big."
Eh? Isss that r-really you, o m-m-mighty one?
Ahh, sso it isss!

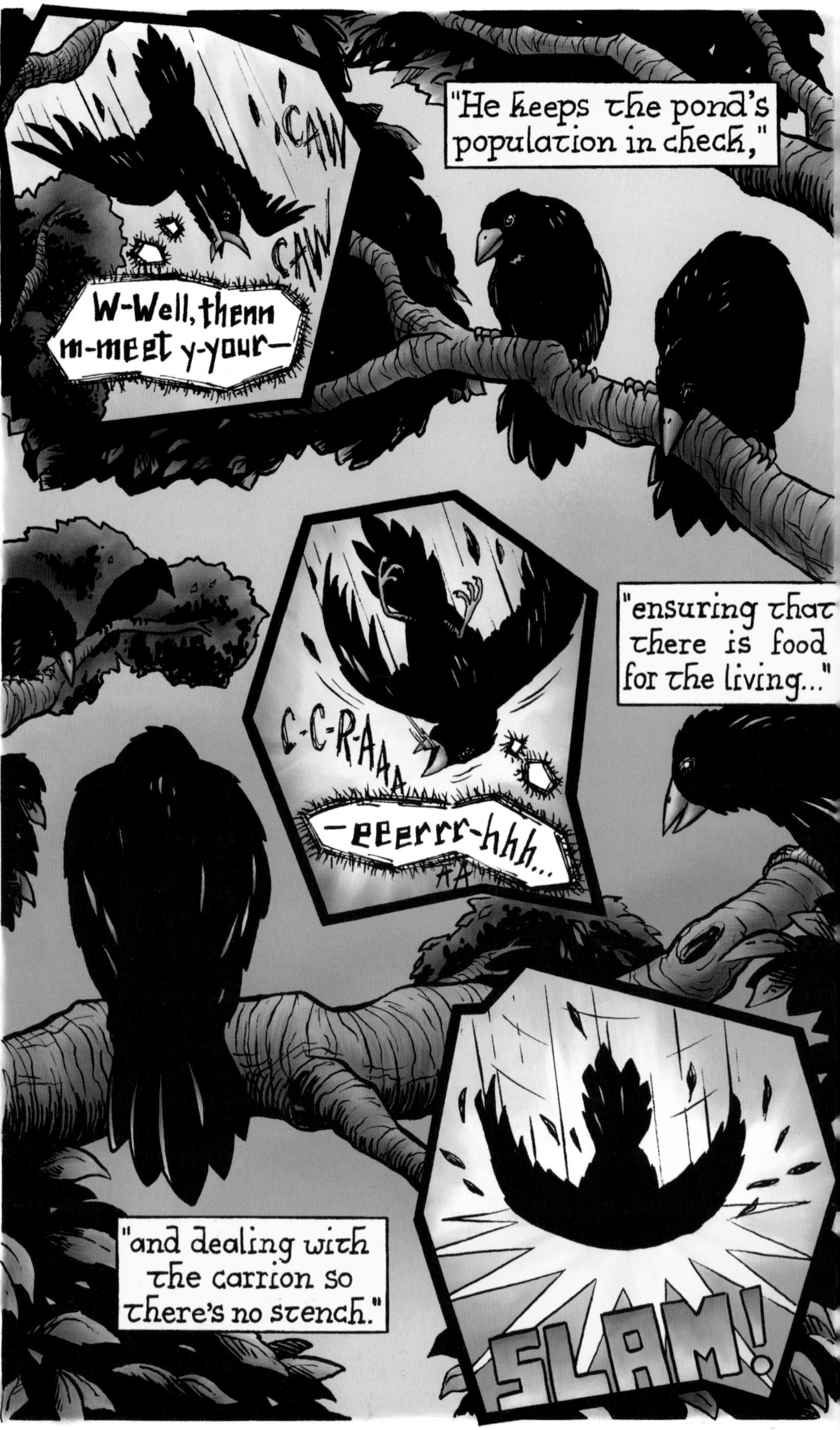
CAW
CAW
W-Well, thenn m-meet y-your—
"He keeps the pond's population in check,"
"ensuring that there is food for the living..."
C-C-R-AAAA
—eeerrr-hhh...
AA
"and dealing with the carrion so there's no stench."
SLAM!

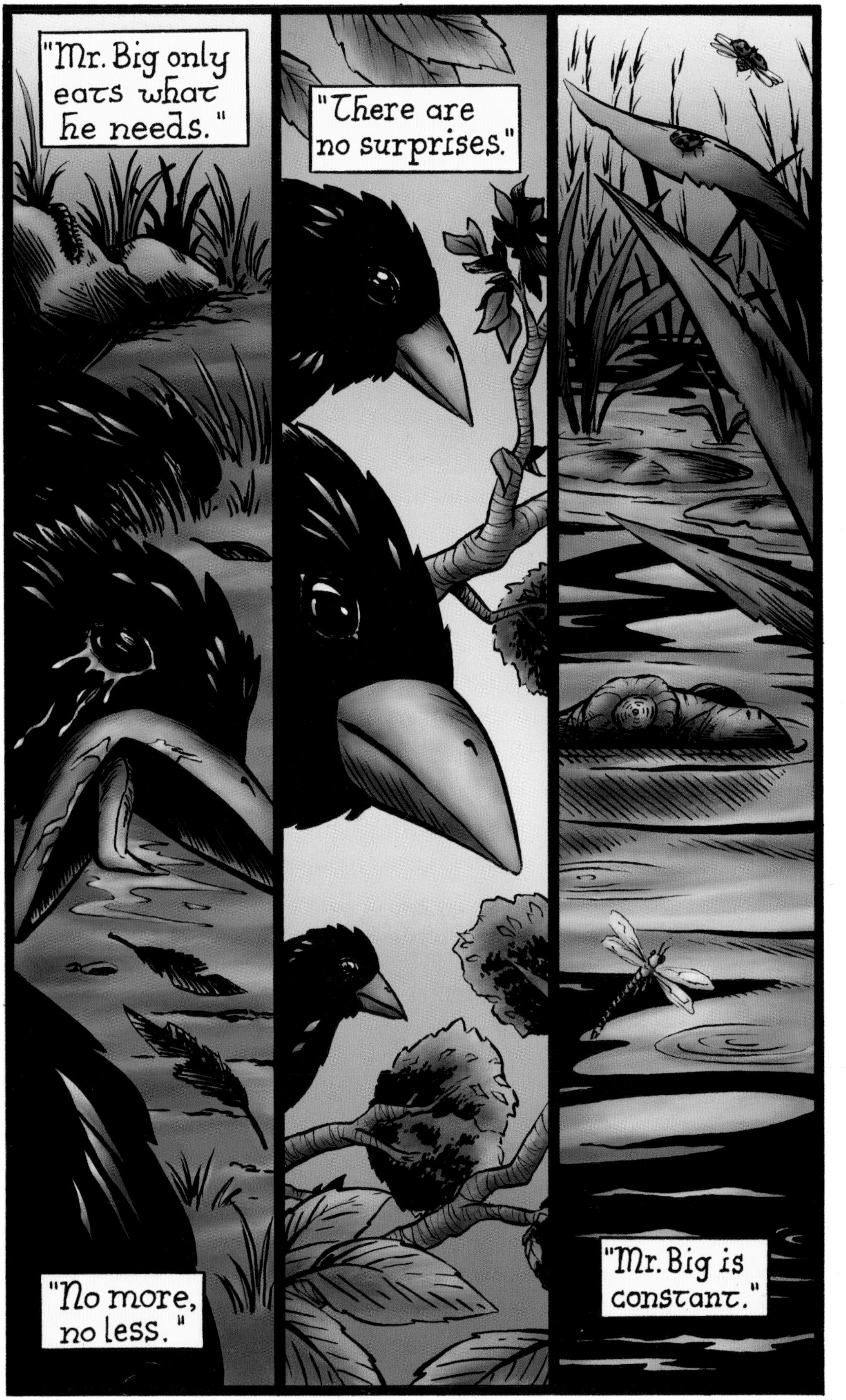
"Mr. Big only eats what he needs."
"No more, no less."
"There are no surprises."
"Mr. Big is constant."

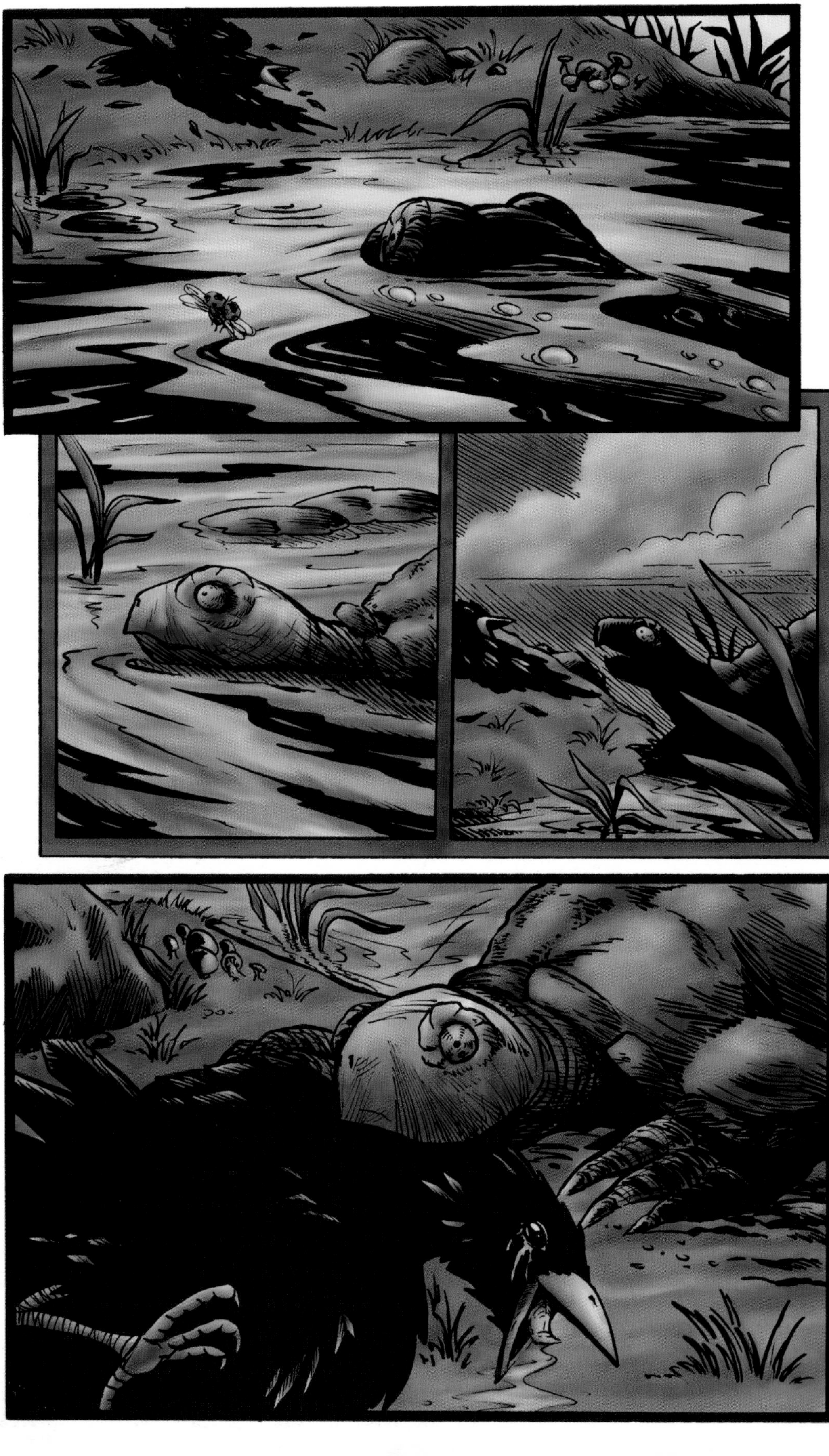

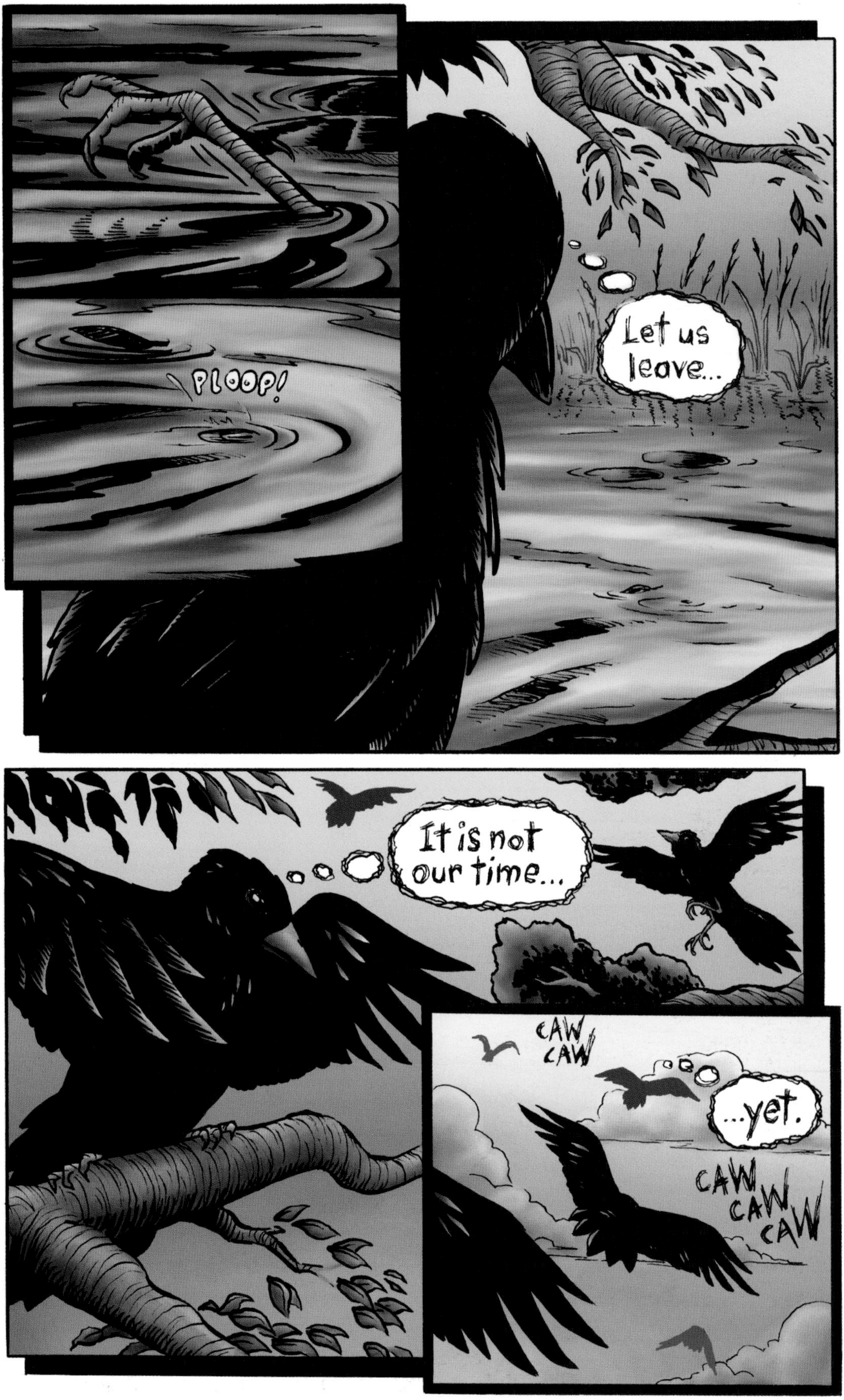
PLOOP!
Let us leave...
It is not our time...
CAW CAW
...yet.
CAW CAW CAW

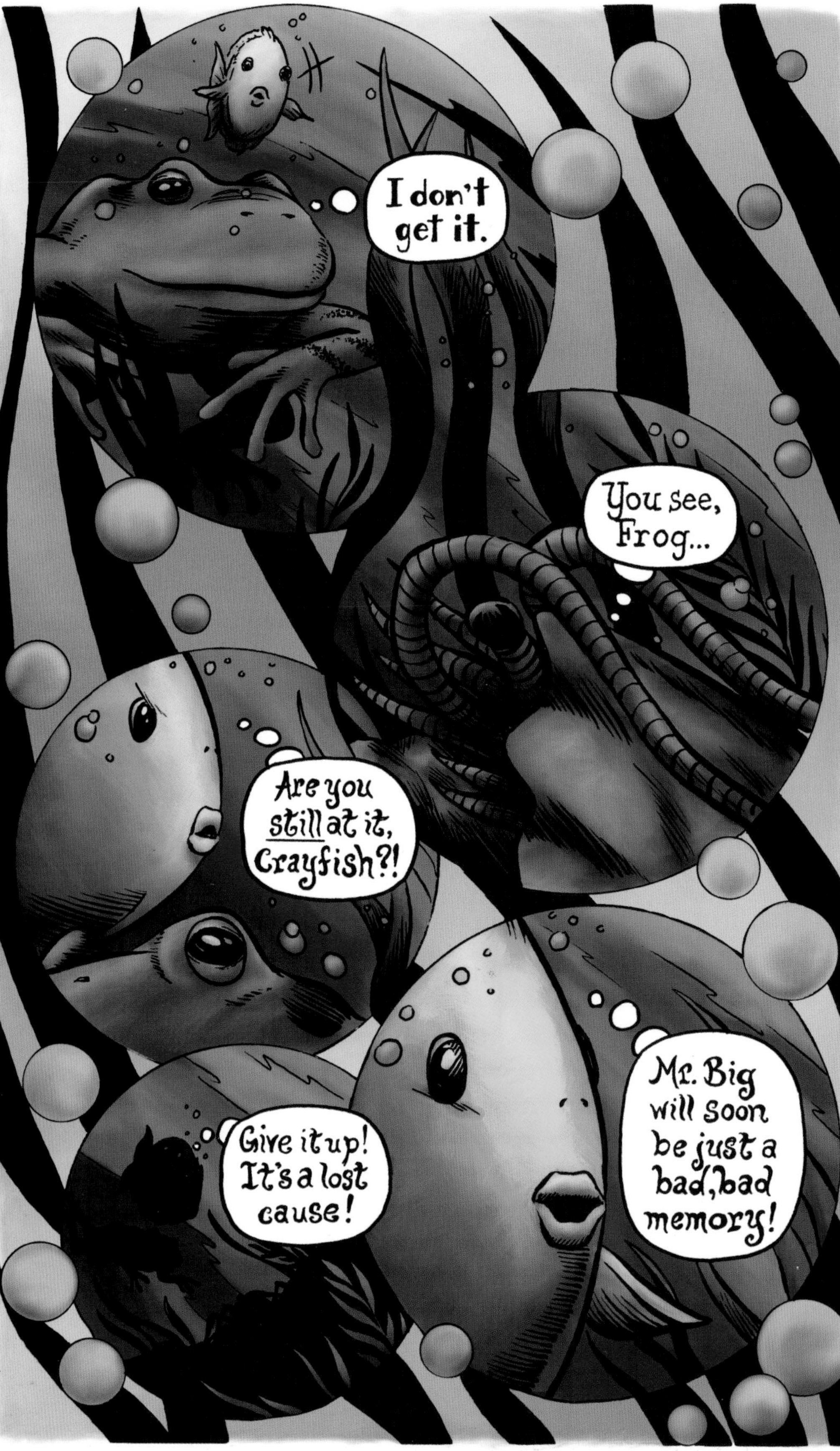
I don't get it.
You see, Frog...
Are you still at it, Crayfish?!
Mr. Big will soon be just a bad, bad memory!
Give it up! It's a lost cause!

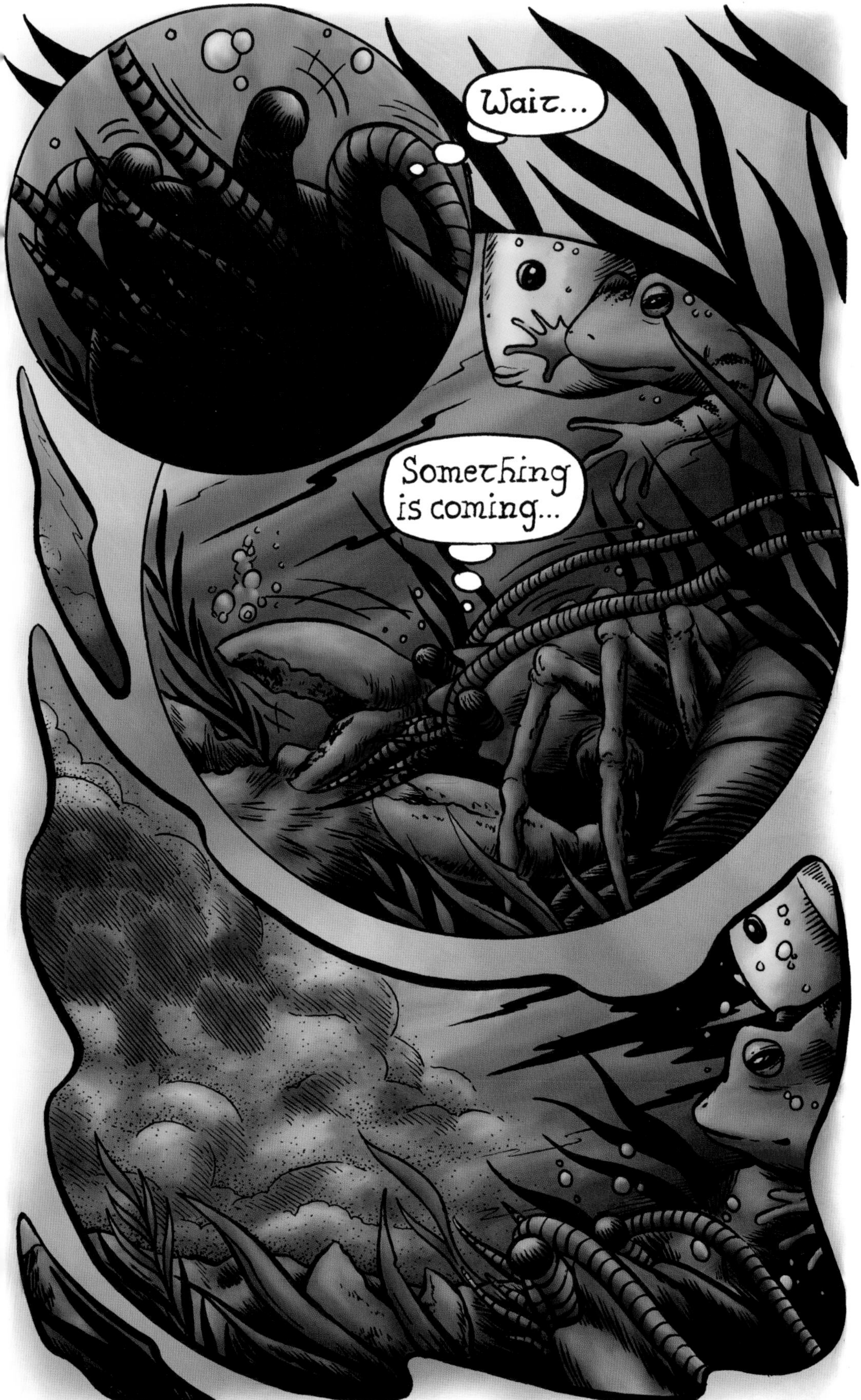
Wait...
Something is coming...

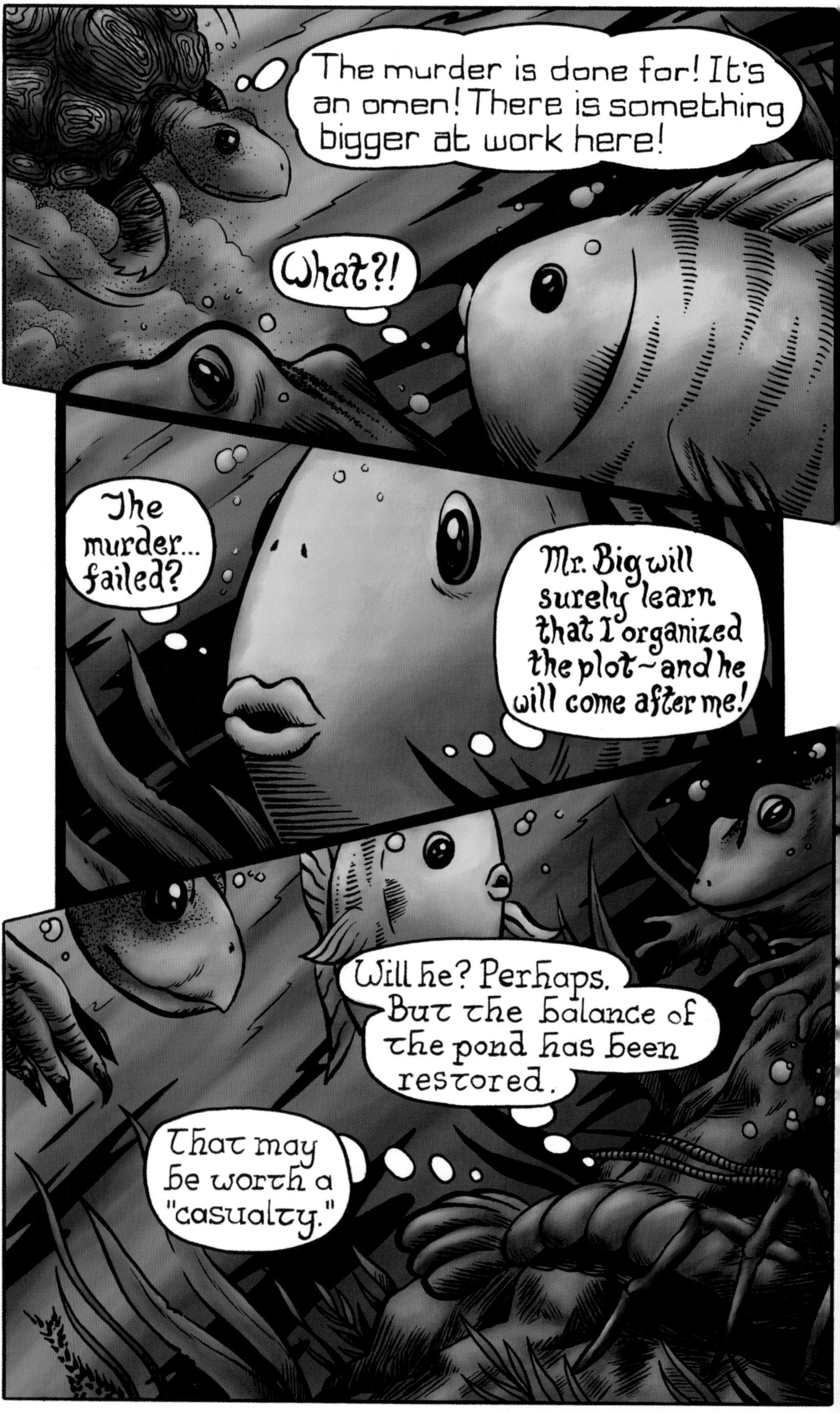

The murder is done for! It's an omen! There is something bigger at work here!
What?!
The murder... failed?
Mr. Big will surely learn that I organized the plot~and he will come after me!
Will he? Perhaps. But the balance of the pond has been restored.
That may be worth a "casualty."

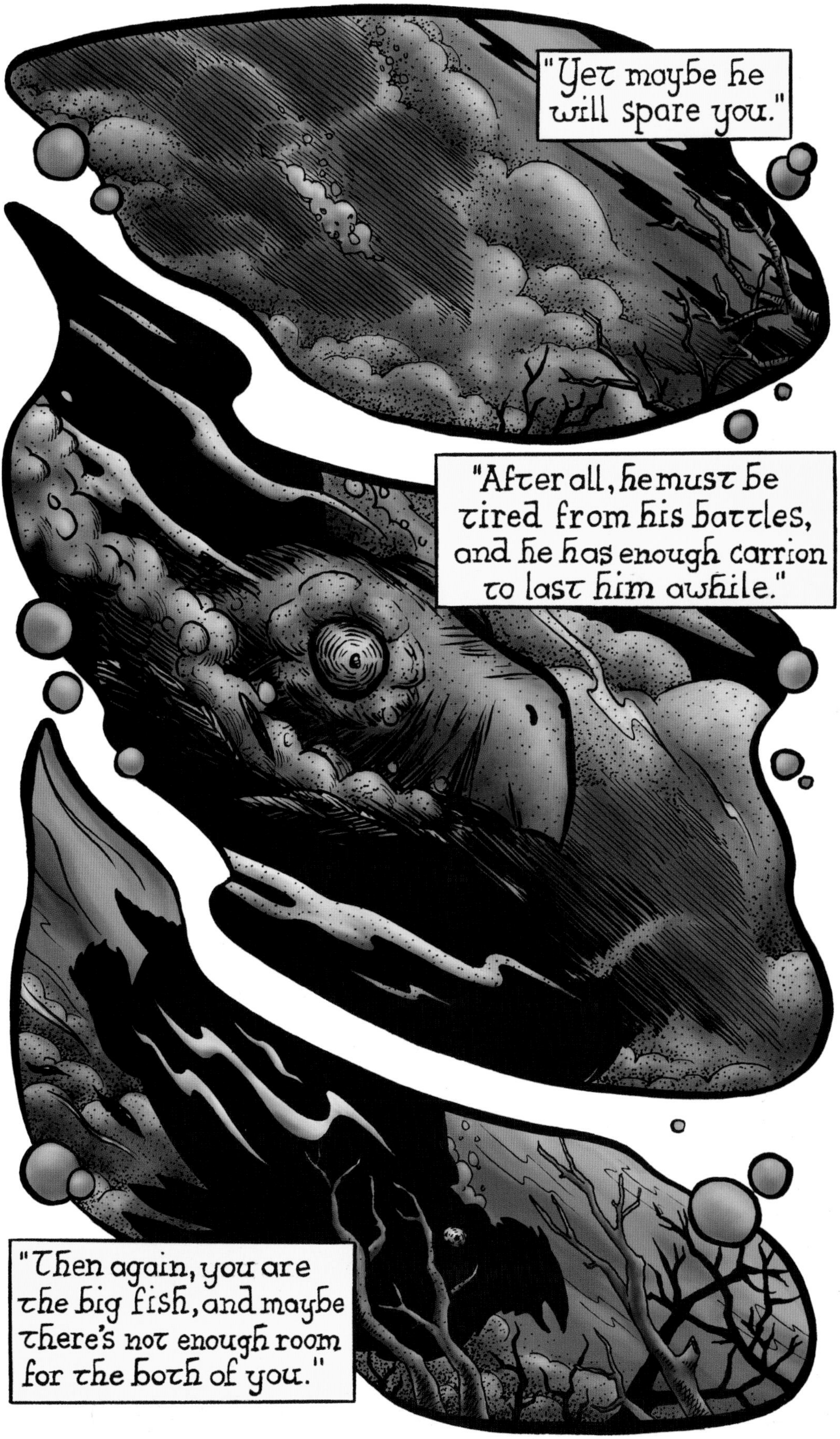
"Yet maybe he will spare you."
"After all, he must be tired from his battles, and he has enough carrion to last him awhile."
"Then again, you are the big fish, and maybe there's not enough room for the both of you."

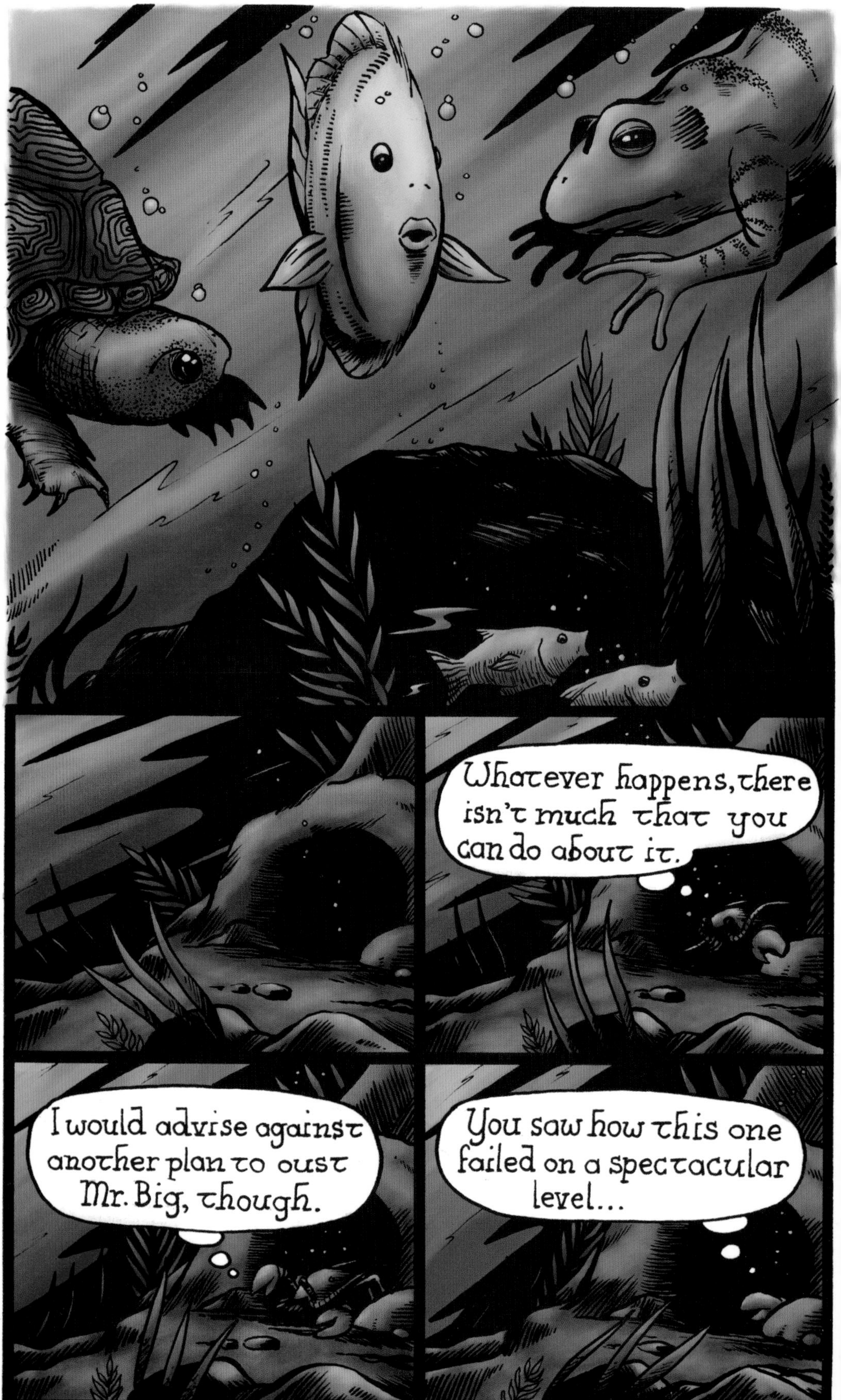
Whatever happens, there isn't much that you can do about it.
I would advise against another plan to oust Mr. Big, though.
You saw how this one failed on a spectacular level...

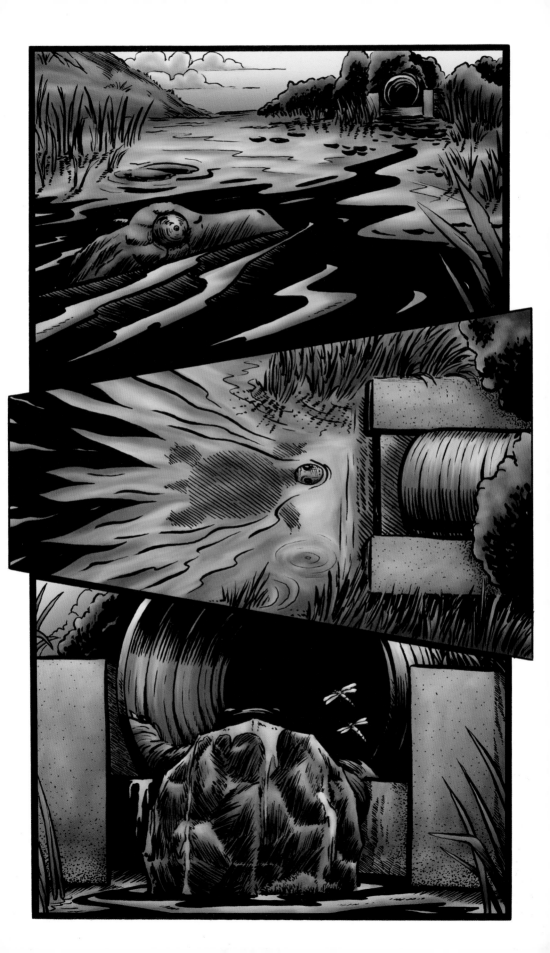

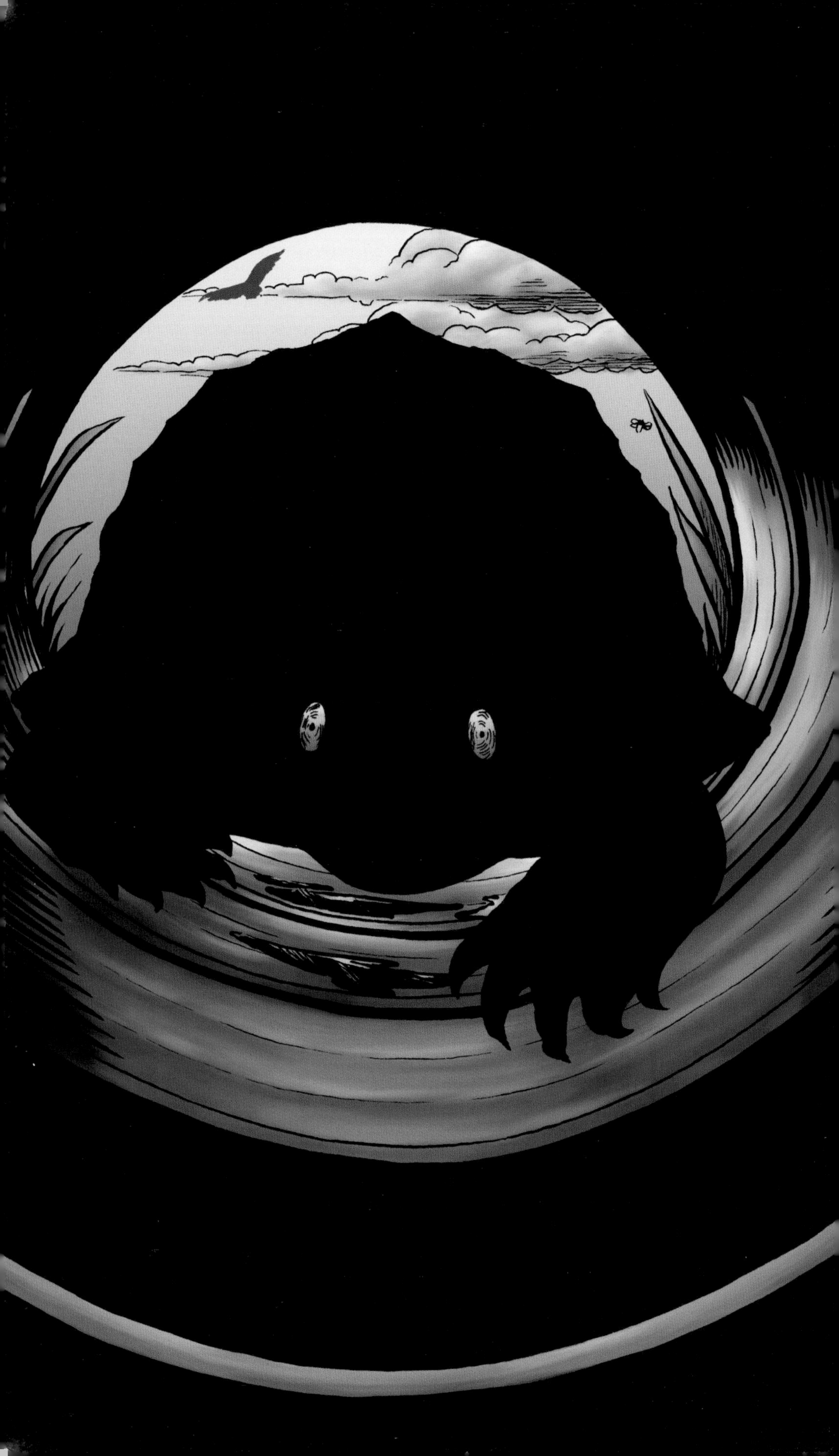

# Afterword

A pond community is a small, self-contained natural ecosystem, which holds a delicate balance of life. At times, animals can be predators, and at other times, in turn, can serve as prey for larger, faster, more aggressive species.

One such animal that participates in preserving this natural balance in ponds and slow-moving waterways of the United States is the common snapping turtle. These prehistoric-looking, aggressive, and largely aquatic animals reach a size of about twenty inches in length and are found throughout the country, from the East Coast to west of the Rocky Mountains, and south into Central America. Snapping turtles can live to a ripe old age of fifty to one hundred years.

In a pond environment, these turtles feed on anything from small mammals and fish to frogs, birds, and plants. Snapping turtles are considered a top predator in pond environments as they have few, if any, natural enemies because of their large size.

Unfortunately, there are those who do not understand the importance of these reptiles and consider them a nuisance. Once a snapper decides to live in a pond, the population of fish, amphibians, aquatic reptiles, and birds can drop at a rapid rate. But a snapping turtle is a natural and necessary inhabitant of pond life, whether you choose to admire or fear it.

Over the past several years, however, a much larger and more sinister problem has come into our local environment.

This problem includes nonnative animals, plants, and other foreign life. The environment's delicate harmony is in trouble because it does not yet have any way to contain the invaders. One such species is the Asian snakehead fish, which has been introduced as a result of the exotic pet trade. This fish is a large and toothy predator that has quickly adapted to the local climate and aquatic environment. In a pond community, a nonnative and aggressive alien such as the snakehead can do a lot of harm to the local animal population, unless a larger, native predator decides to broaden its menu choices.

Another threat is the West Nile virus, which finds life in local waters. A disease organism from Africa, it is typically spread through a mosquito bite. A common mosquito that begins life as a larva in small bodies of water, such as ponds, has now become a threat not only to animals but humans too.

As winter approaches, the life in a pond, whether peaceful or scary, native or introduced, goes into the deep sleep of hibernation for the cold months. This is a good time to reflect upon the sometimes peaceful and sometimes violent natural balance of life in a pond. As spring approaches, however, and daytime temperatures start to warm up, you may hear a splash. Make sure to look around you, because you might find yourself face-to-face with the snapping turtle, Mr. Big!

—Sean Henderson

**Sean Henderson** is an animal keeper at the National Zoo in Washington, DC, where he works with aquatic animals, including reptiles.

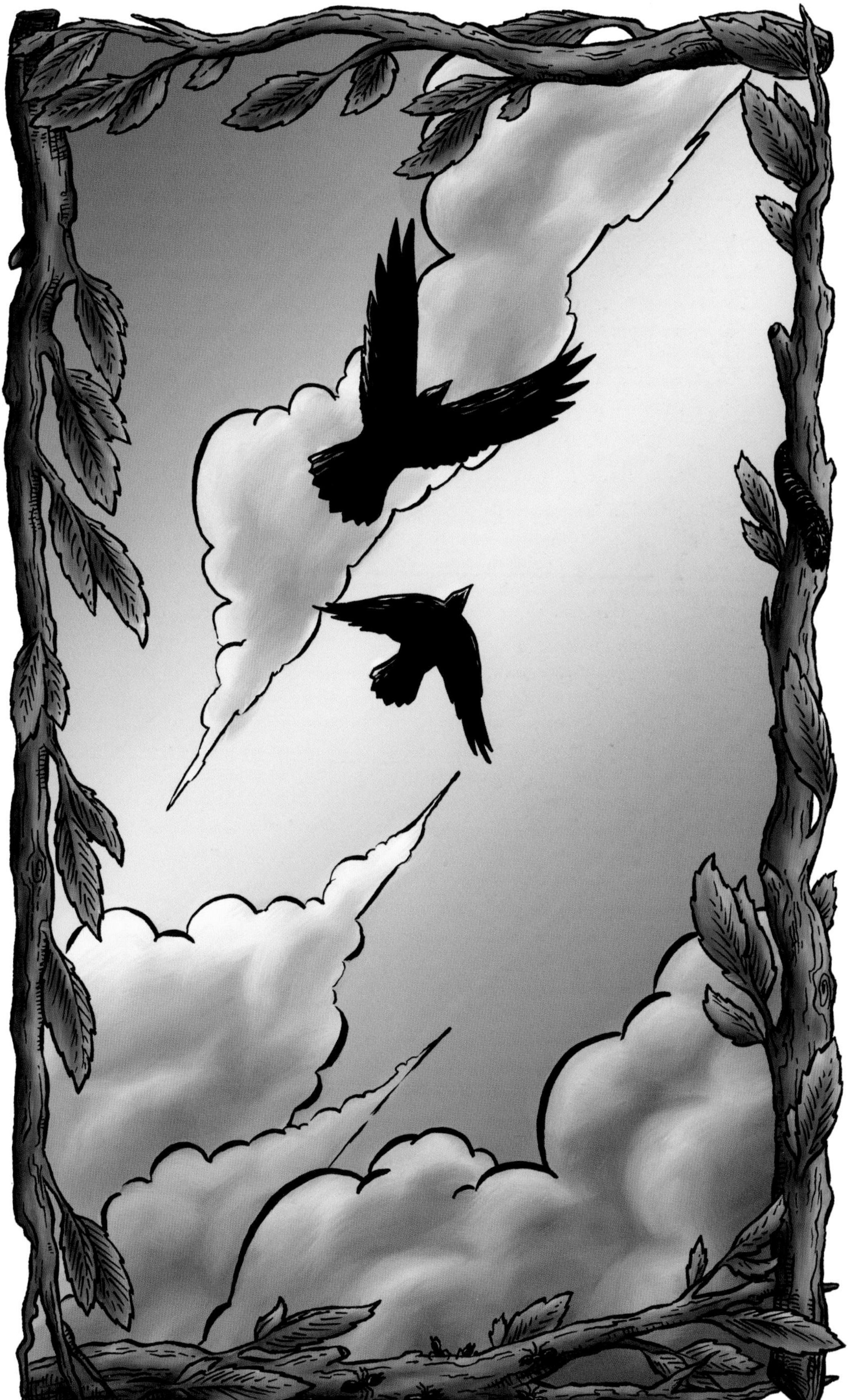

11-12
d
C.D.